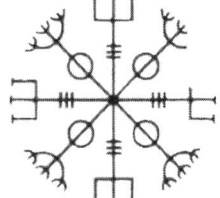

THE WIHTWARA

BY

JAN HARPER-WHALE

This is the first book in a trilogy dedicated to the Ancestors of Wihtland, Isle of Wight, who lived in peace and cared for their island home in a sacred manner. As devout pagans, they knew the land in an intimate way. They were killed in the massacre of 686, led by Cædwalla in the name of Christianity.

The Wihtwara, (people of the spirit) were the last to be Christianised in Britain, of the few that remained!

Extensive research over several years has brought to light some surprising evidence, which, when pieced together has built a story that most surely needs to be told.

These are works of fiction, but backed up by the latest research.

The lives of these people, our forefathers, is truly important and needs to be honored.

Lest we forget.

Ure Ieldran fram Wihtland (Isle of Spirit) begongan und āwarian þes godcundnes ealond. Heora lufian nūðã weorð und heora gemynd gebran ongean.

Bletsunga Beorhte

To Sarah

THE WIHTWARA

Copyright © 2017 Jan Harper-Whale

All rights reserved. This book or any portion thereof may not be reproduced or used in any manner whatsoever without the express written permission of the publisher except for the use of brief quotations in a book review.

Cover Design and illustrations by Jan Harper-Whale

http://www.waking-the-dragon.co.uk

Our Ancestors of Wihtland cared for and protected this sacred land. Their Love is now honoured and their memory now re-born.

Bright Blessings

Jan Harper-Whale

FORWARD

One wise archaeologist giving a lecture at Oxford not so long ago made us all giggle, then reflect quite hard with his pronouncement:

"The only thing an archaeologist can be sure of is that he is wrong!"

He was, of course, trying to remind us that new discoveries in the field are happening all the time and frequently overturn previously cherished, long-held beliefs and understandings. So, we must be ever ready to adapt to change.

Interpretation can be a minefield. What seems blatantly obvious to one person can just as clearly appear to be the polar opposite to another.

Yet some folk do seem to possess a special insight that transcends the obvious evidence to build and flesh out a comprehensive narrative on the framework of the relatively few available clear facts.

You hold in your hands the work of one of such extraordinary insight.

The Isle of Wight is commonly seen as the 'last Pagan place in England', although it was briefly Christianised through Roman times before the population returned to its Scando/Teutonic beliefs and finally adopted its last Pagan king.

This sacred land has long suffered the denial of any Jutish heritage, although there is archaeological evidence these peoples long ago were here, as well as in Kent.

The author is a direct descendant. A Wahl of the Warinni tribe. And this gives her an extraordinary lineage on which to draw, a bloodline, as well as insights us mere mortals outside of the tribe cannot really hope to fully comprehend.

Jan - who I have known for many years as a dear friend - presents this tale to you as fiction, but it is far more than that.

She has spent years researching this project, through which we have had very many discussions on the historical and the sacred, and I can vouch for the immense amount of work she has ploughed into searching out as much historical fact as remains. Just as valuable, however, is the extraordinary insight she has brought to this work, to shine a light into the darker and more mysterious corners of the narrative. Giving it life again.

This is a great read, with well-drawn characters, as it is. A class novel.

But if you have an interest in the deep history of our islands - and especially the Isle of Wight - you will find so much more here to absorb you and pique your appetite.

This volume in its unique style transports you back to a time of gods and goddesses, charms and spells, populated by myriad spirits who had to be respected and placated for the good of the tribe, embroidered with passages of a language not heard in these lands for many, many years.

Herein there be magick!

Maurice Paul Bower
Wight Druids /|\
Newport, Isle of Wight
2017

FORWARD

I have known Jan Harper Whale for quite a few years now. During which time, we have talked endlessly about spiritual matters, and undertaken spiritual adventures together.

Having been in on the start of the book, I have followed it with close interest and enjoyed hearing about the new findings. Jan is a woman of integrity, and true to her belief's. I know many hours of research have gone into this book, and Jan has also been helped by local archaeologists.

Of the book itself, it is in the vein of the storyteller. As you read you are transported back to the early times on the Isle of Wight. Learning about the spiritual and mundane journey of the heroine of the piece, and perhaps some of the practices of that time.

At first when Jan told me that she was going to use a lot of Saxon language in the book, I was a little taken aback, but on reading it adds a little flavour of the time.

Although this book is about days long ago. Some of its themes are relevant to today, and it just goes to show that throughout history some things never change. Perhaps acknowledging the past, we can learn a different way. I believe now that we are on the cusp of that awakening, and the choice is ours, do we go on in the same vein, or change to a better way.

Suzanne Thomas
Producer of the Fountain International Magazine
www.fountaininternationalmagazine.com

ACKNOWLEDGEMENTS

And in deep appreciation to the researchers and writers whose incredible work has fuelled the passion to complete this work:

Stephen Oppenheimer
Tylluan Penry
Stephen Pollington
J.C Medland
J.N. Margham

And to the constant help and support of Alan Phillips whose archaeological knowledge of the island led me to the next step in a wonderful way and Maurice Bower, Druid and journalist who guided me through the peaks and troughs as a wonderful friend. Thank you to my close friends who helped edit, give timely advice and support throughout. Sylvia Charlwood, Merry and Juliet Sargent.

To my daughter-in-spirit Kelly Louise who has gifted me so much, and to my daughters Jay and Aimee, wise-women both. To my dear husband Mitch, who is "my rock": thank you.

ANCIENT (OLD ENGLISH) NAMES ON WIHTLAND

Affetūn	Afton	
Ēastūn	East Afton	
Sūđtūn	South Afton	
Westtūn	West Afton	
Norđtūn	North Afton	
Meolodūn	Ashey down	
Þÿpacumb	Assembly valley	
Beaddingaburnan	Bathingbourne	
Ađolfeshÿlle	Bathingbourne	
Ŏrhămm	Bembridge	
Bicandoene	Bigbury farm	
Hūfēinga	Blackwater	
Etđredecumb	Bowcombe	
Breredingas	Brading	
Berandinzium Hus	Brading Villa	
Wykendeshÿlle	Brighstone	
Brocbeorg	Brook down	
Carisbroc	Carisbrooke	
Chesteborg	Chessell	
Ceofodūn Scyte	Cheverton Shute	
Dēawcumb	Dew Valley	
Fōrdūn	Foredown	
Froggalönd	Frogland farm	
Forsterswelle	Frosthills	
Gemot Beorg	Galibury Hump	
Lāfadūn	Garston Down	
Gārclif	Gore Cliff	
Heldewaye	Hillway, Bembridge	
Lawercedūn	Lark hill - Lordon Copse	
Lucleah broc	Lukely Brook	
Moteresfān	Mottistone	
Mōtstāndūn	Mottistone Down	
Stithes fleots heafod	Newtown	
Plaesc Bearu	Plaish Copse	
Raegehris	Rains Grove	
Ränadūn	Renham down	
Raegecumb	Roe deer valley	
Siăcum	Rowborough bottom	
Rūhbeorg	Rowborough Farm	
Rurigge	Rowridge	
Senclinz	Shanklin	
Scorawella	Shorwell	
Smerdūn	St. Martin's down	
Gārdūn	St. Catherine's down	
Stiepel	Steep Hill Cove	
Sumorbeorg	Summerbury	
Idelcumb	uncultivated valley	
Wæter Geat	Watergate	
Westōferdūn	Westover down	
Westiggedūn	Westridge down	
Walpenneclinz	Whale Chine	
Everlant ēalond	Yar/Bembridge	

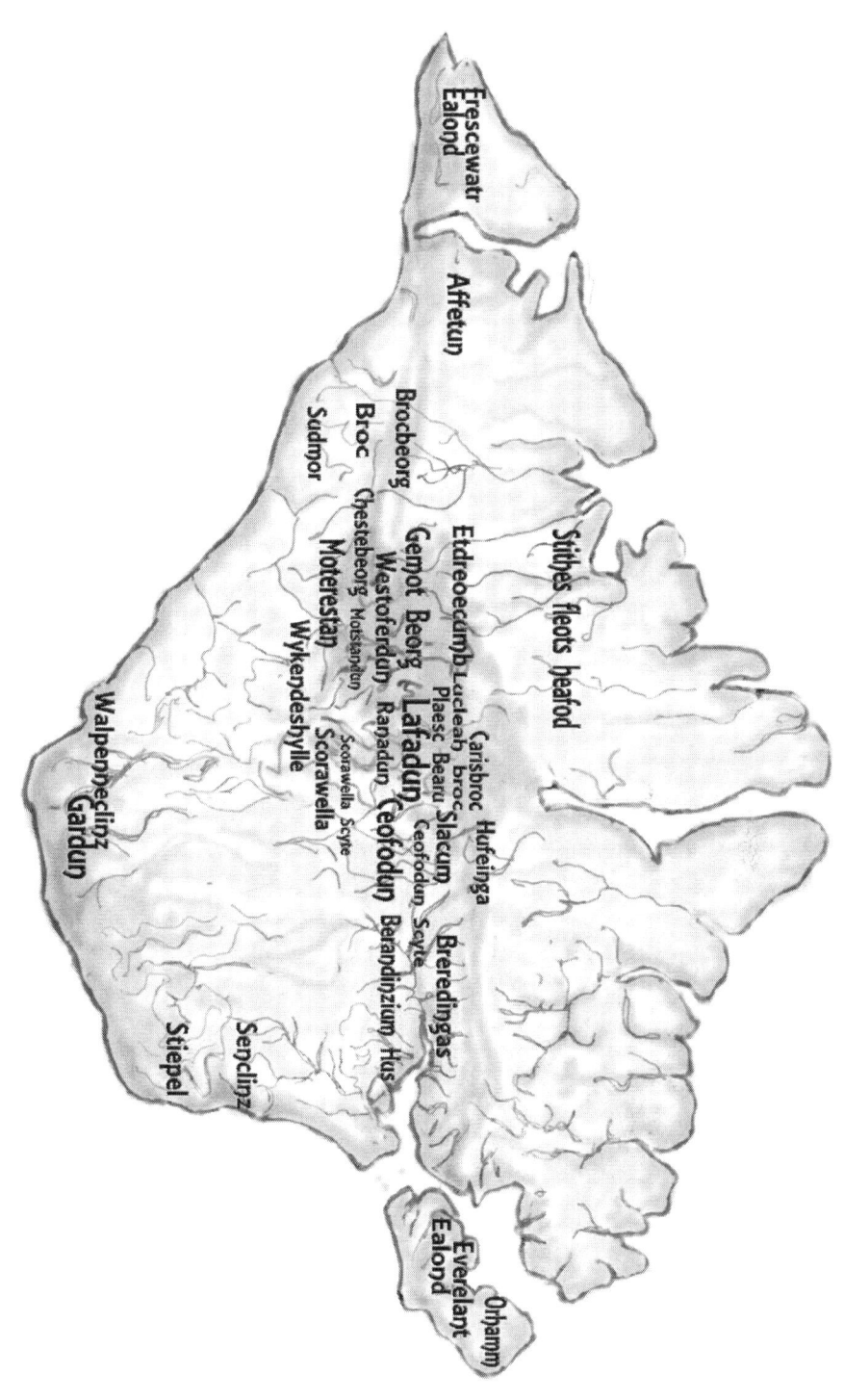

ANCESTOR'S NAMES AND THEIR MEANINGS

Dagrun Wahl......... Day Rune.... Guardian of the stones.
Dagrun Wahl's daughter...... *Lãfa*... Love,
Lãfa's Husband.... *Arkyn*... Eternal King's Son,
Mother: *Gudrun*... divine rune,
Father: *Folkvarthr*.... Guardian of the people,
Brother: *Eystein*....... island stone,
Brother2: *Eyvindr*.... island wind,
Husband: *Eileifer*..... forever heir,
Grandmother: *Ealdmōdor*,
Close friend to Dagrun: *Lífa*... Life,
Friend: *Sãga*.... Seeing one,
Priestess: *Aslaug*.... God-betrothed woman,
Priestess in training: *Eldís*......Island Goddess,
Friend to Sãga: *Alfsigr*..... Elf victory,
Eudose who became Anglii: *Vidgis*.... War Goddess,
Ingavonii friend: *Ingvar*...Ing's warrior,
Married to Ingvar: *Ynghildre*.... Ing warrior,
Descendant of Wodan and King: *Wihtleig*,
Wizard to Wihtleig: *Gandãlfr*..... Fiendish elf,

Family of thralls:
Mother: *Leofflæd*... Agreeable beauty,
Daughter. *Ingríd*,
Father: *Leofwine*... Dear friend,
Husband: *ívarr*.... Bow warrior,
Mother in ceasterwic: *Gudlaug*... God-wife,
Son: Egil.... Little Edge,

Adopted boy to Eileifer: *Eastmund*.... Eastern protection,

Eastmund's father a Rōmānisc: *Eardwūlf*... land wolf,
Elíse's new husband: *Dǽgberht*... Day bright,
Wedding priest: Weofodthegn Ælhstān,

Ingvar's crew:
Wigstan... war stone, *Eofōrwine*... bear friend, *Glǽdwiþ*... bright friend,
Army guard: *Hereward, Acca*... oak, *Cǽna*... warlike,
Hrothgar... famous spear,

Eileifer's messenger: *Kenward*... royal guard,
Dagrun's servant.... *Hild*,

In Wōden's world:
Consort to Nerthus: *Godwulf,* Brother to Wōden: *Loki,*
Priestess: *Hjördis*... Sword Goddess, Elder: *Heiðrūn*... true rune,
Young trainee: *Frídr*... Peace, Teacher: *Eir*... Goddess of Healing, Wet nurse:
Brynhildr... Armoured warrior woman,
Wet nurse 2: *Bergis*... Rescue Goddess,
Night singer: *Huld*... Hidden secret,
Elder to Wōden: *Anleifr*... Heir of the ancestors,
Chief: *Yngling*... Descendant of Ing,
Guardian to Wōden: *Vermundr*... Protector of man,
2nd guardian to Wodan: *Týr*... God of combat,
Forest guardian: *Víðarr*... Forest warrior,
1st accomplice to Loki: *Alfljötr*... Elfin ugly,
2nd accomplice to Loki: *Brandr*... Flash sword,
3rd accomplice to Loki: *Agni*... Edge of sword,
Friend to Wodan: *Bjartr*... Bright, Wōden's guise as old man: *Ōfnir.*

Berandinzium Villa:
Greco/Roman family:
The owner of Berandinzium villa: *Vrittakos Eluskonios,*
His Wife: *Venitouta Quadrunia,*
Daughter: *Aia Duxtir Quadrunia,* Slave woman: *Quintina,* Slave girl: *Tullia.*

Chapter	Title	Page
ONE:	The age of the Avatar	...1
TWO:	Wunder cræft: Miracle working.	...21
THREE:	Þæt Gifu: The Gift.	...29
FOUR:	Þæt Nigt-Gala: The Night Singer.	...36
FIVE:	Ljðð Leoð seiðr: Spell song singing magic.	...47
SIX:	ᛗᛟᛞᛁᚱ Mother I remember you.	...53
SEVEN:	Gerihte fram nearu: Rite of passage.	...60
EIGHT:	Þæt Genemnan: The naming.	...76
NINE:	Wihtland.	...85
TEN:	Wacian: Prayer Vigil.	...91
ELEVEN:	Deað-gerihte: Death rite.	...96
TWELVE:	Geweorðan a Witig cwèn: Becoming a Wise woman.	...118
THIRTEEN:	Nerthus.	...129
FOURTEEN:	Drímeolce Þægweorþwa: Beltane.	...156
FIFTEEN:	Þæt cið are weorþan: The seeds are cast.	...166
SIXTEEN:	Forewítegian æt þæt ðèodscipe: Prophecy to the people.	...183
SEVENTEEN:	Líf begeondan Wihtland: Life beyond Wihtland.	...200
EIGHTEEN:	Þæt Getrýwð rícsians: The Truth prevails.	...219
NINETEEN:	Þæt Sãwol's æthweorfan: The Soul's return.	...230
TWENTY:	Tacitus.	...235
TWENTY-ONE:	Þæt Wihtwara, ðèodscipe fram þæt Sãwol: The Wihtwara, people of the Spirit.	...239
TWENTY-TWO:	Foregísl: Hostage.	...244
TWENTY-THREE:	Þæt Æcerbot Ōlǽcung: The Field Remedy Charm.	...247

CHAPTER	Title	Page
TWENTY-FOUR:	ᚹᛟᛞᛖᚾ Wōden.	...257
TWENTY-FIVE:	Ūtiseta: Vision Quest.	...268
TWENTY-SIX:	Yggdrasil: The tree of Life.	...276
TWENTY-SEVEN:	Wuldortanas: The Glory Staves: The Runes.	...285
TWENTY-EIGHT:	Yngling and Loki.	...299
TWENTY-NINE:	Geri and Freki.	...307
THIRTY:	Þæt nigon wyrt ōlǽcung und þæt wuldortanas: The nine-herb charm and the rods of wonder.	...318
THIRTY-ONE:	Gungnir: The shaking one: and the trickster Loki.	...323
THIRTY-TWO:	Freyja of the Vanir and the Seiðr.	...327
THIRTY-THREE:	Sleipnr: Slipper.	...335
THIRTY-FOUR:	Mecurius:Þæt èacen specul. The great Talker.	...344
THIRTY-FIVE:	Wōden: Þæt èacen hǽlend The great Healer.	...347
THIRTY-SIX:	Þæt dèað fram Baldur: The death of Baldur.	...353
THIRTY-SEVEN:	Hringhorni.	...358
THIRTY-EIGHT:	Þæt wel fram Mimir: The Well of Mimir.	...361
THIRTY-NINE:	Loki.	...365
FORTY:	Wihtland.	...368
FORTY-ONE:	ðã þæt Hãlig Stãn grèotan: When the Sacred Stone weeps.	...376
FORTY-TWO:	þæt Cynelíc ǽwnung: The Royal marriage.	...388
FORTY-THREE:	Sceatt æht: Coin Wealth.	...403
FORTY-FOUR:	Berandinzium Villa: Brading Villa.	...432
FORTY-FIVE:	Abraxas.	...441
FORTY-SIX:	Ealdmōdor.	...451
	AUTHOR'S NOTE.	...457
	GLOSSARY.	...467
	BIBLIOGRAPHY.	...473

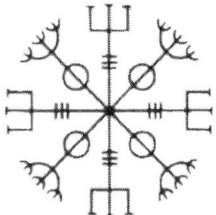

THE WIHTWARA
AGE OF THE AVATAR

Inside our women's sacred place, I sat, or rather kneeled to push myself forward to get closer to her. I hung on every word she uttered. Amidst the smoke-filled place, the fire embers casting low shadows on her crumpled form, I tried to grab the meanings for her words which came slow with great breaths in between. Life was ebbing from her: she knew this to be her last utterance and for her, it was so very important. We had heard it before, but somehow at this time of the full moon, and the Nerthus awakening time, she needed to impale it on our spirits, for us to hold it in times to come, to make it legend.

I am Wahl of the Warinni. My people belong to the confederacy of the seven tribes, we are the defenders of Nerthus, and my people, the Warinni, are defenders of the Stones. And in turn, our defenders are the nearby Geats, the warrior lords of Gotland and beyond. I am no longer in my Ancestors' given land. That is far from here, across the large sea and then many weeks' walk again to be within the rising cliffs and tall tree forests and the islands.

But here on our island home in the warmer climes, our high elder woman, whose life is ebbing, tells of a time there in our true ancestral lands.

The full moon brings the winds, whispering its own story on top of our lady's words. The sky gods are giving her strength as she lifts her arms up onto the wood and leaning forward, her eyes, glazed over with white film, non-seeing, now views a world beyond this one.

"So many, many women years ago, our god was left: a foundling near the water's edge. The water gently rippled over the rush mat that covered his tiny form. As if Nerthus still wanted hold of him. He is Hers always: we know that: he is goddess given and that he will only spend the time in our realm that she permits. Oh, but what a courageous, golden time it was.

"At that sacred time of our year, when we heard Her call: in the midst of the tall tree forest that protected Her domain, kept Her waters hidden from the warrior damage of men, she came to know us for a short time. And we came to worship and love Her. All the men and the warrior women lay down their iron. It was forbidden to fight or even say an angry word. Our Earth Mother, creator of all, surfaced from the waters deep. She greeted us and brought us to her.

"Nothing can be said of that time with Her. It is secret. Only the feeling of supreme love and nurturing stays and is remembered till the next time we are honoured."

Our Elder woman paused to take breath. She coughed with the smoke that now swirled around the women's space, the wind blowing it in spirals towards the high roof and out through the smoke hole. My mother, Gudrun, reached to the dwindling fire and laid fresh dry kindling to spark more flame. We huddled ever closer to our High Elder to keep her with us, to help her in the story telling that would mark our tribe here in foreign lands. She leaned forward to throw a small branch over to the fire: her will to live this moment so strong.

I saw the thin strands of her hair glisten in the firelight, wisps of white that showed her skull silhouetted against the dark. The woven wool shawl hung from her skeletal form: a puff of wind would send it cascading to the dirt floor.

She bent her head into her arms resting on the wooden table. For a moment, we thought she was spent, then with a deep audible breath she lifted her head to the heaven once more and continued.

She called out in a voice not her own:

3

> *"Hal wes thu, Folde, fira modor,*
> *Thu Gebletsod weorth!*
> *Wè cumaþ to gebrèman þa halig wihtes*
> *Ond bewægnaþ bèdu for pas earþan þe we on lifiaþ,*
> *Hir eorðtùdor ond hir eallwihta."*

> Greetings to you, Earth, mother of men,
> You shall be blessed!
> We come to honour the sacred Ones
> And offer prayers for the earth that we live on,
> Her peoples and all her creatures.

"Your forefather's ancestors spied upon the foundling due to his lusty cries! His lungs were fully formed, so they say and could summon the gods before he had learnt our language. Nerthus, our mother reluctantly gave him up. She trusted the elder men of our tribe more than others. We were a peaceful people and it was important to give the babe a foundation of care and love within which to grow. He was to be perfect in all ways and this responsibility of his care was taken so very seriously.

"This Elder father walked out of the tall tree forest that dawn morning to glittering bright sunshine that suddenly flooded our small village. People stopped their work to stare at the noisy bundle, as the man made his way to the woman's round house and lifted the hide flap. Inside, women were already about their work, spinning, weaving and scraping skins. And talking. The noise suddenly stopped: all went quiet for men did not usually enter the women's house.

That only left the hearty bawling of the infant swaddled in a wet rush mat."

"Freyja. Giefan me strengu. Hwaet is þeos!" (Freyja, give me strength. What is this?)

Hjördis, the elder grandmother heaved her frame from the stool, where she was overseeing the young Frídr who was weaving the weft thread of assorted coloured yarn into the cloak being made for her. Her long grey hair, braided, still nearly touched her ankles and as she straightened her bent spine into a walking stance, groaned in a deep voice. Her bones were bent out of shape now and all she could productively do was watch over the younger woman and offer advice with very few words.

But she moved fast at the sight before her and ushered him outside. She took the screaming bundle from Godwulf.

Godwulf released his charge with lowered head. He was the chieftain warrior king of this tribe, part of the great Geats. He was a big, big man. The sun shone through his mass of curled hair and looked like he was a haloed warrior. His grin, now absent, was like a full quarter-moon and his laugh could reach the hinterland of the village. He had fought with so much courage and skill, he had earned the chieftain name early in his life, but he had never hardened his heart and was compassionate to all who deserved it.

Now he was lost for words.

Hjördis stared at him, her intense blue eyes boring a hole in his downturned head.

"Godwulf, beorn Ealdor, beseon aet me!" Warrior Chief, look at me!

"Have you been consort to Nerthus," she asked softly, "and is this the child-god we have been blessed with and has been foretold?"

Godwulf raised his head and stared with piercing truthful eyes at his grandmother elder.

"Giese!" he replied simply.

"Then we have much to prepare!" she said and turned towards her women, closing the hide flap behind her.

The flames flickered low, casting smaller shadows around us and our elder grandmother took a deep breath, and remained silent in her telling. Everyone paused in her silence until she slowly turned her head out towards us, her sightless eyes looking, feeling for the person she needed.

"Where is Dagrun Wahl", she whispered breathlessly," come to me so you alone may hear."

I shuffled forward. She heard me and turned to the noise I made.

"Come closer Dagrun," she whispered, "you need to hear me."

I bent over her wispy skull and gently kissed her. She smiled and sighed and turned to face me.

"Listen and listen well to what I am about to tell you. For you and you alone must carry this knowledge to your children and to their children's children. It is the true legacy of our people and it must never be forgotten. You are Wahl, defender of the stones. The stones carry the knowledge. Listen well dear one."

The high Elder Grandmother gently lay the screaming boy child down onto soft fur. Taking a wool bundle, she gently wiped the water and rush detritus from him. What a lusty child! she thought. The women's hall had become silent since their entry, they had stopped their weaving spinning and scraping to gather round in a semi-circle.

With her head bent low over the child-god, her braids coiled around his muscled little legs, she spoke without looking up: "This child will need two cildfestre mothers. His thirst will drain just one." She turned then and her eyes moved around the circle of women.

"Bergdis", she looked sharply at the young women half hiding behind Eir, the immensely tall statuesque woman with long flaxen hair, braided and twisted round her head. She was the healer who passed on her knowledge to the worthy young ones. Bergdis was her worthy young one but all things herbs had ceased for Bergdis who had entered the birthing house and her term was not yet finished. She had brought a beautiful daughter into the early summer light.

"How is your flow, child?" Hjördis asked.

"Very plentiful, grandmother," Bergdis replied softly, "She is sweet and placid my little daughter, she sleeps many hours and does not disturb my nights."

"Hmm," Hjördis was thoughtful, eventually she spoke," For now, young Bergdis, you may be his first cildfestre mother, for our child-god. Bless him with your milk and he will bless you more than you may ever dream!" She looked around and spied Brynhildr. She was a strong warrior woman with a sturdy build and tree stumps for legs. Never could she be called pretty but her flowing auburn hair spoke of a warrior race to the north who were fierce and valiant in war. She was holding her wriggling babe on her ample hips.

"Brynhildr, are you still giving milk to this monster of a boy?" Hjördis, always straight with her words, gave a sideways grin.

"Giese", Brynhildr replied reluctantly. For her, her cildfèstre time was nearly at an end. She was not a natural mother and wished with all her heart to join the men in the field with shield and spear. She, who could dismount her gelding, run and leap back on effortlessly, with shield and spear, did not relish months more of giving milk to this giant of a baby, even if he was a god in the making.

"Brynhildr", Hjördis spoke sharply," You cannot seem to see beyond the end of your nose child! Suckle this baby, tend to his needs. He will tax you beyond your knowing, but you will be the one to gift him with your warrior courage, your talents with horse and shield will protect him in times to come. But you will also teach him the true warrior way, of going to the killing fields with honour and care only a woman warrior can teach."

"Here! He is yours. Frigga, we pray: Silence this young one with your love."

The level of his bawling had reached new heights: he was already making his mark in the realm, reducing everything and everyone to silence. Brynhildr, for all her reluctance made a beautiful start for this child-god. He quietened almost immediately and soon fell asleep on her breast.

Hjördis turned and sat on her haunches, staring into the fire a long time. The women gradually removed themselves back to their work, knowing their elder grandmother would give them a sharp tongue if they dared to ask any questions. The flames reflected in her eyes, and they moved in understanding. She knew their language. She emitted a low "hmmm" in understanding and slowly, with great pain levered herself to standing.

"Eir," Hjördis turned to see her companion appear from the dark of the house. "Come with me to the sacred pool, and we need to find Heidrun. There is a splendid work we need to do for the naming ritual and all must be with the gods and goddesses' consent."

There were only two places where she might be, for she was either with her bees, or with her goats. She had been chosen at an early age, for both had become her familiars and spoke to her in ways neither man nor woman of the tribe could fathom. She was keeper and guardian of the sacred Mead, and she was needed for this gathering of elders to name the child-god.

Hjördis shuffled out into the mid-morning sun, the ground dust dry for there had been little rain on this, the eve of planting. There were still deep cuts in the ground from the last heavy rains and her skeletal large feet dipped into one and she silently screamed.

"Eir", she hissed," fetch my staff. It is where it always is." And Eir hurried back to the women's house to find it. Hjördis' place of rest was deep within the house; the mound of fur hides was high to rest her aching bones. To the far extreme corner lay her familiars from her initiation rite of long ago, her spear and shield. There resting against the shield was her twisted beech staff, as high as she was many moons ago. Now she was dwarfed by it. It held magic. It would see her across the village without harm now her sight was failing.

Hjördis stamped it on the ground three times, as was her way to wake it up. There were women, now outside with their high upright looms, she could hear and feel the swish of yarn through the warp, and wondered on the design. There were woman now carding wool by the sheep holding house where knives rasped against skin and grunts and shuffles could be heard from both sheep and men. It was the busiest time of year, outside of harvest. She made a prayer to Nerthus for rain, knowing that the women needed to come together and make offerings very soon.

The sun was hot for this time of year, and little breeze. She made her way to the side of the encampment, where the wooden palisade had been created, huge impacted wooden spikes running the full length of the village perimeter. There were hostile tribes to the north that sent warring parties to steal stock and sometimes women. It was, Hjördis thought thankfully, not often and certainly not now, when the call for planting was paramount. Never the less she banged the palisade at intervals three times to protect her people.

She passed by the shade of the giant ceremonial house which shielded her from the afternoon sun. For a moment, her mind went back to the far-gone days when it was being built. A whole wood was felled to build the walls and a further copse of sturdy beech with willow ties to create the roof. She remembered, as a young woman, just initiated and being given the tribute of carving her animal familiars into the wood. Eagle was her first and most powerful friend. She had gone climbing up to the towering cliff, high above the pine forests. There on a lay, amongst the branches, sat her Eagle. She stayed there for days. And watched, not moving until the Eagle looked straight into her eyes and spoke. She then realised she could understand, for thoughts came into her head which Eagle had put there. She learnt to recognise each cry and even the twist of her head. Expressions came next. If she obeyed the distance imposed, her familiar taught her many things.

So, in carving her most precious friend, Hjördis had to be winched and tied to the tree post for the length of time it took to carve her symbol. Then, lower came Raven. It had always been that way; her challenge and test of courage came in the extremes she had to face. She became the Elder Grandmother by living through many of them. But she was not, although she had earned her spear and shield, a warrior woman. Now, in the evening of her years, she felt glad.

Hjördis felt that the gods and goddesses had chosen this tribe and these people to teach the child-god the ways of Nerthus, the ways of compassion and true melding with Nature. But he will be a force of Will to teach! She thought.

Heidrun was at the very edge of the village, past even the forge, which was stone built and facing west. The heat of the forge made Hjördis gasp, and sparks flew as the slæn wyrhta drymãnn, created metal from liquid and beat the pattern into the blade.

We will teach him this, thought Hjördis, for there is magic here and he must master it.

Heidrun was another female giantess, who was a head taller than most men in the village. She was broad and strong with a mass of wheat coloured hair that cascaded down her back tied loosely by a leather thong. Her long woollen tunic was a loose weave, tied at the waist, and buttoned at the shoulders. She dressed simply because most of her time was outside with her goats and bees. Now she was with the bees who were her familiars. Her name Heidrun was older than old: meaning true rune after the goat that made mead for the Einherjar, the spirits of the warriors who died in battle.

So, she was given the tribute of caring for both the goat herd and the bees. And it was with the bees that Hjördis and Eir found her, sitting cross-legged between two hives, bees traveling to and fro around her. Suddenly they flew en-masse away to find nectar.

"They never sting you!" Eir exclaimed, "Why do they not? They would certainly plant a few on me!"

"Why would they?" Heidrun smiled in a full way. "I show them the way to the best flowers and they give me grand honey!"

Hjördis sat down with the help of her staff beside her friend and pupil, looking her straight in the eye, a look that could pierce right through to the soul. No one dare say anything but the truth to the Elder Grandmother.

"Heidrun, my dear, the foretelling has come to pass. The child-god has come and we three must prepare now for the naming and a rite of passage: for this babe is like no other. He will advance faster than any of us are accustomed to and we must be prepared. Come with us now to the sacred pool. I need to speak with the Ancestors directly and to Nerthus. There are sacred things we need to collect: herbs and stones, tree parts and clay. Everything must be in readiness for the full moon. It's close and we do not have much time."

All three women began walking, at a slow pace for the elder Grandmother, and it would certainly be a long journey for her. They were travelling to the most secret of places. Where no man was permitted. Only when the rare consorting times arrived did chosen men make that journey to meet Nerthus.

"Are you sure you can make this journey, Grandmother?" Eir queried.

Hjördis stopped suddenly and hit the ground with her staff six times each one sharper and with more force than the previous one. Her eyes went dark as night and she turned to Eir, who was frozen to the spot, silenced.

"Do NOT make that hole you are digging for yourself any bigger than it is now child, as I for one will not be helping you out!"

"I am sorry." Eir whispered.

"Of course, I can make this journey," Hjördis hissed, "otherwise it would not be taken!"

They continued in silence, no talk was needed or indeed required, for each were deep in their own thoughts. They walked through the deep tall forest of trees that hid the sacred lake of Nerthus; close to this they veered left into a spinney of trees that thinned to make a glade, full of sunshine and flowers and the waterfall that spilled into a deep, deep pond.

The tall grass caressed their legs, and now barefoot they felt the warmth of the earth. Deep contact with their earth mother was needed to focus. A wren sped past Hjördis's nose, she felt the whisper of its wing on her cheek. She smiled slowly and nodded. The goddess was here, she was answering her unspoken prayers and her heart opened and love flew in.
Eir came to stand by the pool first, her head bent, looking into the deep water. Slowly she started to sway to an unheard rhythm. The pool's surface rippled and the waterfall sang as it touched the water.
"My sisters, Hjördis whispered," We need to join in blood oath before we enter the sacred water."
They all came together, slowly untied their shoulder clasps and stood naked, feeling the sun's warmth all over their bodies. And they languished in that for long moments. Hjördis's frame was almost skeletal now her skin parchment thin, loose skin hanging from her arms as she lifted them to the sky.

"Oðdin, èacem Dryhten fram æll:
Fyllan ūre Sāwol wíþ þín èacem wisdom
Þæt lytlíng-dryhlem has cwícian on þeos œrðríce
Èower fōstrian ond èower fæðm hè wædligend

Odin, Great god of all,

Fill our souls with your great wisdom

The child-god has come alive in this earthly kingdom.

Your nurture and protection, he needs.

Your courage and valour he needs.

Permit we become your way to his soul, heart and mind

For your wisdom to become his wisdom.

Hjördis lowered her arms, bowed to the earth and walked slowly over to the sacred spring, the others followed her. They all knelt together by the edge of the water, holding hands and silently praying. They knew the huge importance of their combined task. And they all felt apprehension.

Hjördis spoke up clearly:

> "Wes ðū hāl, Folde Mōdor
>
> Framfíras, æt þu Nerthus.
>
> Ālyfan þes sunu weaxan ðærl in Nerthus onwærdness.
>
> Willan hè bèon finn frèondlíc ond wisdom.
>
> Đearl in feorhbold ond in ferhð.

Hail to thee, earth, and mother of men, to thee Nerthus.

Grant this son grows strong in Nerthus' presence.

Willing he be filled with your love and wisdom, strong in body and in mind.

And so, the wise women knelt beside the water for some time. Silence. Everything was hushed. The only movement was the gentle ripple on the water and the moving of their long hair in the gentle breeze.

Suddenly the tiny messenger bird, the wren, broke out of her hiding place and whisked past the women, touching each cheek with her gossamer wing.

"It is time", said Hjördis.

Take each a piece of your hair as gift to the goddess. I will take the forelock, you, Eir, take from the nape of your neck, and Heidrun, you, dear one, are double sided…take from both sides of your temple hair. We will make the blood oath before we submerge.

Each wise woman took a tuft of their hair, silently wincing. Hjördis then produced a small knife, never used or seen in daylight except for now.

"Your palms, please," she whispered, then slowly slashed across each palm, the blood flowing freely.

"Now we join, blood to blood, hair to hair," she intoned in a flat voice as they held hands together.

"Now!"

They jumped in perfect unison disappearing beneath crystal waters, their hair momentarily floating and swirling around each making a perfect circle. Then that too disappeared.

Everything was silent. Not a chirrup or a swish of wind could be felt. The mother too was holding her breath. The animals and trees silent for this time. But how long a time it seemed. Seconds turned to minutes and even they added to each other. The little wren suddenly flew over the deep spring. And then again back to its hiding place. Suddenly she broke into her beautiful full song, lilting and precious. The silence was indeed broken.

A splash of water saw an arm reach for the surface. Then Eir appeared, opening her mouth and taking a precious big breath of air into her aching lungs. She immediately turned to find her sisters. She was about to heave back underwater, when Heidrun appeared, gasping for air. They both looked at each other in dismay.

"Hjördis. Get her!" Eir shouted.

They both dived, knowing in their hearts that this was a terrible ordeal for such an old woman to face. That she was nearing her passage to the Otherworld, and that this just may bring her there faster than either of them wanted. That she had not shown any fear, nor anything at all that brought this awful thought to the present time.

The number had to be three. Just had to be!

Deep within those waters, Hjördis lay, her eyes open and her breath slowly leaving her in bubbles rising slowly to the surface. In one hand, she clutched sticks and in the other a bunch of herbs, fresh and newly plucked. But her life was fading. One last huge bubble escaped from her gaping mouth when Eir and Heidrun reached her. With each holding her up, they swam back to the surface.

Eir jumped out first and held her arms to catch their precious grandmother.

"Heave", shouted Heidrun.

When Eir had caught hold, Heidrun leaped from the water and both caught her and brought her up to lie unconscious on the grass. For several heart-stopping seconds they looked down at her in total dismay, shock. Her skin hung from her skeletal body like damp paper. Folds upon folds hung there on her lifeless form. Eyes sunken deep into their sockets, she was near dead, and no pulse could be seen at her temples at all.

Then Eir suddenly became present and heaved the old grandmother to her side, banging on her back to expel the water from her tired lungs. Water hurtled out with great coughing and cries of joy from the women. Hjördis's breathing was so weak, Eir turned her on her back and breathed into her mouth for several minutes, making sure her lungs were moving, her heart getting stronger with each breath.

She saw Hjördis was still holding onto the wood and the herbs, so tightly, her knuckles were white. She tried to lever them open.

"NO!" Hjördis croaked, "They must stay with me. They are for her son and I must give them to him when he is ready. I will teach you their true meaning for I am returning to the Otherworld"

"Not yet", retorted Eir.

Suddenly she realised they were all bone naked.

"Here," she cried," Cover our mother with her clothes. I will run back to the village to get help"

She stepped back into her tunic, missing several ties, and disappeared into the forest. Heidrun held her Grandmother close, keeping her warm, and waited. She let her rest, no questions, although she was full to bursting with the vision she received and the glimpse into the future.

She had been given message from the Einherjar, the spirit warriors giving her the role of guardian to the child god. To teach him about the mead spirit, about the sacred goat, but most of all show him the heights, where she herself goes with the goats, but then even higher for he must climb the highest mountain and know of it. The goat will be one of his familiars.

She looked again at the herbs and wood. They came from the goddess, for they were not damaged by water at all. There seemed to be eight herbs, some she recognised but most needed Eir's eye for she was a Læringmæden to the elder grandmother in all things herbs and healing. She had no idea about the nine sticks of wood.

"She nearly had me", came the whisper from Hjördis, "the serpent. I know her now and it is important that I do, for her son must know of the magic. He will, when he is grown turn into a serpent, the water will be no barrier to him and he will return also. He will be given the choice of his Otherworld home."

Heidrun starred at the old woman in silence, lost for words. There were none to be said. Some things just are!

Eir returned with a flurry of helpers, all women, who came with fur hides and woollen wraps, water, food and best of all a horse to carry the elder grandmother home.

"Do not repeat anything I told you, Heidrun. NOTHING!" Hjördis spoke sharply, having retrieved her voice.

"Gíese", Heidrun replied, "nothing will pass my lips. We are in a sacred bond here. I know this full well!"

"Hmm", Hjördis was not in an ambient mood at all. The thought of bumping back to the village, however wrapped up did not please her at all. They all sat for a while and ate the food brought for them. Hjördis just drank a little and Eir and two other women lifted her onto the horse's back. They needed to get her back and administer herb potions quickly

The journey back to the village was swiftly done. The mare brought for Hjördis was a wide backed giantess of a horse, able to take both Hjördis and Eir, she trotted with legs held high, making nothing of the troughs and dips, swerving past the branches as if she was a wild forest horse. Eir held her Grandmother against her, folding her arms around her tightly, keeping a firm grip with her legs guiding the horse home. The sun still sparkled through the leaves, bringing the deep sap green of new leaves alive, and the fresh smell of trodden grass reached Hjördis and she breathed in deep, her shoulders lifting at the effort." I am alive", she sighed as the sun caught the top of her head and warmed her skull, the only part of her showing on this journey home. The warmth of those furs against her skin had stopped the trembling. She was safe. The gods had given her a reprieve purely because she had to stay alive for this child-god. She wished it was otherwise: she was so very tired.

The other women walked back, Heidrun saying nothing and they knew better than to ask. Everything would be revealed when the full council met in the great hall.

… … … … … … … … …

I felt the elder grandmother heave a deep breath. Her shoulders sagged, and she wrapped the fur hide tightly around her. The central fire was nothing more than embers now, and the women just dark silhouettes merging with the wattle and timber walls. No one shifted and there was a great silence within the house, waiting for the following words of this great legend of the Geat and Warinni to be passed on. On this fair Isle of Wihtland, that reminded my elders and grandparents in some part, of their ancestral home, and their other relatives of the Cimbric peninsular, I hungered for the rest of the story, the missing pieces still to be sewn into this sacred cloak.

"I am tired to the bone", muttered the Elder Grandmother, "enough talking Dagrun. I must sleep, so bring the sleeping herbs to me. I wish to vision." I lifted myself off the mound of fur hides and let the elder grandmother lie straight, her bony arms extruding and her head to one side, she said quietly, "Dagrun, dear one, I will tell the rest of our story when we meet again, and you must use all your wits to remember every detail. It is important to remember. Promise me this."

"*Giese*", I replied, "Of course, this is so important to me, Grandmother."

"And for the next part of the story of our child god, you must see Wihtlæg, for it is his forefathers that thread together the weave of the warrior's tale. This will be a challenge to you Dagrun, for you are a young woman seeking the voice of our Cyng. You may be tested of course, so keep your wits about you."

I crept out of the woman's place, lifting the hide flap, and releasing it slowly and gently, so no draft would disturb the elder Grandmother, as I went to fetch her herb potion of vervain, chamomile and poppy, and I was deep in thought.

Crossing diagonally over toward my own small earth house, that doubled as my home and my apothecary, my mind was swimming between ancient past and problematical present. How to get king Wihtlæg to even see me, whose stronghold was situated high on the almost vertical hill, and whose warriors kept vigil against the Romans. It was the most secure place overall of

Wihtland and of course the king was safe there. These Romans, whom most Wihtlanders were wary of, were not trusted and looked upon as an unwelcome intruder. They did not kill or murder hardly at all. No, they had their sights set firmly on the trade and fertile lands that are so abundant on this isle. Trade with people over the big sea was abundant. Skills were so much a part of island life, that people overseas sought our goods. No, these Roman used us, worked us like slaves, even made some of us slaves when it suited them and took all the coin and pottery over to Gaul. And there were far too many of them, legions as they called their army of soldiers, to fight back on this tiny isle. But one day, one day the gods will bring a change, a new breath of wind we will feel and then we will act!!!, I thought as I walked headlong into a tall dark shadow, that felt like a solid oak tree.

"Ahhh!" I cried as my forehead contacted the solid bronze torc this "oak tree" of a man wore.

"Dagrun, my child," said Eystein, who was a good four hands taller than me, and I, who was many hands tall myself. "Why out in this darkness? And deep within your thoughts. What is the problem little sister?"

He wrapped his muscled arms around me: he made me smile, my big brother, and I relaxed. He was my big brother Wahl, with a shock of the darkest brown hair, curled and massed at a plait behind. Most still escaped around his ebullient features, dimpled and lined with crow's feet from far too much laughing. He was the chieftain of my tribe and a famous warrior.

"I'm just fetching our Elder grandmother her sleeping potion. She is singing our legend story, brother, and I am being given tribute to keep it for our generations to come. That is why I am in my head! I also need to find a way to see our *Cyng* Wihtlæg. And how am I able to achieve that, you may ask!!"

"*Hwæt!!*" exclaimed Eystein, "I may find a way for you, but it is near impossible for anyone to gain audience to Wihtlæg right now"

"Our Elder Grandmother has told me that only he holds the song of the child-god's warrior days. And I must know of it before the Romans kill all the Geat and Eudose and Warinni on this blessed Isle." I heaved a sigh of exasperation at the thought of even entering to see the great Cyng. The responsibility was weighing heavy upon me.

"Bah", Eystein retorted, "They will never do that. We will spear them all and throw their bloated carcasses to the sea goddess to finish them off!"

Suddenly, rain drops as large as dewdrops began spattering the ground, I raced into my house, leaped down the steps into the earth cavity to find the potion, ran out with my goat hide over my head and skidded straight into Eystein.

"Sleep well little sister", he said, "I will visit you soon with an answer to your problem, if I can." I ran to the women's house.

I slipped into our elder Grandmother's place, seeing her breathing easy, I nearly left, when she opened her eyes turning towards me, "Dagrun, my potion, dear one."

I lifted it to her shrunken lips, thinking with some alarm that it may see her to the Otherworld before her telling is complete. Maybe *Cyng* Wihtlæg would know, but then no man was privy to women's sacred work, ever!

"I will carry on at the sun's next rising, Dagrun. I will not leave before the story is complete, however much I wish it so."

"Grandmother, do not speak so." I replied, my throat swelling and my heart aching.

"Oh, sweet daughter, the Otherworld is not so far away. A deep breath and prayer will see me come to you whenever you call. You know this." The elder Grandmother sighed in a serene way and drifted into sleep.

I stayed with her. I could not find peace or sleep in my own damp and drafty earth house. I stayed and drifted into a deep sleep also. We kept each other warm and I did not want to miss another word she might say.

I am a dreamer, and the one that visited me this night was lucid and horrifying. Far, far beyond the life that I know now, in a time of a long winter, when copper leaves, curled and crisp, swirl around my feet, wind blowing harshly leaving my hair to sweep across my face. My lips are cold and when I lick them they freeze. They become chapped but more in total fear is my tongue searching comfort and finding none. In a full costume that is fine and beautiful, a style I know not, I am holding onto the Sacred Stone high above the island lowlands. My whole life is freezing into my lungs, and I am fighting for breath. From the sacred Stone, I can see for many miles, over to the downs. On an ordinary day, I would be praying to Nerthus, our Goddess of All, and laying the gifts before her, preparing for ceremony. But not on this day, and I am not who I am now. I am a leader of the people: a queen. And this is the last day of my peoples living on this beautiful Isle, our goddess given home. We are being attacked and we are being wiped from our Earth mother. We are pagan, they are not and they wish us dead.

For over the far horizon come an army of men, soldiers with spears, swords and shields, hardened leather armour and braided thongs on leather leggings. Hundreds of them come to kill everyone. Come to kill me.

In taking my last breath, I see fully the wrought iron mask, engraved and embossed in delicate filigree of copper and silver. I see frozen for all eternity his black eyes, blood crazed and beyond any humanity, the blackest energy, intent on his most important kill. The possession and then ending of my life.

I woke up harshly, inhaling noisily, gasping for breath. Still with that scene fully in my mind, I looked over to see our Elder Grandmother, seemingly serene in her peaceful sleep. "Does she know?" I asked silently: this was a dream of beyond. How far into the future I had no knowledge of that? I decided I needed to ask her.

A thin stream of morning light cascaded into the women's house from the hide flap. A gentle breeze was swinging it back and forward in a slow rhythm. Birdsong accompanied it and I knew the day was as beautiful as my dream was ugly. I crept over to the fire pit in the centre, realising that the ashes still glowed and would rekindle with work and care. Hides all around me moved and shuffled. Women were waking up and starting their day. The sweat that is purely woman arose in the air. Sweet and pungent, it flowed with the incoming breeze.

The kindling I put on yesterday's fire awoke with my breath and I watched the thin swirling smoke rise to the smoke hole. I decided I needed to greet the sun and take in some fresh air. Just as I stood to move over to the big entry flap, I saw a nose and half an eye appear.

"Psst!" the nose hissed. It was my younger brother Eyvindr Wahl, whose nose was as large as his tall, wide frame of a body and I knew it anywhere. He was our giant in keeping with all of us Wahls. We are the "Big People."

"Egil came running to me just now, his mother is in childbirth and struggling!" Eyvindr hissed. No male must enter the woman's place on sufferance of severe pain in many forms from the elders.

"I can't," I replied looking at him, his full face now staring at me, "Go to mother please, I am with our Elder Grandmother. I cannot leave her, really! Ealdor Ealdmōdor is *gesècan þæt ōþereorðe swiðe eftsōna. Nerthus onbídan.* (Elder Grandmother is going to the Otherworld, very soon. Nerthus waits.)

"*Gíese!*" replied Eyvindr, "I will tell her. Do not worry." Then turning back, looked at me with a frown, "I think I know, Dagrun. We must gather a clan meeting, you know this of course!"

Knowing my brother as close as we were in many ways, I wondered if he too had dreamed the future, like me. And if he had, what, in this time, must we do, as the Wahl clan to protect the stone knowledge.

I turned back to the Grandmother to see her move and stretch slowly, her eyes glued together with dried mucus: I watched as she forced them open, eyeballs rotating madly to see the world again for possibly the last time. My heart broke a little more. She turned to gaze rheumy eyes towards me, unseeing, yet knowing, sensing where I was.

"Dagrun Wahl," she wheezed softly, "Come child, sit beside me. Get close now for I cannot shout above a whisper!"

I levered myself down gently to put my ear close to her mouth so she may not strain any part of her unnecessarily.

She heaved a long deep sigh:

"The child-god bawled and bawled for even Ōdin himself to hear! The two cildfēstre women each took their turn to keep the baby pacified and well fed. They succeeded in the second, but the spirit of the child-god was frustrated in this new small body. He took to walking without even scraping his pudgy hands crawling on the earth. Teaching him to feel the Earth became an important part of his education. The baby/child had other plans! His eyes were already staring at the horses, and most certainly the mountains all around him. His eyes were always focused upwards as if reaching for his Ancestors on high, and he remembered them well.

As the rider jumped effortlessly up onto the horse's back, melded with the horse and became one, he could see and feel the magic, the alchemy happened before him and he knew. He understood.

As the lightning seared down to mate with the Folde Mōdor, on the tip edge of the tallest mountain, he saw and understood that magic, that alchemy. He missed nothing. He would watch the bees talk, communicate, work, gather the nectar and understood the intricacies of working life. They never stung any part of his body. Heidrun would talk to him of all she knew as if he understood every word. Sometimes a look of revelation would cross his small face and she knew he understood every word but had still yet to speak a single human word himself.

People, outside of the elder spiritual community, started to whisper that he was backward. Or that he was strange, not "normal." These quiet undercurrents grew until it came to the notice of the elder guardian of the clan. A full elder council meeting was called, to be followed by a community meeting of all. The child-god had to be brought into the clan, and be named, this ceremony being the most important to make him legitimate.

… … … … … … … … …

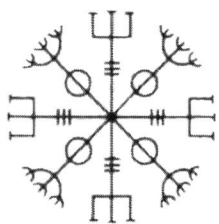

CHAPTER TWO
Wunder cræft: Miracle working

The great hall eclipsed the Elders meeting. It was built to house the whole community. Within its darkened edges, and full shadows, sat the cluster of Elders, quietly, in a circle around the central fire. The door was barred, no-one could enter until the horn was sounded. They had each sanctified and made sacred the area, called to all the gods and goddesses in turn to enter and assist. They were naming the child-god and needed approval. They needed otherworldly insight and above all they needed Hjördis whose veil was so thin she had the ear of Nerthus herself.

She sat quietly, listening.

Eir raised her head, holding her arms outstretched, raising them above her head, the nine herbs in her left hand and the nine sticks in her right hand.

"Wes ðū hāl, Folde Mōdor fram fíras, æt þu Nerthus.
Ālyfan þes sunu weaxan Ðearl in Nerthus onweardness.
Willan hè bèon finn frèondlíc ond wisdom Ðearl in feorhbold ond in ferhð."

Everyone was silent, breathless, waiting... for a swish of wind, a half-heard song from the Otherworld. Nothing.... waiting. Just the intake and outtake of human breath.
There was a gasp and all eyes went to Hjördis.
"*Wyrd byð swiðost!* Wyrd is the strongest!

We are incomplete and she will not come to us. We cannot see or hear her for we are only half what we need to be. If we are only half, how can our child-god become whole?

Wyrd oft nereð unfægne eorl, þonne his Ellen deah. The course of events often spares a man not doomed while his courage lasts."

"What must we do to become complete?" the heavy male voice of Yngling, the Elder Chief, boomed across the divide, the flames of the fire swinging away from him with force of his breath. He was a giant of Geatish blood. His huge frame was covered with woollen robes down to the ankle, not tucked, as his waist had long ago left him for the love of meat and mead. He was beyond ancient, and no-one except perhaps Hjördis herself dared cross him. It was whispered he was directly descended from Ing, the god of fertility, and it was indeed true that he had sired several generations in numbers uncounted. His mother was of the Ingavonii tribe, the water dwellers. His relationship to Nerthus was undisputed.

Vermundr, Týr and Steinn all concurred, shifting on their hides and muttering in agreement.

Hjördis straightened and took a huge inward breath to calm herself: knowing as she did that this represented a challenge of male insistence to direct on all levels the guardianship of the male child-god.

She did it neatly, with quiet confidence and truth travelling with her words across the fire.

"Wè sculan brengan þæt nigte-gala æt hine ond singan þæt ijōð leoð æt ūre cwildseten.
Wè sculan āginnan seiðr wíþ wyrd rapas ond āne þæt spakōna magandōn þeos!
Þær sculan wesan prag.... wefan wrydstafun wyrd sculan wefan þæt for hine.
We must bring the night-singer to him and sing the spell-song at our twilight.
We must begin spinning magic with sacred thread and only the seeress can do this!
There must be a period of time woven on the *Wyrd* staves. *Wyrd* must weave that for him!"

"He must know of his courage, his power, his intelligence and song, which all these things we do now, will give him. Protection of all kinds must be sung and woven around him. He must know the song of the Bees, the Raven, the Wolf, the Horse and the Goat. All these guardians I already know are to travel with him. He must hear the language of the waters and the message of the birds and know the magic of the mist.

Above all this we must tie the magic of the nine herbs and the rods into his being now and for all time. It is part of his destiny."

"So, great chiefs of this tribe, we bid you leave so we may start this work. As you well know every action has its Time, it's season and this is our time for the god-child."

Before there was any space to argue, Hjördis slowly, painfully levered her way upright, taking several minutes to straighten and tapping her staff, the signal for Eir and Heidrun to join her. She made her way to the entrance, the sun peeking through the hide, already casting her shadow back to the male Elders, who sat there, quite speechless.

"Oh, and to tell you also, that our beloved Nerthus has spoken…and she wishes to unite with the child-god and her statue must be washed and brought here along with her gemstone girdle for a short time only", Hjördis said this with her back turned away from the elders knowing the reaction before she had finished.

"Oðdinn's ðōðors! Næfre," bawled Yngling, "That is forbidden. It is against all our Laws. Nerthus must never be exposed."

All the Elders were now standing, waiting for Hjördis to capitulate. She did not.

"Do not worry old ones," she sideways smiled, "you will not be exposed. She does not wish your presence out of Her time. She wishes to unite with the child in her own way, in our tribal land so he may know of her at any time in his life here. Do you now understand?"

And with that she and her women exited the large house, leaving the male Elders to ponder and wonder just exactly how Hjördis had achieved the impossible.

The strong sun assaulted her, as she brought the loose woven wool shawl up and over her head shielding her tired, aching eyes: she had not slept well the previous night for all the spirit talking and the anticipated outcome. It went better than she thought. As her eyes were challenged so were her ears, as the bawling of the child-god got ever louder. She *wanted to sleep, to exit this day, but with a weary sigh knew their task had only just begun. Only when she was given leave by Nerthus herself, could she hand the child over to the men for their initiation of him.*

… … … … … … … … …

In the welcome shade of the women's house, Hjördis cradled the boy child, rocking him gently speaking Old Norse to him in couplets and rhyme and he settled. When he was truly asleep she looked over to both cildfèstre who looked weary and plainly exhausted as both their milk flow was diminishing and Bergis still had her own daughter to feed.

"Clearly, he is not calm or settled with undernourishment being the culprit here," Hjördis spoke to both women, "It is a brave service you give but this boy child is growing faster than any of us thought possible. He is learning faster and making all the physical movements of a young boy not a baby. We will give him more solid food now. Reduce your milk time and replace with barley in goat milk, increase it slowly but I feel very soon this young "boy" will be scampering around on full solid food before we know it!"

Both women let out an audible sigh of relief. Neither had dared to move away from prescribed feeding because he was so important to the clan and to Wyrd.

When they looked back, both child and Elder Grandmother were fast asleep. Eir came over smiling at the sight, and placed a warm hide over both and secured the door flap so no glare of the sun entered.

She looked over towards the women busy working on their looms. Wyrd was calling and could not be put aside. She called Heidrun over and they sat together in a quiet corner making urgent plans so the rite of naming could take place. They could not put it off much longer, both realising how much pressure the Elder Grandmother was under from the Elder chiefs of the council.

"We need to find the nigte-gala, the night singer", Eir said," where is she?"

"I believe she is in the forest still or on the mountain path with her goats." Heidrun replied, thinking it would be near impossible to get to her, if the singer was indeed on her way to the mountain, where she habitually travelled at this time of year.

"If Mani calls to her and Thor strikes at her heart, she will go to the mountain and not look back. Her calling comes now. She will be up there for certain when the birthing rite takes place. That we can guarantee. But for now, we need her here very badly."

"I can ask young Frídr if she will go and find her.", Heidrun pondered on this for it would serve another purpose. "She is coming to her own rite of passage and needs to be offered a challenge to prove herself and discover where she will be in her womanhood: bee keeper or seeress? This would form a good part of it."

"Excellent", replied Eir, "I believe I know where she will be." She leapt up from the comfort of the soft hide pile and strode out of the women's house, careful not to disturb the flap for the two sleeping generations, Hjördis snoring gently.

Frídr was an elfin child: her hair whisper white that fell past her shoulders and swept out like a spider's web to and fro whenever she moved. She had a face full of freckles in the summer sun and was sporting them already in this warm spring air. Eir saw her tending the bees. She knew she would be there for she knew their song.
She heard her singing before she saw her.

"Thor, imbi ist hucze, nu fliuc, du uihu minaz hera fridu frono in munt godes gisunt heim zi commone sizi sizi bina"

Thor, the swarm is out, now fly my beasts, here in the lord's keeping, in god's care, to come home safely...sit sit bees!

Her clear voice spun through the air like an invisible web of sound and most surely the bees heard and felt the song. She, as much as Heidrun, was at one with the swarm.
Eir edged forward, as she knew she was not, and the bees would feel her energy and not know it.

"Frídr," she called, "I have news and a challenge should you wish to take it, child."

"What?" Frídr turned and looked straight at Eir.

"Call off your bees, please", Eir replied, "I have not your bee charm nor your magic and I know we will not have the conversation we both wish, if they are swarming about!"
There were several wicker bee hives placed in a rough circle with Frídr in the centre, softly singing her charm magic. Sure, as day will follow

night, the bees, who up to that point were swarming free, took a straight line almost in formation and entered the hives, deftly avoiding each other in a dance both beautiful and breath-taking.

Eir took a breath to appreciate what she had just seen. Frídr was staring at the ground, hands clasped tight before her. The warm spring air gently rustled the white hair of Frídr. Eir looked over to her.

"Come and sit with me child," she said gently.

Frídr's hands were working, she was tense, and Eir picked up her anxiety. Her hair had fallen in front of her face hiding her expression but Eir knew from her shallow breathing that she was scared indeed!

"There is no need to feel so frightened," Eir spoke gently.
Frídr gave no response.

"You must tell me what is wrong before we can do anything about it!" Eir continued still hoping for at least a sigh or anger to erupt. Anything would be better than introverted silence that gave nothing away.

Slowly, Frídr turned to Eir and accusingly, looked her straight in the face.

"I know what you want of me," she cried, "It is to return to the women's house and help look after the boy child, who is taxing everyone's patience and fortitude! Why do you think you find me here? I prefer my bees, who may swarm at me on a difficult day, to wrestling with the child-god who is not happy in his little body! Everyone is saying dreadful things about him, but no one dares confront the Elders about it."

Eir gave out a long sigh, "We know all that you say, child, believe me we are trying to resolve this situation that has been sprung upon us by the gods. It is not that we ask you to join the other women. No, your challenge is a powerful one. One that will assist us in getting the child-god to know his spirit and his place here. We have powerful magic and charms to perform for Nerthus and the gods. We need you to go to the forest and find the night-singer as quickly as you can. She alone can summon the spirits to bring Wyrd into his life and make the spirit join the body. Will you go, child?"

Frídr relaxed when she heard this, then became excited.

"Yes!" she replied, smiling, "I will get ready immediately. I know now that this will be my rite of passage to womanhood, which I have been fretting about. The forest will teach me many things. And I want to be a singer: I want to learn from the night-singer."

"Her name is Huld, Frídr", Eir spoke smiling, pleased that her journey had not been wasted, "And she will recognise you, I'm sure, for you have the Wyrd so clearly with you and the voice that transcends to spirit.

But you must gather what you need quickly, and take this with you for she will know who it is from and you may have need of it also."

Eir untied the bag she carried with her always and handed the herbs and potions over to Frídr. It carried on the leather Eir's own mark, her talisman, incised and painted in red and ochre, the intertwining of the serpent of Nerthus and the willow tree.

"But you need this for your healing!" exclaimed Frídr.

"Oh! I have others you know, it is no matter to me and it will be very important for you.

"Come and eat with me: the afternoon draws on and you will be working your way through the forest by sundown. Catching your food will be your first and most difficult challenge. We have become soft in our living off the land."

They both sat with a spread of apple, barley cake and pork pieces laying at their feet on rough wool cloth. The afternoon sun cast long shadows before them and warmed their backs. Relaxing quietly, both submerged in their own thoughts, the food disappeared quickly.

"Honey", exclaimed Frídr, "I almost passed it over."
She went over to an upturned hive, the bees no longer working in there, and pulled out a handful a honeycomb. She spread it over the barley cake with her knife, and beamed as she tasted the mix.

"Be sure to take adequate amounts of that honey, Frídr," Eir explained," It will be helpful as bait and as a diversion."

"What do you mean?" quizzed Frídr.

"You will see", Eir replied quizzically.

She pulled the wool cloth into a bundle, straightened her robes and took Frídr by the shoulders.

"Take diligent care, Frídr, May the goddess be with you and call on your Ancestors when you may be in need. They will answer."

She left the young woman clutching her herb amulet with a look of sheer unabated excitement. In truth, she had asked the gods for this and *had given up hope. It is always the way, she thought, that in releasing a thing, you bring it ever closer.*

… … … … … … … … …

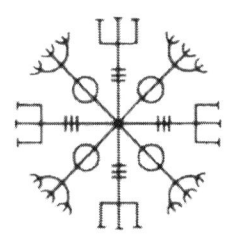

CHAPTER THREE
Þæt Gifu: The Gift

I saw a look of pain pass over the Elder Grandmother's wrinkled face.

"*Genōg Ic tèorian*," she whispered, "Enough I become tired. Let me sleep a while."

"Shall I bring you food?" I asked her, knowing her strength was leaving her and the story must be told.

"*Gíese, Gíese*" she whispered, "Bring some food in a few hours."

I left quietly leaving her breathing softly, hoping so much she would stay with us a while longer. It was early afternoon, the sun, I felt was hotter than normal, the women's house, musty and smoky. There was no one here. Who would be on this spring day? I placed more fur skins over her, and crept out leaving the door ajar to bring in fresh air.

I heaved in a lungful of fresh spring air and let it go slowly, looking up to the sun. In that outbreath, I let go a prayer to our goddess Nerthus and to Wōden, to make her passage soft and easy. To bring her into peace and harmony. I decided to make an offering to Nerthus, mother of all, and walked across to my home, where inside, laying deep in the earth was a gift I had buried for safe keeping, I knew it would be hard to give it up but would mean more for all that. It was a beautiful braecleat, with copper filigree design in the form of my guardian, the owl in flight. It was a gift, and in the new giving, the prayer would flow to the goddess for our Elder Grandmother.

Picking away the encrusted dirt, several years old now, I saw again its making, in the forge of my Father's brother, who sweated profusely, and I remember as a child thinking his skill, his magick was falling drop by drop into my keepsake. And then the filigree of shining copper being twisted and tapped and beaten into the owl in flight. It was my most precious object. I took a deep sigh; How could I do this? It hurt to think I may be betraying my family. It hurt to think I was insulting all the creative work of my Father's brother.

"Dagrun, you know it is never a shame or an insult to offer and gift beauty to the goddess!" Eystein said softly. I jumped and turned to see my big brother shielding what small light filtered into my underground cave home. He of all my family read my thoughts, sometimes before I had even created them!

"And," he continued, shifting his ice-blue eyes around my rough, cow dung and clay built home, "when are you going to take a husband who will rescue your poor dear body from this frozen Hell you have misguidedly chosen to devote your entire life to?"

My elder brother was my guardian in all senses of that word, and I loved him dearly. He was my left side, and my right side and before and behind me. We were bonded from the very beginning of my birth. He was there with my mother and saw me enter this world. It was breaking the traditional law but there was only him to tend my mother and so it became his gift and his burden both.

"It is not misguided! I replied, "How can you say that? I am the keeper of the herbs and charms, I am the healer and to heal I must keep these plants as well as I can. Keep them safe. Would you see me in a warm hall where they will wilt before my eyes?"

"You and your herbs can part company you know!" Eystein retorted, smiling all the while, "They will not shrivel at your parting, but you certainly will if you stay here!"

"And" he continued "you are the keeper of the Stones first, remember that my dear."

"Bah!" I cried in exasperation, for my brother was nearly always right, "I will not marry just for a warm fire, my soul needs warmth too!"

"Then in the offering you might just add a small wish for the goddess to bring your soul friend into your life. I would cheer a mighty chorus if that came to be, dear sister."

"How did you know I was making an offering to Nerthus?" I asked, looking at him with raised eyebrow and a chin stuck firmly out. There was always banter between us, friendly cross fire... on most occasions.

"Do you think we do not know what is happening with our Elder Grandmother dear sister?" he replied. "We have been praying for her. And there seems to be no-one to take her place."

I walked up closer to him, looking at him intently, trying to get behind those unfathomable eyes that gave nothing away. "You know she is shedding not only her worn-out skin, but also her birth right: her Story. She is telling me everything so I can give this to the Stone: always in the keeping of the stone's wisdom." I paused for a moment.

"Will you help me, Island Stone", I whispered, giving his ancestral name.

He looked over my head for a long moment, seeing beyond this realm, then stared into my eyes to see my soul. "It will be my privilege", he said simply.

Eystein made to go out of the door, when something came to me suddenly. I caught his arm.

"May I take your gelding, brother, as I have to make the offering and make food for our Grandmother before she wakes? I have to be there for her: she is relying on me completely."

"Do you mind this vigil?" my brother asked.

"Gods no!" I replied, quite angry at the thought.

"What I mind", I said, "is the gnawing thought that will not fly away, that I may not be good enough to keep this story alive. I t is our tribes' birth right, it is for generations to come! I have not trained to hold so much information!"

"Yes, you can!" Eystein retorted," You have, as all the Wahls have, our own birth right which we carry day and night for all our lives. You do not give enough credence to that Dagrun. We are with the stones, it is in our blood, girl! We carry that ability to hold stories as much as the Stones do. Now! Let us get this gelding for you and be mindful, he is frisky on a day like this one. We all are!"

The spring sunshine held; the air seemed to still, our Mother held her breath for all of creation was about to spring into life. I could smell so many plant perfumes sitting on the still wind, a faint whisper of wind sending them through the air to weave across my nose. Oh, glorious day! I thought. And it was intense.

So was my handling of the gelding, for immediately after I landed on his back, we were skipping sideways and around. I pulled on his reins so hard his lovely head swung sideways, and he calmed. I kicked gently and we were away, speeding across the flat meadow land towards the sea. It was not far, and soon we came to the beach which stretched along to the white cliffs. I hobbled the gelding near the cliff and where there was grazing. Apple mint wafted past my nose and I breathed in deep, noting the need to collect some for my apothecary.

The braecleat was in a pouch inside my shift. Close to my heart, it had become warm and damp with sweat, I lifted it out where it caught the sun and glimmered brightly.

The way down to the beach was difficult, but there was a freshwater stream that gently cascaded to the beach. It was sacred to us. The eternal cycle of water from sea to clouds to thunder and rain met here. And there was a natural deep pool that collected and gently over spilt the rain water as it continued, meandering to the sea. This pool held our gifts to Nerthus. Many silted over. Mine was about to join them.

In the distance were the white cliffs towering above a languid sea. The sun, vivid, created dancing sparkles, which, as children we called the sea nymphs. Azure blue and cerulean blues danced with each other as the wind and tide took them in a beautiful spring dance.

I thought of our Elder Grandmother, and her journey to the everlasting meadow of Nerthus, Neorxenawang, where she would join the Muses in their constant overseeing of our fated lives and our mistakes. I hoped she would find joy there and peace. I would hope they laughed at our mistaken attempts to be "great."

I hoped, with her beautiful soul free again she would be able to visit our ancient homeland, she, who had memories of that place, that we did not. She was, according to my mother, a small child when she was taken, with many others to cast their fates to the big sea and make that extraordinary journey to find a better home.

And I hoped that she would, for a while, walk hand in hand with our beloved Nerthus, mother of all, who cherished us with an unspeakable love.

And those were my prayers for her, as the braecleat slipped from my fingers into the pure water, the sun, for the last time catching it and glinting, it disappeared into the gloom of the deep-water pool.

"*Nerthus! IC bèn forðæm ðe þæt gesund færeld forðœm ūre Ealdmōdor ond gescèawian hiè stillness, blíðnes, ond frèogan in æfre æfterra ealdor.* Nerthus, I pray for the safe journey for our grandmother, and grant her peace, joy and love in life everlasting."

I sat for a while lost in thoughts, until I could no longer feel my feet, and scrabbling up, rubbed ferociously to bring my legs back to life.

I half hobbled, half ran back to my brother's gelding, rubbing his neck and putting my forehead to his in apology. He did not seem worried. The pasture was rich and he had his fill. I walked him over to the bushes of mint growing: they were a signal to anyone that this is healing land. I took bunches from several bushes, making sure there was enough left for all the insects and birds who needed them also.

I jumped on to Forseti's back and he sprang forward, ready for the gallop, so we sped over the land, jumping bushes that suddenly appeared and swerved all the ruts and ditches. Suddenly to my left appeared a familiar sight that immediately opened my heart. The invisible strands that bound me to it, tugged strongly. I simply had to obey and swerving sharply to make my way over the stone circle, the home of our Ancestors of the Warinni and the Geat, Eudose and Suevii that had made this island their home.

It sat in a perfectly flat piece of land, a peaceful meadow that had been made sacred many years ago, before I was born. The sun shone on the circle for almost all day and at night the Moon was given uninterrupted view of our Ancestors' home. It was alone, of itself, unique. Back in our homeland, so my Grandmother would say, there were fields of stone circles, protecting many tribes and hundreds of Ancestors. They stretched forever to the horizon and beyond. I hold this picture in my mind. It is a sacred gift.

Again, I tied my brother's gelding to a good tree and walked over to the circle. The stones were the height of a tall child-tall, for we were known as giants among other tribes. Each stone, an Ancestor. I knew most of their names, as my mother and grandmother had sung them to me often enough at our twilight time of ceremony and honouring.

To go into the circle during daylight was forbidden. No-one dared break that respect.

In daylight, they slept: we worked the day in this physical realm. The twilight is our marker for a day well spent. We honour this time as both a beginning and an ending. So, it is always this time that ceremony takes place. Twilight when we meet in tribal council and when the stories are told. I knew I would be asked to be that storyteller for my people. As I went around the outside of the Ancestor circle touching each stone, I quietly asked for the gift of long memory and clarity. Strength in my speech and endurance in the telling. I do not know if I was heard. But I felt wrapped in a comforting feeling as I left to see to the needs of our Elder Grandmother.

As I galloped back to our village, I saw the shadows had grown so long: I knew I was very late. I kicked Forseti and urged him on. Speeding into the entrance gate I pulled Forseti to a sudden stop throwing up dust on to Mother's tunic, who happened to be standing in the way, a basket held on her hip.

"Dagrun, Bah! She exploded, *"Forðǣmðe bismrung! Þín Ealdmōdor is āweccan*. Your Grandmother calls. Here take this to her."

I swung my leg over Forseti and jumped to the ground, taking the basket in one move and sped over to the women's lodge.

… … … … … … … … …

CHAPTER FOUR
Þæt Nigt-Gala: The Night Singer

I found our grandmother sitting up, or rather leaning on the nearby weaving table that held wools and thread.

Her bony fingers lacing the coloured threads around the hilt of her seax, in a pattern I had never seen.

"Dagrun, daughter," she half turned to lower her lids to register some disappointment in me.

"You have food?" she queried.

"*Gíese,* Ealdmōdor." I placed it beside on the weaving table. She seemed much rested and alert.

"*Ðoncian þu.* Thank you", she replied, "I see the warm sun and the flowers perfuming the spring air proved too much for you *dohtor.*"

"I felt so strongly to go and respect our circle of the ancestors, grandmother," I said, looking to the floor.

"Ah. So, you think my time is so close you can rob me of my food for my old body has no need of it!"

"That is not so", I retorted, hurt at her stinging words.

"Then tell me what is!" she rasped back as she spooned the broth into her mouth. By blessed Thor, but she had her appetite back, I thought.

"I took Eystein's gelding and went to Nerthus, her sacred pool by the big sea. I gifted her my braecleat that is my animal guardian, the owl in flight. I…"

"I know," she interrupted.

"I…. don't understand", I stammered. "How?"

"*Bearn, bearn!*" she gave a deep sigh and her shoulders sagged. Taking a deep breath, she continued in a softer voice, "You block your wisdom and we must correct that, Dagrun. Let me please finish my food. Then we will talk.

Here take this *seax*, it is now yours, *dohtor*, sit with it. Go to the horses, see what they may show you. Come back to me before twilight, for there is still much to tell you."

I left, shaking. The knot in my throat and a knot in my stomach coiled with each other until I felt I was choking. Taking gasps of the now sickly-sweet air, to calm myself down I strode past my mother's *cotlíf*, past the great hall and to the end of our *ceasterwic*, past the ever-hot smithy to our boundary land. The horses were spread out in rich meadowland, as they were enjoying the later afternoon sun. Forseti whinnied as he saw me approach.

I was grimly holding the *seax* my grandmother had given me, and felt my hand begin to tingle. I knew not why, but knowing with my front mind is rarely part of the journey to wisdom and I felt I was on that journey by the gifting of the *seax*. Forseti turned and gently stamped his hoof, stepped backward in a deliberate motion flicking his tail; from side to side as he did so. He stared into me, a full deep wisdom coming from his eyes and I knew I could meld with his spirit. The stamping of his hoof was showing me that the wisdom of the earth mother is beneath our feet always, the stepping back was travelling the backward path and the swinging of the tail was the truth that before and after are running side by side with us now in the present. Forseti, our benevolent god is for justice and peace. I jumped on his back and he slowly led me round the outside of our boundary. Holding onto the *seax* I put my head down to his and shut my eyes.

Lightning shot down from the heavens in a cascade of shimmering fire, zig-zagging to our mother where it exploded in ground shattering fusion. It was the All Father, Oðdin, creating with Nerthus, our mother, a new spark of creation. She was being renewed. She trembled at the touch. The people stood in a circle protecting a man and a baby, in awed silence, waiting.

A massive roar of thunder brought the ball, as it shot from the heavens it swirled to an even bigger mass of light and power. In the blinking of an eye it came and shot into the very centre of a lake that was almost perfectly circular. In alchemy, Fire met Water to create a fusion of steam that encircled the entire lake and swept upwards to engulf the circle of people at the ravine's edge.

A baby was held aloft.

My eyes shot open, in a gasp of air I came to the here and now. I found I had held so tightly to Forseti's mane, handfuls of his hair came away. He whinnied. I hugged him in thanks and whispered words that he knew. I led him back to the meadow with half my mind still in the vision. He had wandered far enough away from our *ceasterwic* to make me realise I had been away for a while. We cantered back. He enjoyed the run and I left him, head down in a tuft of green grass. I looked at the *seax*. It was the weave that elder grandmother had woven that took me to visioning. I was sure of it and knew I had questions to ask before she continued with the telling.

I found her rested and more alert than I had seen for many a day. A fur hide wrapped her in warmth and she beamed a knowing smile when I sat and stared at her, bursting with the need to share the vision.

"*Ealdmōdor*, I was given a vision, but it stopped too soon!"

"No, it did not stop too soon", she retorted, "You stopped it, my *dohtor*. Tell me what you saw."

In the retelling, I suddenly knew the importance of what I witnessed. It was a birthing ceremony in the ancient way, which the gods and goddesses spoke in their way that rarely happens now.

"And the baby, *Ealdmōdor*!" I cried," what was about to happen to the baby?"

"That I am about to do in the next telling."

"And the weave on the *seax*," I continued," What does this weave do. What does it hold?"

"It is *Seiðr*, Spinning magic. *wyrd rapas* is woven with the aid of the *nigte gala*, the night singer. And that is for the telling. Have patience, my Dagrun beorn, and you must learn to trust your inner mind for it houses your soul spirit where the lessons are sitting waiting for you to gain and win your own wisdom. Let go!"

Grandmother rested her back against the shield behind her hides and looked at me with a soul reaching stare and said, "Listen and remember *dohtor!*"

"Frídr sat on her heels with her back against the immense pine that towered above her. She sighed. She had been fairly skipping through the forest but now the wooded mountain towered above her. It made her feel small: infinitesimal. As small as her bees. This feeling she did not like. "Now I know what the bees make of me," she thought aloud. She heaved herself up and continued the tendon stretching climb ever upwards. It was nearing dusk. She needed to find cover, with ferns and detritus to build her shelter: she had enough water for this night, but she hoped to follow the animal tracks to guide her to a stream for the next days.

Eir had given her a detailed guide to find Huld. She hoped her spirit would guide her. She hoped she would hear the singing before she caught the sight of her. Tonight, she had enough food. She made her shelter with a fallen branch resting against the pine and spent the remaining day light overlapping ferns and leaves to make the roof. A bed of shrivelled beech leaves she had collected before she entered the deep forest, became the soft floor along with moss gathered. Last, came the fur hide she had used to carry all her survival things.

Would she light a fire? It was both a warning and an attraction to the night creatures. She decided not. It was still warm from the hotter than normal spring day.

She settled to hone her seax blade and spear point. Then after several protection prayers to Nerthus and to Nōtt, goddess of the night, asking for her help and guidance to bring Huld and herself together, Frídr fell asleep.

The tall, fully grown he-bear did not move silently through the forest, for he had dominion and was not especially hungry. But the shuffling woke up Frídr with eyes wide and breath shallow. All her nerves were pinpricking her weary body into awareness. Then the fear shot in like a bolt from the deep unconscious. And she felt she was trembling so much it made the leaves shake and he would be on her before the seax and spear were ready. But it was useless to think either of these weapons could kill him, unless the gods steered the spear straight into his heart.

And she was alone. There was no man to help her. This dawning would be her last and no rite of passage would grant her life to the Singers.

She knew bear could smell fear. She had to confront it and quench it somehow. Anger might help but it was not her nature. Frídr was not a warrior in her heart. She could no more summon anger than an army full of men warriors to kill this bear. She did not even want to do that.

She reached down into her soul: A feeling of peace when she sang to the bees, that first time, came over her. It was all she could do in the face of it. Frídr decided she would sing to this he-bear, who had now smelled her scent. She could see his darkened shadow form move towards her shelter. The moon escaped from behind a cloud and lit the forest floor and brought a low, shimmering glow to the leaf canopy. Frídr chose this very moment to move out and expose herself to the approaching bear.

At the last moment, she thought of the honey and Eir's words to her. She snatched it up and held it tightly in her hand.

Frídr shone white in the bright moonlight, Mani had heard her. Her white hair moved with her body as she started to sway from side to side. Her face, the pallor of white shell, her eyes wide and fixed on the bear, who was now raised up on two legs, his fur rippling as he stood transfixed at the sight before him. He snorted, his breath steaming from his nostrils.

She sang, so clear and so loud, the vibration from deep within her chest, made her tremble.

"Thor imbi ist hucze, nu fliuc du uihu minaz hera fridu frono, in commone, size, size grèat beran"

As she sang to her bees so she sang to this great bear, but calling his name in place of the bees. He put his head slowly to one side. He snarled softly, showing great teeth, the steam of his breath escaping in short bursts. Frídr sang deeper, swaying all the while. Very slowly she brought the honey pouch out so he may pick up the aroma. He certainly caught it and began to move forward.

With great courage and deftness, Frídr moved forward, changing her song:

"In munt godes gisunt heim zi commone…. æfterhyrgan great beran, æfterhyrgan great beran. FOLLOW FOLLOW GREAT BEAR!

As she threw the honey pouch with all her strength, the bear turned, slammed down on all fours, fur shaking, he followed the honey, giving Frídr a half look, and she ran in the opposite direction, swiftly picking up her seax and spear, and Eir's medicine pouch.

She was just catching her breath when an arm hurled out from behind a tree and grabbed her tightly.

"Ahhh," she shrieked, turning, found herself looking into the eyes of a wild woman. Her hair tied up in a knot with white shells laced around the topknot. They glistened in the bright moonlight. She noticed these same shells hanging from the thorn that held her skin tunic together at the shoulder. She had skins for leggings and fur trim around her waist. Nothing woven except for a braid of deep ochre and crimson threads held on her arm by a beautiful silver braecleat.

"I heard you," she said, with a deep resonant voice, "I am Huld."

"Oh, so thankful am I" Frídr gasped, still taking in a lungful of air, "I escaped the great bear." "I saw it all," Huld laughed, her teeth shining white against her dark skin, "By the Goddess, but you are as white as the moon! That bear had not seen the like of you before. You were very brave, young girl. Are you on your rite of passage?"

"Giese", Frídr replied smiling shyly and looking to the ground, "but also to find you. I have a message from our women. They are calling for your help with the child-god, who is still parted from his soul's spirit and is fretful and angry. He is driving all the women-folk quite mad with frustration. The cildfèstre in particular are fainting with the effort of keeping him fed!"

Huld laughed, a deep throaty laugh that felt infectious, and before Frídr knew of it, she was laughing too, in relief, until she collapsed on the forest floor, heaving for breath.

Huld grabbed her arm.

"Come, young child, we must make some distance between us and that bear!"

They clambered up the deep ravine, studded with tall pine and fir trees. There was no space for talk, just the immense effort in the climb. Frídr was wincing in the pain from pine needles catching into her soles, which were, she decided totally unfit for purpose. Huld had triple layers of leather and wadding protecting her feet.

"Rise above your pain, child," Huld said without looking back, "sing: in your head. Your rite of passage is not finished yet awhile."

It took many more hours in darkness to reach the summit. Huld knew exactly where to go, what footholds were good and Frídr followed her close behind. The dawn, the sun rising in a cloudless sky, came as a welcome relief for them both. And there appeared before them, a narrow flat plane of land that was the very edge of the mountain. The dawn chorus was, even at that height, loud, with crow and raven and jays making their unique calls to each other. An eagle's eerie screech pierced the mountain air, followed by her mate's answer. They were slowly circling in the high thermals.

"Go to the edge, child," Huld commanded, "but please do not fall off"

"My name is Frídr, and I will not!"

Huld smiled. Frídr edged towards a line of tufted grass that marked the boundary to a thousand-foot drop or more. Yet it was more than that, as Frídr gasped at what she saw. The tops of thousands of fir and pine trees marched their way down the steepest incline she had ever seen. She felt giddy for the first time in her life. The eagles called and circled. She knew she was experiencing a sacred sight, a place of the gods and goddesses together. For far, far down below, beneath the mist that was swirling and gently lifting as the sun's heat coaxed it ever upwards to meet the cloudless sky, Frídr glimpsed a perfectly circular lake shimmering in the early morning sun. At such a spiritual moment, Frídr could feel Nerthus, see her ghostly half-form weave across the top of the water. Her mind emptied and her heart opened completely and broke. She fell to her knees.

"Sing! Frídr", Huld commanded, "Become the singer you desire, call to your goddess now you see her!"

Frídr slowly stood firmly on that rocky edge, her feet apart and opened her lungs with her heart and sang.

"Hal Wes thu, Nerthus, fira modor, thu Gebletsod weorth!

IC cumaþ tō gebrèman þa halig wihtes

Ond bewægnaþ bèdu for þas earþan þe we lifiaþ

Hir eorðtùdor ond hir eallwihta"

Frídr repeated the song, louder and clearer. Huld came to quietly stand beside her, then joined in the song. They sang in perfect harmony for Huld was a deep contralto, her earthy notes complimented Frídr's high soprano, almost an octave higher. Their voices soared up into the heavens. And down towards the sacred lake, where, another ethereal voice joined them, a cadence unknown and lilting. It was an echo, a voice made apart from their own. The mist from the lake was rising into a shape that almost formed a woman, imposing and tall, Frídr almost saw her face, the mist sculpturing a nose and brow, and hair that swirled in dove grey colouring. It was so beautiful an image, she caught her breath: and it was gone as soon as it appeared.

Then, suddenly, that ethereal voice came clear into their minds.

Nese cyme, nese gegigan,

Nese ǽfter, nese ǽtforan

IC warian þu Folde Lytlings nèahfædras æt mè

IC onlǽtan þu ǽt wesan frèo

Forðǽm IC am on þu

Ond þu are on mè

No coming, no going

No after, no before,

I hold you Earth Children close to me,

I release you to be free,

For I am in you,

And you are in me.

Huld and Frídr looked to each other and saw confirmation. Their eyes wide in wonder, neither could utter a word. Moments passed. It was sheer beauty that had entered their hearts and minds. Nerthus was within them both and they felt humbled beyond speech. Then she became invisible, the mist beneath them cleared and Frídr saw for the first time, the deep azure blue of the lake and its immensity. Stretching farther than she thought and wider than she believed, this sacred lake, the home of Nerthus, hidden completely from view to everyone except the adepts, shimmered in unspeakable beauty in the now midday sun.

They came back to themselves slowly, reluctantly.

"Down there is a cave," Huld whispered, "Deep and stretching through the mountain. It is the mountain pass through which I will bring Hjördis. She and I will be the anchor, the echo to the singers here above." *She pointed to the rocky outcrop.*

"When, what!" *Frídr asked in confusion.*

"Why, the naming of the child god of course, and bringing him directly into the care of the gods and goddesses. How else will he achieve his Fate? However much we might weave the Wyrd staves, it is through the union with his true guardians that life will be as it should be for all our tribes.

And you will lead them here, Frídr", *Huld continued, scanning her eyes for understanding and compliance.* "All of them, up through the forest where we have just travelled. Do you understand child?"

"But," *Frídr stammered,* "I don't know the way! I will lose them all, truly."

"You just walked all the way up here, child", *Huld choked in exasperation,* "what do you think this rite of passage is about, I would like to say. Nothing is for nothing! You had better learn and learn quickly!"

"I just followed you!"

"Well you can lead the way down!" *Huld retorted,* "And leave markers, as many as you like, and make them large and visible."

… … … … … … … … …

Huld strode into the ceasterwic, spear and shield in hand, looking straight ahead, unblinking, blind to the stares. It was rare for a nigtegala to appear not only in full daylight but to appear in a village at all! Her burnished skin spoke of a life in the wild. The skins that wrapped tightly around her body, spoke of a forest life that most of those living now as farmers had long forgotten. And she needed to wash. Her long-knotted hair was matted. She was not of them. A wild woman. And it set her apart.

Frídr walked at her side, head held high. She was now a singer and she was very proud. There could not have been two more dissimilar women. Day and night, dark and light. These two complemented each other by their diversity to each other.

And they were being talked about.

Huld felt a stirring within her of a long-forgotten feeling of belonging and friendship. She had been alone for so long, part of her was frightened at this new alliance with Frídr. Another part gave a deep sigh of release. Fear of loneliness was a ghost never far away and now that was gone. She smiled and turning to Frídr, took her hand.

They walked into the women's lodge and saw Hjördis, Eir and Heidrun. All three women were huddled together in deep conversation, none saw the two enter. They waited until Hjördis looked up.

"Ahh, my beorns! You have returned to us. Huld welcome!" she gave Huld that rare tooth-gapped smile and clasped her forearm in Elder greeting. It was amazingly strong for such a frail looking grandmother and Huld reciprocated.

"I am honoured Ealdmōdor", Huld bowed her head, then reached forward to kiss Hjördis gently on the cheek. They both embraced in a bear hug that squeezed the air out of Hjördis, and she broke away laughing.

"By the god, Mani, but you are stronger for your forest living, beorn!" Hjördis said smiling.

Meanwhile Eir sprang over to Frídr, searching her eyes for confirmation.

Frídr beamed. "I did not need the medicine pouch, the singing brought Huld to me... but the honey, Eir, Oh my! That was a godsend."

"Hah, I knew it" Eir hugged Frídr, "Are you a Singer?"

"Yes, I am", Frídr replied, turning to Heidrun, "May I ask leave of you, dear sister, for I now know where I belong, and give to you my bees, for your safe keeping?"

"You will be missed, sweostor, and you must visit… often", Heidrun replied, feeling a sudden sense of loss. She had watched over this frail looking white haired, pale mæden since she was small enough to sit on Heidrun's ample knee. A surrogate mother she most certainly was. And why was there not a rite of passage ceremony for losing mothers? she thought sadly.

"The bees will miss you too," she said, "I cannot sing to them the way you have done."

"But they will still make honey, Mōdor!" Frídr cried, using the word mother for the first time. Tears appeared in her eyes and she hugged Heidrun so tightly, some tears flowed from her too.

"Come, come, my beorns," Hjördis called insistently, "we have much work to do this day, we have a child-god to attend to."

"The moon is still full," Huld said, looking to them all in turn, "we will make the wyrd rapas this night. What do we need to include in the seiðr spinning magic and what do I, we" she turned to smile at Frídr, "need for the ljðð leoð, spell song?"

Hjördis replied, "Look to the gods and goddesses, most importantly for all their guidance and protection for the young god in training. Then we must weave arstafas and wrydstafun, the staves of honour and of destiny. We must weave in the nine charm seiðr of the healing herbs and sticks gifted by Nerthus herself, for it is this that will make of the god, a supreme healer. That is his destiny even above his valour in battle.

He can receive the seiðr of shape changing but only if we weave in the stafas for it to become part of him. His goddess Mōdor demands this most of all."

"Tonight, then my sweostors," Hjördis continued, "We will meet at the beginning day, at twilight, and we will walk to the sacred grove to spend the night there."

"Rest well", Heidrun replied.

… … … … … … … … …

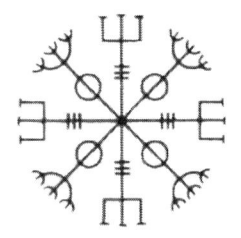

CHAPTER FIVE
Ljóð leoð, seiðr
Spell Song, Spinning Magic
For a god.

The three wise priestesses sat together in a circle, Hjördis speaking softly, so as not to interrupt the preparations of the singers, as they too sat huddled on the ridge preparing for the night ahead. It was frosty, cold, and soon they could see their breath as a mist swirling in the gentle breeze. They had all come prepared with fur skins wrapped around them, but for Frídr, who had no spare flesh to speak of, she was already trembling. Huld wrapped an extra fur around her legs and hugged closer. "Together we will wake the gods and goddesses, Frídr, you will forget the cold and become warm in their presence, I promise you."

Hjördis explained softly, "Listen well, sweostors, for I am giving you weaving to cræft. Do it well for our children's children. I am giving you the child-god's life to be in your care this night.

I have been given his name. It will be woven into wyrd rapas. Each rune is a quality he will be gifted. For good and ill. Each will be empowered at the exact time. He will wear these weave rapas for all his earthly life. They will be guarded by a bronze, then silver torque on his left then right arm. This is what I have been told by our goddess, Nerthus, his earth mother. These are his runes:

The All Father Oðdinn wishes him to gain the wisdom of the Runes and now it is for our child god to work them into magical healing for our people. He will become a great healer. The herbs, Eir, you keep in your safe keeping, sweostor, for the day when he will ask for them. And the nine glory sticks, he will discover.

"Now, the looms before you hold a warp and weft that is unique and magical. Never to be told or talked about, Sweostors."

Hjördis had brought new and unseen looms, worked for her by the smithy with polished oak wood cut to six sides, and silver crafted nails were hammered along the edges to hold the threads. They looked beautiful even more, so that the silver nails shone like elf lights, within the sacred grove.

"Now each thread has spirit power, so with care lay the blue threads from Sun to Moon. Lay the crimson from South East to North West. The green is his Life, it is unbroken so this will be woven without pause and fixed without a break. It is for the Fates to break, not us. This will be woven from North East to South West. The amber thread is for the runes. Work each one into the centre before you weave the Life thread."

Each wise woman sat in silence for a few moments collecting their prayers, their songs and their Will to create the sacred link of the child-god to his guardian Spirits. Then they began.

… … … … … … … … …

The full moon sent shafts of luminous light onto the surface of a pool that was still like glass. The night world held its breath. The women sat in silence with only the rustle of threads being tied to the small looms each woman held on the ground. Threads of amber, crimson and dark blue and green lay on the crisp frost laced grass, in readiness for the weaving. The singers sat away from the women, on a ridge above the pool. Frídr most of all shone in the moonlight. She radiated a pulse that was unique, and Huld loved her for that. Leaves were silhouetted in a silver sheen, for the night goddess Mani was gracing them all with the fullness of a cloudless sky with many stars and a moon to truly sing to.

So, they began:

Wes ðū hāl, Folde Mōdor

Fram friras, æt þu Nerthus.

Ālyfan þes sunu weaxan ðearl in Nerthus onweardness

Willan hè bèon finn frèondlíc ond wisdom ðearl in feorhbold ond in ferhð"

Hail to thee, Earth, mother of mortal men. To thee Nerthus, grant this son grow strong in Nerthus' presence, willing he be filled with your love and wisdom, strong in body and in mind.

"Oðdinn, Fæder fram eall-þu fæðm for se Beorn wè ãcsian þu cuman – cuman – cuman wrōon þu drycrǽft embe hine.

Ōdin Father of all - your protection for the child we ask you to come – come – come, wrap your magic around him."

"Thor Dryhten fram ðunor ond beadu. Þu fæðm ond þu beadu ellen wè ãcsian þu to Giefan

Cuman – cuman – cuman--- þu bord ond bile hè behōfian

Thor, God of thunder and battle - your protection and your battle courage we ask you to give. Come – come – come – your shield and sword he needs."

They sang together, high and low, in perfect harmony, looking to each other for proper cadence and timing. That perfect chanting song rose to the night sky and came back in echo. It flowed back around the sacred grove, and the leaves shook slightly, and the pool's surface rippled gently, and they knew the Ancestors had come, and they knew they had been heard. The three women silently went about their magic weaving, threading all the magic into each warp and weft. Three wyrd rapas for each of the child-god's life stages on this earth.

And so, it continued into the night.

"Bragi, Dryhten fram lèoðcræft ond sōncræft, þu fulfremednes of ferhð ond reord hè behōfian, wè ascian to cuman – cuman – cuman – standan bí his side.

Bragi God of poetry and music, your perfect mind and voice he needs, we ask you to come – come – come – stand by his side."

"Mani ond Nōtt, Dryhten fram þæt Mōnã ond gryden fram þæt nigt. Wè ãcsian forðǽm ðe þu fæðm for se beorn in his swefn middangeard ond Giefan hè niht-gesihð fram þæt wulf ond beran.

Mani and Nott, goddess of the moon and goddess of the night, we ask for your protection of the child-god in his dream world and give him the night-sight of wolf and bear."

And so, it continued through the silvered night, the women weaving and the singers, without pause, chanted into a trance state that took them both above their worldly bodies.

Forseti, god of justice peace and truth, came and wove the strongest thread through the wyrd rapas, giving the child-god a deep love of justice that would, in his destiny, be ever needful.

The goddess of love and fertility, though also of battle, weaved silver, luminous strands around all the women giving them strength and a bonding together that would be unbreakable in the coming years, as guardians of the child-god. The strands separated into three and snaked down to meet the wyrd rapas and meld into the threads.

Hjördis, Eir and Heidrun all looked at each other and gave a quiet gasp in awe of all this happening before their eyes. And continued with the weaving. Never once did they falter, and like the singers had been released from their earthly bodies in a heightened state of consciousness.

Dawn was approaching and night gods and goddesses receded, taking with them, a large part of the energy that was keeping the women alert and alive.

Frídr faltered suddenly.

"Look Frídr, the Sun is rising," Huld whispered, "Sing to the Sun."

The yellow glow of a new day spread across the horizon, in light yellow and shimmering gold. Spreading to the trees, their leaves came alive with the sap green of spring and soon, the birds were singing loudly, leaving the night-singers with an ending.

"*Sunna, sunna, sunna! Gyden fram þæt sunne*

Dagr ond Delling, Drytens fram þæt dæg ræd ond þæt dæg, brengan þū æt se bearn

Cuman – cuman – cuman

Ðoncian þu ðoncian þu!

Sunna sunna, Goddess of the sun, Dagr and Delling, gods of the dawn and day, bring your warmth and wisdom to the child-god. Come – come – come! Thank you all!"

Frídr croaked the last words and fell forward on her hands clutching the grass, head lowered. She was exhausted. All their energy now spent, the women hauled themselves up, Heidrun supporting Hjördis, who groaned low and long as she willed her joints to unlock and her blood to start flowing through her numb limbs.

And what was created after their long vigil and union with the gods? A pile of beautifully crafted wyrd rapas, each laid carefully in line as they were finished. Quite a few for the young child-god and several for the youth god, and only one for the grown man, the longest and most intricate of all, which would be gifted by the Elders when he had achieved his rite of passage to become a warrior. Eir carefully place them in three pouches bound in leather. They began to trudge home, from the sacred grove, to weave their way past the guardian trees and into the forest with all the teeming life of bird and insect, fox and badger. The horses had been hobbled and tied so when they returned each woman caressed and fed them, wiping down and checking their hooves. They had been asleep, heads lowered and back hooves relaxed.

Their day continued.

… … … … … … … … …

"And so, you see, Dagrun, the seed for all our lives was planted that night", the Elder Grandmother smiled and nodded with deep understanding. Everything, absolutely everything of our clan, our tribe, our bloodline was born on that night by the Elder women and the *Nigt-Galas*. What magic, my *beorn*, what magic!" she chuckled.

"Yes," I said smiling, "I understand now the power of the weave you put on my *seax*."

"Oh! It is not just a *seax* any more, *dohtor*. It is a wisdom tool, for you to pass from past to future, both lay within your grasp, side by side with the now."

"I will treasure it most surely", I said, securing it inside my tunic.

"Never be without it, Dagrun," *Ealdmōdor* said, "Now I must rest. The telling will be long tomorrow for it will answer your vision and you will understand your purpose." She turned away and shuffled under the fur hides, muttering,

"And spend time with your mother, *dohtor*. She needs you now." I left and walked over to my childhood lodge where I could already smell a beautiful stew within those welcome walls.

… … … … … … … … …

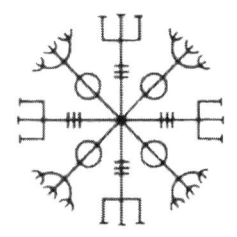

CHAPTER SIX
ᛁᛟᚱᛞᛁᛋ
Mother I remember you

Dagrun found *Ealdmōdor* rested, sitting up and beaming to herself. She looked positively more alive than for many days since. She turned:

"Dagrun, *bearn*, come come, sit by me. So much to say in the telling this day."

"The vision I was given with Forseti," I said softly, "It is the naming rite, isn't it?"

"*Giese*! Yes, beorn, but before that great journey can take place, Hjördis requires a miracle. There was so much bad whispering and disruptive talk from the male elders, she must remove their unbelieving, before even a step can be taken. They cannot believe the first miracle, so they need a second one to open their hearts and their eyes!"

"Pah! Men!" She uttered an old, old ancestor word that Dagrun knew she would never disclose. She continued in a strong voice.

"*Hjördis moved silently over to Yngling, at the shadow end of the day, the light was faltering. The great orange disk sat, motionless, in the crimson bled sky, waiting for the moon to reach her place and the sun to glide into the night. Hjördis tapped the ground three times with her staff and felt the tremor: a thrush, resting on the nearby branch felt it too and flew low to whisk past her face. Yngling felt it not. She was so tired, exhausted from the twilight to dawn's work and she pleaded inwardly* for her bed. This last arrangement made and she would cover her worn-out body with tingling warm fur. Oh, but please, she begged silently, let this elder know his place…for once.

"Yngling, May I have your attention, gecwèman, please!" Hjördis spoke clearly, despite her crippling fatigue.

Yngling turned, his great cape swirling at the knees, and having to loosen it, it to fall straight to the dirt. He towered over diminutive Hjördis, her frail body now shrunken with age, but her eyes flashed and her head sprang up to stare at him full and determined.

He stood against the failing sun and he was in deep shadow. She could read nothing from his face.

"Everything is now in place for the naming rite, which needs to be done so very soon at the dark to new moon. Everything is ready except for you disbelieving, Yngling; I have the deepest wish from our goddess that all must be clear and good and that she will only appear for her son, if all the humans are at one and believing. So, with great exception she is allowing you to be present when she transforms for her baby son, in the great lodge."

There was a sharp intake of breath from the shadow. He looked down, in full thought.

"Giese, yes, I will be there, Ealdmōdor" he growled, softly, "It will be my great privilege to be present." With that he walked slowly off, towards his lodge and Hjördis gave a long deep sigh of relief as she too headed for her bed.

… … … … … … … … …

Many women had been brushing, clearing and cleaning the lodge for two whole days. It was just two twilights to the dark moon, she was a waning sliver of light, as Hjördis looked up to see the clouds scudding past in an impatience she could feel in her soul. Giese, she thought, but we are running close to the wind here, my Nerthus! The journey to the top of the mountain would take at least two twilights, how would the child-god fare on that journey she knew not. And he had to arrive by the first new appearing of Mōnã, their beloved moon goddess and not a minute after. It depended much on the skill of Frídr, who had made the journey with Huld.

She herself had collected the jewelled girdle and the torque of Nerthus, kept in a secret place only she knew. Soon, she thought, this must be shared, for I will be joining my Ancestor Muses. Dah! Think not of that, you silly goat, she silently chided herself.

She had cleaned them with dew collected that morning, and now she placed the wyrd rapas weavings before her, only now in the moonshine did they come alive. She rubbed the magical dew in, singing softly.

"Nigon dropa æt clænsian þu

Eahta dropa æt hǽlan þu

Serfon dropa æt weorþan deofol āweg

Síex dropa æt ōlǽcung þu

Fif dropa æt Giefan þu reord

Fèower dropa æt āsmiðian þu blíðe

Ðrèo dropa æt āsmiðian þu frèogan menniscnes

Ãn dropa æt Giefan þu frègan

Nine drops to cleanse you

Eight drops to heal you

Seven drops to throw demons away

Six drops to charm you

Five drops to give you voice

Four drops to make you joyful

Three drops to make you courageous

Two drops to make you love humanity

One drop to give you love."

Hjördis continued into the night, placing those drops so carefully onto the wyrd rapas, all of them placed in a line, and she sang gently as the dew was rubbed into the cloth. Absolutely nothing was left to chance for the child god and his naming.

Everything was ready. She called Eir and Heidrun, who appeared in the darkening mist with the tall giant of a man, Godwulf, the father. He came with straightened back, so obviously both fearing and anticipating the coming meeting with the Goddess who could, so it was said, fell a human man with just one look!

But he should not be at all fearful, Hjördis thought, looking up at him as he came to greet her, both traditionally, with a handclasp held to forearm, and a deep warm hug that enveloped her tiny body into his. "Of all our tribe of men, warriors and seers both," she thought, "This one had courage, loyalty and nobility shining from him even on this dark night."

"Oh, by gods but you are still the giant of this tribe, Godwulf!" Hjördis laughed, standing back to admire the man who would be changing the Destiny of her people. "Are you ready?"

"As I will ever be", he replied.

Within the great lodge, in the centre stood the huge circular bowl of clear spring water, and it stood next to the fire that had been stoked with new timber, ash and oak and hawthorn. The cildfèstre women, Brynhildr and Bergis stood by the water holding the child-god who was thankfully asleep, Brynhildr, by far the stronger of the two, swayed gently and crooned to the boy child, who was so large of body, his legs dangled over her arm. He was no longer a baby and his awareness was growing daily. He could walk and even stagger to a run before falling flat on his bruised little face, but nothing stopped him and he rarely cried when he fell. Frustration at not conquering the world and all its complexities at a stroke, did however bring a fury of tears. But he had yet to say one word.

Hjördis moved quietly over to brush a kiss on the child's forehead, smiled gratefully at Brynhildr for her good work and patted her arm. She knelt to place the torque, the girdle and the Wyrd Rapas by the water, to the left and the right.

Yngling was in the shadows, at the back of the Great lodge. Hjördis could hear his heavy breathing but she felt his anger even more. She will not come! She thought. This is not going to work.

She spoke quietly to Godwulf, who nodded and went to whisper in the ear of the chief high Elder of their tribe. Within a very few minutes, Yngling came forward and stood, nodding peacefully, by the water and waited. Godwulf stood behind him and it was clear that he had forgone his place, to honour the Elder, who would present the child-god to Nerthus. Within that humble act, all the energy changed, the barriers melted. A great man has sired a great child, Hjördis thought.

And so, it came: the time…a great surge of energy rushed into the lodge, causing many to gasp, billowing in waves towards to the water and the fire. The thick oaken door of the lodge creaked shut and with a great slam, closed. Everything was perfectly still for a moment only.

Yngling and Godwulf quickly moved forward and with two antler horns placed together, lifted a pile of burning wood, sparks flying in a great swirling vortex upwards towards the smoke hole. Glittering embers danced and circled everyone there, all standing holding their breath their faces highlighted in glowing amber, as they looked towards the water pool.

"Nerthus, beloved Nerthus," Yngling intoned in his deep gravelly voice, "Behold your son, come to him, we ask of you, to grant him your divine energy and your eternal love."

They carefully lowered the burning wood into the pool. Steam erupted from the water as the red-hot wood sizzled, in great swirls, getting denser and it enveloped all those standing in a great mist. Still it came, as the oak and ash sizzled, and as the thickness became almost impenetrable, a figure began to form, loosely at first, then the mist seemed to pull evermore tightly together. Swirling into shape and form, the Earth goddess became human. She stood immeasurable tall in a flowing green and blue semi-transparent gown that flowed to the floor and swirled with the mist. Her hair flowed and moved of its own accord, alive in its magic. Her face was so serene, all felt at peace in her presence. She was love, she was the earth mother and she loved them also.

She was smiling, a deep look of love washed over her face as she saw, for the first time her boy child. Brynhildr had carefully handed the child over to Yngling, who stepped forward and held him out to Nerthus, who wrapped him in her embrace. For a few seconds, her face eclipsed the child, her hair covering almost all of him as she whispered words that no-one heard but only to him.

Then as she straightened up, the child-god's eyes opened and looked fully up at her, and he smiled. Then that look was replaced by a look from ancient eyes, a thousand-year-old eyes stared back at Nerthus. He spoke clearly for the very first time on the earthly plane.

"Min Mōdor, Ic gemunan þu

Bèon æt þæt wynstre ond swiðra fram mè

Bèon æthindan ond ætforan mè

Bèon neoðan ond bufan

Ic am hèr Forðæmðe ān scort āna

Ic willan æthweorfan æt þu.

My mother, I remember you,

Be to the left and right of me,

Be behind and before me,

Be beneath and above me

I am here for a short time only

I will return to you."

Nerthus let out a soft sigh, and imperceptibly nodded. She held her precious boy child for a moment longer then handed him back, this time to Godwulf, his father, smiling and touching his cheek.

"Thank you, my wonderful people, for bringing us together. My eyes will behold him once more then I will return to the deep, until I come *again. Care for him. Guard him well for there are dangerous times ahead for you all. You and he will suffer, it is the Wyrd, but he will be shielded.*

"You brave honourable and peaceful people, you must find new lands across the big water, larger than even you know. To keep your honour and your lives, do it!

"Now bring me the wyrd rapas for me to bind him, to protect him."

Hjördis knelt and picked up the smallest weave and handed it to Nerthus who carefully with delicate fingers wrapped and tied the weave around the boy's upper arm.

"The weaves are here for his entire life on this earth. And the torque is his also. The girdle I give to his woman, when he so reaches the age of coupling. Godwulf, teach him well. You must also be with him. You are his earthly guardian as is Hjördis, for his feminine teachings. Yngling you are his teacher of the ancient ways.

"Now I must go. The mist fades as I will too. Many blessings."
Nerthus stepped back into the still swirling steam and faded into the dance of water that fell to the floor in a disappearing circle of energy. And then… silence. Nothing but water droplets lay on the compacted rush and soil floor, to be swallowed by the hungry earth.

And then a voice, as clear as a morning chorus…

"Brynhildr, I am hungry, will you make me some barley porridge, please?" the child-god said.

"Oh, my gods," Brynhildr shouted, "Yes, yes child", giving him her true gap-toothed grin. She scuttled off, knowing there would be a torrent of words to follow this first miraculous utterance.

"Well Yngling," Hjördis turned to face the elder chieftain," Is that miracle enough for you!"

"Giese", Yngling rumbled into his beard, staring at Hjördis with some respect glinting in his eyes. "We have plans to make, quickly Ealdmōdor. The dark moon is only days away."

"I am aware, and we will be ready. Choose your men with care, they will be guardians to the child-god throughout the journey, of course, Godwulf must be present. We leave tomorrow twilight."

… … … … … … … … …

CHAPTER SEVEN
Gerihte fram Nearu: Rite of Passage

"And of course, Dagrun, *beorn*," The elder grandmother twisted around to stare deeply into my soul, so that I looked intently at the floor rushes, seeing a fleeing insect, feeling I would like to hide also "It was a large task indeed to gather food, shelters, all manner of things, to provide a safe journey for the child-god, but also create a rite of passage for the boy, who was fast outgrowing this boyhood. It was meant that Frídr take the leader role. Huld knew exactly why.

Remember, the veil between the worlds was so much thinner then, the people so much closer to the earth spirits than they are now, with the invader Romans here on Wihtland, squeezing out our souls like so many of their lemons. But then, so many years ago, the past and future were within touching distance with the present now, so for the child-god to revisit his recent past and to see his future, this was the true meaning of his journey to the mountain top, and it simply had to be Frídr who took him because, Dagrun, she was *fægr*, fey, completely of that near and far world that holds all our secrets and our wisdom. She was walking with one foot in our human world and the other with the *fægr* ones.

And it was her rite of passage also, to bring herself into full understanding of her birth right. So, she had to become the leader very quickly and assert her rightful place within a frightening group of elder grandfathers and chieftains whose egos were higher than the mountain they were climbing."

"Oh, *Ealdmōdor*," I sputtered, suddenly finding my voice, "*Ic dreogan þes èac!* I feel this too. My challenge to see *ūre Cyng*, our king, frightens me!"

"Your guardian brother will assist you, I'm sure," she assured me, looking at me with those hooded eyes that said everything and nothing.

"Remember *lytel sweostor*, little sister, this time is also your rite of passage, opening before you, whether you wish it or not! Now listen well to this last telling, for you must take it deep into your soul, for it needs to be given to our ancestor stone. It will be the only record left of us, my *beorn* in the times to come."

Elder grandmother settled into her fur hides, looking over to the fire, which was in embers now, and the thin trail of smoke snaking up towards the smoke hole was feeble, the twilight was upon us and the chill entered my bones as she spoke, "Dagrun, *sweostor*, pile more wood onto that shrivelling fire, *gecwèman*, please, my two teeth will clatter too much in this telling!"

She was only skin wrapped around old bones now: all muscle shrivelled like the fire.

Her bright light would be extinguished soon, and while her spirit flared, so must this fire. I scurried around finding good wood, dry and fragrant. There was so little now to keep her here. A bright fire would be a pleasing memory.

The flames, orange coloured, danced around her face, shadows formed in a duo of light and dark, that dance of life we all must know. She smiled, a deep warm smile that made everyone love her. She was determined to go to her Muses sisters, victorious: nothing less would do.

"Listen well, for it is in this part of the telling, we find the truth in the life they were living.

Frídr stood silently, away from the men and their pile of weapons. They formed a spectacular circle of shields and spears and swords, some inlaid with gems of garnet and ruby. The craftsmanship of inlaid silver and copper at the hilt of the swords and the shaft of the spears spoke of ancestor symbols and animal augury. Delicate filigree intertwining patterns of the goddess serpent in silver shone in that late sun, and the boss on the painted shields honoured the raven and wolf.

But Frídr saw none of it: her eyes trembled in a world unseen by those warrior men. She stood with arched back and head held high for the consummate concentration she needed to be gone from this physical world. To see with her invisible eye was almost overpowering.

She saw a man walking towards her, in the forest. His head down, concentration furrowed his brow as he stared at the animal track he was following. Over his shoulder were a brace of Hare. Suddenly he looked up, almost seeing her, shook his head and continued through her. She saw a pack of wolves beginning to howl in the tall firs beyond and knew that was a meeting to come. A raven flew over her head and cawed three times turning his head towards her. His silky black feathers ruffling in the breeze, which picked up speed to become a whirlwind. This, she knew meant challenge. And then she saw the bear: that bear looking towards her with deep intent.

The child-god was staring directly at her, being held by Brynhildr, his cildfestre, away from the gathering men, and he pulled directly on Brynhildr to take him to Frídr. They walked over and he stood silently looking up at her. And then gently took her hand. She seemed like a ghost, a white apparition next to the brown-haired burly young child, yet together they were one, as the child-god's eyes took on that flickering unseeing look, that spoke of the parallel world.

The men stood around the weapons, Yngling evoking the ancestor's guidance and help in their journey up the mountain. Calling upon Oðdin to direct them in the right ways. And Nerthus to sweep her protection for the child-god around the boy. They all stood on the beach of their island home, away from the tumbling surf, and turned towards the mountain, whose peak they were heading towards. It was eclipsed in deep mist. The mountain, on this early evening, seemed almost black, threatening, the trees overshadowed all life and had donned their night colour. The smell of fir-cone resin drifted down towards them, luring them forward. The naming ceremony for the child-god was about to begin.

Frídr suddenly opened her eyes and smiled down at the child-god.

"We have to collect some honey, will you come with me?"

"Giese!" He shot her a wide grin and trotted off, knowing exactly where to go.

"Forstoppian, forstoppian!" yelled Yngling in his deepest booming voice, that was known to bring warriors to their knees. "Where do you think you are taking the child, Frídr. Stop and come back here. NOW!"

"Honey!" the boy shouted, without turning around, "We need honey, lots of it!"

And that was the very first myth of this god in the making, that even before his naming before the gods, he stood up to the biggest known warrior and descendent of Ing without a bat of his eyelid and went to visit the bees.

They both returned with pouches of honey, wrapped in hide and tied well with thick leather thongs.

The men were huddled in a circle, bracing each other from the gathering wind off the water. They would be glad of the forest protection. And as they saw the two return, they began to gather all the weapons, hides and water they all needed for the journey upwards. They began the trek, swishing through ferns that carpeted the steep incline towards the first trees. Yngling led the way, followed by Vermundr, a giant of a man, of Geat descent and a known protector of proven loyalty. Behind him came Tyr, who was a valiant warrior who had amassed many kills for his young years.

Frídr, the boy-child, Brynhildr and Bergis followed behind, some way back, until looking up, Frídr saw the men's shadow forms merge completely with the forest. The women were carrying all manner of things that had taken some time to arrange.

"Bí þæt gods forgeswerian! By the gods forswear," she shouted after them, "but they are entering the forest all wrong. Pah, an infection on their hides I give!"

"YNGLING! Turnabout I say."

Frídr ran up the incline, provisions bobbing on her back. The child-god was at her heels, singing "Yngling Yngling, your hides are infected with wyrm!"

Brynhildr and Bergis were still some way back, tying and arranging the bundles.

"Yngling", Frídr yelled now, "Forstoppian! You will get us all lost. The way to go is this way", she pointed at an angle that clearly showed a path, the same as she took with Huld. She stood waiting for them to return, feet apart, hands clenched at her side, her white hair blowing madly as the deepening wind took it swinging across her face. And those deep blue eyes took on a look of steel, glinting harshly. Frídr had shed her skin, she was now a fægr warrior. And let no man mistake her gentleness for weakness.

Yngling was clearly furious, as the long strides he was taking made his robe tangle in the ferns, and he was made to fling it up over his shoulder. As the giant, he was, he made ready to stoop down over Frídr, her delicate frame swamped by even his shadow. But something in her eyes stopped him dead.

He straightened and looked deep into her eyes. She did not flinch.

"Hmmm, you are Fægr. Why did no one tell me?" Yngling looked around at the other elders for support. He fingered the braiding intertwined in his long beard, clearly thinking of some answer that would save his ego.

"I would have thought it obvious," Tyr said, more to Frídr than the elder chieftain, who now swung round to face the young warrior with anger contorting his features. Tyr was a match for him and he straightened and tensed up, ready for the first blow.

Yngling cocked his head to one side, looking at Tyr, then without any warning burst out laughing, great guffaws echoing through the forest.

"Well", thought Bergis, "Even Huld and Hjördis will hear that at the mountain pass. Every creature in the forest will be hearing that!"

"The path we take is over there, you will all follow me" Frídr commanded.

A small but powerful little hand clasped hers, she looked down to see the child-god smiling up at her, "I am with you," he said, "Some adventures we will have." Frídr smiled to herself, for she knew now that she had passed the first part of her own rite of passage. She owned her birth right which no-one could ever take from her and in doing that one act of courage had given the child-god the beginnings of his.

The party followed the two Fæges, and soon tendons were being sorely stretched as they snaked through the fir trees that were themselves clinging on to the steep incline with sinewy hairy roots. The light was now fading and the gloom intensified. Frídr had already collected several of the markers she had left. It seemed she was feeling her way through with hidden senses.

Frídr knew they had to continue even in the dark, as their journey had started much later than her first trek, and in this she knew time was running out. They had to reach the summit by the next moon: the first sliver of the new moon showing in a cloudless sky was how it had been shown to her.

The men are so clumsy, she thought, they have no forest skills and the birds gave warning of our entry and just flew away. We need the birds to come, we need Raven.

"Forstoppian", she shouted, "We rest now. I wish to speak with the men."

She had found a clearing that was nearly level, and set out some food for the boy. He was ravenous and as he ate his cheeks blew out with the meat, Bergis scolding him to stop and chew his food.

Frídr, her white hair glowing in the misty dark, made her way over to the elders, all three now hunched over their shields and spears, drinking from a water-filled skin. Tyr handed it to her and she was so grateful for her thirst was great. She felt the cool water fill her body and only stopped when she felt completely renewed.

Frídr rested her arms on her knees and looked down thoughtfully for a few moments. Then she looked up with determination and care.

"Elders of our tribe, you have forgotten how to walk in the forest. Your feet have become heavy and noisy. When did you last spend time living here? Has your world become so comfortable that you need not hunt anymore? This night we need silence for the child-god will travel to the near world to meet with his guardians. They in turn will need to travel with him here in our world, and they will do neither if we do not respect their world or indeed our own!

"We need Raven to help us this night, for we must travel through darkness. Even with the markers I have left, we will get lost."

It was not difficult to see Yngling shaking with supressed fury. Clearly, he felt threatened by this young elfin girl. And more so because the child-god obviously had chosen her over the tribal chieftain. Tyr spoke up before Yngling could respond. "We will leave you, Frídr, to your meeting with raven on your marked trail. For us, it will be better to hunt and find food for us all."

They shifted from their circle, heaved their weapons, spears, shields and swords to trudge off into the darkness. "Still too noisy", thought Frídr, "and still waking the whole animal kingdom. We will be fortunate indeed, if there is food for the morning."

The forest became theirs again, although she distinctly heard Yngling whisper to Tyr to stalk close to the child-god and not allow the party out of his sight.

Frídr found another marker and knew they were now in the deepest part of the forest. Little known to human, they were coming close to the near world, the spirits of long ago ancestors had melded into tree form and animals, plants and forest flowers. The energy altered to become wisps of barely felt breeze, and whispered voices. They were climbing still, pulling their weight up by handfuls of low branches, hanging low to the ground, but the stiffness of the pines and fir were chafing. They had layered their feet with leather, bound tight with thongs, but now Frídr called a halt and pulled layers of leather from her bundle to wrap around the child-god's hands. They were red and bleeding across his little palms.

"Tch! Beorn, you are hurting, lytel-swǽs," Frídr caressed his swollen hand, the left being worse, "you are wynstra! Left-sided, I should have known. Here, I will rub this salve in, and wrap your hands up. Try to use your right hand for a while. Are you tired?"

"Oh nã! I will tell you", he suddenly pointed with his free hand, "Look, look, over there. Do you see that shining thing?"

His eyes were shining nearly as brightly as the green fluorescent glow before them, close to the earth and accompanied by several others.

"We are at the beginning, the entrance to your near world, Beorn," Frídr whispered, "Begin to see with your hidden eye now." The glowing lichen formed a direction and Frídr felt herself completely drawn to follow. The child-god picked up one of the glowing lights, it was a tree lichen secured to an old piece of bark.

"It lives on the tree, Beorn, do not remove it lest the wyrd will leave." He held it on the palm of his injured hand. "My hand is tingling", Frídr!" he laughed, "and itching, my sore is mending!"

"Ha! So now you learn, now you know the forest heals us, every plant, tree, flower and herb will heal us all. You have healing hands, our god-in-the-making!" Frídr laughed. She knew the spirits were very close.

The tiny lights were enclosing them, the smell of the forest became thick, fir and pine resin clung in the still air, forest detritus gave off a pungent aroma that soaked into their lungs. She could not see beyond the glowing lichen, they were encased within the wyrd.

"Sit with me, Beorn," she whispered, "be very quiet and still your mind, think of nothing and open your hidden eye. What do you see?"

Silence.

For an untold time, there was just the slight breathing in unison, and the shaft of misted breath snaking into the dark void. She held his hand, and suddenly she felt it tighten around hers.

"Ohh," he exclaimed, "I see Raven, yes, oh and now two, three all coming and shining their black eyes on me. What big beaks and shiny feathers!"

"Shhhh! Beorn, listen," Frídr hissed, "you learn from what they say, they will not speak if you keep talking!"

Silence.

Frídr saw clearly his eyes were unseeing of this world. They were moving rapidly as in a dream and she stayed still, waiting for him to return. She suddenly decided to enter the near world as she felt her guardianship was needed there.

She felt her spirit wrap around the young fledging as he stared unblinking at the Ravens, all gathered to greet him, in a dance of clicking claws on the hard ground and a myriad fusion of darkest purple, subtle crimson red and the deepest blue intertwined in the shiny black feathers. They cawed each in turn, and the young child-god nodded and smiled, holding his head to one side then the other in intense fascination. He understood and the ravens were loving it.

One stepped forward and scraped his claw along the ground to the left of where they were sitting. It was day in the near world, the early dawn sun, shining, and before the child-god, lay a patch of plants and a sapling of an apple tree with one beautiful succulent apple hanging from the thin branch. He leant forward to grab it and it shone brightly in his hand. The Raven cawed, the child-god nodded. He placed it on the ground and looked at his hand. It was healed completely. So, now he gathered the other plants around him. Each Raven cawed in turn, giving him the name and property of each powerful herb. The old soul within the new young body revelled in the knowledge. Mugwort, Waybread, opened from the East, Lambs cress, Attorlothe, Maythe, Nettle, Chervil and Fennel. And the Ravens were ecstatic.

Frídr felt a shift and she stepped away from the child-god. One Raven padded forward and extended his wing towards the spirit boy. In touching him, he became raven, and flew exultantly upwards to the pinnacle of the tallest fir tree then hopped onto the pine, cawing all the while. It occurred to Frídr too late that he was in danger.

"Change me", she screamed, "Change me now!"

The Raven pulled her to him and together they flew aloft, wings scraping the branches of fir and swerving the sharp pine, the early sun glinting swiftly in their eyes as they raced upwards. The boy raven was injured, too much by the pine trees that he had not the experience to duck and dive. He was belly flopping downwards at gathering speed, crying helplessly. Frídr's heart broke badly within a second and she realised for the first time how much she loved this boy. The whole of her world will love this boy if only she could save him. Near world or physical world, the result is the same.

"Catch him!" she screamed, "He will die for the lack of our care!"

They both dive-bombed downwards, unaware of the scratches and cuts the sharp austere trees made on their spirit bodies. Streaks of light, dark green and brown sped past them.

Suddenly they were beneath him and together they caught the fledging raven in their outspread wings and all three slumped to the ground in a spread-eagled heap.

Disentangling themselves, they looked to the boy raven.

"Eat the apple of wyrd and you will heal" commanded the Raven. The boy Raven opened his beak and worked furiously at the apple. His strength grew back.

"He will be forever striving upwards in his physical life", the elder Raven sent the thoughts into Frídr's open mind. "Mountains are his spiritual home now"

"He will be a supreme healer of men. He will be valiant in the field of battle but he will give much time to healing therein. He will shape-shift to be in Raven form, and carry the souls of the dead from the battlefield to Valhalla. There will be great dangers that he must overcome. But in all this he will walk with the highest loyalty around him. There will be no-one in your world who will not admire, honour and worship this god.

From this moment, we are his guardians in both worlds. Go now. You both have a meeting with Manni. There is great danger ahead. Stay ever to close to him and one will arrive who will save him as you did now!"

Frídr shuddered, then opened her eyes to the apparent world of the physical. The chill of the night air trapped her bone and muscle in a shock of freezing cold. She gasped with the suddenness of it and turned to the child-god, who was shivering and trembling uncontrollably.

She shed her fur wrap and put it around his shoulders.

"You need human warmth, beorn," she muttered, "We must find Brynhildr."

They threaded their way back, using the glowing lichen as guide markers and soon heard the two women talking in earnest.

Brynhildr and Bergis both shrieked with relief and joy when they saw them, scattering the night birds, protesting in all directions, the cacophony waking even the hibernating ones.

"He has travelled to the near world for the first time," Frídr explained," He needs warmth, this night is freezing and he is in some shock. Brynhildr, wrap him up around you, gecwèman dèore frèond, please dear friend,"

Brynhildr immediately took the child, who was still trembling, teeth chattering so talk was impossible. She wrapped him in a large fur hide around her, in sling fashion, so he was tied to her back with only his leather-bound feet showing. Soon the child god was fast asleep.

They trudged on, ever upwards, breath heaving in the frosty night air. Not one complaint, not one grumble came from the cildfèstre of this incredible boy. Their silence was broken only by the swishing of the held branches, that aided them ever upwards towards the mountain's precipice.

It was professed to be the most sacred of mountains. It brought instant silence when first seen from the precipice. The forest owned the whole circumference, from lake's shoreline to a near vertical ascent upwards to the summit. Clouds surrounded the summit for most of the day. Snow covered the gorge in an incredibly beautiful tapestry of white against the dark green foliage. But now in early spring, only a few areas were white. It was said that opening out onto the summit floor, only a few metres wide, was the first glimpse anyone had of the height and breadth of the gorge and it stunned the human to absolute silence, thereafter the gods took over.

… … … … … … … … …

They had found a dry area to lay their weary bodies in rest. Brynhildr unbound the sleeping boy and laid him next to her. There was an intense peace that surrounded them and they felt safe and in friendly territory. But it was for a shockingly brief time.

Frídr had not forgotten that the men had been stalking them. So, in their hunt for food they had brought an ill wind. They would bring danger to the young fledging child god.

It was the smell that awoke her, in the depth of the still night. Her eyes shot wide open and through the gap in the trees where they were huddled, she saw unmistakably the towering dark form of bear. He was dribbling from his slack jaw, and it was blood. Her heart pounding, she forced her body to absolute stillness.

There was a sudden shout, a yell from Tyr when Yngling came blundering towards them through that same gap in the trees. The bear dropped on all fours and followed, growling in a low persistent snarl

"Get the boy out of the way," Yngling shouted, but before anyone could move the bear was upon them. It was the very same bear and in an instant, where time stood quite still, both Frídr and the bear recognised each other. The boy now very much awake and eyes wide, came to stand with Frídr, who shielded him with her arm. He was so small against the size and weight of that fully-grown bear, but he seemed unafraid, fascinated more in the great animal that, still on all fours, swayed slightly before him. Frídr began to sing softly, that same magical chant that had calmed the bear before. She whispered to

Brynhildr to get the honey bundle, without turning her head, still staring straight at the bear, keeping their eyes locked.

Then, there was a sudden swish. She felt the energy of the spear as it past her just above head height. Then the thud as it entered the bear. It was not a clean shot and the giant shuddered and howled then screamed, head pointing to the heavens, his face contorted with astonished shock and pain. He stood high on his hind legs now, and the child-god gasped at the sheer height of him. His little head craning upwards, his face also contorted in pain. Frídr realised in that split second that the boy was empathising and in great danger.

"Naaaaa!" The child-god screamed.

Life sometimes hangs on the fulcrum of wyrd, to dip one way or the other. All things slow to fill the void of choice making that all life invites. Instinct makes the choice and it is survival that triggers the change.

Before Frídr could move, the tall sinewy form of Vermundr jumped in before them, seax in hand, to deal a death blow to the heart of the great bear. It was clean and swift. The bear, for a second looked disbelieving, that his life was forfeit, then his great form crumpled to the forest floor.

The child-god moved towards him, and knelt at his great head, the bear still barely alive.

"Èacem geberan in frið feran þu. Great bear in peace go you", his ancient soul whispered, while he stroked the bear's head gently, watching as life ebbed away from him, his great eyes becoming blank and blind.

Frídr moved forward and pulled the spear from the still body, blood now oozing from the gaping wound. She turned and marched up to Yngling, stretching out the spear to him in defiance.

"That was an unnecessary kill", she stated, "That bear was known to me. You have forfeited the child god his life guardian, his protector and friend in the forest!"

"Daaaah! I saved his puny skin!" Yngling bellowed, "You dishonour me child!"

"No", she replied, trying to remain calm, "You put his life in danger. It was not a good shot, you wounded the bear only."

Yngling could say nothing more, he turned and strode away into the dim coming of dawn, as the sun slowly rose for this new day.

Vermundr walked over to Frídr. "There is cooked hare waiting for you all in the clearing. That is what brought bear to us, hunger. I will stay to clean this up. I will prepare the fur for the child-god and will meet you on your way down. That is the best I can do for him. He will be in shock. This was not meant to be."

Frídr shook her head, looking to the forest floor, trying to find good words. But there was nothing to say. It was done.

"Ðoncian þu, thank you Vermundr. Will you be his guardian in this life? His bear guardian of the forest?"

"Giese, it will be my honour Frídr", he replied, smiling.

… … … … … … … … …

"In so saying, Vermundr became the boy's right hand to Frídr's left hand. Together they guided him through to manhood" The Elder Grandmother looked to me in satisfaction. "And those two matched each other in so many ways, they became soul friends. Then lovers and brought lovelier *Fæges* forest dwellers to a dwindling race.

And for you, Dagrun, the very same applies. Are you learning, *beorn*, from this telling?"

Elder Grandmother scanned my face for clues. "Well"! I thought, "I know what she is about to say!"

"Do I have a soul friend waiting to become my lover?" I interceded before she could put it her way.

"*Giese*! Precisely, well do you?" Elder Grandmother looked at me from under fading lashes, raising an expectant eyebrow.

I hesitated, knowing the answer would give a long admonishment, descriptive of my long-term life without a lover and I really did not relish how I would reply.

"Oh Dagrun", *Ealdmōdor* sighed heavily, "the Wahl is a dwindling race, my *beorn*, and while you bury yourself in your herbs and healing balms, that gift you have been given will eventually die with you. Do you understand? You are the guardian of the stones, it runs in your blood so very strongly and there are few of you. Still fewer in times to come. Remember your dream?"

"What", I exclaimed, sitting back so harshly I knocked the small of my back against the boss of her shield, leaning against the wall, "You *know* of my bad dreaming?"

"*Giese*, of course, I sent it to you. It is from *Wyrd*. It will happen and you will be part of its weaving in many years to come. What you do now will ripple on its own *wyrd rapas* to the future time. Think on that well my dear."

I sat in silence, caught up in the memory of it: the horror of the invading soldiers with spears and shields, the bitter winter day and the death: the total death. I had not spoken to a soul about the dream for I thought it had been brought by the Dark Mare of night instilled in infancy, and it sat in the deepest recess of my mind.

Ealdmōdor leaned over to me and whispered gently," Go to see our *Cyng*, Dagrun…soon. Go to Wihtlaegsbyrig and speak with him."

I will", I replied softly.

"Now", she said wrapping her fur tighter around her shoulders,

"I weary and the telling is nearly done. Listen well Dagrun."

"Meanwhile, Hjördis, Heidrun and Eir were making their way through easier terrain. Huld had led them to the hidden opening through the mountain. It was masked by two ancients, almost impenetrable Yews with holly guarding the base. Huld led the way, crawling in places where the Holly was thickest. She had placed charms at the entrance and spoke a chant that dulled the prick of the holly leaves. She sang softly all the way through and it was a genuinely pleased Elder Grandmother who emerged at the cave entrance unscathed and smiling.

"Thank you, Huld my dear", Hjördis said, holding her arm and bringing her into a grateful hug. "I hope this is how the rest of the journey will be"

"Giese, Grandmother. It will be."

They entered the cave in silence, it was a sacred place to Nerthus, for there were several water courses and lakes within the mountain. It was where her boat was moored near to the opening at the other end. How long it would take, Hjördis knew not, but it would be much shorter, and level for her old bones, than the trek the younger ones had undertaken. Then she thought of old Yngling. "He will hide his exhaustion with temper and bluster," she thought, "that is little Frídr's challenge for sure and I hope she succeeds: both her rite and the boy's rite of passage depend on it."

Huld and Heidrun were busy lighting the tallow torches and when the shadows danced and bounced around the cave walls, they walked on. It became colder as they travelled through. Hjördis wrapped another fur around her shoulders. The young ones did not feel that cold spike that was biting into her bones.

She saw several glistening shapes on the wall and realised with a gasp of delight that it was a crystal cave. So much energy was throbbing from these walls, she felt her whole body become enlivened. She touched the quartz and knew it was of an enormous size. They all walked in silence, saying their own inward chants to the goddess for this beautiful place.

They had travelled for a considerable distance, sometimes bending low for the ceiling descended downwards sharply and twice they had to crawl. This was Hjördis's toughest part of the journey, but not one word of complaint passed her lips.

Eventually, not being able to chart the time of day, Huld called a halt. They were in a large cavern, the undulating walls reaching up to an incredible height, slimy to touch as water trickled down to form rivulets that fed the lake before them. Yellow ochre and deep brown mineral seams snaked around each other forming beautiful patterns. This dance of Mother Nature kept Eir silent as she scanned each wall following the path of the intricate designs. There were huge crystals jutting out from the rock face. She swept her hand along them. Prisms leaned against each other like giants holding up the Earth herself.

"Oh, Nerthus Goddess!" Eir whispered and sank to her knees, holding her hand to the giant crystal that radiated a refracted glow from the light of the torches.

The atmosphere was pulsating with energy. The women joined together and chanted. This was a holy place. It was secret and belonged only to the Goddess. They asked in their own way for permission to be there, to carry on and to leave the cavern as they found it.

After untold time, Huld said softly, "we can re-fill our skins with the water. It is powerful water, magical. We must then leave, for the power of this place will overwhelm us and we will get sick".

And so, they continued until they reached another cavern. Dry earth greeted them and there was a circle of pure light shining down from an aperture high above them.

"We are nearly there, sweostors," Huld said," We can rest here. It is safe and warm. My reckoning is that it is nearing dawn. We have walked through the night. Now we can rest, sleep and wait for the new moon rising and for Nerthus."

It was only then that Hjördis sagged. Only then did she know the exhaustion that overcame her, had been waiting to claim her, old as she was, and aching in every bone, she also knew that the Goddess energy in the crystals and the water had rejuvenated her so much, she was ageless. It was an extraordinary feeling. She slept so deeply she dreamt of nothing.

… … … … … … … … …

CHAPTER EIGHT
Þæt Genemnan: The Naming

The three women formed a circle around the child-god, as they walked into the dawning of his day, and as the ground levelled out gradually, they knew they were nearing the summit. The trees became sparse, and they caught hints of a broader horizon. The sun now fully up, sent shafts of light, now they could see all around them. When he tired, they made a chair with their hands for him, joking in turn when he wriggled too much or saw a beautiful bird, stretching to reach, overturned and tumbled to the forest floor. The horror of the night diminished with the warmth of the sun. But Frídr caught a frightened and pained look pass across his face and knew it was not gone at all. The boy said nothing.

Her heart broke some more, and just as he empathised with that great bear, so she too was empathising with this poor tragic boy, whose Ancestor spirit demanded far too much from him. Fragile little human spirit! she thought. He was caught between two worlds.

The Raven guardians were forever present, if only in the background. They would make their presence felt, she knew, if danger was near.

Yngling was off and away elsewhere, keeping with his own company and choosing not to accompany the women. Tyr was protective of them and walked at the rear, for he wanted to be near the boy. He knew he would pass on very decent warrior skills to the child-god, and they would unite in friendship. In battle, he would be his oath sworn guard.

So, the party journeyed on.

Godwulf, the boy's father had taken a different route. He knew the mountain well. He knew the wolf family that roamed there. They were his guardians, his familiars and imperatively, he wished his human son to know them also.

Frídr had heard the wolf call in the distance, though now they were becoming louder. She sensed two calls, one wolf, the other, a human wolf-call, knowing intuitively that the meeting she had foreseen was about to take place. In full daylight!

Raven suddenly appeared ruffling his feathers in the bough of the nearby Fir. Cawing loudly, Frídr had two thoughts enter her mind. One that Godwulf was near, the other that the white wolf would pull forward to greet the child-god. The leader of the pack was chosen. The boy, sitting bolt upright, suddenly jumped from his human-chair perch and scuttled off into the trees. Frídr leapt after him. Tyr ran after her, spear and seax in each hand. Both looked to each other.

"Do not use those!" Frídr said looking at the weapons, "This has been foreseen. Godwulf is nearby. He knows what is about to take place. He has arranged this."

Tyr was grateful she had warned him, for he was in full hunter alertness, knowing the split-second decision between life and death was throbbing at his fingertips. He would not have forgiven himself if a repeat of the previous night occurred again.

Suddenly they stopped and bent low, creeping forward in a wolf walk, arching their feet to sound the ground with tip toes caressing the ground in total silence. Not a twig was broken in their movement forward. The boy was standing still, staring ahead, for before him, not 20 lengths away stood his father, his hand resting loosely on the head of the most beautiful noble-looking white wolf. The wolf's tail swished gently, and Frídr thought she could see him smiling.

"Lytling, mín fæle sunu, child my beloved son, come forward." Godwulf spoke clearly, gently with his eyes wide with love pouring towards his son. He had waited with great patience for this moment. He had forfeited so much time he would have had with his son, and given him to the wise women. He had stepped back. He had said not one word of protest, or haranguing the women, his heart had begged from him.

"Come and sit with me and your Guardian Wolf. His name is Vídarr, forest warrior."

The boy moved forward, slowly, not taking his eyes from the wolf, who was sitting still on his haunches. As the boy came within touching distance, Vídarr, the white wolf, gently lowered his sinewy body to a crouch, so that the child-god did not feel threatened and that he could sit with him. The boy reached out and caressed the wolf's ear, then the top of his head, getting confidence as he did so. Soon he was stroking him and smiling, words whispered, ancient and beyond hearing reached the wolf but not the humans. The child-god's flickering eyes showed he was beyond the physical present and in the near world of the Nature spirits, where he would be close to the spirit of the white wolf, who had also closed his large ice blue eyes. Only the gentle flicking of his tail told a wordless story to the people standing watching the miracle before them.

Godwulf was kneeling, head bent in a prayer that clearly was sending heartfelt gratitude to Nerthus and to Oðdin, the miracle nearly complete and the father re-united with his human son. Then he too led his spirit-self to the near world, and joined his son and his guardian wolf in a trinity of peace and trust.

There was complete silence. No-one moved or uttered a word, they were entranced watching this reunion and bonding which secured the spiritual safety of the young god in the making. It was a privilege beyond words. They were all his earthly guardians in one form or another, and silently each one was laying down a vow to protect, respect and honour in every way possible, the child-gods growing years and beyond. For Tyr, he knew his allegiance would last a full lifetime.

Knowing the battlefield as he did, Tyr also realised the extremes he would face and the tests he would endure to protect his lord. But he would not gainsay a single day of loyalty and protection. That was how deep and enduring the laws of his tribe worked.

It was enduring, without time, everyone melted into the moment… until it was broken, snapped, and ripped apart like a spider's cobweb by a blind and ignorant human, Yngling. He crashed into the enclosure like a boar sniffing a kill. He had not related to this moment, his spirit closed and bleeding in some part of his mind.

Before he could utter a word in defence or ignorance, Tyr sprang forward, stood before him in anger,

"Come, Dryhten, out of here now!" Tyr hissed, pushing Yngling back and back until he was behind the trees and out of sight.

The boy, his father and the guardian wolf were all shaken out of their spirit selves too suddenly. The child-god, shaking and crying was being held closely by Godwulf. Vídarr was growling deeply and the crouch became a steady wolf creep forwards towards the two shadows behind the trees. Ears pinned back and those ice-blue eyes intense and unyielding, Vídarr would have torn Yngling limb from limb.

"Naaa," Godwulf commanded, "Back Vídarr. Wolf, stay still!"

Vídarr halted and with a huge outtake of steamy breath registered his frustration, he remained still, then turned and came back. Looking at both humans, now his spirit guides and friends, he flicked his tail, and sauntered away to re-join his tribe and family.

Sunna was making her journey to the hinterland and the shadows were growing, leaving only a short margin to reach the summit and the climax of this journey.

… … … … … … … … …

Hjördis, Heidrun and Eir followed Huld through the remaining cave tunnels. The shadows extended showing the sun was retreating for the day. They were in silhouette, gliding as shadows themselves along a level and dusty dry floor. As moisture and water were left behind, the three women felt curiously adrift in their sense of place. They walked silently, in prayer to Nerthus, their Earth goddess who was peace and love in her Divine aspect. No-one doubted, no-one gainsaid her magnificence, only their own human frailty and in this unique sacred communion between the Gods and man, for the honouring of the child-god, only the human side may split it all asunder. They had no idea that their Chieftain, Yngling had caused a split already.

Huld paused and turned around to face the women.

"As we turn this corner ahead, you will greet the last and most sacred of the water lagoons. It leads out to the entrance of the lake. It is here we must wait until the moon goddess Mōnā appears in the night sky. Only then will we be able to greet Nerthus."

They walked in silence, in deep contemplation and not a little anxiety. For in this moment, they were being given a unique opportunity, a rare *gift from the gods, and as always, an unrehearsed moment, that allows a deep truth to enter the human spirit.*

What they encountered, on turning the sharp bend, created a collective gasp of pure astonishment. At the end of an almost perfectly circular lagoon, lay a boat moored at the exit, leading to the immeasurably fathomless lake encircled by forest that grew into the clouds above.

The last of the evening sun shone through the narrow gap, which, they all realised, from the outside would be completely invisible. It threw rays of orange, crimson and deep yellow on the softly rippling lagoon.

The women sat, heads bowed, waiting.

… … … … … … … …

She appeared as the very last of the sun's coloured rays left the lagoon with a mere hint of their vibrancy.

Even in the now dark shade of the cave, she shone with a luminosity that came from her Spirit. She was spirit, yet here, at this moment, entirely human. Her face was calm and perfectly featured. Her hair so long, it curled down her back and almost to her feet. It was garlanded with flowers that none of the women knew. Her gown was gossamer fine and flowed with each movement. She was wearing a silver torque, and arm bracelets, inlaid with jewels. The only visible clue that she was not completely human was the supremely feather-light walk that made her glide along the dusty floor of the cave.

The women followed her in silence. When they came close to the moored boat, she turned and smiled brilliantly at each of them.

"Mín hold ond lufíendlic cwèn, begongan þín beornas- þu willan warian þæt frèogan ond behygdig fram þæt weaxan Dryhten. Warian ofer his færeld æt wǽpnedman.

Nūðã, þu sculan āwarian mè, þín Folde modor, for Ic willan bèon gemètingheofon Dryhten, Thör und Oðdin.

Wariam mín ealdor ðrǽd æt mennisc ǽht und frèogan swã Ic motan æthweorfan æt þæt lagu þæt gemètan wíþ menniscnes ongean."

My loyal and loving women - carers of your men - you will guard the love and intent of the growing god, guard over his journey to manhood.

Now, you must protect me, your Earth mother, for I will be meeting both Sky gods, Thor and Oðdin.

Hold my life thread to your human power and love, so I may return to the waters to meet with Humankind again"

Hjördis, exhausted though she was, felt a surge of energy pass through her to the other women, who looked equally astonished. Smiling gently, Nerthus moved towards the boat, which had a human passenger, a man, holding the oars.

"*Þes is mín gerèðru monna hwã willan stíeran min gebeorglíc æt þæt wæterscipe middle. Þu sculan ālǣtan ūs æt þæt wæterscipe efes.*

Weardian wæccen sweostors!"

This is my oarsman who will guide me safely to the lake's middle.

You must leave us at the lake edge. Keep vigil sisters!

Nerthus carefully climbed into the waiting boat, the three women to the stern. The man, shrouded and unseen, sat in the middle and began to slowly push the boat away and into the centre of the funnel of water that led outward towards the awesome lake ahead.

Twilight was upon them. The thin sliver of the new moon peeped from behind gathering clouds, then to shine clearly in a circle of unbroken night sky, it seemed as if a halo encircled this sliver of an infant moon. It gave off its own brilliance, as though the fullness of it was in waiting. Hjördis thought silently that she had never seen such a new moon as this.

The soft swish of the oars brought them out to the edge of the wide expanse of the lake. It faded into the distance, like the open sea. Only Huld had witnessed it, the other women had not, nor ever seen the open ocean either. The boat beached gently against the foreshore tiny pebbles and sand.

Hjördis, Eir and Heidrun stepped from the boat. They gathered together, held hands and prayed as they watched Nerthus the Earth Goddess, at the prow, facing towards the expanse of water, becoming smaller as the oarsman rowed.

… … … … … … … … …

Godwulf, now leading the group to very summit of their arduous climb, had the child-god in his care. Now the union had been made, it was natural for the child to be with his father. Yngling came up at the rear, followed closely by Tyr, whose gaze never left the chieftain's arrogant stride. The hostility was bristling around the old man, prickling the skin. Tyr wanted to tie him up. Leave him to the wolves.

Twilight was upon them now, and as Frídr fulfilled her personal task of bringing them to the summit, safely, the new moon appeared, a sliver of light that had a magical halo around it.

The small level ground they had gathered upon led to a sheer precipice. Frídr and Brynhildr gathered wood to create a fire that would be both a calling to the gods and a barrier not to go beyond. As they were building the logs up, Brynhildr went to the edge and gasped at the sheer height they had all climbed. Below, far below, she saw the minute figure of a woman on a boat moving towards the centre of the huge lake. She could not see the edge of the other side. She had never seen so much water surrounded by forest before.

Then suddenly to her left she saw three women standing together at the edge of the foreshore.

"Frídr!" she exclaimed, "It is Huld and dear Hjördis, and Heidrun. They have made it sweostor!! They have arrived!"

The two women linked minds together and joined with them far below. Hjördis and Heidrun suddenly looked up and waved. The power was complete and they all knew.

The night sky began to gather huge clouds. Deepening with every moment, Godwulf could feel it begin to crackle with building energy.

"Hit is sœl", *he called. It is time!*

He picked the boy up in his arms, caressing his cheek. He spoke gently as he took away his fur hide, giving him naked to the gods. "Lytling bèon forð" Child be still.

Standing as close to the fire as he could, Godwulf raised his child up, arms stretched high, giving him body, mind and spirit to the gods.
The flames of the fire silhouetted the child-god and his father against the night sky. They both stood out in flame gold, iridescent in reds and yellow hues. Statuesque, standing still, they waited.

"Oðdin", *Godwulf roared, his echo reverberated around the mountain enclosure.*

"Oðdin, Fæder fram eall-þu fæðm for se Bearn, wè ācsian þu cuman, cuman, cuman wrōom þu drycræft embe him" Oðdin, father of All- your protection for the child-god. We ask you to come, come, come, and wrap your magic around him.

Now the sky became electric. Tongues of light flashed behind the dark clouds, snaking back to source. Power was building up to a crescendo of strikes that began to zig-zag to earth. The clouds rolled in a rhythm set by the gods themselves. And the humans in this orchestra felt immediately diminished, powerless by the building of the sublime source of all. They all felt the presence of the gods. It was building beyond anything they had experienced before in ceremony or magic.

"Thor Dryhten fram ðunor and beadu", *Godwulf roared again. The word Thor echoing around the mountain top.*

"Þu fæðm ond þu beadu ellen wè ācsian þu to Giefan- cuman, cuman, cuman-

Þu bord ond bile hè behōfian" Thor, God of Thunder and battle. Your protection and your battle courage we ask you to give. Come, come, come, your shield and sword he needs

With a sudden crash of thunder that did not leave a second for the lightning strike, a massive ball of shimmering swirling light crashed into the lake itself. And the world shook.

There was that alchemical moment of fusion between fire and water, the very beginning of the Earth herself. And in that fusion, came a growing mountain of steam, itself creating a pathway, a form and a dance, all to its own rhythm. It grew ever upwards, towards the heavens and towards the gathered humans on the mountain top.

Hjördis looked up, realising why Nerthus had asked for their protection.

"Now, Sweostors!" she cried, "Hold fast for our Goddess, she is but mist and steam. Keep her image in your mind and do not let it go!" They held in a tight triangle, linking arms, heads bowed in the deepest prayer.

Above, the mist swirled and formed into the Goddess herself, her hair swirling in a fusion of blue and of fire red. Her eyes glowed deep into the human soul and she turned to a man shadowed in the background.

"*Yngling*," she roared, "Þu are forwyrcan! Þín gielp beswican þu!" Yngling, you are forfeit. Your arrogance betrays you!

Her eyes flashed and a deep ray of molten red, fired towards Yngling, hitting him directly at his heart. With a gasp, he collapsed to the ground clutching his chest, still breathing and conscious, but unable to move. And there he lay.

Nerthus turned towards the child, and his father, as she flowed towards them both, her colour muted to turquoise and blue. She reached out her hand and stroked the child. Her whole luminous form wrapped around both humans for untold time. They disappeared within her energy.

Then as her energy began to flag, she summoned all her remaining strength, her eyes flashed, and her mouth opened wide, looking to Thor and Oðdin, she roared his name at last, echoing and reverberating around the whole forested lake…

WODEN!!

… … … … … … … …

CHAPTER NINE
WIHTLAND

My Elder Grandmother sat upright, eyes closed, still her spirit was in that place and I had no mind to interrupt her. It was a very sacred moment. For her these were precious stories told in her childhood, and like me, chosen to hold them. I was glad she did not open her eyes to gaze at my gaping mouth and staring eyes. Those eyes had a hundred questions behind them. It was pure prudence and patience that kept me from saying a word.

Instead I sat, pulling all that she had told me into my soul. I tried to memorize wording, descriptions, everything that was needed for the re-telling. Before long I was swirling in a mass of sentences and letters: it became a thing of the mare of night. A scramble of wool yarn left in the bottom of the basket: forgotten and useless.

"Stop fretting, *Beorn*," came her calm voice, through my confusion, "Pictures, you see in pictures, Dagrun Wahl. It is part of your tribe's heritage. Use it! Pictures and feelings are the gateway through to the deeper brain where words are stored of long ago. Nothing is forgotten. So, practise, dear one. You will find, the more you bring those pictures into your front mind, the more you will get the words and with them the feelings. Remember, above all, our Spirit Ancestors work with pictures as do the ancestor stones."

"*Ealdmōdor*, what happened to our Goddess Nerthus, and what happened to the oarsman?" I asked plainly and almost insistently. It was my first burning question.

"To both these questions, I will answer in time", she turned to face me with such a haggard look that held depths of compassion, as if she knew so much she could not tell me.

"I need to rest now, my *beorn*", she whispered, "build up that fire, I am feeling the cold seep into my bones."

I looked to the dwindling fire. We had sat for many hours in this last telling, and it took several layers of small wood and much blowing at the embers. At last, I could put good wood on top of the fire, fit for an elder, it glowed in the dark of the lodge.

Our *Ealdor Mōdor* had made a sacred space in the lodge for herself, as the laws allowed. No other women had entered to their usual places. The emptiness held an echo of the weaving, women's talk and laughter. Hollow husks of life in those empty spaces now and it suddenly clamped down on my soul. And the deepest sorrow held them there.

She felt it also.

"*Ealdmōdor*, " I asked, "Would you wish me to fetch food for you? Are you hungry?"

"Dagrun, my child. I would wish you to gather the women and bring them here to their lodge today, this twilight. But first ask your brothers to come at once. Even if they are doing an important task. This is more important. They will understand. Go child!"

I grabbed the urgency and tried to spring to my feet. My knees buckled under me and I heard our grandmother cackle softly. Limping out, I asked her if she needed light and she shook her head.

Again, as for many days, the sun shone brilliantly in a cloudless sky. I was sure the women were glad of that, being out in the fields all day, they would be bronzed. But I could not feel glad or happy. I felt numb. I felt a deepening soul-pain that was inching its way to every part of me. Coldness gripped my heart. Our *Ealdor Mōdor* was dying and we both knew it now.

I searched for Eystein in all the usual places with no luck and fretted he may be on a spring hunt with the other warrior men. Our *ceasterwic*, our village, held the first settlers from our homeland, and the growing number who have travelled here since. It is said those first people fled after invasions from tribes who wanted our land which was lush and abundant, hidden as it was by lakes, teeming with fish and forests full of deer and boar. It is true. I am the fourth generation to come here for the tales of this sacred island came back to us in trade visits, and how like our own it is. It made the journey possible.

For the night singers see a sacred thread Nerthus left for us to follow. We have followed. And it led us here. I wonder if those Romans feel the same *fōtswæö* of *Folde Mōdor*. My feeling is they are too greedy; men full of trade and profits to ever feel the earth tracks at all.

We can, however, honour our gods and goddesses, for these Romans have no interest in our spiritual ways, only our physical bodies and how much they can leech from every one of us.

Our people are the confederacy of seven. Reudignians, Aviones, Anglii, Warinni Eudose and Eote, Suardones and Nuithone. The Warinni are the guardians of the stones and my family, the Wahls are the largest and tallest family.

I returned to the Now, and a red hot *seax* stabbed in my heart and broke it some more. For our guardian and mother for so long, so many years, was about to leave us forever to meet her Muses and her Ancestors. My present reality, the view in front of me, the village, the lodges with their smoke twirling upwards to a cloudless sky, the children playing in the dirt, began to tear like a dry autumn leaf and become fragile and vulnerable.

"Ahhh, Dagrun, move!" I shouted silently to myself, and shot up to find my brothers.

I made a dusty cloud, on the parched earth, leaving a trail swirling behind me as I strode towards our *tunstede*, the men's part of our settlement. Some children left to play, too young for the fields, shrieked and kicked up more dust, swirling and dancing in a haze of brown air. I switched my head around and shouted to them, throwing my arms up when they took no notice. Then realising I wanted no enjoyment in my world, not this day, not by anyone and knew the childishness of that.

I passed beyond the women's lodge and the wool and dying *hū*, dodging the dying vats that had been brought outside for the prolonged warm weather to fix the wool faster. I had poked my head in to the wool *hū*, expecting to find my mother there.

Except for the children, the *ceasterwic* was deserted, the sun had claimed all who could walk to the fields. I marched on, past the smithy, unbelievably unattended by Hrodgeirr, who rarely left his forge. A boy apprentice was standing guard, half-heartedly pounding at a developing *seax*, the coals clearly needing bellows before they reduced to ash and embers.

"The fire needs air: bellows," I shouted as I walked on, not waiting for a reply.

I needed to find out where everyone was. I made for the horse meadow for I was certain Eileifer would be tending the sacred horses. A good spear throw into the meadow was the most beautiful pied stallion, his tail gently swishing in the warm breeze, a low rumble and neighing coming from him as the tall slim figure of Eileifer, bent over, was slowly brushing his coat in a rhythmical way, his long hair swaying, and as I got closer, heard his secret language joining in with the horse.

I could not break into this union, it was not permitted. But I had to attract their attention somehow. I waited for a few minutes, then picked up a stone and threw it aiming for a few yards in front of them.

The horse, in a split second, blew out a lungful of steamy air and gently pounded the earth with his hoof. Eileifer looked up. I raised my arms in apology and walked forward.

"*Swã sarig*, Eileifer, so sorry," I shouted, "It is urgent. It is *Ealdmōdor*, her time has come. She is asking for my Father and brothers. Where are they?"

"In the Hall, Dagrun. There is a council taking place, an important one."

"Why are you not there?" I asked.

"Because the raising of my arm will not change the outcome of this matter!" he said hotly, "I would rather talk to this beautiful and very wise horse here. Do you not agree?"

"*Please go* and find them" I implored, "Grandmother needs to see them now!"

"*Giese*!" he replied and handed me the brush before rushing off he added," keep brushing till I return. It will be your apology to *him*!"

He was gone for longer than I expected, and the smooth motion of the brushing helped to send my mind over to the Hall where I saw a heated argument flaring like spikes in a white-hot forge fire, between my father and a man I did not recognise: the man looked foreign, not Roman, but certainly from across the large sea, possibly Gaul or Belgic. He dressed like a rich man and I sensed he had come from Wihtlaegsbyrig where the Romans now held a camp.

I kept brushing the pied stallion, his coat now glinting in sun reflected waves as his skin rippled under the brush. I tried to keep my mind from travelling to the women's lodge and our *Ealdmōdor,* for the stallion's sake and just as I had given up and felt the huge crushing weight of sorrow enter my soul, I saw Eileifer returning at a fast run.

"Dagrun", he cried, "Your father and brothers have gone to the women's lodge. He said you must now gather the women from the fields. Bring them to the lodge. The funerary rite has begun."

I crumpled at the words at last spoken. He came to me, in a warrior embrace, to give me courage and I took it, thankfully, heaving a deep sigh as I looked up at this man who walked in both worlds.

"*Ðoncian þu,* thank you", I replied softly and ran to the fields that lay scattered for many spear throws on our tribal lands. Some instinct made me look back, and I saw Eileifer staring after me with an intense look of care and love on his shadowed face.

I saw my mother first, at the near field, weeding out for the young barley shoots to gain strength.

"There are some healing herbs here daughter, I have bunched together over there," she smiled as she continued to pull and shake the green stems, kneeling on the rough turfy soil.

"Oh, mother stop please! *Ealdmōdor*..."

"Ahhh, *NO* ", she cried, jumping up, shouting in pain as her knee joints wrenched and came to wrap her arms around me. It was then that I gave up being brave, and heaved breathless tears into her hair and onto her shoulder. I thought I had no air left in my lungs and my mother's wrap was moist with tears. She stayed in her warm embrace until I was calm.

"Oh, Dagrun, sweet child," she whispered as she gently wiped the tears from my face, "you have bravely and loyally been *Ealdmōdor's* right hand and left hand these last of her Earth days. Now we must ask you to be brave for a few more."

She held both my arms and pulled me straight.

"Do not let your sorrow put the dark night on all she has told you in the telling and allow your soul to forget", my mother stated firmly, "for it is you that has been chosen from all in our people. That responsibility will stay with you all your days and better it be now that you accept it fully. We will be looking to you Dagrun."

She called to her women and told them quickly to split up and take the adjoining fields to tell the others and meet her at the lodge.

She came back with me. Her strength supported me and I loved her.

Our *Ealdmōdor* is the ancestor stone to which all our heartbeats go, each day. She upholds our tribe, with her council, with her healing and with her ancient wisdom. And she is always there like the stone circle where our ancestors lay. Where she will lay after the funereal rite and our goddess Nerthus has welcomed her to the earth.

… … … … … … … … …

CHAPTER TEN
WACIAN: PRAYER VIGIL

Thunōr sent his crackling arrows down to meet with our Mother Nerthus and Sunni dipped behind thunderous clouds to hide. Our warmth from her gone. It was ominous for us in our threatening hour of *deaō*, death. But Nerthus shimmered and gave off that heady beautiful perfume, intoxicating for those few moments before water drenched everyone. She was thankful.

The raindrops, as large as those in *sumor* soaked us all as we trudged homewards to the women's lodge. Many of us ran past the large fields of young shoots, which now would grow fast. Mud slopped into my sandals and the thongs dragged into the puddles and flayed up my legs. We would have shrieked with laughter had it been another day, any other day! But we had our heads tucked down to our chins, grimacing and silent.

In the *ceasterwic*, the children ignorant of the doom-laden day shrieked and laughed in the mud pools that were expanding quickly in the troughs of hardened earth.

We came to the women's lodge, shivering and drenched. All of us stood, uncertain what to do. My father had heard us and quickly eased out.

"Dah", he exclaimed quietly, "Gudrun, *cwèn*," he said to my mother, "Get you dry, you too Dagrun, for our *Ealdor Mōdor* does not wish to be dripped on. She has been asking for you *beorn*, be quick!"

He looked over our heads to the other women, "You too. All of you put dry clothes about you before you enter this lodge"

I rushed to my apothecary cellar wishing I could indeed find some dry clothing. All I could find was a linen under vest, a mouldy over kirtle and my apothecary tunic that was covered in old stains from herbs and potions and smelt terrible. But they were dry and they felt wonderful.

I eased in quietly to our women's lodge where the dearest of ancient elders lay dying. I stood silently for a moment. The fire was built high, now the weather had broken and we could all hear the pounding of rain upon the thatch roof. A few drops managed to hit the fire sending a sizzling steam swirling up to the smoke hole. It was not quiet. It was not the peace we two had enjoyed in the Telling. My brothers were talking quietly to her, as she lay flat on her back now, covered to her chin with hides, the fur shimmering in the firelight. As the flames danced, shadows flitted across her shrunken face, her breath slow and sometimes ponderous, sometimes stopping, where my brother immediately leaned forward to catch her words.

My life began to slow with hers. Caught in that void between life and death where time does not work. I determined not to cry.

Eystein looked up and beckoned me over. My mother, now standing behind me, gave me a push. I sank to my knees beside our grandmother and kissed her gently on the cheek.

"Dagrun, beorn, my beautiful child", *Ealdor Mōdor* whispered, "I am so happy you have come." She reached for my hand. Hers was just bone now. I held it lightly, feeling her skin as parchment of the thinnest kind. It felt brittle.

"Dagrun," she continued now twisting her head to look me full in the eye and even now more so, she penetrated my soul." "I have spoken with your guardian brother. He will gain you entry to speak with our *Cyng* Wihtleig and you must follow his instruction exactly. Do you understand?"

"*Giese*", I replied, choking back tears.

"Gudrun", she beckoned over to my mother to join us and the men withdrew leaving three generations of women together holding our hearts close for her last moments.

The other women came in dry and silent and gathered around. A low chant began, slowly gaining in sound until the whole of the women's lodge sang in tribute to their *Ealdor Mōdor*. As the sacred chant lifted ever upwards, soft crying could be heard. I held fast, looking into my grandmother's eyes and holding our love. So very softly, she gasped and a rattle was heard in her chest. Then the life drifted from her eyes and she was gone.

… … … … … … … … …

Ealdmōdor lay in her shroud of gossamer fine white linen. The women attended to her in absolute silence, each knowing the part they had to complete in this burial rite. The fire was extinguished, a practical thing to occur, to keep the women's lodge cool. Her body would not be moved until the pyre upon the sacred hill was completed by the men of our *tunstede*.

Riders had been sent from us, the Warinni, to all other *thegns* and earls. To the *Cyng,* our king, and too the native people, the Durotrige, with whom we had good relations.

We did not send our message to the Romans. They were not interested in us. If a Roman did come, their energy would doubtless cast a shard of mistrust, even anger, into our sacred ceremony for our beloved *Ealdmōdor*. Neither she nor the Norns would be thanking us for that.

At her head, her guardian feathers lay, shielding her soul in waiting from invading dark spirits of the Elves. A delicate full wren rested on her forehead and her closed eyes. She is a messenger bird from Nerthus and mightily wise. My mother placed a full Heron over her heart, and it spanned her entirely, the elegant wings folded around her. The shimmering grey feathers caught the sparse light that entered the lodge. A wind entered and the heron ruffled and shook slightly. We gasped. It was the bird spirit entering and we bowed in reverence. Heron is the most sacred of our guardian birds. For our grandmother, she was her heart, her soul and her mind, for Heron is also a guardian of the runes and her tree is oak. I had seen my grandmother change before my eyes when she embraced Heron about her and now she was taking her to meet the Norns in her afterlife.

Thunōr kept opening the skies, and the rain fell heavily. We were bound to the lodge, in almost complete darkness, keeping vigil for Ealdmōdor. But our men were getting soaked. Their task in this rite was to fell sound trees, though green and new, would act as the outward shield of the pyre. The sacred woods of oak, ash and alder were kept deep underground, tinder dry and covered. The grain and wood store was placed very close to my own underground apothecary *hūs*.

I let my spirit free, travelling to my home. I saw my father, Eystein and Eyvindr each disappear down the dark hole in the ground, marked only by the woven shafts of heavy wood, covered by clever detritus. They lifted out wood logs covered in fur hides.

Ranged around the hole in a half circle were the kinsmen of our *tunstede* dripping with Thor's water. Both my little brother and Eileifer were there, heads hanging down, their hair knot of the seer and storyteller, now hanging loose over their faces, bobbing as they moved to catch the fur bundles as Eystein heaved them upwards. They were placed in a waiting wagon, harnessed to a pair of mighty oxen. Both bundles and men would shortly make the journey skywards, up to the sacred grounds where our Ancestor stones lived. It was where our very ancient ancestors had buried their dead and it was on the powerful Nerthus treading, where she had walked to leave her footprint, and it spanned across our island from East to west. Our *ceasterwic* lay in the valley below, close to the big sea, and our *Cenningstān* stood hidden within our stone circle, our *byrgels* within a small copse of trees. We knew the Romans had their own gods to worship, Mithras the bull-slayer, and there was much talk about that in the mead hall from time to time. But we also knew their overriding and most powerful god was money, with their Caesar's face on all the coins and if they deemed it necessary for their money-making, they would think nothing of taking our burial stones and using them in some "villa" of theirs. We kept our burial place secret.

I came back to the lodge and our *Ealdmōdor*. The women were praying very deeply. I joined them knowing that our prayers must be heard. To beloved Nerthus I chanted: to Woden and Thor, Tiw and Frigga. All those gods and goddesses who on seeing our sadness would stop the skies from falling on us, this day of our Grandmother's burial rite.

But my mind wandered off and I thought unkindly, immediately regretting it, that in the Telling, if they could muster Thor and thunder to create that wonderful alchemy for Nerthus, they can also undo it! Stop it! Indeed, our Ealdmōdor was nearly as ancient as Woden himself!

I watched as my mother placed the last of the guardian birds over *Ealdmōdor*. The beautiful full black raven lay about her.

It was then that I crumpled. I was not strong enough, I was weak and as my whole body began to tremble and shake, the tears I had long held back, welled up and coursed down my face. Silently I cried in despair. My mother sensed me and looked up. She crept over and simply wrapped me in her arms and held me in her tight mother embrace. She saved me.

… … … … … … … … …

CHAPTER ELEVEN
Deaō Gerihte: Death Rite

As Sunni wove her way towards Nerthus' grove, the rain ceased. Mōnā rose slowly as we made our processional way up the steep incline towards our highest point and where we were closest to the gods and goddesses. Those same oxen that had carried the men and wood upwards, earlier in the rain, now carried us. *Ealdmōdor* lay on the many hides secure on the wooden bed beneath. She was protected from wind and rain by hides over her: her guardian birds kept secure. We sat either side, six women whose love and loyalty would keep us at her side until the true departure of her spirit. We were the *Wacian*, the vigil keepers.

My dear mother sat close, next to me, head bowed in constant prayer. Next to her, Aslaug, god betrothed woman, who was close in years to *Ealdmōdor,* as wise, yet younger in her eyes and her soul refused to age. She still worked in the fields with the young ones, walked miles each day and was never ill! She was stricter yet very funny. She helped my mother in difficult birthings. She would be the next *Ealdmōdor* to us all in our *Ceasterwic*. On my left side sat my dearest, closest friend, Lífa, Life, who had become my right hand in many visits to elf-shot and ailing people. She was learning very fast and I trusted her deeply. In turn, we both kept good council with Sāga, who was *Fey* and could pass between the worlds. She became a *nigt-gala* early in her life and of all my women friends, she reminded me most of legendary, Frídr, in the telling of Woden. She was sitting silently, her closed eyes moving rapidly. I knew she was not here, but in the near world of spirit.

Eldís *Island goddess,* sat quietly on the other side of Aslaug. Indeed, Eldís rarely left the elder's side, for she was in training. She had a spirit energy we all felt and saw. We knew she would become a very powerful leader in time. We respected her beauty but also her total humility. She had grace within her beauty, for she was very beautiful.

But oh, how those oxen worked for us! It was an uphill winding path to the Ancestor ground. Troughs made by many previous journeys had left deep ruts in the sodden soil. The rain had ceased but the ground held that water, not giving it up to Sunni or Thor. It held it greedily for Nerthus.

We were swung to and fro in an endless motion that if we were on water I would be certainly losing my stomach contents. My mother held out her arms to cover *Ealdmōdor* as she swung and lurched. It was not an easy journey as we climbed slowly higher. Sunni escaped from behind a dark cloud that threatened rain, yet she chased it away. Her rays shot down directly onto *Ealdmōdor*, who shone like a beacon of light. And that is how we entered sacred ground, the gentle hills before us shimmering in that light and the sea below dancing in a thousand silver sparks. The wind lowered to a breeze. The clouds fell away. All the gods and goddesses were there and I could feel the energy grow deeper, sharper and more powerful. They were waiting. The Norns waiting for their *Sweostor* to come to them. I suddenly felt lighter, and I saw my mother look over to me and nod very slightly. She knew. Our *Wacian* was moving into the *Deaō Gerihte* in full ceremony. At the long stone, the entrance to the ceremonial procession to the pyre, stood our two-warrior women, Vidgis, an Eote who came to live in Anglii, and became part of the confederacy, and Ynghildre, who was descended from the legendary Ingavonii, and was an Anglii warrior married to Ingvar.

Both women stood very tall and erect, broad of shoulder and carried both shield and sword. They were guarding the burial vase of our *Ealdmōdor*, which stood in waiting at the stone of our ancestors and all people who came must pass by them showing fealty. They both nodded gracefully as we passed. No words spoken, just the commitment passed to each other of respect and honour.

They looked so much a part of the tall stone, leaning over as it had done for many, many twilights, seeking union, or looking to the horizon. I was suddenly, shockingly pushed into my vision of that terrible battle and bloody ending in tomorrow's world, I knew naught about!

My mother caught the terror dancing across my face, and she frowned, wondering, but unable to say anything. I pushed it from my mind.

The last part of the processional journey became much easier for us and our oxen. Soft undulating ground met us and it was level until the very end, where we dipped down only to come up again right in the place of the ceremonial pyre.

The sun was leaving us, and a myriad colour in her departure was beautiful. Crimson, deep turquoise and orange played with each other over the land that soaked up their colour in a last celebration before twilight and Mōnā took Nerthus into the night. The low gorse bushes that spread all over the high ground took all the last of the sun's rays in their vibrant yellow flowers. I made a mindful task to collect them, for they were potent in their healing.

As we came closer it was easy to see the tall sturdy pyre, in all its readiness, with our *Cnèomagas* standing before it to welcome *Ealdmōdor*, in this, her last journey. They came forward, as we achingly shifted down from the wagon. They now took over the guardianship, gently hoisting the wooden platform upon their shoulders, linking arms to form a bridge strong enough to carry her these last spear lengths. Against the setting sun, with deep long shadows falling behind them, our men carried *Ealdmōdor* towards Sunni, elegantly, slowly and with great love, towards the wood.

The tears welled up. I fought them down, swallowing hard. Lífa moved forward and linked arms with me, Sãga the other. We held each other close.

The men gently placed her down in her final resting place, as the great woman we all knew. And how her form would change so very soon.

I now could look around, after my stiff and numb legs came back to me. In the distance stood a group of *Londlèod*, the Durotrige, whose native land this really was. They lived beyond in the sacred ground to the west of us. Some still lived in the dense forest that had taken most of the north and north-east side of Wihtland. They had come dressed as the guardian animals of the forest with fox, deer wrapped around them, and one had a crown of Boar tusks. It was their ceremonial masks, they came in deep respect but did not approach us. We did trade with them and they had welcomed our people all those twilights ago. They had an uneasy truce with the Romans, but we all wondered how long this would last.

Eystein looked over to me and walked up to me, gently taking my arm, leading me away from the women.

"Dagrun, *sweostor*," he looked down on me, from his towering giant's height, "*Ealdmōdor* loved you dearly. She spoke of you before her passing and gave me instructions. It is timely you hear them now."

I looked up at him, frowning, for at this moment my whole soul was elsewhere.

"You need to listen well", he continued, "Our *Cyng* will be here very soon, and he will grant you a hearing. You must listen carefully and do not anger him in any way. He is angry enough for the whole Eudose nation now, and small matters can irritate him. Also, *Ealdmōdor* gave a guidance for you to abide by. You will take for yourself one guardian bird that you feel a heart song with.

"What", I exclaimed, heaving out a breath of disbelief, "How can I do *that*, now at this moment?"

"You must *beorn*!" Eystein insisted, "for it is how her spirit will talk through the guardian bird directly to you. Think what a beautiful gift this is. Think about your task before you, Dagrun. *Think!* And choose your feathers now. There is a gold torque for you and for your children's children, Dagrun. Take it now. It lays at the feet of our Grandmother." He walked back to his kinsmen, without looking back. Eyvindr saw my distress and walked over. His understanding and compassion, not least a big brotherly love, supported me and we walked over to Ealdmōdor together.

I leant over and gasped for she was uncovered now, the lifeless face serene but completely empty. The shadows deepened her wrinkled skin and cast an unearthly pall.

"Feel with your heart", Eyvindr whispered in my ear, "And take your time. She is seeing you now and she has one eyebrow raised already. Have a care *sweostor!*"

I groaned inwardly and tried to see with my heart. My mind scrambling for attention on such a major decision. Yet it was instantaneous, I was pulled to Heron. Our regal, wise bird of the water and of land. She covered Grandmother's heart and her wings stretched around her frail body. What care, what loyalty I thought. Above all Heron was close to the Gods in all things. She was guardian of the Runes and her tree was Oak. She had, like her one footed stance, one foot in the world, and one foot in spirit. She was Woden. She was calling to me and I silently returned her call.

"*Giese!*" I turned to Eyvindr, smiling in relief, "It is Heron, brother: it is heron!"

As the sun finally disappeared below the line of the white cliffs, the songs began. The *nigt-galas* took this beginning of the death rite into themselves, and their souls took over. Sāga and Alfsigr "*Elfvictory*" sang the ancient song together. Both looking towards Ealdmōdor, they poured out their hearts to her.

101

"Nerthus, Nerthus, Nerthus! Ūre ælfsūenu Fodör Mōdor
Ūre Ealdmōdor sāwol is fūs æt ālǽtan þu.
Fram clǽne heorte hèo is
Fran ðearl hyge hèo is
Fram lufiendlic sāwol hèo is
Norns, Norns, Norns!
Ealdmōdor secan feolan æt þín heal,
Hèo willan hlihhan wíþ eadignes.
Hèo willan wesan frèo
Lōcian hiè becuman
Norns, Norns, Norns! Openian þín heal.
Giese! Giese! Giese!"

Nerthus, Nerthus, Nerthus
Our Grandmother spirit is ready to leave you,
Of pure heart, she is,
Of strong mind, she is,
Of loving spirit, she is,
Norns, Norns, Norns!
Grandmother seeks entry to your hall,
She will laugh with happiness,
She will be free,
See her coming!

Norns, Norns, Norns!

Open your Hall,

Yes, Yes, Yes!

They both sang in harmony together. It was a beautiful energy for our hearts to enshrine this moment. And as I looked over I saw the dark shadows of the Durotrige becoming larger, they were getting closer to our gathering, and then I heard their low rhythmical drumming. They came in full respect of our *Ealdmōdor*. She would be so ecstatic about this, for she had often made it known that we were visitors in their land. Especially since no blood was spilled in our first coming to Wihtland, and they had accepted us because we are Nerthus worshippers and a very peaceful people.

I looked to Aslaug and my mother standing beside her. They were both smiling and Aslaug nodded to me. We three Warinni women held our arm aloft in tribute to the Durotrige *Londlèod*, who, along with the Regni on other *èalond* of Everlant, were here on Wihtland when the Romans first came.

As the night deepened, our kinsmen began their songs to the All Father, Woden.

Eyvindr, my younger brother, came towards the pyre with Eileifer, (forever heir) kinsman to the sacred horses and fey, and they began to sing in a low soft voice.

Oh Wōden, Fæder fram Eall

Befealdan þín frèogan ond wisdom embe ūre Ealdmōdor ealswa hèo feolan þín heal,

Gewadan wíþ hèo æt þín heorð æled

Fram clæne heorte hèo is,

Fram ðearl hyge hèo is,

Fram lufiendlic sāwol hèo is

Oh, Wōden brengan hèo blíðnes!

Giese, Giese, Giese!

Oh Woden, Father of All

Enfold your love and wisdom around our grandmother, as she enters your Hall.

Walk with her to your Hearth fire,

Of pure heart, she is,

Of strong mind, she is,

Of loving spirit, she is,

Oh Woden, bring her Joy,

Yes, yes, yes!

To say our kinsmen were wholly with Nerthus would be a lie. There was an undercurrent of tension amongst them, especially the young men. They were being drawn to the ways of the men of *Cant*. Our *Cyng* was a warrior Nuithone and it is said the blood line of Wōden ran in his veins and those of his family. And it is fair to say, our men were embittered with working twice as hard for half as much, the Romans taking all they needed to feed their endless cohorts of iron centipedes. Our *halig*, blessed Wihtland, so rich of soil and forest, fish, salt and minerals, was being stripped.

A mighty trouble was brewing in the cauldron!

The singing ebbed and flowed as a tide would come and withdraw. Mōnā shone down making the sea shimmer in its path to the land, where soft shadows against bush and tree were made. Suddenly a brilliant white owl appeared, flying low over our *Ealdmōdor*, in slow motion, she looked on us and circled around to a nearby tree. She sat and waited.

We could hear wolf in the distant forest, calling. The night creatures had joined us, as had many of the kinsmen from our neighbouring *Ceasterwics* and *Tunstedes*. I could see a bobbing trail of rush torches snaking up the undulating hills into the far distance. Many people were arriving to take part in the *deaōgerihte*. There were small numbers in the rest of our Nerthus confederacy, but they had, through council, joined together in one larger settlement in the next valley to us at *Cæferdūn*.

I looked over to the west and saw another glowing snake of light weave its way towards us. And I knew instantly that these were the small but powerful hearth warrior Geats who had settled in the outlying western ranges of Wihtland. They had all pledged their loyalty to our *Cyng*, yet kept their distance from the Romans. They were oath-sworn and if called would instantly come and give their lives for their *Cyng*. I knew who they were because their lights were much higher, heads higher, for they, like the Warinni, were giants. And we all had profound respect for them as they were a highly noble people.

The chanting was reaching a pause, a moment of echo, as the traces of sound were taken by our near ancestors on a wisp of sudden wind, through the veil to the waiting Norns. That pause brought two shadows towards me, Eyvindr, my dearest younger brother and Eileifer, the sacred horse kinsman, also Wōden-born, a royal in waiting.

"You know the *Cyng* is coming Dagrun," Eyvindr whispered in my ear, "With the Geats, he is amongst them. He rarely stays at Wihtlaegsbyrig, for the Romans have rebuilt around the keep, they are taking control as they always do!"

"He is staying close to the Durotrige," Eileifer said, "They have reached an accord, a peaceful and amicable treaty, for we all now see we have one common adversary, who came uninvited to Wihtland and who has steered all towards the upkeep of their legions and their cohorts of soldiers."

"Ahh, *Giese*," I replied," So that is why they are entering from the west!"

"Dearest Dagrun," he continued, finding an opportunity to wrap his ample arm around my shoulders. Smiling inwardly, I did not mind in the least.

"We all know your forthright speaking. You are adept at digging some big holes for yourself to fall in. On this occasion, dear one, keep quiet. Let me do the talking with our *Cyng*, for I know his ways. We are kin, and I know his patience is thin. I believe he will be leaving our Isle soon. There is a gathering in *Cant* of the *Centingas* the Men of *Cant* and he needs to be there for his *Cynedōm* is in the east of Britannia and in the Cimbric peninsular also"

Inwardly I sighed in frustration, outwardly, the slightest shrug was my only comment.

Eileifer did not surrender his embrace, he held a little tighter and I found myself leaning in to him and turned to smile up at him. He was a Eudose after all, so they were very tall people. He returned my smile with a deeper one and something stirred deep within me, and for a second I lost the sorrow of the night.

Mōnã had created a low shimmering haze of light, she was, in a cloudless sky, offering the way to the oncoming gathering, punctured by the bright lights of the torches held aloft. Thunōr had silently given his consent by offering not a breath of wind to bring any clouds. So, the night was starred and Nerthus and all upon her held their breath: waiting for our *Ealdmōdor* to begin her passage to *Neorxenawang*.

There were countless people of all tribes now waiting in the shadowed glare of many torches. Now the chanting from both Sãga and Eyvindr began slowly in harmony, joined by Eileifer, who had moved to join the *nigt galas* in this last lament. As I looked over to the eastern horizon, I saw the unmistakable glow of the dawn, Sunni was awakening and the torches needed to touch the pyre so very soon.

Our *Cyng* must be the first to bear that torch and he was still arriving. Everyone looked to the western approach as people shifted to make a pathway for him and his oath sworn warriors. He was, by common assent the most regal and stately of all. He was immeasurably tall, at least a head and a half above the tallest Geat, Eote, Eudose or Warinni. And all his gold he wore about him, from the torque to the armbands and rings, shimmered and flared in the bright torchlight. His hair now silvered with age was thick and plaited. His beard was plaited in several bead-adorned lengths, and swayed with his broad, long-gaited strides. The Geat warriors moved almost in unison behind him, so, on this dark night of long shadows, they appeared as a long swaying serpent, moving almost effortlessly along our sacred Nerthus dragon line.

I held my breath in awe, and then unexpectedly elf-shots of fear hit my stomach which knotted and churned.

"Grrh!" I shouted within, "Let this not mar my *Ealdmōdor's* final parting" And I fought to quell it.

Our *Cyng* had arrived and my mother and father shunted me forward with both my brothers. Our *Ealdmōdor* was Warinni and we were her closest family. My father would hold the torches with the *Cyng*.

And so, it was, on this night turning to day in our *Lenctenmōnaþ*, as the night became day in springtime, the *nigtgalas* ended their night-long *Wacian* with a tribute to Sunna for gifting us a new day. The *Cyng* stepped forward with a burning torch handed to him by one of his oath-sworn, who, head bowed, retreated slowly. My father came forward and with a bow to the *Cyng*, they both proceeded to stretch forward and put tinder-dry sacred wood to the flame. Without rain, it caught and flared almost immediately as if the Norns wished it over. We all felt, in the total silence, the irrevocable transition from body to spirit as the flames licked higher as our beloved *Ealdmōdor* was caught and taken.

I leapt over to retrieve the Heron, which had been placed for safety under the fur hides on the wagon. I held her close to me and felt a shudder of feathers moving gently, and I felt life come into her. I felt spirit energy course through my body in wave after wave until I was tingling with this new awakening. I think I was smiling, for both my mother and Aslaug were beaming over to me in acknowledgement, not for what I had just done, but that the new spirit dawn had opened for me through my *Ealdmōdor*.

Sorrow left me completely to be replaced by joy.

… … … … … … … … …

It would be near the next twilight before the mortal remains of *Ealdmōdor* could be placed in her burial urn, and when Sunni made her way westward to sink below to meet the Ancient ones at Headon Warren, casting a last intense glow towards Mōnā in union and promise of the next day.

The close relatives of *Ealdmōdor* would remain near, as I watched and felt the intense flames engulf her fragile body, we all knew her soul-spirit had long fled, but for us with flesh and blood still around us, those remains were as precious to us as the air we breathe.

The *Cyng* stood with Eystein, my brother and my father, talking quite intently. Those of the Geat warriors stood a few paces behind in a cluster, quietly talking but forever staying close to the *Cyng*. He stopped talking and looked over to me. I was still clutching Heron and brought her ever tighter as my heart fluttered, missing several beats. I found myself fighting for breath. Eyvindr and Eileifer instinctively came to stand beside me as the *Cyng* approached.

"Well, Dagrun Wahl of the Warinni", he growled through his thick matted beard that moved and swayed with every syllable, "It would seem our *Ealdmōdor* graced you with The Telling, as much as she was able that is….", he trailed off leaving a hole to be filled. How we filled the vacuum would no doubt determine whether I would achieve the goal set for me.

Eileifer moved forward. He bowed low, one knee bent, the other held forward in respect to high rank. He had been taught well.

"My Lord," he uttered, not looking up, "The Wahls of the Warinni have always held the guardianship of the sacred Stones, through time in our old land and in this our new home. Dagrun is now that guardian with the passing of *Ealdmōdor*. And it is her responsibility and role to know all The Telling. It will safeguard our spiritual ways for all generations to come and she will pass all knowledge to the Leaning Stone yonder for all time to come. My Lord"

I was staring quite open mouthed at Eileifer, for the intensity of his words reached my heart. I felt Heron shudder and knew the spirit of *Ealdmōdor* was with me. He straightened up and looked with an open soul, into my eyes, and I knew my own soul stretched out to meet his. We were being joined by *Ealdmōdor!*

"*Giese, Giese*", came the royal reply, "Of this Eileifer, "forever heir" I am well acquainted. That will be accommodated under certain conditions. But it is the ever-present moment that is my urgent concern, not hundreds of twilights away!

Eileifer, you are about to forego your birthing name and enter true manhood! The name "Forever heir" will no longer be yours. I will be leaving this beautiful isle, in all honesty, never to return! This has always been a home to visit and while the Romans hold sway, and we do not have the numbers of warriors to break them, we must erstwhile hold a certain peace and wait......*Gíese*! Wait, for they will inevitably leave our shores and when they do, our people, our *Cynedōm* will ascend in honour to call these isles our true homeland.

Now, I am making you client *Cyng*, Eileifer. Gather around you all those you trust completely with your life. Make them your oath sworn hearth warriors, as I have my Geat *Gebroðor*.

Kneel before me, Eileifer, Eystein, Eyvindr and you Folkvarthr, you too, old sire. We have need of your wisdom."

The look of frozen horror on Eileifer's face matched the sagging of his body.

"My Lord, *gecwèman*, please, forgive me, but I am a keeper of the sacred horses. They are my life responsibility and..."

"Enough, young fledgling *Cyng*!!" the old man roared, his beard swaying as he made towards Eileifer, bearing down on him.

"Your life with horses is finished. Do you understand? A much higher and more significant role awaits you and you are not permitted to gainsay *me* your *Cyng*! I need your peaceful spirit to rule over this island in my absence, keeping to ways of our beloved Nerthus, for a peace must be maintained, against a meaningless war that will rob the island of good men. Give your horses over to someone else!"

Before my mind could stop the words, I uttered the inevitable, which would alter the course of my life.

"I will look after the horses, my Lord," I said clearly and after those words were said I felt a certain peace enter my soul.

"That is settled then! Now kneel kinsmen and honour your new roles in life"

Wihtlæg immediately brought his hand over to hold the hilt of a sword that nearly reached the ground. The hilt was studded in garnets and a filigree of silver intertwined with the bronze. Both shone in the morning light. On the side, was an ornate fixing of a ring. This then was the Woden sword. The ring giver sword. With a mighty swish and loud grating, it was released and held aloft. Sunni caught the metal and sent slivers of light around the men, now kneeling before their Cyng. Wihtlæg laid the sword upon the shoulders of the men, speaking with a deep resonance, the prayer and offering to the god and goddess.

"Fram þæt mægen of þæt Eall Fæder Woden

Ond þæt frèogan fram ūre Gyden Nerthus.

Befæstan þín getrýwlíc beornas æt rǣdan rihtíc, bèodan eornost ond lifian wíþ inwyrean.

By the might of the All Father Woden,

And the love of our goddess Nerthus,

Entrust your faithful men to rule justly,

Command honestly, and live with honour,

To you Eileifer, Woden born and *Cyng* in waiting, you will be client *Cyng* of Wihtland to the end of your days.

To you Folkvarthr, you will be *Hèahwita*, High Councillor of Wihtland, and wisdom giver to the end of your days.

And to you, Eystein, you will be *Ealdorðegn*, Chief Thane of Wihtland to serve your *Cyng* to the end of your days.

To you, Eyvindr, you will be *Ealdorman*, Earl of Wihtland, to serve wisely and keep good and kindly council with those around you. Create what wealth you may for the good of all."

The sun's glare on the Woden sword at each levelling to the shoulders of my kinsmen sent blinding shards of light upwards, a truth to be spoken, was *wyrd* and Woden made *drýlíc*. It was a magical moment in the lives of our *Cynn*.

Aslaug came over, in her new role of *Ealdmōdor* she seemed taller, more regal and for her, quite solemn.

"I do believe," she whispered softly in my ear, "that our *Ealdmōdor*, now free of her pain-wracked body is joyously working her *wyrd drycræft* on all of us!

We'd better have sharper eyes and even more a sharper wit about us, Dagrun. She will be your right and left hand now in *sāwol* as you were hers here on earth. Her gratitude to you will be felt *beorn* be sure of that. Hold Heron close to you. There is an intricate filigree being woven by the *wyrd rapas,* dear one, that is very powerful. Be alert, my dear"

As she walked slowly back to her young apprentice Eldís, whose beautiful eyes were even now glazed over as she was in *Sãwol*, I felt a shudder from Heron and a growing feeling of apprehension. I knew I needed to learn fast, and be ready for what lay ahead.

And that happened in an instant, as most moments of glaring truth do, leaving not a moment's pause to reflect and decide. We were in the grip of *wyrd*, standing as we were at the smouldering pyre of *Ealdmōdor* with our *Cyng*, so rarely seen, creating a royal house from my Warinni *Cynn*.

It came in the form of a shadow within a shadow, or so it seemed, with Sunni's brazen glare creating deep dark shadows, he appeared almost by *drycræft* from Wihtlæg's long flowing cloak. He was wizened, old beyond measure, or so it seemed. His hair was entirely unkempt. Neither knotted nor braided as most men of our kin do to keep their long locks tidy. It fell in tangled wisps, and his bent backbone made this matted hair almost reach to his skinny waist. Oh, he was so thin! My first response was to feel sympathy for such a poor soul, but how that feeling was squashed by the look of his head shooting up and his deep penetrating eyes, stripping my soul bare, for him to appraise. Those eyes were to become my torment and my saving. I knew that this was the reason for my fear and my only protection was Heron.

"So!" he growled in a low guttural voice," This is the stripling *mæden* who thinks to become *Hwata,* a soothsayer!"

I looked at him with disbelief, and took an inward breath.

"I am Dagrun Wahl of the Warinni people who are part of the confederacy of seven who worship the goddess Nerthus and I am a healer and guardian of the Stones, as were all my *Cynn* before me, my lord!"

"*Giese, Gíese,*" Wihtlæg interrupted, now focussed on our conversation," My *Wítega* Wiseman already knows of you Dagrun. He is to be your teacher and *Hwata* in the next part of The Telling. Listen well and do all he says. Be respectful of his standing. I will be receiving reports, stripling *mæden*," he chuckled.

It could not have been worse, but sensing with resignation, the role I had been placed in and the relationship with this grizzled little man was inevitable, I responded as best I could.

"My Lord," I answered back as politely as I could, "As I am to be your pupil, may I know your name?"

"I am known by many names", he replied, considering me again and shrivelling my soul, so that I hugged Heron ever tighter, "Some not so *Ælscienu* beautiful! You may call me Gandālfr, fiendish elf! And there are conditions to this umm... contract, "he continued, obviously enjoying my discomfort, "You will leave that Heron gift behind when we have council and will bring your younger brother, Eyvindr, to all our meetings until I say otherwise. He is more adept than you are, stripling. And until you reach maturity in *drycræft* he will be by your side. Do you understand?"

"*Giese*", I muttered, feeling smaller than I had ever done in my life. Our *Cynedōm* was built on the sturdy stones of honour, respect and honesty. All these aspects created who we were. Now it seemed, to this little wizard, they counted for nothing. Some other, yet unknown attribute had become more important. My safe and comfortable ground was beginning to sift away like so much sand on a windy beach. What lay beneath I knew not. Oh! I thought, I need the sea, more than ever before. But I had to stay until Sunni was taken by the horses to greet Mōnā. A long wait for someone who was desperate to be alone with the waves and beloved Nerthus.

... ...

The sun finally sank below Headon Warren to the west. Wihtlæg had long gone, now just a diminishing speck on the undulating hill pathway to the western coastline of Wihtland. But his parting words to my big brother Eystein had echoed through me and I still found them worrying.

"Eystein, keep a strong weather-eye on our young *Cyng*," he had stared directly at my brother as both were of equal height, "He has a noble and strong heart...with a deep soul. But there is unrest growing on Wihtland. Some stupid thrall-thinkers believe they can outshoot the Romans. Lamentable! To keep balance and peace, he needs must strengthen his backbone and I will look to you to guide him through these challenges."

Eileifer was amongst those disappearing dots on the horizon, for Wihtlæg had decided to take our new *Cyng* across the water to meet with the Centingas in *Cant*.

He managed a sorrowful smile and the briefest touch of my hand. My heart broke a little more and it marked the final blow to my shattered spirit. I had the challenging task of creating a union with the sacred white horses, who would be soul-split at his disappearance. And I was being "removed" from the safe family nest step by step. Maybe I was that stripling *mæden* who thought so high of herself that the fall was just around the next bend in the river!

I sat alone, away from those remaining of my family. Thunor had taken streaks of deep colour, orange, red and magenta, and flung them across our world from edge to edge. The sea reflected them back in shimmering colours at the close of day. Mōnã appeared, quietly, silently, in the dusk sky and I sent out a prayer of safekeeping for my loved-one, who did not even get the chance to prove any love to me or for me to show him my growing love! I was lying down, so close to the gorse bushes, I could breathe in the heady perfume that was healing me of my sorrow. And the deep yellow flowers, I picked and held them to my heart, imagining that yellow gold flooding my broken heart.

"Dagrun", Lífa's voice broke into my silence, woke me from a serene dreaming, "The warrior women are arriving from the leaning stone with the burial urn. It is time for the final honouring *Sweostor!*"

Lífa, forever my closest friend, strode up to me, kicking some dry grass up in the air to land on my face. "Ah, you see Dagrun Wahl, you were miles away, kissing that gorgeous Eileifer all over his handsome face!"

"Ohh don't, Lífa, it hurts to think we will be apart for how long? Who knows with Wihtlæg, for he may decide to take him further on to the Cimbric peninsular, across the Germania sea, never to be seen again?"

"Dah," Lífa scoffed, "He will return in no time, if you keep yourself busy, with me at your side, healing all those elf-shot folks and delivering babies. We are coming up to the big birthing season. Always seems to multiply in *Þrimilce-mōnaþ,* the month of three milking, it must be the dark nights of *Winterfylleth,* October, that brings so many babies into our spring world!

"You've got all that to look forward to", she chattered on, trying to lighten my spirits," Wager you, he will be at your side by *Winterfylleth* and you can create your own kith and kin!"

I jumped up, grinning at the very thought and grabbed her hand as we walked together back to our family in the closing stages of the *deaō-gerihte.*

… … … … … … … … …

Sifting through the still warm ashes made my heart plummet to new depths. I found *Ealdmōdor's* first finger ring lying around charred bone. It was to be buried at the *Cenningstān,* the touchstone, that marked the entrance to our stone circle far down from here, past the water meadow, and in the willow copse. I reached over and retrieved it, sending a prayer to her as she watched over us. I felt her near, and inwardly cried my pain to her for the harsh and cruel words of that little elf wizard, who had replaced her loving touch.

I lurched back as the clear words came into my mind: "Time to grow a skin, my *beorn!*"

All her mortal remains were lovingly placed in the urn, with gold and breacleats, lying on top. We trudged off, our Warinni *Cynn* to sit in the wagon and be bounced relentlessly back to our *ceasterwic* and the men, choosing to walk, made their way to their *tunstede.*

We would place her in the women's lodge so she may see and hear us, no doubt making her powerful presence felt when we transgressed or just to make some mischief! The time for her final burial would not come until her next earthly birthday so the cycle would be complete and *wyrd* honoured.

… … … … … … … … …

My first thought was of the white horses. And as we entered our *ceasterwic*, bum-sore from the harsh rocking of the cart through deep ruts in the dried mud, as if we had all rode stallions across the hill-tops of Wihtland. And to add to that, Thunor gave us a soaking. The clouds built up thunderous layers, deepening by the moment. They scudded across the sky, but not fast enough to miss the horse meadow.

With huge raindrops thudding into growing puddles, I leapt from the oxen cart, briefly waving to my maiden-friends, and ran, past my *Wyrt-hūs*, herb-house, weaving around the cloth dying lodge with its huge vats of red, woad and green dye sitting outside, and past the smithy, briefly being hit by the onrush of heat escaping from the forge fire. I jumped the woven fence marking the edge of the white horse pasture land and saw nine drenched horses already waiting to be led to their warm stables.

But they backed off when they saw me, not their guardian-keeper, but a "stripling-*mæden*" soaking wet with dripping hair hiding my eyes and hunched against the rain.

"This is most surely the worst kind of introduction for them," I thought. What to do?

With good fortune on my side, the one horse who had joined with me those twilights ago, remembered, and beating his foreleg gently on the turf, came forward bowing his head for a stroke and a nuzzle. It was a releasing moment for us both, and a fast relay of images scudded through my mind of that day we both knew.

I opened the gate before the waiting horses and they made their own way into the thatched and warm stables. Each knew their own sleeping place. It was a wonder to watch. I bunched fistfuls of fresh hay into each of their feeding skins, then with a shock, realised the extent of my new commitment. They all needed drying and grooming! Before I could reach my bed, they had to be fully cared for. Muttering low to myself, I found musty worn blankets to cover them all while I worked on each sacred horse. I began with my friendly one, also realising with a shock, that I knew not one single name that Eileifer had chosen for them. My spur of the moment decision was a totally thoughtless one, I decided sadly.

The only way was to meet them in spirit. And so, as I brushed them slowly and lovingly with Eileifer's hog hair brush that he was so proud of, the night wore on, and I was blissfully unaware of its passage. Each horse had its own story to tell. We began with that. Two of the much older horses had arrived here as foals on a huge boat, brought by Romans, and sold to a merchant here on Wihtland. As far as the Romans were concerned, black stallions were the honoured breed, for fighting in battles. The bigger the better. These strange white horses would not fare well on the battleground. But for the Warinni, and all the confederacy peoples who are united with Nerthus, those white horses are precious in every way. And if we cared for them as I was now charged to do, they would reward us with so much wisdom and foresight outside of our smaller knowledge. They talked with the goddess. They knew the gods and were favoured by them. It was a fortunate and good union.

So, as I was reaching the last horse, who was not strictly pure white but pied with beautiful grey and brown flecks, I noticed Sunni rise to give us a new day. This horse along with his sister were both younger and they had lived over the water in the fenlands of the Eastern coastline. This is the land of the Anglisc, who were part of our kinfolk, and they too honoured the white horses. But these were not pure enough for them, so they were sold to a merchant travelling to *Cant*, and so these horses made their way to Wihtland.

I trudged back, with morning dew wetting my soft shoes, making me feel even more exhausted and I wearily thought of the day ahead, realising that there were potions to make up, herbs to gather and mulch, and most probably an unforeseen birthing or a relative *síclaān*. I would forgo the herb gathering and snatch some sleep.

Sinking down onto my straw and deep fur hide bed, with my favourite lavender and chamomile filled pillow, I sunk into darkness within a heartbeat.

… … … … … … … … …

CHAPTER TWELVE
Geweorðan a Wítig Cwèn. Becoming a Wise Woman.

"Dagrun! Wake up!" Lífa screamed at me, eyes bulging, hair like serpent mandrill's, teeth, brown and rotting, a smell so viciously awful, shooting from her gaping mouth, I turned in revulsion.

"Nah!" I shouted, twisting my head away so sharply. My eyes shot open to see Lífa starting to shake me awake. "You were one terrible, smelly dragon woman in my dreaming, Lífa!"

"Hah, 'tis not I, smelly horse-woman, 'tis you, who have chosen to live with horses!"

I turned my nose down and smelt my over kirtle and tunic. It did indeed stink of smelly horse sweat and worse!

"Ahh,", I grunted, leapt off the hide covers and searched within the pile of fresh clothes for something to change into. "Why the fretting, Lífa?" I asked as I tore off the horse-dung clothes.

"You may wish to hurry, Dagrun, young Ingríd is beginning her birthing."

"Ah, *Frèyja Giefan mè strengu*! but it is too soon, her time is when Mōnā is full at *sèremōnaþ*, a full moon and half away from now!"

"*Giese*, I know." Lífa turned to look for all the herbs, charms, amulets and water.

"Is their water pure there?" she asked.

"Bring Ale", I replied, "I do not trust that water where she lives. It is on the edge of our *cæsterwic* and the pasture animals, the sheep, graze too near that stream."

I bent over my own washing pail slinging chilly water onto my face to bring my sluggish mind back to me. I scrubbed ash onto my hands to scrape all horse detritus away. Finally, an astringent bottle lay beside the water and I poured some in the pail to finally rinse my hands.

"We must bring this pail for cleaning", I turned to Lífa, who laid it ready.

I was keenly mindful of the *drycræft* aids, all the herbs and poultices that would be called upon. I sent a prayer to Freyja, our goddess of birthing to make me remember all those things we needed. That outpost where Ingríd was waiting, was too far to countenance a return journey for something forgotten. And I knew this birthing, if indeed that it was it was, would be fraught. Too soon, I thought, far too soon and it is her first. She is small of hip, and too bony.

"Lífa, please fetch some clean linen over there, for I doubt we will find any over at the *hūs* of Ingríd" I spoke while searching my *drycræft* bundle for essential, important talismans and amulets. I placed my birthing braecleat that had been *drycraeft* empowered inside the bag. It had gold engraved broad pins that held a hemp string of cowrie shells, crystals and beads that stretched across my shoulders and hung to my belly. I found, most importantly, the female boar tusk encased in silver and the link to the Vanir and to Freyja, whom I hoped would dearly come to assist us. For without the gods help I feared the babe, the girl, or even both might die.

I sought fresh penny royal, parsnip root, and henbane with coriander seed. I needed old bacon and speedwell even hollyhock. I bundled them into the deerskin bag I held at my waist. Finally, I snatched up a leather covered piece of hardwood oak. "She will need this to bite on for sure," I muttered to myself.

"Shall I bring the poppy potion?" Lífa asked.

"Dah! Of course," I replied, rushing up my steps to be met by a dry and hot afternoon.

I suddenly stopped dead in my tracks, Lífa banging into my side.

"I have not eaten since before the *deaō-gerihte*, my stomach is seizing into tight knots. I must grab some food."

I hurtled down the steep steps into my underground home and searched for those dried apples I had intended to give them to the horses. There was some hard cheese wrapped in linen. That would suffice for what was to come. A very difficult long labour indeed!

I had a large hide bag which could contain all the medicines and Lífa carried the water and the linen. We set off at a fast pace, hoping to reach the outlying *Hūs* in good order. Many spear-lengths later, we heard the cries before we saw the *Hūs*. We broke into a run. Poor little Ingríd I thought. And indeed, she was in a lamentable state. The contractions had clearly taken a hold. Her face was beaded in sweat, her long fair hair lank and wet. She had kicked the linen away from her and I saw immediately that her womb was distended in all the wrong ways.

"Have offerings and prayers been made to the gods?" I asked looking over to the husband, her father and mother.

"*Giese, Gíese*", the husband replied quickly, looking terrified and worried, wringing his hands uselessly.

"Then make yourself useful and make more! To Freyja and Frey, to Wōden and Thunōr."

"Mother, I need another pair of hands and I'm sure you wish to stay."

"*Ylde* Men, be gone from here! I will recall you when you are needed. And make a big offering to Sunni and deep prayers for it is She who will birth this baby, be sure of it!"

I felt Ingrid's swollen belly and knew I was right. The baby was laying sideways, the head needing to go sun wise to the west to be head down in the birthing canal.

"Ingríd, my dear *beorn* hold strong. You must not bear down. Take this leather and when the pain hits you, bite hard! And breathe quick and low. We will turn this baby round, but you must help us"

She looked up at me plaintively and nodded, holding the leather oak in her teeth. Her waters had broken and the linen was soaked in her womb water and blood. Lífa quickly replaced it with clean sheeting, so glad was I, that it had been brought.

I unclipped my *drycræft* hemp loop which was created to sit at both breasts and stretch over the whole belly. Within it, the gods could enter.

Lífa had been boiling the pennyroyal and milk to create a seal.

"Lífa I am needing the seal now", I whispered to her, for from this point all talk was banished. It was the time for the gods.

I took the deepest breath:

"Freyja, becuman, becuman, becuman

Wraðu þes níw sāwol sceawian ond dreogan Ealdor!

Becuman, becuman, becuman."

Freya come, come, come help this new spirit see and feel Life.

Come, come, come."

"Ing, warian Dryhten of Ingríd, Wraðu þes bearn ond Mōdor in níw Ealdor!

Becuman, becuman, becuman"

Ing, guardian god of Ingríd, help this child and mother into new life.

Come, come, come."

"*Freyja fēgan wíþ ūre fǽle Sunni.*

Niman þæt eofor tūx ond glíden wíþ þæt beorn æt þæt west.

Becuman, becuman, becuman!"

Freyja, join with our beloved Sunni

Take the boar tusk and move with the child to the west."

I took a wide mouthful of the sealing liquid and with my teeth clamped, blew a spray all over the belly of Ingríd, and around the *drycræft* ring.

I hissed the S vowel of the rune Sōwelo, the sun, and as I inscribed a protective circle in ash outside the *drycræft* ring I called in power of Sōwelo and then drew in ash the rune at the unborn baby's head and again at the base of the birth canal.

"sssssssssss Sōwelo sssssssssss Sōwelo sssssssssss Sōwelo,"

I saw the power enter and saw the baby shift. Ingríd bit down harder to stifle a scream. She was showing such courage. The gods could see. I took the precious boar tusk and laid it within the circle and saw the baby move again.

I slowly began to move the tusk westwards, slowly, slowly invoking Sōwelo.

Sssssssssss, I sprayed more pennyroyal onto the belly of Ingríd.

And the baby moved. The *beorþor* was happening!

I heard a voice so clearly say, "Assist!" The tusk was nearly at the vertical point at the birthing canal. I leant forward and held both hands at the head and shoulders of the *brōd*. And with a huge push from me and a swish of power from the gods, that dear little one shifted into the birthing canal and Ingríd let go a shattering scream and slumped back.

Her breathing was easier if shallow. She was exhausted as this had been going on for many hours before the call for help reached us.

"*Mōdor* of Ingríd, what is your name?" I asked as I saw clearly, her eyes well up. She wiped the tears away quickly with the back of her hand.

"Ingigerdr" She said, smiling at last, at the relief of seeing her only daughter live when she had feared worse.

"Ah, Ing's enclosure!" I replied, "So you have our god with you too it would seem."

"We are all thralls, *Wítig Cwèn*, we were re-named by our master Ingvar."

"Huh!" I exclaimed, "I did not know Ingvar held thralls! Tell me your story *Mōdor* and my name is Dagrun Wahl, please"

The poor woman sighed deeply, for in the telling there was much sorrow.

"We were all in thraldom in the place where buyers and sellers bid for human bodies. Over the Germania sea. Our master was cruel and treated Ingríd very sorely. My husband was eaten with up with anger and bitterness, but we were powerless. They were going to take us to Gaul to Freyja knows what! Ingvar took great pity on us. He bought us all in kindness. He is Ingavonii and close to the Eudose, by the big sea. He is wed to the sea. We took to his boat and after a time in *Cant* we made for Wihtland. We thank the gods daily Dagrun for our good fortune."

"*Giese*, I see clearly," I replied looking sharply into her eyes, "but why are you all so lacking in food and good shelter?"

"Ahh, because Ingvar for all his nobility is lacking also. He is miserable on the land, Dagrun. He married an Anglii woman whom you know are all farmers at heart. But he has no interest in the land. He sickens to be on the sea again. I think he doesn't have blood running through his veins, but pure salt water!"

"Ah", I mused over this, "Now I think I understand. His land is vast. Yet I see only a portion fully under the plough and crops growing."

"That is not the worst of it!" Ingigerdr replied hotly, her brow furrowing into a deep frown, "The Romans are exacting a higher yield of grain from us as the soldiers build up in Wihtland. There is a growing ferment amongst the thralls who remain in slavery.

We cannot survive on what is left. We *could* do if this land is managed well. This is a fertile land, Dagrun, the best for us all. We can give what the Romans ask for and have enough for ourselves. But we are powerless."

I thought about this for a moment and decided. But unlike my old self who would open her mouth and let it all come tumbling out for anyone to pick up and make another story, I held still.

"I have thought of something that may help you and your family but I can say nothing yet. Leave it with me, Ingigerdr"

"What is your birth name?" I asked as I reached for the cheese. I was beginning to feel faint with hunger.

"Leofflæd," she answered her eyes widening, as I was surely the first person in many a twilight to have asked her. I had a plan!

"And your husband?"

"Oh, he was named Leofwine, it means dear friend and he is a kindly man for sure!"

"Ingrid's husband?" I ventured. I felt I was dredging up memories that caused some pain to this poor woman.

"He has always been known by his given name of ívarr, bow warrior, and he is just that! If ever there was a hothead to tackle these Romans it is him. He is slight and can run as fast as a west wind. He knows the forests well and can kill an animal from many a spears length."

"And does he love your daughter?" I ventured.

"To his dying breath he does!" she answered.

Good, I thought. I had heard all I needed to hear. I could not create a new life for these people yet. Until Eileifer returned to me and my higher status made sure. And my father comfortable in his new role, I could only plant the seed of the "freedmen" for them and the benefits that would create.

"Dagrun, please come and share some pottage with us, you must be hungry!" Leofflæd said, smiling, showing brown and broken teeth in a radiantly beautiful smile.

She is her name, I thought sadly.

I settled to a bare watery soup of few vegetables and very old barley. But the bread she offered was good, warm and newly baked. Another new thought entered my head. She would be a very good baker in her own right.

Ingríd gave out a low moan.

"Ahh", I turned to Lífa. "Boil up the pennyroyal and milk, please. We need this *beorn* here before Sunni meets with Mōnã."

I gave the potion to a very tired young girl and before very long her belly seized and she cried out.

"Bite on the leather, girl," I insisted, "I will tell you when you can give it your all. Not just yet."

"My back is hurting, Dagrun", she moaned.

"Lífa help me tie the *drycræft* in place" So we both bound the ring securely and hoisted Ingríd to her feet.

It was her first birthing and she shrieked, not knowing what we were doing.

"Ingríd, do not fear, *beorn*, you are going to kneel for us. And hold onto the table edge."

"The baby will have an easier journey and you will not have an aching back!"

Soon the pennyroyal took full effect and she was gasping for breath in between ever closer seizures of her belly. I looked at her opening. It was wide enough now and I could see the head.

"Ingríd, on the next one, push with all your power."

Gritted teeth and high shrieks followed, then by two more.

The head was down.

"Ingríd, listen *beorn*, you must not push anymore. Take the oaken leather *now!* Breathe quickly, come on! dear one, you can do this!"

With a sudden gush amidst high screaming the baby arrived, bloody and waxen. And with a hearty cry to melt any old heart this baby girl met with earth and Nerthus smiled!

"'Tis a girl, Ingríd!" I cried. I cut and tied the cord with strong hemp. I washed her over with wet linen that had been sitting in the astringent water, and handed her to her proud, exhausted mother. Her beaming smile was a joy to witness. And I sent up a prayer to Sunni, Freyja, Ing. And as always to our Nerthus for their help, and thankfulness. I felt truly blessed to be a *Witig Cwèn*.

Ingríd had already put her daughter to the breast. She will make a good mother, I thought. It gave me time to see any ripping that would no doubt have happened, and sure enough there was. After a while and before the after-birth arrived, I decided it was timely to honour the ritual of the father holding and offering his baby to the gods in thanks.

"Call the men in and put them out of their misery", I called over my shoulder. I felt her womb for the after birth. She was exhausted and it was being sluggish.

"Lífa, my dear *wencel*, do we have brooklime and hollyhock in the sack?"

"We do Dagrun, *Witig Cwèn*" she replied with a slow grin breaking into a chuckle. "Here."

The hide flap swung open and bright sunlight cascaded onto mother and baby giving them a Sunni *sãwol* glow. It was most serene and beautiful. She had favoured them.

Ívarr hurtled in and stopped dead as though one of his arrows had pieced him straight in the heart! Slowly he stood to full height and a smile as brilliant as the sun spread across his face. It was called Joy and he came forward to look lovingly at his new daughter.

"Take her ívarr, you have the right to show her to Sunni, to the gods now. She is yours."

He took the swaddling *beorn* cradling her carefully in his arms. He held a look of pure devotion as he took his daughter out into the afternoon sun.

I returned to Ingríd who was lying still, eyes closed.

"Ingríd, we have one more push to make as the birthing sack must come away. Here take this and it will make fast the ending."

She pulled an ugly face at drinking the strong-smelling herb potion. And who did not, I thought. It was foul tasting but it worked.

It took a short count for it to take effect and after a big constriction of her belly the sack slithered out and it was all done. I placed a healing poultice on her *gecyndelícu*.

I bound it in place with linen strips, hoping it would heal. I hoped her milk would flow well. I hoped she would not get milk fever. All these worries for the slight little mother who had the courage of a boar!

I placed the birthing sack and the cord in a linen sack and told Leofflæd to take it to her sacred place, bury it with prayers for the gods to look over the child all her life.

"It is most important you remember Sunni and Freyja. It is they who have taken up guardianship of the baby. I do believe Ing has stepped back."

I carefully unbound the *drycræft* ring placing it in cleansing water with the boar tusk offering a prayer of thanks. I placed them all in my hide bag that hung at my waist. We gathered all the herbs and potions, the astringent water ale, and made our way outside. My last view of ívarr was of him proudly holding his daughter up skywards, the shafts of sunlight striking his new-born daughter with warmth. And then her mewling loudly asking for milk. I was glad to see he did not hesitate and turned to take her back to her mother.

As we left I called back "Tell me when the naming ceremony takes place please. And do not forget. I will see about your hardship and talk with my *fæder*."

"*Giese*, we will," shouted Leofflæd, smiling at us with that toothless grin in such a beautiful face.

… … … … … … … … …

"I am exhausted, Lífa," I turned to pull a face.

"The goddesses were so present back there Dagrun. It was powerful, *Wítig Cwèn*!"

"Hah!" I exclaimed, "I doubt that weasel of a little wizard would agree I had any power at all."

"He has been sent to test you, Dagrun, truly."

"I know," I replied making another face, "*Ealdmōdor* told me I needed to grow a skin!"

"She is rarely wrong. You must learn to stand up to him in a way that empowers you not him."

"Hmmmm", I replied, "I suddenly have an over powering need to see the sea, ride the horses through the waves as far as the white headland and loosen this exhausting day. Will you come *sweostor*? What say you?"

Lífa had already quickened her step. Before Sunni disappeared behind the Headon Warren, our hair would be full of salt, our legs aching with the speed of the mount and our cheeks aching from laughing.

… … … … … … … … …

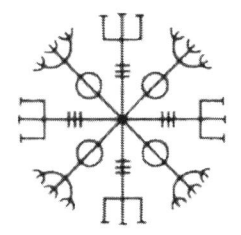

CHAPTER THIRTEEN
NERTHUS

I was treading a twilight path soft and sweet, with the night perfume from the hedges. Of herbs and bright flowers. Wild rose shaken by the bees filling me so much that my purpose for walking out had left me.

I stopped to breath in this twilight air. Sea breezes wafted across and I twinned the flower perfume with seaweed aroma, strong and astringent. How I loved this Wihtland home. We were nearing that magical time of *Þrimilce-mōnaþ*, the month of three milkings. Sunni and Thunōr had been very kind to us for the sun and the rain had come in equal timings and our crops were sturdy and growing well. This was a sacred part of our year when we celebrated in procession and rite for Nerthus our Mother Earth. We always chanted for her appearance. We gave huge offerings in the hope she would gift us in her human form if only for a while. And I knew, having been given the Telling, that she could come. So wonderful a being was she that shone with a bright light. We always chose a *Cwèn* amongst us with whom she may twin. And I also knew that the only woman strong enough and pure enough for Nerthus to enter was Eldís, our young *Ealdmōdor* in training. She had come of age and had passed into womanhood. So, her spirit was ready and her soul deep and old enough to respond.

It was also a time of couplings. Of love expressed and shown. Secret trysts, spells and much hawthorn worn and chanted to so that the heart-ease white flowers would gift and blossom a new romance.

And the *seax* of loneliness twisted in my heart once more as I stopped dead in my tracks. I missed Eileifer more with each passing twilight. It seemed endless. And with no message given to me. No thread of intent to attach to my heart. It was slowly breaking. He may well have been forced to travel back to our old homeland in the Cimbric peninsular. For all that I knew. It had been several generations of Warinni since any of us had seen that land!

And I knew I would be heartily miserable through the entire *gerihte*.

I heaved my mind back to the present moment. I could delve into the demands of the procession and try to forget.

I was on the edges of the *Tunstede,* seeking out a boy Eyvindr had told me about. He had a natural gift with horses and was not working in the fields. His father had been approached and was willing to let him come to me to be trained as stable boy for our sacred horses. I could not in all truth be the sole keeper. They would suffer in the end and Eileifer would not be thanking me at all. I was anxious that nothing would come between us. In his absence, I felt part of me broken away.

Eyvindr suddenly appeared out of the growing night, wrapped in a woollen cape.

"*Brōðor*, why so dressed for a winter's night?" I asked, looking up at him as he winced in some pain.

"Elf-shot or worm, I know not which!" he groaned, "attacking my throat and chest."

"Home for you!" I declared, "Ask mother to attend you with *feferfuge* and some pennyroyal poultice for your chest. Go!"

"The boy's home is over there", he pointed to a well-kept dwelling that was large and had a good roof, "*Mōdor* has tended to the child over the years: he has a broken body but a strong spirit."

He turned to leave as I blurted out beyond control.

"Have you had any message from Wihtleig or Eileifer?"
Eyvindr searched my eyes and wrapped his arms around me in a huge brother bear hug that robbed me of air.

"Patience, *sweostor!* Learn it or it will come to try you for sure as Sunni rises."
I winced inside and gave him a half-hearted smile.

"Oh," I remembered, "I need to talk with father about the family living in the hinterland. Ingvar's thralls."

"I will tell him" Eyvindr muttered as he slipped into the night.

… … … … … … … … …

The room area, inside the *hūs* was very large and well-lit with goose-fat wall candles. Fresh floor rushes hit the nostrils with rosemary and dried lavender. Sleeping areas were divided off with patterned and embroidered hangings. But what stopped me in amazement was that this *hūs* has its own baking oven set at the far wall with an especially built stone flu to take the heat away from the furnishings.

All of us Warinni baked our bread in a family oven set away from the trees and *hūs* and where we baked a week's supply of bread for us all.

Here was something I had never witnessed. I suppose my shock which quickly turned to fascination. It made the telling easy for Eardwūlf, the father, who was a trader born and bred. He was from the Southern Eudose, part of the Ingavonii. Their life was on the sea. It made them excellent boat builders, travellers and merchants.

And the Romans took to him as he took to the Romans. He had become a *Rōmãnisc*. And he loved to trade. Anything that came into his hands he would find a buyer. A market that would provide enough coin for both him and his Roman masters.

Wihtland offered up opportunities with several trading ports and the important link to Gaul and beyond. This had been established aeons ago.

The *Rōmānisc* family had a life set apart from the rest of the confederacy of seven. But they had a sorrow. And for the most part they were kind generous people. They had respect accorded to them. They helped where they could. But no amount of generous help, chanting or spell-working could bring back the full health for their son which they craved beyond any wealth and trade. Eastmund had lived ten summers or thereabouts. He had survived a shocking birth and lived despite the twisted bones and head. He had not grown out of the deformity. Rather it became his signature.

He was relentlessly bullied by his peers. His father did not cushion him from the beatings and taunts, hoping he would grow several skins and become a warrior of sorts. But anger did not enter Eastmund's soul. Silence did.

He retreated from the harsh human world and sort out the friendship of the animals who did not judge him in any way. The horses big and free became his muscles and backbone.

And so, as I sat taking food with them I realised Eastmund was perfect as a helper for the sacred horses. I needed to find out if he understood the language necessary to build trust with them.

"Eastmund would you be pleased to come and aid me and Eileifer in the care of our sacred horses?"

He looked up eyes widening in astonishment. And then he nodded and nodded some more until his whole head of curly hair was shaking in the candle light.

"I will take that as a *Gíese!*" I stamped the table in acknowledgment. I held out my other hand to the mother Friduswiþ for a uniting clasp in friendship, honour bound.

And from deep within me I felt a butterfly of excitement stirring so small yet powerful. Now I was sure *Wyrd* was at work. I had altered my path in this one action and *Ealdmōdor* was smiling down on me.

"Come with me to meet the horses after the *Þrimilce-mōnaþ* rites", I said, smiling at the young boy who would indeed become my left hand.

… … … … … … … … …

Sunni rose in a sky free of clouds on this the first day of *Þrimilce-mōnaþ*.

All the women had been baking in our oven the heart shaped breads to gift to Nerthus. They would offer them at the leaning stone and on the pathway to the sacred guardian oak. It was the gateway to the Norns and world of spirit. From small and delicate biscuits to large and deeply decorated cakes the chanting had been born into the bread. All the prayers on the breath of a score of women. Asking for health for their children and husbands. For a keen harvest and peace in our time. For the younger women, a heartfelt spell for love to greet them and to be swept away in the arms of a handsome man!

We were dressed in our best. Blues and light greens fluttered in the light breeze that had sprung up. In honouring Nerthus it was our day also. The men were on the back foot.

Their role was one of support. There would be seven priests from each of our tribes and two Eōte priests making nine. All iron and weapons were put down. Everything had to remain in the *Tunstede*. The priests would guard and escort our *Cwèn* up the hill to the leaning stone. From there to travel to the sacred grove in the forest of bright stone. Eldís would be purified and anointed with scared herbs to await the coming of the goddess.

Eldís appeared in a shaft of pure sunlight. Aslaug at her side. Our new *Ealdmōdor* was grinning and making the spring in her step as that of a young girl. She was eclipsing her aging body.

Eldís was glowing in a pure white flowing gown that had been lovingly made by the women of the weaving lodge. And intertwined at her neck and sleeves and hem was a knot of *wyrd rapas* in blue and green single stranded dyed hemp that was *Drýcræftig*. It flowed with every movement and shone with a light that was iridescent.

Eldís had a band of flowers intertwined in her hair. It flowed in waves down her back. She had been cleansed and her hair was swinging in a freshness of the newly washed. It glinted in the sunlight and we all were struck dumb by the complete beauty of our young goddess in waiting. We did not know if Nerthus would come to her. But one thing was certain. All the women had crafted with their utmost skill and the tenderness of that work radiated from Eldís. Surely, surely, she would come, I thought, breathing in an unexpressed excitement. This day could become a Telling before the night fires for many twilights to come.

It would be the *Þrimilce-mōnaþ* procession to outstrip them all.

Eyvindr had been chosen as priest for our people, the Warinni. From the Reudignians came an older priest. I had learnt this from my brother who had travelled from Brigantia, across our narrow waters to join us. This older priest made much of the celebrations over there. They were larger and the processions longer and the much-established secret grove fiercely guarded leaving no doubt that we would be passed over by our Goddess. He endeared himself to not one soul amongst us. And my brother was muttering charms under his breath for his swift removal!

His arrogance knitted a thread of discord amongst us and I too joined my brother in strengthening those removal charms.

Aslaug had felt the growing tension. She moved forward to step in front of the aging priest. Her smile now fixed. Those piecing grey eyes, like tempered iron, stared right into his soul and found it wanting!

"The Warinni greet you, *hālettahn þu*. It is our honour to have you here at our *Þrimilce-mōnaþ* procession for our Earth Mother Nerthus." She clasped her bony hands in his, smiling with a knowing look.

"And it is also an honour to give you the very highest accolade. Knowing as you must that you are a stranger in our midst and therefore you become the haloed sacrifice made to our goddess in her sacred and secret pool of wisdom. Your journey to spirit world will be much applauded and your name sung around the night fires."

I watched in fascination as the shocked and frozen expression turned to sheer horror on the craggy face of this elder priest. He suddenly realised his life was about to end. This had not entered his mind as it had been many twilights ago when sacrifice had been stopped here on Wihtland. No-one disrespected the Grove and there were too few men here to afford a needless sacrifice. But he did not know this and it must still be practised in the larger lands of Brigantia.

He ripped his hands away from Aslaug. In stepping back away from her he shrank before our eyes into a quaking huddle of a man. He was stripped of his armour of arrogance and what was left became a trembling and terrified worm.

"Ahh, I beg your indulgence. I must leave, I I… suddenly feel most unwell!" he stuttered looking not at Aslaug but at the ground before him.

He turned and left, his sandals flapping on the dry earth at the sheer speed of his exit.

The air around us cleared and even the sun seemed brighter.

"Dah! Good riddance", Aslaug exclaimed, "Eyvindr, sweet *cnapa,* we are now one priest short. Please go and find a young male with a pure heart and a clean soul to join us. There is no need for priestly training. Look what we have just endured! I would wager this young soul will be far better for us and Nerthus will rejoice. But hurry we are lagging in time."

As Eyvindr ran to find the likely "priest" I noticed the remaining priests. The seven from our neighbouring settlements were huddling in a tight group and I could see a hard discussion with much arm raising was taking a hold of our peaceful gathering.

"Aslaug", I turned to face her, "That awful priest had cast a spell on all this! There is dissention over there. Why is it that the men always ruin things for us?"

"Only certain men with unhappy souls, Dagrun, remember that. They are half of our humanity. And we really cannot live without them."

She strode over to the men in priestly clothes and spoke quietly. She was calming them it seemed.

"Oh! By the gods" she exclaimed when she returned, "but sometimes I do believe we women are from another place, another time, for I cannot make men out! They earnestly believed they were going to die this day at the sacred grove and have forgotten our pledge of peace to all on this island home of ours!"

I thought for a moment.

"We have a large tribe if we gather them all together, Aslaug. We should do more gathering together. For I feel we are all living in separate little *Ceasterwics* and *Tunstedes*. We are not united as we were in the old homeland. Why, I do not know. But something is separating us from each other. I shall invoke a pledge and vow to make us come together before Nerthus."

"Some tribes are small, like the Reudignians and the Niuthones, who number but four families over in the Chestebeorg settlement. But the Anglii are like us, and the Aviones. We should gather Aslaug, for our strength lies in unity."

"I agree with you Dagrun, *sweostor*," Aslaug looked at me with such warmth. I almost wanted to hug her. And again, the spirit of *Ealdmōdor* came so close to me I could feel her breath on my cheek. Then the Heron wing, the last gift from her which I carried with me, ruffled for a moment. I was sure. *Wyrd* had visited me. The Fates were looking down on us. Where this would take us, I could not fathom. But knew only that it would be for our good.

… … … … … … … … …

We had entered the *beort stān*, the bright stone circle, which lay in a deep valley, enclosed all around with ancient beech that clung tenaciously to the escarpment. Their knarled twisting roots encased the earth with intricate beautiful threads of beech wood. The old beech trees were just turning to that exquisite sap green. The sun shafted through their young shoots. They became emeralds glinting in the noonday sunlight. We had gathered, all our tribes in this sacred place, for the ceremonial procession to begin. The *beort stān* was our entrance and when the noonday sun embraced the large stone our ancient ancestors had created, she came alive with crystals glittering around her whole surface.

It had been passed to us in the Telling that this stone was the gateway to spirits. To the great Wisdom held within. And I trembled at the energy I suddenly felt when she came alive. A fear I could not explain coursed through my body. And it left me breathless.

"What ails you *sweostor*?", Sãga reached out to touch my hand.

"I do not know, Sãga", I replied feeling the sweat grow on my hands, they felt clammy to the touch. "Some energy touched me from *beort stãn*. It is from the near world and it is powerful enough to do this to me!"

"She is calling to you, Dagrun, most certainly pulling you into her realm. Have a care. When you reach the Grove, ask Nerthus for guidance and her protection."

I looked intently at the standing stone now, trying to feel what this was about. But nothing came.

I sighed deeply, knowing also that *wyrd* was calling to me. There was nothing to be done but follow.

"Look", Sãga said, "The women are beginning, we must join them."

We moved towards the scores of our women now encircling the stones. They were kneeling in prayer and chanting our honoured song to the Goddess, while they dug the earth before them to bury the sacred heart cakes.

Our *Drímeolce cwèn* stood in front of the *beort stãn* as we encircled her. The priestesses and *Wítega cwèn* began dancing in rhythm around her and the stone as the full noonday sun shone down on us.

"Erce, Erce, Erce,

Folde Mōdor fǽle Nerthus Mōdor fram eall,

Gèara, Twuwa, ðriwa

Wè gifu ūre ferhð cicel,

Gèara, for hæfest fram fyllu,

Twuwa, for þæt gesundfulnes fram ūre ðèodscipe,

Ðriwa, motan þæt frèogan ond frið weaxan ðearl.

Bletsunga Beorte

Bletsunga Beorte!

Erce, Erce, Erce,

Earth Mother, beloved Nerthus, mother of all,

Once, Twice, Thrice, we gift you our heart-cake,

Once for harvest of plenty

Twice for the health of our people,

Thrice, may the love and peace of our people grow strong,

Bright Blessings

Bright Blessings!

They sang their hearts into the offerings and began placing them in the earth. Their chant continued and we danced, swirling gently around the stone, arms held aloft, fingers intertwining with Sunni's rays so they too danced on the stone, bringing us all into one rhythm. The feeling of peace descended on us all. We had reached the place of Nerthus and we were ready to continue to the Grove.

When all the offerings were in the ground, we placed our hands upon the *Beorht stān* in communion and thanks.

Without warning, a shot of pure terrifying energy took my body in its grip. The air left my lungs in a thunderous whoosh and my heart stopped!

I felt I might have died. I tried to open my eyes, they were held shut by a force. I had never experienced anything like this in my training.

I shouted out, but nothing came from my mouth, it was rammed shut. If anything escaped, it was a hiss of high pitched terror.

Quite suddenly, without warning, I was released from this invisible force. I opened my eyes and looked in shock at what was before me. Not this land, not this time. The ancient beech trees were mere stumps, the escarpment bare, with just gorse and thistle growing. Our stone circle was no more. As I reached to feel the reassurance of the *Beorht stān*, my fingers touched thin air and I stumbled backwards, falling to my knees.

The earth was cold. It was a winter's day, and dark thunderous clouds scudded across the sky. Thunōr was in anger. I began to pray to Nerthus for her help.

Then I saw two figures working their way towards me in a hurry. As they drew closer, I made out their dress and appearance. My heart missed a beat, and I felt that terror I experienced with Sāga wash over me again. These men were not here to be kindly and they looked so foreign.

One was a portly figure in a long brown ankle length smock. His big belly wobbled as he strode down the escarpment. Even more shocking, I saw he had no face hair at all. I had never seen a man without hair on his face. It was a mark of manhood in my world. And he showed two chins! One that also wobbled as he walked. His hair was short and cut close to his ears. Then he bent down suddenly to take a stone out of his sandals. With a gasp of horror, I saw his head had absolutely no hair growing on it, but bare to the skin in a perfect circle.

He was carrying a large square scroll, so thick it needed hard leather to hold it together. I had never laid eyes on anything like this. The strange man had a large jewelled cross hanging from his neck, which swung wildly as he made his way towards me.

He was waving the strange scroll at me, his podgy arm stretched out.

He looked ridiculous.

But the man who strode beside him filled me with terror. He was a warrior. He had a long Saxon sword dangling from his waist. It was bejewelled and no doubt bloodied in many a battle. He wore a hardened leather armour that came to his waist and below intertwined metal that chinked as he walked. Emblazoned in bright dye on his leather were the symbols of the Boar and the Wolf.

He was Wōden's warrior. Why was he coming for me in that frightening way?

His face was struck in a cruel snarl, his knotted beard swinging in the harsh wind.

"Harlot! Whore, Witch to the Devil himself, "the beardless man shrieked, "We have found you out! Here at the Devil's circle. Practising your spells and wicked ways! Recant NOW, I ask you to join the Christ's fold, or you will be forever damned to burn in the Hell's fire!"

He was so foreign I did not understand his language. Then I realised it was his accent. It was from far north in Britannia

"I would do as he says, Harlot!" the warrior snarled, or you will wish for death before I have done with you!"

He charged forward and grabbed my hair, twisting it in his thick knuckled hand, until I shrieked in pain. He laughed and twisted more. Then he grabbed my arm twisting it behind my back so I was at his mercy. He had not shown one ounce of kindness towards me.

He pushed me towards the beardless man.

"Kneel to the priest Wilfrid, now!" he shouted in my ear, his foul breath choking me.

"Repent your evil pagan ways and become a child of Christ."

"Kiss the Bible", he demanded.

I turned up to look in his face. Those eyes were as black as the darkest night and sunk in cruelty. It was a face I would never forget throughout all my days. It was he that was the evil one, not I!

"I will only kiss the *Beorht Stān* of our beloved Nerthus, for my pagan way is more precious to me than your bible or your Christ!", I uttered through breathless speech, robbed by weakness born of fear."

I heard a swish and grate of that sword being released from it scabbard.

I shut my eyes and shrieked, "Noooooooo."

Then suddenly, my entire world went black. Then I realised that the warmth of Sunni was sinking into my frozen body. I opened my eyes to see the shocked faces of my friends looking down on me, with the warmth of the *Beorht Stān* on my back.

I was shaking with relief at being back with my people in this time. In this sacred place. What I was shown terrified me beyond thinking. But now, at this moment, I had broken the energy of love for the Nerthus ritual to be complete.

I looked up from where I was straddled on the ground to see Aslaug glaring at me, her hands crossed at her waist, her head to one side.

"Dagrun Wahl", she shook her head in disbelief, "you have picked the very worst time to practise your stone guardianship skills. The energy is broken. You screamed…. why?"

"*Ealdmōdor*, the *wyrd* took hold of me. I was taken to another place and time! I am so sorry I shrieked, but I could do nothing else. What I was shown is meant. I must learn to ask *wyrd* to take account of our timing and our rituals. It was not meant to be dishonoured."

"Then we must sit another time and you must recount this "adventure" to us in a Telling in the women's lodge" Aslaug said in a kindlier manner.

"Come *sweostors,* let us chant to Nerthus as we walk to regain the energy she needs. Dagrun, you must remain here, *beorn*. Regain yourself."

"No, no please," I exclaimed, "I must needs be with Nerthus, for what I was shown is part of us, our tribe, our whole way of life and the danger that lies ahead!"

"I will stay in the shadows, please, but I know I must be there", I pleaded.

Ealdmōdor stood stock still, staring intensely at me searching my soul with her iron-grey eyes.

"Very well", she murmured, "But please only join us when you are free of this blackness. I still see it swirling around you. Pray to Freyja to take it from you child."

As I looked to the trail of receding figures. My tribe, folk of my kin, Sunni gracing them with ever more heat and shining rays, I collapsed into a mournful heap, hugging my knees. I tightened into a ball. My eyes rammed shut as I relived those frightening moments. I had been brought up to love and respect all, as Nerthus asked of us. All the tribes of seven on this beautiful island home had laid respect and honour as first amongst us. The warrior blood was not coursing through our veins. The *Centingas* had this, the men of *Cant*. But they were small in number here on Wihtland. Their *Cyng*, through Wōden's bloodline made them royal. My beloved Eileifer was of royal blood. How I wished him here at this moment!

I tried to step back from my fear, knowing this to be a glimpse of a future time. We all knew *wyrd* ran a course between our lives, past, present and future. The *wyrd rapas* intertwined these in a sacred web. So, I relaxed into this knowledge.

It seemed the man with the pot belly and no face hair was an agent of a new faith to reach our lands. It was not a peaceful loving faith. This faith saw our ways as dangerous, hence the warrior, and that it's energy of death and killing had overtaken them. Killing was accepted.

My heart turned to ice and my belly knotted into painful strictures. The horror made worse for the total of absence of bloody war in my life. We even accepted the Roman, small as they were, stationed over on the east of the island. Intent only on ferrying their soldiers to Britannia. I had heard of bloodshed. This at second hand telling from travellers and traders who came through this way on their way to Gaul.

They spoke of a few battles taking place many twilights ago, along the East coast. The tribes' people had risen in anger against the might of the Roman sword. I worried constantly for Eileifer, who was in *Cant,* where the *Centingas* men, also native to the land, may decide to revolt against the Roman legions. Wihtleig and Eileifer were *Centish* men, who had brought their *Nuithone* society with them. They had created all men and women as freedmen and there were many respectful laws. They were consummate traders and craftsmen. This was the bedrock that kept them apart from the warring tribes. But I wondered for how long?

    I uncurled my numb and aching legs. My calves were tickled by the rough grass. Taking a deep breath, I re-entered the stone circle and made my way over to the *Beorht stãn* keeping a spear's length away. I knelt and prayed deeply to Freyja for release. Nothing happened. Then I prayed to Wōden for he was said to be the god of war. Although I knew in my heart, from *Ealdmōdor's* Telling, that he had a deep compassionate nature.

    A deep voice entered my head.

Feorh hyrde fram þæt eald fæder stãn-cèpan gíeman:

Forhtian wyllaþ brengan Ellen ond Ellen wyllaþ

Warian þū ond þín ðèodscipe fæstan in þín treow.

Ūre Folde Mōdor ãcsian þes fram þu.

Bletsunga Beorte fram þín Eall Fæder,

Life protector, Guardian of the ancestor stone,

Take heed: Fear will bring courage, and courage

Will hold you and your people fast in your faith.

Our Mother Earth asks this of you.

Bright Blessings from your All Father!

For a moment, my breath was taken from me. From empty lungs, I took a huge breath and in letting go, I felt the blackness and terror leave me. I became calm and in that calmness felt my *Ealdmōdor* come and brush my cheek. The Heron wing fluttered in answer to my unspoken thanks to her and to our All Father. I held them both close me. A growing feeling of love enveloped me and I knew I was ready again to re-join the women in the Grove.

I remembered only fleeting images of that walk to meet my kin. The rays from Sunni were coursing through me to keep the warmth in my heart alive. The glints of light on the sap green leaves waved before me. The shimmer of the sea, and the swirling of larks' high in the sky with their song so elegant, met with the waves of warm air around me. It was perfect!

I caught up with them quickly enough. I sought out Sãga for a friendly hand to hold. She looked at me, questioning silently my return.

"*Þín Eall Fæder* he came and took the black energy from me!" I whispered and smiled, "It was wonderful, to be sure!"

"You look radiant Dagrun Wahl!" she exclaimed, linking her arm in mine as we strode forward. And I nodded and smiled at the others who had always looked out for me.

For now, I thought… I am shielded.

The sacred grove of Nerthus was hidden within tall and ancient trees. The carriage holding the throne, taking our *Drímeolce Cwèn* to her appointed place, continued with the priests walking behind. The oxen, now finding the ground flat, picked up a speed that lilted the carriage to and fro. Eldís sat erect, her face inscrutable. She swayed with the motion but not one expression showed on her beautiful face. The white gown flowed gently, the *wyrd rapas* glinted at her feet. Barefoot and without any other adornment, she looked ethereal.

Silence….no words were spoken as Elíse and the priests became as one with the forest of trees. They disappeared. Sãga, my mother with Aslaug and myself followed several spears lengths behind. The low-lying branches of the giant beech caressed us as we passed. The smell of forest earth, anemone and garlic, filled the air. Butterflies skipped in a dance around Sunni's rays.

It took a while to walk through the forest of *Hāligwielle* at *Scorawella*. The spring which eternally fed the pool where Nerthus may emerge from her serpent form, lay hidden within deep tree-root and foliage. The path was narrow and the carriage just squeezed through. Elíse brought her cloak around her to keep away the branches. Her head was now bowed in deep prayer. A tension was beginning to grow and I tried so hard to keep the recent images from breaking into my calm.

The carriage had come to a halt. The oxen, now relieved of their struggle were led away. They were separated, one being tied to a post where a large bowl was placed. The place of sacrifice to the Earth Goddess. It waited quietly, unknowing, chewing on the grass.

Before us lay a truly beautiful ancient oak, so old its branches had become huge pathways. This oak straddled the rushing waters from the sacred spring. Its spirit lay in complete communion with Nerthus. It had forsaken the journey upwards to the sky to meet with Thunōr or even Sunni and Mōnā. It was so entrusting, this old oak. It had stretched it branches even to the water's edge of the sacred pool itself, as if seeking only to unite with the goddess. But it was fecund, healthy, and the sap green new leaves hung everywhere, like small emeralds. Sunni was nearing the journey to night. So, we waited, silently for a few moments. True twilight was Nerthus' time, when Sunni embraced Mōnā, briefly, before leaving.

Aslaug turned to me:

"Dagrun, you must wait over there behind the oak. Do as I say!" as she saw my face twist sharply in protest. I moved away and sought a wide branch to sit comfortably. The night would be long and now I was separated from the ceremony, it would be much, much longer!

All I could do was pray.

Fǽle Nerthus, Folde Mōdor fram eall-

Gehlýstan mè IC bidden þū

Ætiewan mè þǽt ondgit fram þæt gesho̅ mist wolcens mín ingehygd

Forhwōn am IC coren

Gehlýstan mè IC bidden þu

Ure ðèodscipe behōfian æt feōndscipe ond ānlæcan swā ãn.

Wraðu ūs!

Beloved Nerthus, Earth Mother of all-

Hear me I beg you.

Show me the meaning of the visions!

A fog clouds my understanding-

Hear me I beg you.

Our people need to unite in friendship as one.

Help us!

And as I sat hunched up with head down, repeating my prayer softly, intently, I was lost in the near world of spirit. The chanting to Nerthus increased to a crescendo. All the voices were in harmony now, united. I looked up to see Eldís was gone from this world. She had her eyes closed. She remained frozen like ice on her throne.

I returned to my praying that was too personal, too removed from the circle of priests and their ancient chant. It continued for many heartbeats. Then a horrendous bellow came from the stricken oxen whose throat was severed, rent the world apart. It made the chanting freeze. Silence, except for the slap of warm blood pouring into the bowl. And the snorting from the fellow bull who smelt his death and was terrified.

The whole grove was still. Not a breath of wind nor the cry from a bird. Eldís shook momentarily, shaken by the sacrifice. She began to compose herself.

Then so easily, so slightly, there came a mist. A blue tinged mist that deftly caressed the serpent oak, twirling around the knotted and roughened trunk branches closest to the pool. Intertwining with a purpose of binding, the mist deepened and intensified so the hue became both blue and the sap green of the oak leaves. I saw the serpent oak shake through its entire body, as if woken from a long sleep. Together serpent oak and mist slowly danced and swayed in silent sacred union.

It was a wondrous moment for all of us humans present. We were risen to a higher plane, closer to the gods, closer to the Norns and Wōden, Freyja, Thunōr.

"By all the Gods," I thought, "She is coming!"

The union continued for many heartbeats, as we watched, entranced and at total peace.

Then so slowly and as easily, the mist curled away and wrapped around itself to become a form growing above us, and above the low-lying serpent oak.

And so, it intensified and became more solid. I dared look up to see an exquisite face of a woman form in front of us, hair flowing like tendrils in turquoise and green, eyes that shone with the brightest light behind them and a smile to caress and love us. Her gown was gossamer thin, like woven spider threads and it gently swayed of its own, in a still forest that held its breath.

A voice in my head, soft but clear as a lark in song, spoke:

Mín fǽle Foldè beorn team

IC ārian þu in þín wilsumnes ond frèogan for mè ond mín sunu Wōden.

Þin sāwol is ðearl ond clǽne

IC brengan a ærende.

Gehlýstan wielle!

My beloved Earth children,

I honour you in your devotion and love for me and my son Wōden

Your spirit is strong and pure.

I bring a message.

Listen well!

The circle of priests had formed an ever-tighter circle close to Eldís, not wishing to miss a moment. I could only see her head, which, as I stared, was still, devoid all expression. She seemed dead. Her face had gone a deathly pale.

Suddenly in a single heartbeat, the form of Nerthus spun into a tight whirlwind of energy and swept towards Eldís with a speed that defied description. Faster than any arrow shot I had ever seen. She was eclipsed in mist. I saw the mist enter her mouth, her ears, and her eyes. And any other enterable orifice, I was sure!

Her hair swung out, her face grew large. She grew in a dimension I thought impossible. She became a giantess in front of our eyes. Her hands were grasping the sides of the throne. I thought for a moment she would rise and walk about us. I held my breath.

Then her eyes opened. And they were now Nerthus' eyes, completely.

Eldís was no more. Her mouth opened wide and spoke with a voice so deep, so loud and resonant, we were pinned to the ground to listen.

"Ancient peoples of the seven tribes. You who have forsaken your homelands to live on the sacred Isle of Wihtland, bring with you a covenant which will soon come alive. In your children's time and in their children's time, a force will bear down on all who worship mother earth. All who live within the gods' love and who stay close to the near world of spirit through love of our animals and flowers, plants and all living creatures. This force will try to annihilate every human who worships nature or force them into their religion because they see their way as supreme. They believe they have dominion over all living things and they fear the gods of nature.

They will fear your strength and they will kill you because of it.
There is one amongst you who has seen this, who is now hiding in the shadows.

Your prayer has been heard. Dagrun Wahl of the Warinni, protector and defender of the Stones, come forward, beorn, you of all here, must hear my words."

I starred, speechless and unable even to move, as eleven pairs of eyes bore down on me. Gradually, a space was made in the circle and I moved forward to step into the most iridescent light I had ever seen. Eldís shimmered in this light. But it was our goddess Nerthus who commanded her mouth to move.

Dagrun Wahl, your forbears are close. Your Ealdmōdor is never far from your side. My son Wōden has spoken to you. Have courage. You carry the blood of the stones within you. Walk into that power, my dear. Know the stones, their spirit, and their strength. They are waiting to give you all that you need for the years ahead. Let them into you, too. See the pictures they hold for all time, without fear. Teach your children all that you know. Bring them to feel the stones as part of themselves. For it is they who will pass our knowledge onto the earth children many eons from now.

Be certain of this. The flame of our spirit, the ways of the earth mother will be brought to nothing but a flicker, in times to come. It is only by recording our knowledge in the stones that our ways will be re-born again.

And now in this time, the covenant will only survive if you all join. All the tribes here on Wihtland need to speak and feel with one accord. And this too must be passed down to your children.

You may believe the Romans are your common enemy. Dah! But they are nothing compared to those who will arrive on these shores. The Romans tax your bodies and steal your wealth. Those coming will suck the very spirit from you and it is only when the spirit of the people dies that the nations will fall to their knees.

Hear me well!"

For several heartbeats, the forest and everyone within the grove was frozen. Not one person even dared to breathe. I just starred ahead, in shock at what had transpired. I felt sweat breaking out all over me. And before I could stop, I began shaking. I was going into shock.

But that soon stopped when I looked over to Eldís. Within one heartbeat, Nerthus made an exit from her host that felt like the entire world had imploded in on itself. It felt as if even the serpent oak was pulling its branches away from its roots. The sacred pool swirled, its iridescent light creating a whirlpool which swallowed all energy to disappear without a trace.

And Eldís simply slumped. She was waxen and still. No breathe was coming from her. Her head hung at an odd angle and her hair fell into her lap.

I broke free and ran to her, gently lifting her head up to see lifeless eyes staring down.

"Help me", I shouted over my shoulder, and soon felt the arms of my mother take Eldís.

"Take her to the pool!" I cried. We carried her and laid her by the waters' edge. I dipped my hand in and sent waves of water over her face. I thumped her chest three times, quickly, then again.

"Eldís," my mother shouted in her ear. "*Beorn*, come back to us, your job is done and done well"

I swished more chilly water over her face and thumped her chest again.

Suddenly I felt a shudder, and her body contorted in pain. She screamed out, long and remorselessly. Then she slumped back into my mother's arms, breathing but barely conscious. I felt she was fighting for her spirit to return. Her soul was in deep shock.

"*Mōdor*, she will die if we cannot bring her soul back", I looked to my mother in desperation. "I do not have the herbs here!" I cursed inwardly at my stupidity. I had changed into more ceremonial clothes for this occasion and left the work day clothes with all my dried nine-herbs and glory sticks attached to the belt I always wore…except for today!

I left my mother cradling Eldís and ran to the others. They had grouped together in a tight circle to support each other.

"Help us! Please," I shouted as I approached them. "Aslaug, Sāga! Eldís' spirit is lost. She will die if we cannot retrieve her soul."

"We need herbs aplenty." I called to the priests. "Find wild garlic, fennel, feverfew and sage, three catkins and gorse flower also. All of them are in plenty here. Eldís' life depends on this."

I saw the young man Eyvindr found to replace the false priest. I knew him vaguely. I went over to him.

"Run with all speed to my father and Eyvindr. Tell them what has happened and that we need fire. Tell them to come with all speed, and bring a pot! To the others, tell them to prey well."

I went over to the serpent oak, laying still and supine on its watery bed. I knew the oak carried many lichen host. Some were poisonous to us if taken inwardly. But when this lichen was smoked it reached out to the soul more than any other. After scrambling around the convoluted bulbous lair, I found the right one. I crunched a bunch of it in my hand, smelt the strong aroma, and said thank you, several times.

Mōdor was still cradling the limp Eldís, whom I doubted would ever be the ethereal beauty of just a few moments ago. She would live, I knew, but the changes that had taken place in this grove forever seared onto our souls. We were in part splintered away from the past, and in this moment, were being forged together in a new alliance.

I thought it had been an eternally cruel way to get the message to us, but now I suddenly realised that Nerthus' actions were, as with all spirit ways, entirely immaculate. She was creating a unity between us forged from love for our daughter Eldís and common humanity.

There came a crashing through the trees. My father and Eyvindr appeared carrying a pot and flint fire. They ran straight to Eldís.

"*Fæder,* we need a fire and the pot needs to boil quickly with herbs, when the priests come back with them. Elíse will live, but we need to bring her soul back to us. She is in deep shock."

"What happened?" Eyvindr starred at me, frowning in mounting anger.

"Patience, brother," I replied, taking a deep breath in. Shock was ever close to me and one more thing would surely see me shaking like an aspen leaf again. "I will share the night's telling later when we are recovered. And remember we still have the *Drímeolce* celebrations at Headon to reach before dawn arrives!"

We all heard the scrunch of several footfalls coming towards us from the forest depths, waking those creatures now asleep and scaring all others!

The priests came armed with handfuls of the right herbs. I breathed a sigh of relief. Now we had all that was needed to help Eldís. *Fæder* had started a good fire. I needed smouldering embers to smoke the lichen. But first I needed to soak Eldís' head with the feverfew mulch. Laid over her brow, I pressed the juice in, chanting words to the plant.

Then came the boiling of the garlic. Many bulbs went in and the smell was powerful. Sage went in also and I mulched some green leaves to set aside for later. Eldís began to moan. The feverfew was pulling her mind upwards towards the light. She pulled her head from side to side as if trying to expel something. Indeed, she should be, I thought. I asked *fæder* to bring the garlic decoction over. I had to put it in her now, for I knew she had been elf-shot when Nerthus left her. I did not have the nine herbs or the glory sticks of Wōden to expel the evil. But garlic, especially from this sacred forest, *Hāligwielle* was powerful enough.

I knelt over Eldís, poor lovely women, who did not deserve this trial placed upon her. I brushed her hair back, away from her face and her ears. Her hair was splayed around her angel face, now deathly white. And the flower head band was tangled in between. I eased it out and placed it in the sacred pool. It floated aimlessly for a second and then sank, suddenly, as if sucked into the depths by an unseen hand.

Deep dark energy was flowing now in this forest and I felt the presence of spirit in many forms.

So, I turned to Sāga and whispered she should become *Nihtgala* and sing the *ljðð leoð* to bring the garlic-heart forward.

Sāga began softly, then her voice grew to echo into the forest. It reached the heart of *Hāligwielle* and trees, flora and animal stopped in this moment of *wyrd*.

"*Ǣt þu hramse wyrt þín heorte ís ðearl ond mihtigu.*

Þu hwã willan èhtan þes æfblèd ūt!"

And she sang again, and again:

To you, garlic herb

Your heart is strong and powerful,

You! Who will chase this elf-shot out!

And the priests with my brother Eyvindr joined in.

When I knew the garlic spirit had come, I began.

The garlic potion, now cooled but still very warm, sat at my side. I removed the feverfew and brought the oak lichen smoke to cover her whole face. I took a large mouthful of the liquid and clamping my teeth, bent forward to see the crown of her head. I gently lifted her head, tilting it forward slightly. She moaned.

I hissed the potion onto her crown, twice. It dribbled down her forehead and rivulets spread down her cheeks. Eldís mumbled and moaned, turning her head away. Then she settled, breathing in shallow gasps. I took a breath and said the words, low and strong, in a voice that was not my own.

Swã nygon weorðan eahta ond eahta weorðan seofan,

Ãgãn!

So, nine becomes eight and eight becomes seven.

Go!

I took another deep mouthful of the astringent juice. It stung my gums and set my teeth on edge. Still holding the limp head of Eldís I sprayed onto her eyes. For a flicker of a second they opened and took the potion. She squinted them shut and flung her head from side to side.

Swã seofon weorðan siex ond siex weorðan fif,

Alætan!

So, seven becomes six and six becomes five,

Leave!

Another bitter mouthful was shot into her ears, as I turned her head slowly to each side. I felt a strength come back, for she fought me and resisted. Was that her or the Elf fighting?

Fif weorðan feower ond feower weorðan ðrèo

Ãweg wíþ þu ǽf!

Five becomes four and four becomes three.

Away with you, elf!

Now we were nearly done, so nearly clear of the malevolence.

So, I tilted her head sharply backwards, for the *drycræft* to enter her nose, the last but one opening that saw the elf-shot in. And another bitter mouthful I sent swishing into her nose. She shook and gasped. Eldís was returning to us at last. Her eyes opening momentarily and with recognition, a knowing came into them. I nearly shouted out!

Swã ðrèo weorðn twa ond twa weorðan ãn.

Faran!

So, three becomes two and two becomes one,

Go!

So gently I brought her head up, nestling in the crook of my arm, and brought the remains of the juice to her lips. Her eyes fluttered and she accepted the cure, drinking two mouthfuls before she spluttered, her eyes opened in knowing and Eldís was back with us.

I silently gave thanks to as many gods as I could name, but to Nerthus I gave my soul commitment.

"Dagrun, dear *sweostor* I have seen…"

"Shhhh, be still dear one, later, we will share this later", I whispered, drawing her close, I hugged her and tried so very hard not to cry.

… … … … … … … …

CHAPTER FOURTEEN
Drímeolce Dægweorþung: Beltane

The procession trudged its way out from the sacred grove in a muted dialogue rendered into whispers. Eldís was sitting slumped on her throne. Her tangled hair was falling in clumps to her waist. There was no joyous singing on this *Drímeolce* celebration. She looked as if she had been ravished. And indeed, she had! My *fæder* was in deep conversation with Eyvindr as they both struggled to carry the sacrificed oxen between two branches tied with thick hemp rope. Shoulders hunched against the weight, even for these giants, they found it hard going. My *fæder* was no longer a young man but loath to admit the greying hairs and the aching bones that had begun to plague him.

I longed to get Eldís into the clear night sky with sea breezes to wake her up.

Aslaug walked up and wrapped her arm around my aching shoulders. I was damp with forest sweat and my tunic stuck to my back as Aslaug laid her arm on me. It had been an exhausting time.

"I have wronged you Dagrun Wahl of the Warinni. I beg your forgiveness for all my words and actions hitherto directed to you in arrogance and ignorance. I am shamed!"

"You are a *Sãcerde*, a wise woman in our midst. You do not boast of your skills. In fact, I believe you would rather put them down. But this night has forever changed the choice you thought you owned. You do not own it, Dagrun. From now you must follow the path *Wyrd* has set for you and indeed for all of us."

"I feel weightless in a flowing river, Aslaug, alone and afraid. Wōden told me fear will bring courage, but to see the whites of the eyes of your enemy and feel powerless is terrible!"

"I know nothing of what you are saying, Dagrun!", Aslaug frowned at me, not comprehending.

"I believe Eldís saw this also, *Ealdmōdor*," I replied, "but now is not the time. We must let go of the *Ælfsiden*. Bring a smile of joy to our worried faces, before all our kinsmen, waiting over there, will hold fear over this night too."

"Oh aye," Aslaug said, breathing out the tension into the night air, "Marriages must be born this night, love on a heart-arrow, born. Old love re-kindled for merry old souls are we!"

"Humph!" I countered, "You speak for yourself!"

"We must clean poor Eldís. She looks a mess!" I continued, trying to quell the utter loneliness that had crept in. It grabbed my heart in its remorseless squeeze, bringing a lump to my throat so dense, I was lost for breath,

Eileifer! I screamed silently, I cannot bear this, Come home!

Aslaug and *Mōdor* went to encourage Elíse. They combed and tidied her hair. Sāga had made a new flower crown for her. She sat up straight and nodded her thanks, whilst taking a quick glance over to me. She smiled, a wide brilliant grin that opened my heart and broke it in the same moment. She was a *Sãcerde* too.

As *Mōnã* shone her pale light down on us, we emerged from the forest to see groups of shadowed figures, our kinsmen, waiting patiently. Their torchlights casting deep shadows and flickering in the breeze that had sprung up. Clouds were gathering and we needed to speed our way to Headon, where the fire for the oxen was waiting. Everyone over there must be having great hunger pains. We were in danger of creating a fallen night and that would be a disaster.

A fresh ox was brought to the wagon, and we marched on, towards *Cealcstãn*. By now Eldís was recovered. And more so as Aslaug recounted what had happened. She realised she had been truly honoured and blessed. The rich telling that must surely follow on many mead-hall nights would bring her and her family countless tributes for twilights to come.

We marched down from the hilltop walk near my home, *Sudmōr*. And then back up to the Leaning stone where more heart cakes were buried by the women from the Eudose and Anglii.

I could see the flicker of a distant fire. This created an urge in us all to move on swiftly. Before we knew it, there before us, up the steep incline to the highest point on the western edge of the Isle, lay the sacred ground of our Ancestors. We were at the head of our serpent Nerthus. We had come from her heart. And now, in the darkest of night, we had come to her head. Where all intention is born. Where every creative impulse is given shape and form. The celebration of creative love was played out here.

And I, in this celebration of love, felt utterly alone. I moved away from the gathering crowd who descended on our *Cwèn*. I became a watcher. The oxen that had survived this night were led away to feed and rest. The one that did not, was expertly skinned and gutted, and hoisted onto the large spit over an enormous fire. As its flesh became scorched, fat began to drip, caught in the trough beneath to be spooned up again. And so, it went on.

Elíse was guided, so closely by Aslaug, who never left her side. They made their way to the centre of the immense circle that was made to honour the *Cwèn*. Firelight flickered across her but her face was still bowed down. There was just silence now, a shuffling of feet on the dry earth and a murmuring of intent. All the menfolk of all our nation tribes were called upon to come and honour their *Cwèn*. So, it had been told for many Tellings. She was Nerthus. And how little they knew that she was, for several heartbeats, the Goddess herself. They came to kneel and kiss her hand, wishing for themselves a long life, free from war. Or otherwise, for those hungry for the battlefield. They numbered but few in our island world. And to poor Elíse, her face still bowed, it was a struggle, another protracted pain, for she had seen that future, like me, we shared that ugly moment.

I felt very selfishly relieved, that I was not alone in living with this burden. We would, needs must, share those terrifying moments and likely more that may come.

Then a shudder came over our dear young *Sãcerde* and she lifted her head. I saw her body straighten, and her smile radiated to everyone in that circle of honour. Even the fire seemed to glow stronger. An inner force was feeding her in this moment. She became Nerthus. And so, the men came. Slowly and he was the last of all, came one such young man. As he came closer, I could feel the connection between him and Elíse. He was looking so intently at her, I could feel the love radiating towards her. But she was a *Sãcerde* in training. It was not permitted for any priestess to have a husband. They were given in their entire body to the Gods and Nerthus.

When he reached her, her eyes widened to meet his love. It was clear, his hand reached up take hers to kiss in honour, and then Elíse pulled him up so they were facing each other in mutual, overpowering desire. And she kissed him. A mutual gasp passed through round the circle. Breaking this protocol was deemed serious. Aslaug looked on, an impenetrable expression on her face. She was inscrutable, neither giving her permission to the couple, nor denying them, yet she must know how much this was needed. Elíse needing healing and this young man's love, so obvious, would go some way to achieving that. Aslaug looked away. They left to disappear into the shadows.

Without warning a wave of jealousy simply crumpled my stomach into knots, and I felt so very alone.

After Elíse was released, the drums began.

They were playing a heartbeat that coursed through every vein and demanded a dance. So, everyone began swirling and leaping, shouting, laughing, creating an energy that would grow to the heights. Mead was flowing and our kinsmen swallowed the amber juice aplenty.

Some say it is mead that courses through the veins of the Eudose and Anglii. And I could not disagree this night!

Then, as intentions of the single men turned to love or lust, the heart arrows began to zing through the night sky. Finding the right maiden was a risky endeavour to be sure, for all were in shadow and if the heart arrow, made from blunt compacted hemp, hit another quarry, then the mistake must be honoured. Arguments ensured and quarrels settled in good humour, mostly. The adventure of the night lay in the hunt!

But I was removed from it all. Feeling sorry for myself, not able to uplift my sorry spirits to honour the celebration.

Suddenly without any warning I felt a sharp pain on my shoulder, and, as I looked down, I saw a heart arrow, bent out of shape and of no use whatsoever. Oh, the bad joke of it, I thought, as I determined to insult the sender and send him on his way. I picked up the arrow and turned to see which unfortunate man, with a bad aim, I would berate. There was a deep well of anger building up that would erupt very soon.

Then, I saw him. He was in shadow against the brilliant fire light. But enough for me to know, and I took a sharp breath inwards and just ran.

Eileifer! How could it possibly be!

Tears were welling up in my eyes before I reached him. His long, strong arms came outstretched and I just dived into his warmth, his tight embrace, and stayed there, sobbing the pain and fear away, into his woollen cloak. And he let me stay there until all the sorrow was cried out. Then, gently, he took my face in his hands and bent down to kiss me, long and so beautifully, I experienced a bonding of our souls and such joy that totally eclipsed the last harsh twilights.

"Dagrun, sweeting," he said softly, "Where has my spirited young lass gone? I have been gone but two moons and come back to find a scared and frightened young thing!"

"Ohh, Eileifer, please don't be like this!" I suddenly realised how like a child I must seem to my Cyng! "Please allow me to tell you all that has happened since you've been gone."

"You may, of course. You have my leave", a huge grin broke across his serious royal face. His dimples appeared, and I loved him more. "I am and always will be your "horse-talker", Dagrun, remember that always, especially when my royal status inflates me up like a puffball, ready for puncturing! You will always hold the needle!"

We sat away from the noise of the celebrations, hearing only our own voices and the crash of wave's below. And I told him every detail. From the disagreeable Gandãlfr, whose nickname for me was "that stripling"! Whereupon Eileifer took out a linen rag and began mimicking the mopping up of all my tears soaked into his robe. Whereupon I hit him in the chest and we kissed some more, taking away the insult.

I told him of the family of thralls on Ingvar's homestead and how he was wasting away his land rights. I described the hunger of that family. Eileifer grew serious, and when he frowned, a deep darkness covered his eyes and for the first time I saw the warrior in him.

I told him of my vow to see a lawful, compassionate community grow under a new common name, so that we would become a united tribe again, as it was in our old homeland.

He slapped his knee in serious agreement. He pledged a *Thing* to take place at the ancestor stone circle, for all to attend where the new accord would be registered and made law.

I was quietly ecstatic, for we thought as one, and I knew our union would be blessed with mutual happiness.

"You know, Dagrun, I have studied and learnt much in *Cant*, their laws are powerful and fair. The tribes are in good accord, for they have trust in each other. It is trust that makes a powerful union work. Break it and all is lost."

"*Giese*!" I replied, "These Romans have power, but no trust. Nothing is grown from fear except more fear. They will never get the best from us!"

"Ahh, *Gíese*," Eileifer replied with a sigh, "I have come with news of the Romans. Their numbers are growing in *Cant* and along the eastern coast. They are settling here Dagrun. They are building great *hūs'* they call villas. The only thing they will not take from us is our spirit, our union with the gods. They have their own gods they sacrifice to, called Mithras."

It was then I told my *Cyng* of the *Beorht stãn* and the vision. Of Eldís being made host to our beloved Nerthus, and the goddess's soul-shattering prophecy.

He sat stock still, his cloak folded in his hands. They were nervously working at the decorated hem. His only sign of tension. But I noticed a nerve in his sculptured face twitch at the cheekbone. His eyes were shaded, long beautiful lashes shadowed on his cheeks. The back light of the fire accentuated every bone. His hair was deep brown with red streaks, thick and only slightly wavy. He was of Wōden's blood and a rightful *Cyng* of Wihtland. And I loved him to a heart's beat of death itself.

He looked around at me as if reading my mind...and my heart, for no expression that ever crossed my face was missed by him!

"Dagrun Wahl of the Warinni, Defender and protector of the Stones," he intoned in a royal voice, deep and resonant, accompanied by a delightful grin spreading across his face to light up my life, "Kneel before your *Cyng*!"

He then stood to his full height, arched and so tall: I caught my breath again. By the gods, he was beautiful! I thought.

I knelt before him. Waiting. Then I heard that terrible grate of metal on scabbard. Oh no! Not that. The images came flooding in, distorting my face in fear and agony.

Before I could take another breath, he was kneeling before me, his hands tenderly holding my face.

"I beg for your forgiveness beloved!" he cried, "I would never do single thing to hurt you and here am I doing just that!"

He took a deep breath, then said quietly with care, "Dagrun Wahl of the Warinni, I take you for my *Cwèn*. Whose life I put before my own. Whose love I will honour until death. Whose love I will nourish. Whose comfort and peace I will fight for until death." He bent back on his heels, and looked straight into my soul.

"Eileifer, *Cyng* of Wihtland," I replied, not taking my eyes from his, tears welling up till I commanded them silently to go, "I love you to my last breath. I will honour your love and I will nourish our love to my dying breath. Now… please can we go *somewhere!*"

"Oh, Dagrun Wahl! You vixen", He laughed, and held me in a tight embrace, kissing wildly, his tongue exploring as my belly became aflame with want. There was just no stopping this. We left and disappeared into the darkness. We explored each other with our tongues, every part until he came to my other lips and with arched back, I screamed in ecstasy as he lifted and entered me fully, throbbing and pushing until we were both spent. Curled in mess of discarded robes and tunics, we lay coiled together as one.

The outer world sliced through our dream like a seax.

"Eileifer, *Cyng* of Wihtland, where are you? you crazy horse-talker" came a furious deep throated holler from an angry kinsman. Show yourself, or we will tap another shoulder with the sword and have us a new *Cyng*! "

We dressed quickly and made our way towards the fire and the oxen, now roasted and ready for slicing. Eileifer had his arm about my shoulders and I felt as if I had come home and was safe. It was a unique, beautiful feeling, and as my face mirrored my feelings, Eileifer turned to smile down at me as onlookers gaped and smiled and nudged each other.

My *Mōdor* came forward and excitedly grabbed both my hands in hers and kissed them, before leaning forward, to kiss me on the cheek. "Perfect! My *beorn*", she whispered before kneeling before her *Cyng* and soon-to-be son.

"My Lord, we are so pleased to have you back with us", she intoned, head bowed.

"Gudrun, *Mōdor* of Dagrun, I am overjoyed to be back!" Eileifer almost shouted, "Be standing you honourable woman and let us carve this sacred beast. We are all starving, I'm sure!"

He carved the sacred oxen with his own *seax*, huge chunks dropping into eager hands, dripping with hot fat onto fingers that jostled with the heat. I stood back and watched his face, firelight flickering across features, intent on the task. That chiselled face I loved beyond words. The dark red-glinting beard he kept neat, against the usual warrior's way. He looked every inch a new kind of *Cyng*. He smiled and joked with every one of his kinsmen, who came forward to feast. It was the chosen task of the *Cyng* to feed his people. And Eileifer was willing to that task. He will be more than a "client *Cyng*", I thought. He will be on this sacred Isle. He will not travel the big sea to find adventure in the unknown and dangerous. He is a *Heorð Cyng,* a hearth king. And I, soon to be his *Cwèn*. What will that mean for me, I thought, as I moved closer to him? Will I still be the healer for my kinsmen? Will I be the *Sācerde*, and will I remain true to the stones that my Ancestor's voices lay within?

As I moved up to him, intent on helping with the feast, he turned, looking down at me from his incredible height and smiled long and strong at me. And then, that magical secret smile followed. And it meant only one thing as my belly was set on fire. I touched his arm, and then set about giving the meat to all who were now queuing for food. It had been a long night and still the celebration and dance continued, pot upon pot of mead found hungry mouths and even the quiet and shy kinsmen were becoming boisterous. The overly loud kinsmen were becoming intent on shouting down *Thunōr* himself.

One thought became clear to me. All our tribes were here. Some travelled many spear lengths to get here, and it showed. Before me in the flickering firelight, was a united and happy clan of people, who were easy with each other. If we brought them all together for that all-important *Thing* at our Ancestor stone circle, an event not heard of here on Wihtland, we might achieve the first vision of Nerthus to become one people once more.

I determined to bring it to the fore, as soon as I could get our family together in a small circle, this very night, god's willing.

And so, it came to be, firstly by my *Fæder*, Folkvarthr, who was now *Hèahwita* High Councillor and my elder *brōðor* Eystein who was now *Ealdorðegn,* Chief Thane,

That my dear mother had shared the whole telling of Nerthus in the sacred grove to them, of the goddess's prophecy, which I had only just succeeded in pushing to the deepest recess of my mind. And that this telling had begun the *wyrd rapas* that would be woven into our lives for generations to come.

And it was here at the head of our Sacred Serpent, where creativity sits and the essences of our intentions are born, on this twilight of the *Þrimilce –gerihte*. It was all in the hands of the Norns and we could only follow.

… … … … … … … … …

CHAPTER FIFTEEN
Þæt cíð is weopan: The seeds are cast

My father had created a smaller fire away from the riotous and happy kinsmen, who were in their cups, to be sure. Any unclaimed maiden was a blurred focus and stumbling intent. I was joyous that I had been claimed.

I looked over the headland to the glistening sea, far below. Mōnā was strong and full. She created a silver pathway to her hearth. She hung low in the sky and I felt her silvered arm almost reach down to meet with Nerthus.

The Gods were in communion, and so were we.

Fæder had brought the family circle together near our Ancestors mounds. They too knew the power of this land. It was high *drycræft* magic. My father gave an offering to them of meat and mead, asking for guidance and their protection.

Eileifer came striding in and sat on an old weathered and beaten tree stump. This was a high point on Wihtland exposed to the might of Thunōr and lashed with the rain and winds. But this night was balmy and calm.

"My kinsmen, we are on sacred ground here, may our choice of words reflect this ancient wisdom that lies at our feet."

"Eileifer, our *Cyng*," my *Fæder* began, "You may not have been given the telling that happened only a brief time ago. But I am begging leave for my daughter, Dagrun, to tell us all of the coming of Nerthus and her prophecy for our kinsmen."

"Folkvarthr, my trusted councillor," Eileifer beamed towards him, "the telling has already been given, in brief, by a very distraught woman, if I may say! I soon put that all to rights!" He looked over to me with eyes twinkling and dimples showing. My heart simply erupted now, and I met his stare with fire in my eyes. He looked back with the same fire for just a second. "Oh, by the gods", I thought shouting within, "but I love this man!"

"Perhaps she may re-tell it to those who were not present", he said kindly, while fully aware that I was blushing and not at all prepared.

I took a deep breath and re-counted the whole rite, starring at the glow and dance of the flames before me, as I heard mutters of shock ripple through our circle. I dare not look up as I knew I would falter. I felt a strong warm arm come around me and knew Eileifer had joined me, supporting and loving. I found the strength to continue.

When I had finished, I looked up.

"And all Nerthus asks of us is unity", I said with as much passion as I could muster.

"We need to join as one people. For all our ways are close, we are joined already, I do believe."

"*Giese*!" came a reply that echoed around the circle. Everyone could see that a chain is as strong as its weakest link. Our deep compassion and love for nature's way of living was more important than ourselves and those slight differences.

"Let us look at what our numbers mean," Eyvindr broke in with an intent expression, as if he had seen something on his mind, and wanted it discussed now.

"The Anglii match our numbers very nearly and together with us, the Warinni, make up a big tribe. The Anglii are very good farmers, they have given us the large plough, making our yields very high. We, the Warinni are craftspeople and healers, and guardians of the stones. Our treasured and royal Niuthones carry our God Wōden's blood coursing through their veins.

Then we have the Eudose, southern Jutes, who some call the Ingavonii for their blood line goes directly to Ing. They are our higher, treasured peoples, to whom we pay tributes for bringing us here in their big boats. Without them we would still be marooned in our old homelands, most probably hung up in trees for the crows, by the warrior Franks or the Danes. The Ingavonii are not high in number but live high in our esteem.

Then we have the much smaller tribes, Reudignians, the Aviones, Suardones, each with their own tribal ways that may differ from our own, yet still needs to be honoured by all."

Mōdor leant forward, pulling the ample folds of her skirt around her legs, then stretching her arms forward palms uppermost, almost in supplication to the gathered menfolk.

"We need to ensure all needs are met to create a peace within us. We need to build a new and larger hall that will take all the peoples at any time" my *Mōdor* said forcefully, using her fore finger to make the point.

Giese! Came the common reply. The whole idea had met with approval. I could see in my mind the most enormous, beautifully crafted mead hall and meeting lodge ever seen on Wihtland! And it meant focus, with many busy hands from all the tribes working together to create unity. It could work!

"So now my friends," Eileifer looked around the entire circle, "before Sunni makes her appearance, let us make a ruling that we meet to call a *Thing* at the Ancestor circle to formally create our One People *Cynedōm*."

"*Giese*", came the loud response. And so, all was set. And as we slowly dispersed, we each offered our gratitude to the Ancestors, privately in whispered words. And I walked with my *Cyng* into the darkness and joy beyond words.

… … … … … … … … …

I awoke in ecstasy, the sun filtering through sap green leaves to blind me in its intensity as I felt my loved one play with my other lips, fondling my breasts. He moved up to kiss me with moist lips. Then entered me and we mulched the wet earth some more, sweat mingling and joy being reached with that little death in unison, a cry of love united.

We were deep in the forest. I had no feeling of the day, only that Sunni was lifting upwards and it was probably mid-morning.

I turned and kissed my Cyng, dragging my fingers through his beard, "It is time we should return, beloved, or we will be missed."

"*Giese*, so we should... Ahh Dagrun, but this is perfect, why must we diminish it?" Eileifer turned to gaze at me and it took all my strength to break away and get up, pulling my moist and grass stained clothes over me and sighing at the amount of scrubbing it would take to remove the stains from what was my best celebration gown.

Eileifer frowned, then sighed and stood to dress himself.

"I will make certain you receive the very best gowns my women weavers can make. You wait Dagrun, you will be happy with those gowns waiting to find their owner!"

We made our way through a less trodden path to meet with the wider one most folks use. A breeze met us, out in the open again and dried the moisture from our clothes. Like another ending, our lovemaking drifted away on the wind. The trees rustled their greeting and the birds were in full voice, chattering to each other.

Suddenly from nowhere the slightest fluttering of delicate tiny wings caught my cheek as a wren shot past me to settle briefly on Eileifer's head, before shooting away.

I knew, with certainty opening my heart, that our *Ealdmōdor* had come to us, to bless us and I knew that she had seen all, and was pleased! Her Wren had been given to her, as her "hidden-eye", her third eye sitting on her brow. We had been bonding our love at the serpent's head. The wren had shot through the veil and blessed us completely. Eileifer was stunned for a moment, then his beautiful smile spread across his face and into his eyes. Time stopped for me then, just for a heartbeat. That beautiful moment frozen in Wryd, would stay with me, through untold strife in times to come.

I knew then, that we had been before and would do so again. We were soul partners over many lifetimes. And it was in this moment that Eileifer realised it also.

As we walked together nearing the hillside of the ancestors, to take the main path back to the *ceasterwic,* two figures emerged from the forest on the other side. Closely bonded, I knew before I could see their faces that it was Elíse and your new lover.

She looked radiant and very happy. All the trauma gone, laid to rest. She looked so different from the Elíse who had been in training to be a *Sãcerde* and without asking her, I knew she had made a choice. I did not blame her at all. The way of the *Sãcerde* is harsh enough without having the terrible nightmare she had just lived through, placed upon her, alone and without little help for her heart's ease. I was feeling bereft until Eileifer appeared and healed the pain. So now Elíse had her soul support.

We embraced, warmly, as friends. It was beautiful to feel this wonderful soul able to reach out to us all in an entirely natural way.

"Elíse, dear *sweostor,* welcome to the world of men!" I said smiling warmly at the young man who stood tall, elegant and so much a good match for beautiful Elíse.

We both started laughing, and were soon joined by our men, reliving our mutual lovemaking in secret.

"What is your name, my lord," I asked, considering him and finding quite an old soul lying behind his youth. He also had a hint of nobility. I saw his hands were not worn from slaving in the fields for they were long and slender.

"Dægberht, my Lady," he bowed before me. I was surprised just how much I enjoyed being bowed to!

"I am the grandson of the last *Cyng* of the Reudignians. I am the last remaining, there is no other after me", he looked down briefly before giving us the rest of his story.

"My forebears came in three boats across the Germania sea. They were built badly and two did not survive the harsh journey. No one came after us to Wihtland. It is why our numbers are small. I have a small steading in the valley along from you. I am a craftsman. I make the Wihtland pottery. And I am a storyteller. You may have seen me in the mead hall from time to time.

"This may be so," Eileifer smiled, "And it is good to see you here now."

All this while I was thinking about poor Elise. How would Aslaug be with this new situation? I could see a conflict arising between Elise's new love and her commitment to the calling to Nerthus, which was intended for a whole lifetime.

I saw a deep rift with Aslaug becoming a strident and harsh one with Elise.

We walked down to the *ceasterwic* together, two couples in love, marked by the smiles of deep contentment.

The pathway to *Sudmōr* was steep and pitted with ruts made with the dry weather as Sunni toasted the mud. We fairly ran down the incline like young striplings, trying to out race each other, and it was in this chaotic tangle of flaying arms and legs, amidst the echo of laughter and shouts, that we bundled into a waiting Aslaug. The *Cyng* of all Wihtland swiftly straightened into a semblance of dignity, pulling that wayward hair from his face and smiled, an awkward grimace. He was in truth a young man, as his name was a signature, royalty-in-waiting, Eileifer had always, until now, been in the tallest of shadows, to the great Wihtlæg.

Aslaug took several paces backwards, standing and staring at us like an ancestor stone, whose face had been chiselled in grim lines to frighten and censor those brought before it.

Elíse looked tense, her head bowed. Dægberht held her closer, both lovers waiting for the eruption from the "ancestor stone" herself. But Aslaug said nothing, just turned and walked away, the swish of her skirts, the only sound.

We all were frozen to the ground, and in defence of Dægberht, who would be the guilty party, took hold of Elíse's hand, kissed her palm deeply and wrapped her in his arms only to hear her muffled tears, her body shaking in pain and misery

"Eileifer, my lord, I think we need to hurry homewards, for there are councils to oversee, and your beloved horses need your presence. There is little we can do for our friends here. It is for them to pray for guidance."

I moved over to Elíse, hugging her, whispering "Come to me this evening dear one. We need to talk."

We made straight for the white and sacred herd of horses, whose presence Eileifer admitted he had missed, almost as much as me, he said with a dimpled, cheeky smile.

"Then you will be pleased to know, they have not missed you!" I retorted.

"We bonded. Did you know that? And I have found a dutiful, pleasant and I believe *"fey"* boy to become their trusted companion."

Eileifer turned to give me a dark look. The sun disappeared from his face. I knew I had hurt him, deeply. Nothing I could say or do would repair it. It was then that I realised. He had boundaries that must never be crossed. His sadness was my pain, twice over.

"My lord, forgive my stupid outburst. I would never hurt you. It was in return for your jesting. My cheap arrow shot!"

He stopped and turned, bringing me close to him, he took my face in his hands, and held them there, their warmth was overpowering, radiating into my cheeks.

He leaned down and kissed my forehead, gently, driving love into my muddled brain.

"Dagrun, my *Cwèn*, know that I will forgive. But your respect is a given, and must not be diminished by "cheap arrow shots." If I said to you, that on occasion your childishness, as much as I love it, will be a forfeit, you would agree….no?"

"Oh, by the gods!" I exclaimed, "you are right my lord. And with all that is coming to our people and how the goddess has honoured me, I must honour her in return. I will put my childish ways behind me"

"No," Eileifer murmured, in my ear, "Keep it covered, *gecwèman*, but unwrap it from time to time, for us, just us."

And with that, my heart melted and I was set on fire again!

We entered the stables, where the sack of dried apples was stored, hanging up on the timber wall. As I reached up he took me. Swirling down to hit the straw together, we loved and joined amidst the tickling straw. This time our lovemaking was full of laughter and childish fun.

He met with all his horses, each one giving him a joyous welcome. The dried apples mulched and devoured, his hands wet with horse spit. He patted and stroked, nuzzled those who spoke with him. He was head to head with the great white stallion whose age defied us, and then came the hoof stamping, snorting and tail swishing.

Eileifer broke away.

"He is telling me the mother earth is changing. They can feel it now. But we two-legged fail to feel this change coming. We skip too fast over our mother, he says. We will suffer for it again and again"

"What change?" I spoke up alarmed that it may be the vision coming now, to our lives.

"Drought I believe", Eileifer said softly, "drought, then famine. Or too much rain, which will mulch our crops. Torrents of rain in this valley will flood the *Ceasterwics* and *Tunstedes*. If we act now, we may save us from the famine that may follow."

"Dagrun my *Cwèn*, your days of being a *Wítega Cwèn* and *Sãcerde* are not yet over. Yet I had seen you, sitting contentedly at your weaving in my great hall, big-bellied with our child, your women around you, making our *beorn's* clothes"

"I will have a special cold room built, layered with stone where you can keep your healing potions and herbs, but above I will have a solar, a room where Sunni is in her power, where you will heal and work with your ailing visitors!"

"Oh, Eileifer!" I exclaimed, so overjoyed, "I will be so glad to leave my underground cell! It is a sore and cold place to sleep."

"I have been astounded that you have survived at all in that dirt hole you call home!" Eileifer laughed.

As we strolled towards the mead hall, we saw a little lad bending to clear horse muck from the field.

"My lord, it is the young stripling boy I spoke of. His name is Eastmund.

"If it pleases you, we should greet him, *Giese*?"

Eileifer nodded, and I felt a surge of uncertainty come over me. What if he does not take to the boy? Or the boy may not feel comfortable with him. Although I found that idea strange. Who could fail to like my *Cyng*!

And so, it was, we found ourselves an unlikely trio of horse-lovers who needed to like each other before any contract made the light of day. I hailed the boy, who came loping over, his gait awkward and ungainly. That huge mop of straw-coloured hair, curly and knotted, bounced sideways with each lurch of his twisted limbs.

I saw in peripheral sight, my lord glance at me. I could not gauge his feelings.

Eastmund came to stop before us, shoulders sagging, as if expecting instant reprimand followed by pain.

Instead Eileifer knelt, so he was at eye level with the lad.

He reached forward to pull the mane of straggled hair from his eyes. Eastmund flinched and instinctively stepped backwards. Cruelty had embedded into his poor life for so long, he may not even remember a loving touch from any man.

"Eastmund", Eileifer said softly, "look at me. Straight in the eye, *beorn,* and tell me what you see"

The young lad took a long time to obey, and I expected my *Cyng* to command obeisance. But he did not utter one word, just waited patiently for Eastmund to lift his gaze away from the dirt. In the very shyest of ways, one eye peeked from behind his locks. It was shockingly blue and quite piercing, as if his soul when opened, went searching for truth. This lad still lived in hope. His eyes were not all glazed over in forlorn sadness.

I felt hope stirring, that this contract between man and boy would be a rich one for them both.

Suddenly, Eastmund spoke, a slight lyrical voice, with a cadence that was almost like a song.

"You see beyond what is," he said, softly, but with clarity.

Eileifer rocked back on his heels, and pondered the boy before him. Eastmund's deformity would be something of a physical hindrance. Caring for the full herd of sacred whites demanded physical fitness. Would he be up to that challenge?

I knew Eileifer would be travelling along these lines of thought before he reached his decision.

"That was well said, young sir," he commented, head slightly to one side as if weighing it all up finally to reach a decision. He reached forward to hold the lad by the shoulders, and this time Eastmund did not flinch. Eileifer brushed the tangled hair from the lad's eyes.

"If you are to live, eat and breathe with my sacred companions here, needs must, you show respect to them by meeting them eye to eye. How, in the name of all the gods, can they reach you if you hide your very soul from them? You will have your hair sheared, then we will meet again, whereupon, we will put you through some paces. Go with my *Cwèn* now, to have the job done, before I change my mind", he said, but with a definite grin. He had decided.

And so, we went to carry out the *Cyng's* ruling! And an excellent job it was indeed. After I had hunted down my *seax*, honed to a sharp edge, I sheared off those locks. Eastmund was never to be seen in quite the same way again. He sat on my stool, in the cold dampness of my underground *hūs*, taut and overstrung like a doe in the hunt. But I was pleased with him, for his face was beautiful, even-featured and clear of pox. And I told him so. His smile was broad and strong. I knew then that the horses would bond with him.

I sent him back to his mother, belly full of warming porridge.

I then waited for the evening to draw in, with those myriad colours and darker hues settling on the trees and bushes around our *ceasterwic*. I waited for Elíse. It was twilight before the hides brushed aside and she entered, tripping lightly down my earthen steps to sit on the pile of furs, set by a dwindling torch of goose fat that was furling acrid smoke upwards to the hole above. The breeze set the smoke swirling around our faces, causing us both to squeeze our eyes shut and cough.

"Lest you think you may have made a faulty choice in our illustrious Eileifer", Elise commented, "Just look around you "earthworm" Wahl, at your *hūs* under the earth!"

"Oh, I simply cannot abide this as a home of any sort!" I replied, "And Eileifer has told me of the solar he will make ready for me in the grand hall!"

Elíse sat still, head bowed.

Smoke from the tallow goose fat was eclipsing what small light there was filtering in from the diminishing Sunni. This was not the right place to talk.

"Elíse, let us go to the Ancestor stones. The night is calm and not too cold. Here, *gecwèman,* please take this hide", I handed her a thick pelt of roe deer, "And I will bring some bread and cheese. What say you?"

"Yes," she murmured, her head still bowed. Then she looked up, her eyes were streaming with tears from the smoke and gave me a broad smile that lit up her face. I could clearly see why Dǣgberht was smitten. So rarely had I seen this *Sãcerde* woman smile. Now her real beauty was emerging and her choice between lives was in process.

We stepped quietly upon the earth in our journey to the Ancestors. No words spoken, for both of us were deep in thought with our own problems. The night was upon us, Mōnã only a sliver in the cloudless sky, and we had no carrying light. I cursed quietly. Yet we both knew our way. It was the smell of herbs and flowers that gave me direction, for I was so familiar with them. The path was made easy. Garlic lay to our right, the forest way, and spearmint hugged the coastline as we veered left. The blossom of the blackthorn that loved the rugged edges, had hung on and gave me a line of earthy perfume towards the stone circle. It lay behind our ancient goat willow copse. Our Ancestor stones were not big. Some, according to our elders, had been brought from the homeland to here, to rest with earthly remains. My *Ealdmōdor's* stone was here, and I knew exactly where she would be, heron fluttered as we got near.

I gave an offering of cheese, for she had always loved cheese, and settled the heron wing in front of the stone.

> *"Mín Ealdmōdor, mín heorte is full-þæt þu āre neah*
>
> *Gèoc ūs an earfoðlic anginn*
>
> *Brengan swutol-gesihð foroðǽmðe Elíse*
>
> *For mè, Ic ācsian āne þu bèon a heorte bèatan āweg"*

> My Grandmother, my heart is full- that you are near.
>
> Help us in our difficult undertaking,
>
> Bring clarity for Elíse.
>
> For myself, I ask only that you be a heartbeat away"

The heron wing fluttered again and I placed my hand upon it, closing my eyes, hoping she would come... But nothing happened. I felt a swift pain and felt suddenly alone. Yet I knew she was close, the heron wing was our meeting point.

"Elíse," I turned to consider her soul, for this was not a shut-off place anymore. She had opened her heart. "Tell me everything you saw: from the moment Nerthus joined with you. I believe *Ealdmōdor* is listening to every word we say. Leave nothing out *sweostor"*

Elíse stared straight ahead, eyes not focussing on this world, but far beyond.

"It felt like my soul, then my whole body was sucked away, Dagrun. At a speed, I have never known. Everything was light then it got gradually darker. The world I opened my eyes upon was so very foreign to me. It was nothing like this one, where we are sitting now. So much was different, almost unrecognisable. I did not belong in this world.

"I was standing in a field of barley, it was threshing my legs in the stiff breeze, and it tickled. Sunni was high in the sky. Larks were swooping overhead, offering a beautiful full-throated song. I was so taken with that energy, I failed to notice a large group of men. They were walking towards me over the ridge. Their clothing was rich, golden cloth flowing behind them in patterns of blue and saffron. They had snow white linen gowns, full to the ground. Some had great hats, golden and patterned in blue.

I knew it was some ceremony. Maybe like our *Drímeolce gerihte* but worlds away from us. A tonnage of coin had created those gowns. Rich men were before me. And each carried this strange looking cross, some in plain wood, others, near the front, were created in bronze and were jewelled. They were chanting, praying while they walked straight towards me.

I looked for somewhere to hide, kneeling to hide amongst the barley. But, you know sweet Dagrun, we could never be good at becoming invisible, us Warinni, our height always gives us away!

"So, it came as a shock to realise, as they came within sight of me, that no one said anything. There were no shouts, or cries of "Get her!" or even "Who are you?"

"They could not see me. I was a wraith, an "unseen" one. So, they walked through me, and as they continued, I came upon an entirely separate set of people. They were our people, Dagrun, and they were enslaved. All of them. They stood two heads above the others, who were equally robbed of their freedom. Some *Rōmãnisc*, and several were Durotrige, by their hair and dress. But the haunted and ravished faces of our kin will haunt me all my life Dagrun. They were going to their deaths.

"I stood and watched them drag their feet forward, heads bowed. They were chanting quietly. I could hear they were praying to Nerthus, to Wōden, Freyja, with their souls laid bare.

"I did not see one Roman, indeed, as I looked over to the horizon, I saw the ruins of Berandinzium villa, which the Romans have only just started to create here, now in this present time.

"I realised I was standing in a future time. They could not see me because my soul was present but not my body."

"That was being used by Nerthus."

"I walked behind them, trying to reach their haunted souls, but I was a watcher. Suddenly one of our giant Warinni kinswomen looked up and looked back. She focused on me. I knew she saw me, or perhaps a fleeting glimpse. I recognised her, Dagrun, she is of your family, the same look and hair. But much thinner. They were being sorely treated. I felt her sorrow as if it were yours. And I cried tears that did not flow to the ground.

"They were dragged to the meeting point which was a deep-water pool. And all around were the strange men, chanting louder. The poor imprisoned people were herded close to the water's edge. A group of soldiers appeared who were not Roman, and dressed in swarthy leather and metal. Large *seax* hung in their sheaths almost to the ground. They had shields bossed and painted, which were slung on their backs. They had metal hats on too, but plain, not engraved.

"I wondered why they had been summoned there at a ceremony of such a strong spiritual nature. It did not take many heartbeats before the horror became apparent.

"The men in the decorated hats were shrieking at the enslaved, one at a time, to recant their evil, pagan ways and embrace "the lord." If it was a *Giese*! Then they were given this uneven wooden cross to hold and pushed in and under the water. It took a very long time, and I thought they were just drowning them. But eventually they were hauled out, choking and heaving for fresh air. They slumped to the earth, probably thanking this new god for their life.

"But our people, our giants, all of them, Dagrun, they would not do this plunging into water and taking the cross. And even the woman, who is your kin, did not. She was proud and held her copper -brown head high. They took them all, those soldiers of death, and put them all to the sword. Dagrun, the earth became red, and the barley tainted and sodden.

"We, the followers of Nerthus, who put down our iron to keep the peace true, were sorely betrayed that day, in this future time!"

"The woman", I spluttered, hardly able to pronounce a word, so stricken by the vision Elíse had shared, "You say she had copper-brown hair. She is then a child of ours, my Eileifer and me…. for the hair is of the Wōden born. That she is slain…. oh, by the gods but this *wyrd rapas* is the hardest thing to bear!"

"***Hwæðre beran hit þu sculan!*** But bear it you must!" came the deep melodious voice of *Ealdmōdor*.

We both looked up to see her standing, shining, flowing in energy before us and smiling. All the parchment wrinkles were gone, a radiant young mother stood before us now. I became swallowed up with joy, a lump in my throat prevented speech, and I so wanted to touch her. But knew I must not even try.

"*Dagrun, Beran hit! Ond ne lǽtan hit astíðian þu æt a brèað twig. Hit is tō cyme ond þu sculan wesan ðeorl!*"
Dagrun, bear it, and not allow it to wither you to a brittle twig. It is coming and you must be strong.
Elíse, þu sculan níed faran wiþ þín heorte-
Hwæðre wesan ofer-stǽlan fram hwæt þín heorte is sagu
Bã ǽ ãre gōd"
Elíse, you must needs go with your heart. But be convinced by what your heart is saying.
Both lives are good."

In the pitch-black darkness, *Ealdmōdor* shone like a star. And I would not blink for fear of missing a second. She had come with all her energy, for us, two young women at the crossroads of our lives. I knew it would not happen again. With the shallowest breathing that almost stopped, I watched her. Her eyes gave me all the messages I needed. And I watched her fade, so slowly, and knew she was pained to go. Her eyes remained, loving us with all her soul.

Then she was gone. And the world became truly black. With only the sound of our breathing to comfort us. We wrestled with our thoughts, wriggling helplessly, like some abandoned little fishes on the torrent of time in the river of *Wyrd*! They were mocking, laughing at our sorry, tiny lives. The Gods were not with us this night.

I turned to Elíse.

"So, what will you do, *sweostor*?" I asked softy, seeing her furrowed brow and eyes closed to the apparent world.

A long silence followed. A white owl suddenly glided swiftly out of the trees before us. It was heading straight for us. Our heartbeats quickened. Her large eyes were glowing white and amber in the darkness. No sound came from our sacred bird, only the wisdom passed to each of us, in flashes of understanding. Then she suddenly swerved to disappear away behind us, intent on her nightly foraging.

"The sacred Owl comes to us with some wisdom. She foretells of a profound change, Dagrun," Elíse said, her eyes now wide and clear.

"It is Dægberht who has claimed my heart, and my head can but watch! I chose on this *Þrimilce dæg*. Dagrun, I have known nothing but the way of the *Sãcerde* for all my life. It was ordained by *Ealdmōdor* and now Aslaug holds the power. But I am not strong enough to carry this. You witnessed what happened to me at the Grove. How, without your *drycræft,* I would have joined Ealdmōdor in *Neorxenawang*.

I feel complete when I am with Dægberht. Do you feel this with Eileifer?"

"I do," I replied, "Exactly so. You know in the depths of your soul, it is right. But you know for all the shared love, it is sometimes never enough when the world around you are against such a match. I have such a challenge to face, in just a few moons time"

"Why so!" Elise shot back, not a little surprised.

"The old *Cyng*, Wihtlæg," I replied, "he holds the power to prevent such a hand fasting, and he will, if the poisoned elf Gandãlfr has his way!"

"Who is he, this little demon in our midst", she shot back.

"Someone I must do battle with to expose his dishonourable ways. Until then, our love for each other, will hang in the balance."

"We are both facing similar challenges, but Owl came, Dagrun," Elíse reiterated, "and our lives will change completely. But I must secure mine carefully. I have decided to wait. I must make my peace with Aslaug. She needs to honour our union. And Dægberht is only a fleeting time known to me. You have known Eileifer for many moons. It will deepen our love if it is true, and diminish it of it is not. Am I testing him cruelly, Dagrun?" she asked plaintively.

"No," I replied, "You are being wise, and *Ealdmōdor* is smiling! So, don't be afraid, for I saw him just a little while ago, and his love for you is as deep as the Germania sea…and maybe just as tempestuous. Be prepared for that, Elíse. I too am beginning to learn the ways of men and sometimes they think only with their *wǽpen* between their legs!"

Elíse erupted in adorable laughter that soon caught me. The night air echoed with our chorus, until wet-eyed and ribs aching we collapsed on the warm earth silently thanking *Ealdmōdor* and Ancestors for their help.

And so, it was, that the large gathering of the Suevi at our Ancestor stones, was preceded by our own very private council, which changed our lives forever.

… … … … … … … … …

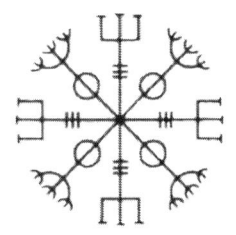

CHAPTER SIXTEEN
Forewítegian æt þæt ðèodscipe:
Prophecy to the people

Many messages had been sent to the seven tribes of the Suevi. Some who held many kinsmen, and held their own meetings in their mead halls. For others who were so few, it was sent by word of mouth to the *hūs* of the leader, who told his neighbour. In our ancient homeland, the Suevi held dominion over most of Cimbric peninsular. We had a confederacy and our laws were just and fair: most of our people were freedmen and we followed Nerthus, our Earth Mother.

Here on Wihtland, our new home, with the unwanted presence of the Romans, we had splintered, retreated for our own safety, unsure of any power we still held. In the peninsular, our power was supreme because we were united and kept a wonderful peace. It was broken only by invaders after our land, or by greedy *Ealdorðegn* after more land, cattle and horses.

And those invaders, plus the harsh weather and floods over our land, made us seek the danger of the Big Sea and travel to the unknown.

Wihtland is better in all ways to our old homeland. The weather kinder. The summers hotter, with just cool winters and two crops some seasons that kept our bellies full, and the crop sufficient to feed those Roman centurions too! Or so I am told by our elders.

And it was those *Ealdormen* that called for the *ðing*. There had not been one called in all my life. They were a council of the past. Only in the direst circumstances were they ever called, and within the sacred Ancestor circle. All decisions made there were binding for all Lifetimes, meaning they could not be changed or amended at will by anyone within the Suevi host. So, it was very important to speak clearly, have honest intent and claim the outcome for the absolute good of all.

The All Father Wōden would be called, Nerthus was invited with Freyja and Frey, Thunōr and all the gods were asked to attend and bring their wisdom and foresight.

Drycræft needed to be performed to protect the circle from *Ælf* and *Wuduwosan*. This task would be given to the *Sācerde*, Aslaug, Elíse, Sāga and most probably myself. Eileifer and Eyvindr were tasked to perform *drycræft* for the men. Although there may be others from the Anglii or Reudignians who would come and work their own *Wyrd* to protect the circle.

Would our old *Cyng* Wihtlæg be present and with him, his horrible little shadow, Gandālfr, I wondered, for if so, the challenge that *Ealdmōdor* foretold would be much nearer!

… … … … … … … …

And so, it was, that the grand hall was built. Its chosen place was high on the *Etdreðecumb* ridge, a highly sacred area. The path to and from it followed the serpent line that Nerthus had set with her footprints on Wihtland. All the men were called from the fields. Timber felling and shaping of the logs were done by as many men as could be spared from the Suevi host. Green wood dictated by availability predominated the building. But the main supports were seasoned, weathered oak that had been stored for such an outcome. The grand hall would creak and groan into being, a living thing, and one we would honour with carvings of spirit animals and guardians. It fell to my *Fæder* and my big brother, Eystein to billet, work, feed the men who arrived from the field, supervise the building and, because they were giants, were expected to shoulder the largest logs, the heaviest oak. They built that grand hall between them and they lived every minute to the full.

I knew this land of *Etdreðecumb*. The forest woods that surround the land are full of the beautiful Larch, the woman's tree. The only evergreen to turn its leaves at the end of summer, gifting us a full weaving tapestry of intense colours. Those oranges and browns of all shades and brilliant yellow were lit up on a Sunni day. With the magical Gorse, the deep valley glowed with that vibrant yellow for nearly all the seasons. The potion I make from the flowers has a perfume so feminine, it takes your breath away. Gorse is a wonderful healer, and it will bring sunshine into the darkest heart and cure all manner of ailment when combined with sister herbs.

It is also the *Cynedōm* of the *Fæges* and all care must be taken in offerings and gifts, for assent to be gained. Sāga and Elíse would weave their *drycræft* through their domain.

Sāga went quickly into quiet action, Elíse at her side, carrying the tiny mead cups, honey pots and herbs. and with a bundle of hair used for threads by the *Fæges*, they waited.

Sāga as *nigt-gala*, blew gently on the night air, her song of the *Fæges*, hoping they would hear and come. And indeed, come they did. Three in number, small and luminous. Their hair flowing in a starry, silver white, and their feet never still, as if their energy moved the leaves and pulled the twigs. Sāga told them of the need for building the great hall, and why it was deemed good to build it in the valley of the *Fæge* as it was directly on our Nerthus serpent line.

"So now you have discovered why we live here." they retorted "We can move through the *Wyrd* with ease here. Come for three nights. We will give a yeah or a nay on the third night."

So, Sāga and Elíse returned the following nights to sit at each *fæge* domain with mead and honey pots, soft songs and little rituals. On the third night, they appeared and gave their assent.

"We approve of your essence of intent. We will not pester you and your great hall with our *drycræft*. Be assured of that. But neither you nor your great hall will survive. Both gone in times to come. But you already know that do you not? We are glad we moved sideways in *Wyrd,* away from you humans and all your destructive ways.

The women nodded, sadly looking down to the dark earth at their feet.

"But what you do now, people of the Suevi, soon to birth a new name, will hold strong the beliefs of Nerthus, our Earth Mother. You will be the very last, and it will be recorded in the ancient stones to be re-birthed again many aeons from now. So, go well, we bid you farewell"

And they left in a whisper of the night.

… … … … … … … … …

Our great Hall was speedily erected, rough-hewn timbers beaten into place. Grudgingly, the splintered green wood groaned. The oak was alive with protest. So much so, I went to the Oak Spirit and asked for his help in determining a peaceful outcome for this Hall to house our Suevi host. But in my heart, my gut intuition, I knew as my sisters did, that it was but a fragment of our race of giant people, hastily created, and just as quickly destroyed.

Mōnā graced us so much that night of the host gathering. She was so bright and full that she cast a faint shadow behind us. We had no need for smoky tallow wands. There was the sound of feet moving, rustling bushes, everywhere. The animals retreated from their kingdom to hide in the darker shadows of the night. Soft mutterings and occasional laughter filled the air. The Suevi were on the move. And most wonderful of all, several had their hair tied in the Suevi knot. Deep emotions from long ago, and I knew not from where they came, welled up in me. And my throat tightened in the wonder of it all.

"*Ealdmōdor,*" I whispered," See this! See our people coming together." Heron rustled before me, where no wind whispered a breath. I knew she has heard me. It made me feel so close to her, to our Ancestors. And I determined that if we remained close to our forebears, who had sight far outreaching our own, we would walk the path of Nerthus to the end times.

I felt nerves slithering around my belly, and a taut stricture in my head threatened to become a full-pained ache. I was here at this throne before my time. Our turning out as a united family was important to secure the "*Gieses*" of the Suevi. And in pure deference to our long-forgotten tradition, except for my dear little brother Eyvindr who had always worn his hair to the side, we had worked our locks into the tightest knot high on our heads for the first time in many moons.

I swear it was the reason for my aching head. But the Suevian knot is the mark of the Suevi. And we intended to give it full honour this twilight.

I stood, smoothing my best gown, which had not a hint of forest green about it. It had taken until noonday to scrub it clean. Eileifer suddenly took my hand and squeezed it, giving me that secret grin of his. All the scramble of nerves evaporated under his gaze. He looked magnificent. His copper-brown hair pulled tight to his right, the knot elaborately interwoven with braids of green and red, the strands trailing down with his hair-ends to shoulders that had hardened leather pads. They were embossed with raven and wolf, interlaced with the intricate knot work of *Wyrd*. His leather breast-piece was an emblazoned, beautiful working of Nerthus as goddess and serpent together. The colours of blue and green interwoven, representing both earth and water. They were evenly balanced and glowing bright in the firelight of the central fire. Torches that were hung on the wooden walls the length of the mead hall sent shadows dancing around everyone.

My mother looked radiant and half her age, as the knot tied to her left, as was mine, had small plaits woven in, with a plaited knot of hair and braids woven together, sitting high on her head.

My *fæder* just looked uncomfortable and I knew as soon as this council was done, he would be undoing his greying knot, and letting his straggly hair fall.

Eyvindr was well, just Eyvindr, storyteller and *Wita,* who had just spent a fair time laying protective herbs and whispering the prayers to keep our hall free from malevolent spirits.

He nodded to Eileifer, who said in a deep voice,

"It is time, open the hall doors to our tribe and bid them enter."

As our people trailed in to take seats near the fire, or to stand in the shadows, I noticed immediately the look of shock by some of them, at our appearance. Particularly the elders of our tribe who remembered the old days. There were some who exclaimed, others who smiled and shook their heads in agreement.

"*Giese, Gíese!*" I heard muttering from many, as the tribe gathered.

Our kinsmen had arrived early, from the valley near to the *Etdreðecumb* ridge. They had lined the pathway, in respect of our *Cyng*. Before me had walked Eileifer, my *Fæder* and *Mōdor*, Eyvindr and Eystein and I had made my way to join them. Eileifer had smiled and caught my hand. His leather breast plate had been so meticulously rubbed with goose grease, and it shone like a metal, on this full Mōnã night. The spirit-animal guardians embossed on the leather, almost stood in relief, ready to growl and roar in approval or otherwise.

This was the moment of truth, for in accepting this commission for change, our future, as a race of people would be cast by a *Giese* or a *Nã*.

"So be it, my *Cwèn*," Eileifer muttered as if reading my thoughts, "This is our moment of truth." And he looked down on me with a look of such deep love. I knew our union would withstand the mightiest tempest. We would survive.

We sat in the well-lit hall, with standing torches on either side welcoming our entrance, as did the kinsmen who had waited along the pathway, with the stamping of feet to the well-meant cheers as we had entered the great hall. A huge fire has been lit in the very centre, surrounded by mighty oak planks, as green as a new born babe. No sparks would ignite this structure for many a moon. My *fæde*r had lugged these oaks in, and I saw him wince at the memory to be promptly nudged in the ribs by my brother, who was twenty-five summers his stripling!

The floor had been lovingly cleaned, swept and laid with new rushes found at the water meadow of *Sudmōr*. The women had gathered and laid fresh rosemary, and thyme to bring a fragrance at every footfall.

Our walk from *Sudmōr* had been many a spear length. But it had been a beautiful early twilight walk. I had heard the rattle and creak of wheels and thud of oxen hoofing the ground, bringing those whose bones could not manage the trek.

We experienced nothing from the Romans. When we reached the high point of the valley, where the Hall had been erected, we could see the *Wihtlægsbyrig* stronghold in the distance. It was now the staging post of those Romans destined for Britannia. Everything was movement with them, but come the dawn when they appointed Romans to stay and be erstwhile rulers of this island, we had no powers over that, no matter our royal bloodline. It counted for naught. We traded or we died.

We all halted within the very entrance of the hall, silently asking our Gods and Goddesses for a just outcome. Their presence at the sacred stone circle would wholly determine the outcome for the Suevi. I looked up and gasped at the sheer height of the roof above our heads. I turned to see my *Fæder* smiling broadly at me. He had engineered this. The eaves were higher than in any hall I had ever seen. And the broad oak trunks used to buttress the roof were wider than any seen before. It was a Grand Hall indeed!

"I think I may be removing myself to set up home here," Eileifer whispered in my ear.

"*Nā!*" I hissed back, "This is too damned close to the Romans. You will end up a *Rōmãnisc*! Man- who- talks- with- horses!"

"Well said *sweostor*," my brother burst in, "Too close to those Romans and they will take your horses from under your very nose."

"Ah no", Eileifer retorted, "My horses are safe. They are bone white. Bad omen as far as those Romans are concerned. They worship black, any animal, any kind"

We relaxed into the "thrones." Well to be more accurate, hastily adorned large chairs, brought from the woodsman who crafted pieces for many other *Hūs*. The embroidered coverings were beautiful with images of Nerthus with the green-forest as blues and turquoise trimming the edges. Eileifer's covering had Thunōr with clouds charging across a blue sky. We sat on our women's challenging work, gently, with reverence. Glad to rest our legs after that long trek from *Sudmōr*.

Torches that lit the hall flickered over carvings freshly created. Guardian's wolf, boar, and especially a most exquisitely sculptured raven now adorned the hall. The presence of Wōden was felt strongly. The Telling was in the offing, unfinished. It needed a conclusion. Until Wihtleig returned, it would remain so. Maybe I put out an unconscious prayer that night, for that part of the *wyrd rapas* was starting a weave that would test me to the depths of my soul.

"*Þu are eall wilcume mín ðèodscipe æt þes heall*", Eileifer sounded out strongly, bringing me back to the Now,"

"You are all welcome, my people to this hall."

"*Æt þes geðeaht, in þeat clomm fram níwol frèondræden wè are ofen-hlèōðr in þæt frið of Nerthus*"

"To this council, in the bonding of deep friendship, we are united in the peace of Nerthus."

There was standing room only, the mead-tables leant up against the walls. So, the stamping of feet on the fragranced floor sounded the welcome back as did the great aroma of lavender, rosemary and thyme that wafted upwards to claim many noses and brought nods and smiles. The Suevi knots bobbed like gulls on a choppy sea.

I looked at the kinsmen before me. Their shouting now reduced to gabbling in small groups, each one seeming to have at least two loud-mouthed "leaders" vying for centre stage. Eileifer joined by my *Fæder* shouted for silence. It worked.

Æmta!" Quiet!" They roared.

Gradually silence prevailed.

"There are grave matters come to us that we need to discuss here tonight", Eileifer spoke with loud resonance I had not heard before, "But first, there will be two Tellings, so that you all understand what is before us.
"Both are from our goddess, Nerthus. A warning we need to take heed."
"While in the deep spiritual place of trance at the *Drímeolce gerihte* Nerthus came to us in human form. She took the body and voice of our dear *sweostor*, Elíse. Her warning came to us, who were gathered in the sacred grove. Also, Elíse herself experienced in spirit, a vision that foretells a likely future of our people."
"I will ask the *Mōdor* of my *Cwèn* Dagrun to come forward to give the first Telling"
My mother slowly came forward, always in the shadow of my mighty, but kindly *fæder*, her role was not one of the storyteller.
She coughed and straightened her back. Looking straight ahead, she began to speak her truth.
"People of the Suevi, we who are born of giants, that their blood runs in all our veins. We are proud to hold that ancestral blood. So, it is, that my daughter, Dagrun, soon to be *Cwèn* of Wihtland, has been given the gift of defender and protector of the Ancestor stones. And it was to her that our beloved Nerthus directed her words.
I will give you a close re-telling. For be in no doubt, our goddess took a mighty effort to reach us with this vison and warning of our likely future."
The hall became hushed, not even a snuffling or baby-mewling could be heard. The tension could be sliced with a *seax* and my *Mōdor*, I saw, was trembling. Sharp flickering shadows from the

fire and random sparks were the only visible movement. The heat from the ceremonial fire, and all our collected bodies was growing to suffocating levels. But the doors could not be opened until the council was complete and decisions made.

"*Ancient peoples of the seven tribes, you who have forsaken your homelands to live on the sacred Isle of Wihtland, bring with you a covenant which will soon come alive. In your children's time and in your children's, and their children's time, a force will bear down on all who worship Mother Earth, all who live within the gods' love and who stay close to the near world of spirit through love of our animals and flowers, plants and all living creatures. This force will try to annihilate every human who worships nature. Or force them into their religion, because they see their way as supreme. They believe they have dominion over all living things and they fear the gods of nature.*

They will fear your strength and they will kill you because of it.

There is one amongst you who has seen this, who is now hiding in the shadows.

Your prayer has been heard. Dagrun Wahl of the Warinni, protector and defender of the Stones, come forward, beorn, you of all here, must hear my words."

Dagrun Wahl, your forbears are close, your Ealdmōdor is never far from your side. My son Wōden has spoken to you. Have courage. You carry the blood of the stones within you. Walk into that power, my dear. Know the stones, their spirit, and their strength. They are waiting to give you all you need for the years ahead. Let them into your heart, too. See the pictures they hold for all time, without fear. Teach your children all that you know. Bring them to feel the stones as part of themselves. For it is they who will pass our knowledge onto the earth children many eons from now.

Be certain of this. The flame of our spirit, the ways of the Earth Mother will be brought to nothing but a flicker, in times to come. It is only by recording our knowledge in the stones that our ways will be re-born again.

And now in this time, the covenant will only survive if you all join. All the tribes here on Wihtland need to speak and feel with one accord. And this too must be passed down to your children.

You may believe the Romans are your common enemy. Dah! But they are nothing compared to those who will arrive on these shores. The Romans tax your bodies and steal your wealth. Those coming will suck the very spirit from you and it is only when the spirit of the people dies that the nation's fall to their knees.
Hear me well!"

My mother heaved a great sigh, her job complete. She turned and swept back to her seat next to my *fæder*, who was glowing in pride for his wife, and promptly put a loving arm around her.

But in the hall, there erupted a cacophony of voices all wishing to be heard. I doubt that such a proclamation of the future had ever been given. Everyone knew the interweaving river of *Wyrd* could and would pass through time, our past, present and our futures all accessible to those who seek that knowledge. It was a given. No one would dispute it. A great flurry of questions hit our ears. So many kinsmen were clamouring for detail. When, where and how?

I knew Elíse would be asked to step forward next. She was hiding in the shadows, quite literally. I turned to my *Cyng*, "I will go in Elíse's place," I whispered, "She has only just returned to our mundane world but a very brief time ago. She could not withstand this!" I swept my arm across to show the raised voices and emotions.

"Exactly so!" my *Cyng* muttered. He then stood and banged his *seax* hilt against the boss of his shield, shouting again for quiet.

All eyes were now on me, and I stood, straightening my back as *Mōdor* had done, seeking internal strength. I turned quickly to pick up heron and held her over my heart. "Help me, *Ealdmōdor*" I prayed silently. I began hesitatingly.

"The words and the feelings that were impressed upon me by our beloved Nerthus were of seeking unity now in this present time. For the future is woven, and certainly changeable, by our actions now. You are all aware of the interweaving of *Wyrd*. It is moving within and around our waking time and our dreaming."

"So, to be quarrelling and splintered now like a rotten piece of wood, on this night of all nights is disrespecting our goddess! Stop this!"

"When the Bright Stone took me to a time beyond this one, I was shown a harsh religion that would not accept any other but its own, for all our people. It is far away from now. So much was altered in the landscape, something that would take lifetimes to achieve. But it was not good, as far as I could judge. So, we need to hold ourselves tightly together now in this time."

"It is why we wear the Suevi knot. It reminds us all that we are a strong confederacy."

"And it sets us apart from those who seek only war. We are as strong as our weakest link. More than this we must teach all our children the way of Nerthus, the Earth Mother. For it is in their time, not ours, that this vision shall be played out."

"I was a pagan then in that forward time, the Bright Stone had been smashed to nothing more than pebbles and all the Ancestor stones were gone. The ancient beech rotting stumps. The strange man with his uneven cross, and the warrior wanted me to give up Nerthus, give up the Earth Mother. I would not and they were about to kill me when I was pulled back to the Now."

"Elíse was shown our people, our children, being herded like cows, to a deep-water pool, where they were forced to deny their nature spirit and accept this cross. Some did not and they were taken and killed."

I stumbled on the words, choking back tears as I looked over to my *Cyng*. He stared back with a sudden realisation, for I had not told him this part. And his eyes shaded with untold grief.

"One thing I feel sure of," I continued, my belly and heart knotted in tension, "There will be many more of our people braving the rough Germania sea to join us here."

"Our numbers will grow. To be united now, strongly, will bind our future people to us, the Suevi."

There were murmurs of assent now rippling forward from the back of the hall. And then a banging of the mead cup followed by another.

Giese! Giese, came the assenting voices of the Warinni.

I found myself smiling, then laughing in joy. I sat down and was immediately enfolded by my *Cyng*, who kissed me passionately in front of the whole *Ceasterwics*, and was gifted with roars of approval.

"We have assent", Eileifer stood up and scanned the hall for any who might oppose this drawing together of the tribes.

"I am calling a *ðing* at our Ancestor circle, a full moon's time from now."

This produced a silence. From our elders, a memory stirred within, of *ðings* held in their childhood in our old homeland. And for our younger kinsmen, confusion. This was a novel word, an unknown in their Wihtland lives.

"For those of you too young to know," Eileifer continued, "We have a tradition in the Suevi to hold a special council within the sacred circle. This is to determine special Laws and Commissions that are binding for all time. The gods are called. Truth, and with that profound respect, is called for to fulfil that purpose. Not only must it be agreed by the people, but also by the gods"

Eileifer allowed the murmurings and quiet discussion to continue for several heartbeats.

Then, from the rear of the hall, came a clear voice

"And what of our unwanted and hostile invaders, the Romans. What of them I ask? Will they too be invited? I think not! But our silence will provoke a reaction from them. For surely silence maybe our greatest weapon, but it also our greatest weakness. The unreal imaginings of the mind are fed by silence."

"We are not proposing to arm our men, become the warrior" Eileifer countered, strongly, "But we are becoming "one people" again. Becoming the Suevi host. We wear our hair in the traditional way. That is all that will be apparent to them. To us it is empowerment, but the empowerment is not towards hostility, more towards an inner spiritual strength. It is what we are being asked to do by Nerthus. What earthly business is it of those Romans? Let them worship their Mithras, their bull and their gods. We are not threatening them in that way."

"Besides, we are few. Even when united. If we still had the numbers of our host when we were in the homeland, it would be very different! But we are as we are."

"*Giese, Gíese,*" came the overpowering reply from the hall.

So, it was done. The first part of the commission for change had been won.

As the softening energy began to fill the hall, everyone looked to the mead barrels, cups began filling and songs were sung well into the night. I saw a small figure step forward, a babe in arms, mewling quietly. I knew immediately who it was.

It was Ingrid and her *Mōdor*, Ingigerdr who now stood before the *Cyng*.

"Eileifer we have one more matter to attend," I pointed towards the two women. "Ingvar keeps them as thralls. They are starving because he has no interest in keeping his fields well. He is an Ingavonii and hungers for the sea."

"I propose that you make them freedmen, they can work their fields and feed themselves well. The *beorn* is ailing look!"

"Is Ingvar here?" Eileifer scanned the hall. "Eystein, please find your mead companion. Tell him the mead is about to flow."

I beckoned the women over to present themselves to the *Cyng*. I was shocked to see the *beorn*, who had not stopped mewling. She was pale and looked as though little weight graced her bones.

"Ingrid, where is your man, Ívarr?" I asked

"He is with his bow in the forest, my *Cwèn*, I am sorry, but he hunts to feed our *dohtor*"

"That is a dangerous hunt" I replied strongly, stroking the babes head in concern, "You know that forest is Durotrige land, and we respect their right to hunt and live on the game there."

"We are hungry and we are desperate!" came her reply, rocking her *beorn*, without settling her at all.

The huge door of the hall creaked open and in came the giant that was Ingvar, a full head taller than my brother Eystein.

Eileifer stood and walked to Ingvar, clasping him a bear hug, slapping him in comradeship. He talked quietly to him for several heartbeats, then with his arm firmly around his shoulders made him turn and face his thralls.

"Ingríd and Ingigerdr" Ingvar said plainly, looking them straight in the eye, "you and your family are free to work the fields as far as the forest on one side and the cliffs, on the other. You will plant as you wish, harvest all the crops for your family and any surplus will be in tribute to me and of course the damn Romans. And while the fields are planted and you wait for the harvest, you will receive all you need from my stores. As of this moment you are freedmen!"

For a second, the women were too shocked to speak. They stared in disbelieve. Then Ingigerdr fell to her knees, heaving a sputtered thank you through sobs of tears. Ingríd broke into the biggest, broken-tooth smile I had ever seen from her.

"Ðoncian þu mín Dryhten," Ingríd spoke clearly, "Now my family may grow, and if it is the god's will, my next boy child will be named Ingvar after you, who gave us our freedom."

Ingvar promptly issued his own gruff thanks, but everyone could see he was moved and pleased by that gesture and the good outcome of it all. Those near and in hearing of what had transpired brought their mead cups down on the hall bench, in appreciation, and of course, this could only mean more mead.

Suddenly, the large oak doors crashed open with a harsh thud by two kinsmen forcing them both apart. It made the inrush of breeze pull the flames of the central fire towards a cluster of families, who shrieked in surprise. And the hall quietened to a hush. I stood motionless, frozen in time as I knew who had uncermoniously burst into our council.

Wihtleig strode forward, followed by his shadow, the poison-dwarf, Gandālfr. Wihtleig bristled with supressed anger. But the little dwarf smirked, openly, obviously enjoying a scenario he had probably engineered.

The elder *Cyng* stood, with his furred legs woven with leather thongs to his huge bulbous knees. They were set wide part with his hands knuckled in defiance on his hips. I noticed he swayed as he began his harangue at my beloved, gentle *Cyng* and wondered if he was in his cups and wholly drunk.

"*Þurh þæt Dryhten? Hwæt Giefan þū þæt riht æt forsuwian þín eald Cyng?*" he bellowed for all to hear.

"By the gods, what gives you the right to ignore your elder king?"

"What lack of respect is this? I know not what this council is for."

"And why is that stripling woman is sitting at your side like your wife, like your queen!?"

Eileifer stood before him, arms at his side, fists clenched, trying to keep a calm mind before answering his Uncle.

"*Fædera,* I have sent messengers to you in *Cant,* describing why this commission for change is taking place, and as for my *Cwèn,* for that is who she is now, I have also sent a messenger giving you this wonderful news!"

As Eileifer was explaining all this to Wihtleig, I looked over to the dwarf, who had left off smirking and was averting any eye contact with me or anyone else. Wihtleig was oblivious but Eileifer was not, he saw both the smirking and the sneaky eyes. As I sprang up to speak in Eileifer's defence citing Gandālfr with grave suspicions of heinous conduct, he thrust his arm across me and I held silent.

What followed was beyond the worst nightmare, as Gandālfr swiftly tore me apart with accusations of a dark and terrible *drycræft*.

"I have a witness to this dark magic," his stringy voice was strident and cracking, but which still filled the hall, as I watched the faces of my kinsfolk darken and caste their eyes to the rush floor. "It is purely her twisted mind that has brought all this to us, here and now. What you see before you, my Lord!"

My mind was perfectly sane, and I desperately tried to make some sense of his poisoned harangue. Then I settled on the memory of that priest, who by his sheer arrogance was sent away. But did he scurry off? Or did he remain to spy and twist into pernicious knots that revelation from Nerthus and why we needed so badly to bring unity to our people?

"If my *dohtor* has a twisted mind" came the booming voice of my *fæder* "Then we must all have a twisted mind! For there is not one single kinsman in this hall who does not respect and love this kindly, devoted healer of her people! And she, the defender and protector of the ancient stones deserves better than this!"

"Hū duiran þū bismer mín dohtor, mín cynn, þæt Warinni.

Begietanþū aweg-gewítan!"

How dare you insult my daughter, my family and my kin- the Warinni. Get you gone!"

There came a low murmuring of assent within our gathered host. Yet not loud enough. For here was our elder *Cyng*, who could not be easily challenged. Respect was a given amongst our peoples.

I began to tremble, and saw the floor rise to meet me. Then all went black.

… … … … … … … … …

CHAPTER SEVENTEEN
Líf begeondan Wihtland: Life beyond Wihtland

I felt my eyelids flutter, and shots of bright light scurry past my eyes. Then complete darkness came to claim me again. I heard the voices of Eileifer, blurred, not clear, yet sounding near hysterical, with the voice of my brother trying to calm him. Then nothing. I let the blackness take me. The visions and dreams that entered my mind were horrific. Distorted and ugly faces leered at me, laughing, then left to be replaced by Gandálfr himself, laughing in triumph. I tried desperately to escape, but they claimed me as theirs as I tried to avert my eyes, force myself away. It was that desperation that brought me back to the Now, *Wyrd* was testing my will.

As my eyes finally opened to meet the intense stare of Eileifer, his eyes staring into mine, all the nightmare visions vanished into the mist. He kissed me gently and whispered beautiful words in my ears, just for me. I smiled, then groaned as the pain hit me like a hammer. It had been a hard knock as I had hit the floor, yet it might have been much worse. The oak planking was very green and bounced with my head.

"Dagrun, my love" Eileifer said softly, "My stubborn and rather stupid uncle is not dismissing his *Warlocan* and insists on a hearing to decide the matter."

I sank back onto the soft fur hides and groaned. Through my pounding head-pain, I saw an horrific scene of claim and counter claim where the winner would disassemble all we were trying to achieve. The vicious lies would take root given enough turgid water to grow into a fact we could not fight.

"Then we must discredit him", I croaked, "Some water please." Oh, the deliciousness of that spring water coursed down my throat, bringing me back to life.

"Eyvindr, is he here?" I asked looking around, almost swimming back into the darkness with the pain. He stepped forward from the shadows. It was twilight and the dwindling rays of the *Mædmōnaþ Sunni,* created a tiny light.

"Eyvindr, this is most important. You must find that priest we banned and turned away at the *Drímeolce-gerihte*, for I believe it is he who has twisted the truth on the orders of Gandālfr!"

"Eystein, big brother," I had hoisted myself up to rest on my elbows, "you need to fly to *Cant* to where Wihtleig stayed. I believe you may find credible evidence that will damn that *Warlocan* and his terrible lies. But speedily brother, take Ingvar, it may be quicker by sea, and there is no one better than he to beat the tides and ride the wave. His spirit will soar at the very thought of freedom from the land!"

"I must feign illness for longer than is real, I fear, but I cannot do it for long. Ask Lífa to make a potion that will induce a deep sleep."

And so, Lífa's potion of poppy and the smallest belladonna with betony sent me into *Wyrd* where I journeyed for an untold time.

I was told the whole story a few moons later when all had been accomplished. Eystein found Ingvar in his *hūs,* worse for wear on an amphoræ of wine, bought from the *Rōmānisc* for a sack of barley. His wife, Ynghildre was sorely testing his addled mind with a barrage of sharp words in Anglin, of which Ingvar knew nought.

It was, Eystein said, the funniest scene he had witnessed in many a moon, and had to retreat into the twilight to exhaust his lungs with laughter.

When all was calm he returned and explained the mission to Ingvar who jumped from his seat to find his sailing tackle and clothes, while a speechless Ynghildre stared at her rebelling *ceorl*.

Eystein had brought his gelding for Ingvar. A mighty horse to take his height and weight. So together they mounted and galloped for the harbour, where Ingvar had his *cnearr's*. These two small boats were built for speed, for skimming the waves under sail and able to tackle high waves and fierce winds. The stronger the better for Ingvar, whose blood raced with the wind.

The Raven, the *cnearr* he chose, was also built for twelve oars, to maintain a speed in becalmed sea. Ingvar had built it himself. His was of a seafaring family going back many lifetimes. Raven was oak-built with a huge centre stem to take the weight of the long mast. He had used larch in part of the clinker as it was light and could keep up a good speed. There was no better boat to get them to *Cant*. Both fore and aft were identical, designed to reverse quickly and rudder moved at will. This boat could be beached under dark if necessary, with a false keel to take the drag up the sand to woodlands. There was no iron on this *cnearr*. The wooden pegs of seasoned oak and the twine binding were soaked in moss and beeswax. The huge square sail had been woven in squares of strong hemp with wool edging to hold the ropes without fraying.

"I must rally my men", Ingvar chuckled, knowing the lambasting that would follow from irate *cwèns* about to lose their husbands to a bearded giant with the rolling gait! He strode off into the gathering dusk. Eystein, my dear brother, headed for the mead hall to summon up his courage to face the waves and the wind, and whatever else awaited him in *Cant*. He was not a willing seaman, nor did the sea treat him well.

Ingvar returned with less men than he hoped.

"By the gods and the All-father," he swore, after a good swilling of mead, "these *cwèns* have their men by the short hairs, by the Valkyries they do!" To Eystein, this did not bode well, and he studied the men that had left their wives and family to be with Ingvar. They appeared steady and loyal. Hearth companions sworn to defend their sea captain. Whatever was before them required skill and courage. He knew Ingvar so well that he had plenty of both. He prayed to Wōden that his fellow seamen had the same.

"I know you are not a capable seaman, Eystein, my dear friend", Ingvar rolled his eyes heavenwards as if he saw the problems ahead, "But I need you to man the tiller on my command, and to man the sail also with Wigstan, here," he turned his head to the sailor on his left who had years of seafaring engraved on his face. He smiled and this broke his face into the ridges, pits and troughs of a well ploughed field, with two eyes that shone at you like Sunni on a cloudless day. My brother liked him immediately. And from this adventure, he gained a loyal friend and oath-sworn companion.

As they sat in the mead hall, cups at the ready for filling, the talk centred on the tides and the wind as both were needed to match the need for speed. The harbour was a creek, hidden by trees on all sides and only able to moor the smaller boats with a shallow draft. Raven was lolling in the mud, as both boat and crew waited for the tide.

The evening wore on, and the banter became slurred. It was a great relief when Ingvar announced in broad Fering, a language kept for such moments, and which few readily understood that the tide was turning and they should prepare to set sail.

Thunōr had graced them with a stiff wind, a westerly that would billow out the sail and see them scudding eastwards. Ingvar planned to hug the coast as far as he could. But his heart was set on more adventurous waters, which tipped the edge of *Cant* and would pull them northwards.

They all clambered into the creaking hull, its elevated stern and aft swaying in the night sky. There were no carved sculptures of guardian animals at either end, just a finished swirl in oak to mark a masterly clinker construction that ended in a perfect point. It pierced the sky and connected them with the gods, just by its design. Eystein, sitting on the nearest plank, realised the truth that Ingvar was as made for the sea as the sea was made for him! Ingvar interrupted his thoughts.

"Well, *leof frèond* you can sit here with me while my men hoist the mast. One false move from you and your brain might be jelly on the galley floor! And you need to learn fast. I am a man short. You must know how to react fast and know what you must do in an instant, so listen well Eystein, our lives may depend upon it"

"This tiller here", he continued, pointing to the angled, beautifully carved oak, "controls the rudder that steers my *cnearr*. I am giving you first watch, on the easy water so you can find your heart matching that of the Raven. She responds well. Learn the drag of the tide and how much to turn that rudder, and remember it is opposite to your turn with the tiller. And when the sail is up, we will, with the gods help, be fairly bouncing over the waves, so you will man the sail with Wigstan. Do exactly as he orders you. The Raven needs me to steer her."

Eystein, my *dèore brōðor* managed to steer Raven, on that dark night, with the hint of dawn glowing on the eastern horizon, keeping her away from the sandbanks towards the open channel. The wind picked up as they left shelter of the creek.

"Eystein, move!" Ingvar commanded, "Join Wigstan now, we are about to fly *mín frèond*"

It took two strong men each side of the sail to bring it up. Thick twinned ropes were bound and looped each end of the oak yardarm that straddled the sail. It was thinner but was still a massive weight all the same. Eystein heaved with the men to bring the sail up to sit on the mast. It could swivel with rope commands of tightening and the releasing of four sets of ropes. Eystein's face was a picture of confusion and fear when confronted with this. Wigstan swiftly ordered his man to shinny up the mast. His feet locked onto the oak as he moved upwards. Eystein craning his neck to see the man with rope and tackle, saw him bind the yardarm to the mast in a clever twist of knots and loops to secure it. And yet keep the oak beam mobile for all the manoeuvring of sail needed to skip round the rip tides and great swirls of deep water that lay in that rough Germania sea.

Wigstan gave Eystein the largest grin, his eyes shining in the dark. Eystein relaxed a little.

"Listen well, *frèond*", he shouted, "It will get a might noisy. Hold both ropes, one in each hand. That one for your *wynstra*, the other your *rihthand*. When I shout loosen/tighten *wynstra*, or loosen/tighten *rihthand* you do it till I say *forstoppian* and tie it down to that cleat!"

It was then that Eystein looked up to see the immensity of his task ahead. And he starred, open-mouthed, to see the huge raven in flight that had been painted onto the sail. As the sail flapped so the Raven came alive and flew. It was breathtakingly beautiful.

Ingvar had been watching his mead companion the whole time while steering the Raven, and he smiled.

Eystein turned to see him. "Who did this, Ingvar, my friend?"

"Well", he replied, stroking his beard, "it was not my *Cwèn*, that is a fact.... let us just say, the wonderful women of the weaving lodge, who created the sail and dyed and worked in the Raven. Good huh!"

"*Wynstra*! Now tighten!" came the shout from Wigstan, and all other conversation died on a breath, as the wind picked up and Raven began to fly.

… … … … … … … … …

Ingvar has steered Raven through the small water. She was a graceful *cnearr* under billowing sail and Eystein had mastered the tasks Wigstan had thrown at him, so he was relaxed and enjoying this adventure. Then it all began to go horribly wrong for him. Tipping the headland of *Cant*, by the afternoon of this first day, Ingvar altered course to head out into the Germania Sea. Waves began to meet Raven and send her upwards, her tip to kiss Sunni in the cloudless sky. The buffeting was enjoyed by these hardened sailors, but my brother could not join them. Within several heartbeats, he lurched his head over the side, the ropes being taken over by one of the oars-men.

His stomach broiled, leaving just rancid spit to meet the waves now spilling into the *cnearr*. He was utterly diminished and quite humiliated. The sea had not treated him kindly and probably never would. Still Ingvar headed out to sea. Raven pitched and rolled, but never once keeled over dangerously. This *cnearr* was a beauty in the water.

But Eystein was beyond caring about the beauty of design, his chin resting permanently on the edge, waiting for the next heave on an already wasted stomach. He did not notice the reason for Ingvar's sudden change of course.

Another boat, a small speck, but getting ever larger, was on their horizon, leeward to the coast of *Cant*. "We have three, no four possible choices as to the intentions of our followers," Ingvar announced to no-one, as all were concentrating on their own tasks.

"For following us, they are", he continued, "and they may continue to chase us to the old homeland coastline and it would put days onto our journey. What say you, Eystein?"

My poor brother, on hearing his name, turned a sweat laden head, his suevian knot dripping in saliva and stomach contents, to put a searching eye on Ingvar.

"We cannot wait days for this, *frèond* my *sweostor's* life depends upon a swift conclusion. We must land soon, I do beg you!"

"Drop sail and turn about," Ingvar shouted, obviously not happy with this choice. A good hair-raising chase would have been his preference, "oarsmen, prepare to backward oar Raven. We go to meet our adversaries."

"That does mean you also, Eystein," Ingvar muttered as he went to man the tiller. Eystein heaved himself up, and slumped over the waiting oar. Keeping in rhythm with the men distracted his mind, and in time he was making good the oar, as they paced through the water.

As the boat hove into view, Eystein breathed a sigh of relief. It was a *fær*. It was not Roman. That would have presented unknown problems, for the Romans enjoyed nothing more than being dictatorial, harassing at best, or simply capturing all on-board for the slave markets.

He saw these people were his kinsmen of *Cant*. *Centingas* (Centish men) or Men of *Cant*).

"*Wes ðū hāl!*" came the shout from the captain, "Does the *Ealdorðegn of Wihtland* Eystein Wahl be within your boat?"

"*Giese!*" Wigstan replied, flashing his bright smile, "Do I know you?"

"You should do!" came the reply, from the captain laughing into his beard, then looking up, shouting at Wigstan, "you old balmy sea-dog! Have you lost your memory along with your wits? For I have lost count of the trading we have done together in our younger days, and the women we enjoyed too!"

"Hah! It's Bjartr! Well *eald frèond*, your *Ealdorðegn* is here, right enough, but a might worse for the sea journey. Not a good seaman is our Eystein!"

My brother well remembers the worst part of this tortuous journey, and the look of sheer dismay that Bjartr gave him. He later described my brother as akin to a sea monster dragged up from the depths, green of gills and dripping with slime.

He took him on board the *fær,* where he settled in a heap, with furs wrapped around him.

"I don't think you will see this man aboard any kind of sea-going vessel ever again!" Bjartr shouted over the crash of waves, "I bid you farewell, enjoy the rest of your journey, kinsmen."

"Eystein, you need your coin to barter for a horse returning to Wihtland", Ingvar shouted, shaking the purse in the air.

"Keep it, my *frèond,*" came the hoarse reply from under the hides, "It is your payment, take it to trade in Gaul or Belgicus."

And so, Ingvar, with his sturdy crew, oared outwards towards the open Germanic sea, seeking the adventure all Ingavonii crave. He was at peace and he was fulfilled.

After a while, as the *fær* settled into calmer waters, and Eystein took first sight of land, his stomach settled, he could take breathe without heaving and he turned to ask the burning question of this new kinsman.

"How did you know I might be on board the Raven?"

"I did not", came the reply, "here take some clean water." Bjartr was a Suevi, Eystein felt sure he knew this kinsman.

"You are Suevi?" he asked.

"That I am. As well you know, for we each see ourselves in the other, when in a foreign land. I have just chosen to live on a bigger island and you have picked a much smaller one, but more powerful in other ways. We recognise the *drycræft* of Wihtland. But it is only those chosen to live on the isle, that thrive there. That is how it has always been and always will be."

"Now, to the matter in hand," he said, digging into the large pouch tied to his leather belt, "See this, if you please. It was given to me by the messenger your *Cyng* sent some while ago, as proof, the boar and raven emblem of the Wōden born. He has a terrible tale to tell. It is best left for him, I think."

The sun was catching the bronze glints of his red hair that plaited to the side and matched the beard. He was a giant also and fair filled the little boat, manned by only four crew.

"I guessed the Raven *cnearr* would be the one holding you. The messenger gave me the task of watching and waiting for you. He knew you would come."

Twilight was settling in to greet the night and Sunni was sinking to meet Mother Earth in union. Deep, dark colours of blue and purple with snatches of orange glimmered on the shingle beach and curlews called into the dusk.

The little *fær* beached. The four-man crew dragged the boat up to secure her safely. Eystein followed Bjartr up into the trees where horses were waiting, while the crew bade their farewells and disappeared into the night.

As they unhobbled the two mighty geldings, the two sons of a pure-bred copper coloured stallion, Bjartr untied their feeding bags and turned to Eystein.

"The love for your *sweostor* must be great indeed. You do know the danger you face on this journey?"

"Believe me, *frèond,* if I could make that homeward seaward journey, I would. But I fear my innards would never recover. So, where do we journey to meet the king's messenger?"

"We are going to *Cantium*, the enemy camp if ever there be such a place in *Cant*. The Romans have made it their own. Villas you will see, Eystein, large and ever growing. It seems they have an unquenchable appetite for showing wealth in coin and brick and intricate flooring. They employ master craftsmen from all over Europe. Your royal messenger is hiding right under their very noses. 'Tis the best place to keep hidden."

"Why is the enemy Roman?", Eystein asked, "Wihtland has peace under their rule since Vespasian and his son built good trading relations with us. They do not harry us too much and we do not harry them!"

"Ah but that is the very intrigue, Eystein. It is best I leave the telling to the royal messenger himself, for I would not want to muddy an already turgid pool."

They galloped onward under a darkening sky, Eystein becoming aware of the very essence of time itself, and how it was dripping through his fingers into this turgid pool of someone else's making. Gandālfr! the puss-filled poison dwarf! Why? He shouted to his fogged mind. As they skimmed past low-lying beech branches, hanging perilously in their path, and which both geldings seemed to know, swerving to avoid them with skill. Eystein found a burning question troubling him deeply: Why was Wihtleig, a famous warrior king and Wōden born seemingly blind to the devious ways of his erstwhile dedicated and "loyal" wizard? What had Gandālfr done to instil such blind respect?

As the full face of Mōnã suddenly appeared from behind the deep near-black clouds, gifting a shimmering edge to the leaves as they hurtled past, they gratefully broke free of the forest. The dunes before them carried the geldings on an easier ride to *Cantium*, which lay in a shallow valley edging to the sea.

It was said that this was the very first landing of Cesar with the first Roman legions. And as Eystein scanned the emerging town, he was taken aback by the narrow pathways and cluttered *hūs*, where two horses could barely pass without knocking a passer-by. They had entered the poor sector of *Cantium*. The slave population was housed in squat, filthy *hūs* that had yet to be graced with hypocausts.

Moreover, his broiled belly was assaulted by the stink emanating from the very air. He gagged and fought back acid tasting nausea from an empty stomach.

Bjartr took his horse a sharp left, whereupon the pathway widened to a stable yard. He turned to Eystein and spoke softly, "You look like a stranger who does not belong here, with your Suevian knot! Here, this cloak will hide you well. We walk from here."

"I am thanking my goddess heartily for her grace in guiding me to Wihtland and not here!" Eystein retorted, "By the god's this place is a stink hole!"

"You should be offering a prayer to those of your kinsmen caught into slavery, *frèond*, for theirs is a truly wretched life. Think on it *gecwèman*!"

He followed behind Bjartr in silence, pondering the other side of the Roman face.

The buildings further away were all well-constructed with wooden slated facings and tiled roofs. There were shuttered windows that Eystein took first sight of and was impressed. Then there were those buildings that had a green coloured glass making up the window, more affluent and more on show, but nonetheless beautiful to look at. Yet they stopped at none of these.

They turned down a darkened alley way, shadows meeting shadows, into near total blackness. Bjartr stopped abruptly, knocking three times at a door. Then twice. The door opened ajar. A tender light escaped into the alleyway.

"*Gecwèman* quickly!" came the voice from within. Bjartr stood for a second, scanning both directions to ensure they had not been followed. Eystein for the first time felt a rush of fear course down his body to knot his guts. He felt faint with extreme hunger.

In the tallow fuelled light, through swirling eye-watering smoke, he caught the eye of a tall giant with a mass of red hair crowning a young face. But whose other eye was blackened and bruised. He looked down, shoulders slumped, sitting heavily on the nearest stool. Eystein realised that his eye was not the only part of his body that had been beaten. He steeled his stomach and his resolve, for he was gathering a deep anger about the whole situation.

Bjartr moved forward to gently clasp this auburn giant on the shoulder. He winced imperceptibly.

"Kenward, introductions are in order," he turned, "This is the chief *Ealdōrthegn* of the Warinni, part of the Suevian host. Eystein, this is our royal messenger to *Cyng* Eileifer. He has a telling that will shock and most likely make you want to murder a certain dwarf!"

"But first, we must eat! I know my stomach is trying to eat itself, so only the gods know what yours is up to, Eystein, my *frèond*!"

Eystein nearly collapsed into the waiting stool, and looked gratefully at the *Cwèn* serving a steaming bowl of barley porridge. Kenward stood up and opened the hide flap, and as the swirling smoke escaped out into the night, a hearth and home came into view. It was a small neat room, with a curtained off sleeping area where Eystein could hear the gentle snoring of children in dreamtime.

"Kenward," he began, looking closely at the youth. "My *sweostor* Dagrun Wahl, newly coupled with our young *Cyng*, is lying grievously insulted and maligned by Gandālfr, who, it seems is intent on causing not just mischief, but a bigger onslaught on the honour of my family the Warinni and maybe the entire Suevian host. Why?"

Kenward brushed the mass of curly hair from his eyes.

"You see this!" he exclaimed, "This was an attempt to kill me. It failed, as you can see. I am in hiding, for my knowledge will, at worst, make forfeit the life of Gandālfr. Or at best, under the compassion of his *Cyng*, he will suffer a ruined reputation!"

"So, begin your telling" Eystein lent forward, "And know from this moment onwards, you will have the *Cyng's* protection."

"Many of our kinsmen see the old *Cyng* Wihtleig as a mighty oak," Kenward began, slurring his words, in obvious pain, "Tall as a giant, true to his word and indestructible. But within that old oak is a rot growing. Gandālfr, the supposed wizard promises to cure him of it, send the *wyrm* asunder. He has worked his *drycræft* before on a cousin of Wihtleig, and deemed it a remarkable success. Wihtleig believes in him as he may be dying. It is clouding his vision and his judgement."

"*Giese*!" Eystein agreed, "I have suspected this also but tell us the whole story, if you know of it?"

"I can only guess," Kenward replied, "but I believe this dwarf plays both sides, and his only driven course is for coin and glory. I know he has been giving the Romans accounts of your commission for change, and the unity growing within the Suevi on Wihtland. He has reported to the Christians, Roman Christians, of your rites and ceremonies. He has certainly chosen to be allied to the Attribates and the Belgic who both see you, the Suevi, as Rome lovers"

"We are not! We honour Nerthus!" Eystein exploded, "Our ways are those of peace. We honour the Earth Mother above all. We do not love Rome! Their ways are foreign and some are downright disgusting to us."

"*Giese*! We know," Bjartr burst in, obviously angry also, in defence of the Suevi host.

"But please tell us, why the attack on you? Why did Gandālfr arrange for that? Was it Rome or the Attribates? These Christians!"

"Above all, he fears the power of Dagrun Wahl", Kenward replied, "He had my dear *frèond* murdered to prevent the knowledge of the union with *Cyng* Eileifer. He must have been given a big bag of coin to warrant this horror."

"But on whose orders?" Eystein asked, for he saw this turgid pool of corruption spilling out to poison so many lives, not least his *sweostor* Dagrun and Eileifer, whose lives of happiness together had all but begun.

"Who has the most to lose?" queried Bjartr.

"I put my coin on this table to say it is the Romans, but those Christian Romans whose god excludes all others and demands retribution under the name of heresy."

"They certainly fear the followers of Nerthus and Wōden. And there are many of us who do, in Britannia now. Why try and destroy a young woman's happiness who only serves her kinsmen with healing *drycræft*?"

"She is much more than that, Eystein, as well you know!" Kenward retorted.

"We need proof, Kenward" Bjartr elicited, "for without that, all this is just hot air blowing out into the night"

"I can provide that proof," Kenward replied quickly, "We buried my poor *frèond* in the dead of the night, but I still have his bloodstained vest with the royal emboss and coin sewn in. He was killed in a terrible manner. I have a witness to the plot also. She is a thrall serving in the local *popina* and overheard the evil workings of Gandālfr, whose voice she recognised."

"That is well done, but will she come with us to Wihtland?"

"You can ask her yourself" Kenward replied.

As he spoke, a head appeared, full of waving auburn curls that cascaded down the curtain, and a shy smile from that small girl - child, gave Eystein all the proof he needed that she would indeed be travelling back with them.

"We must find two extra horses, then," Bjartr said.

"She will travel with me, she is no weight", Kenward said with a smile, "she would wish nothing more than to be secure on Wihtland. She has heard there are no *thralls* living there. She would be a *libertus*."

"That is true," said Eystein, "consider it done!"

"Then we must leave now", Bjartr announced, "We need the darkness now for it is our only *frèond* in *Cantium*, it would seem. We honour your help and sanctuary of course" he added, smiling gratefully to this poor family, surviving in the dark and stricken depths of the "hidden" *Cantium*, Caesar's pride in Britannia.

The horses had been led out of the stables by the man of the *hūs*, who had silently listened to all the debate and responded in his quiet way.

"Go well", he said huskily to both Kenward and the small girl, who was little more than a child. Kenward had wrapped her in a large woollen shawl. She was encased in his arms as he held onto the reins. It was to be a harsh, difficult journey for her. If she was caught by the Romans, it would mean her death.

Bjartr demanded a fast pace, taking them back to the forest, for safety, but heeding the need for speed, careered past the low-lying beeches until the horses were foamed and tired.

"We are out of the immediate reach of the Romans", he turned to the girl and smiled," "We can rest, water the horses by that stream."

"We are now in Regnenses' land, and they will know we are here. They have the very best trackers."

"Are they with Rome?" Eystein asked, as he pulled a fistful of dry grass to rub down the horses.

"Some are, others not", came the enigmatic reply." I am going to find some food, if you might like to build a small fire, we may eat, then move on."

Bjartr proved to be an excellent forester, as well as an able seaman. Eystein sent a grateful prayer to Wōden for weaving this guardian into their lives. Before Mōnā had reached the fulcrum of her nightly journey, Bjartr retuned with two dripping rabbits. Together with the turnips the *cwèn* had plopped into the bag, they would provide ample fuel for the remainder of their journey. A small cauldron was produced from Kenward's bags, with a trivet. Before long a steaming rabbit stew was made ready.

They sat on old logs, or on the mossy forest floor, around the fire. Kenward gave the shy, slightly built maiden first helpings, wrapping her up in the shawl. He was overly protective of her. Eystein wished to find out why.

"You, young maiden, have shown great courage in coming with us this night," he began, sitting next to Kenward, "what is your name so I may forward it to the *Cyng* when we reach Wihtland?"

"Bertr, my lord" she replied in a whisper. A look of hope passed across her eyes, then was gone, replaced by vacancy as if her soul was in retreat.

"What was your life like under the roof and protection of Wihtleig?" Eystein asked

"I can furnish you with some harsh facts on that matter, if you wish," Kenward turned to Bertr. She nodded.

"Bertr is the slave of a Roman consul, who practises the new Christian religion, in secret. He sold her to Gandãlfr in exchange for information about the followers of Nerthus and what he perceives is dark *drycræft* on Wihtland. I believe he is behind the murder of the royal messenger, my friend and oath sworn hearth companion. Although I doubt this will ever be proven. I could not save him, but I can save Bertr. She was used by Gandãlfr for amusement to any visitor who would pay ample coin. He is every inch the poison dwarf that people charge him with!"

"I have heard enough to condemn Gandãlfr," Eystein exploded, "Let us get back to the island with all speed."

"Covering our tracks before we depart is a given!" Bjartr ordered, observing the naïve travellers already mounting their steeds. And so Eystein, muttering apologies under his breath, booted the still glowing fire to dust, careful to place leaves and detritus over the fire circle.

But it was a wasted effort, for as they galloped out of the safety of the forest into open heath land, they saw the darkened silhouette of six horsemen, waiting, studying them from the ridge.

"Agh!" exclaimed Eystein, "What is this before us now, a welcoming party or a killing rout?"

Bertr stifled a shriek. Kenward wrapped her up entirely within the large woollen shawl. It would have looked like he was carrying home a boar, but for the fact that the fine woollen shawl was far too good for a dead boar!

Eystein stepped his horse up to Bjartr, "Are they Regnense?"

"Hard to tell", he replied, but before he could go on, the blackened figures made their move with arms aloft, holding spears, as they charged. Now poor Bertr screamed high and long. The terrifying sound echoed into the night.

Eystein and Bjartr crossed their chests in unison, to hold the hilt of their swords in readiness. But the horsemen came to a sudden and jarring halt, just two spear lengths away.

The bearded and plaited man, who seemed to be the leader spoke out in a dialect so very different from Warinni that Eystein barely managed to understand.

"Who is it that dares to cross Regnense land without permission?"

"I am Eystein Wahl, *Ealdorðegn* to the *Cyng* of Wihtland. I am on urgent royal business and I had no time to seek permission from your lords." Eystein dismounted, knelt, and presented his sword to the leader as a token of peace.

"I offer you my sword in peace." It was a great gesture in defence of their safe passage. The leader studied the sword, smiled, then accepted what was a beautifully crafted family heirloom, so suddenly forsaken, Eystein momentarily drooped. But there was no help for it. The girl's life was worth much more than a piece of metal.

"And who is that bundled in the shawl?" the second man asked, pointing a misshapen and grubby finger towards Kenward. He had been quietly studying the group before them. "I know you" he said pointing at Kenward. "You are the messenger who comes though these parts, but always alone. Why the party?"

Bertr was forced to peek out from behind the shawl.

"Ah, a slave maiden with a coin price on her head no doubt!" said the third man.

Kenward then swiftly dug into his bag to produce a large and heavy pouch of coins. He rattled them at the Regnenses.

"Here take this to save her head!" He threw the pouch over to the third man who accepted it with a rotten -toothed smile.

"You will have our protection through Regnenses land" said the leader, until you meet with Belgic, who are your allies. Stay away from the coast path, for they are *Rōmãnisc* and will have links to the Romans from whom you are trying to flee."

He turned his horse giving the girl Bertr a wide smile, nodding in appreciation of her bravery.

And for Bertr, a sudden release from all the tension, the impending horror, gave way to tears of relief. She could at last see a new horizon in her young life.

With their protection assured, the small band of riders skirted the forests, rounded the ancient yews, where the archers made their bows. It was green undulating hills, soft moorland and sparse *tunstede*. And so, they barely met a soul. The interior of *Sûð Seaxe* was unpopulated. The Regnense had kept to the coast where trade with the Gauls and Frisians proved more profitable. And so why should they move inland? It was this realisation that made Eystein grind his teeth. His oath-sworn and precious sword had been given away for nothing. The Regnense scouts had duped him. An unforgivable act within tribal honour and courtesy.

And as they neared the border with Belgicus, he saw his chance for retribution, as the scouts suddenly re-appeared on the horizon, dramatically waving their spears. Eystein thudded his heels into the horse's flanks, instantly speeding into a gallop. Bjartr realising the hostile action could escalate into bloody injury, chased after him.

As they neared the men, the leader of the Regnense jumped from his horse in one leaping movement, to land feet apart, holding Eystein's sword before him. He was laughing so much the sword shook in his grip. Eystein immediately leapt from his horse as they ground to a halt. He was seething, with fists showing the white of his knuckles. Bjartr fully expected the giant

Warinni to floor and pummel the man into the ground. Bjartr knew he could not bring the giant down himself. He barely reached his shoulder, and so he leapt in front of Eystein instead, screaming…

"*Giese ācwellan gif þu sculan!*
Hwæðre eall ūre blōd willan socian þes elðèodig molde!"
"Yes, kill them if you must!
But all our blood will soak this foreign soil."

He was pounding Eystein's chest with every word, as he walked backwards with every footfall of Eystein's.
Eystein bellowed….
"*Þu sweord ðīefð!*
Þu are forwgrean fram ārian und þu āwerinan þæt twā-nebb fram Loki!"
"You're sword thief!
You are forfeit of honour and you wear the two-face of Loki!"

He was starring wildly at the Regnense, who began to back away realising the imminent danger.

"It was a jest! Here, take your sword!" the man, now alarmed, spluttered, pushing the ill-fated sword into Eystein's chest.

"Take it, by the gods, we have no time to dwell on this" hissed Bjartr, turning Eystein around, his precious oath-sworn sword gripped tightly in his fist. They mounted and galloped away from the thieves in scout's clothing, into the friendly land of the Belgic. They rode into the dawn of a new day, reaching Portchester by noon. A *cnearr* already laden with goods, whose captain knew Kenward, was easily persuaded to take them the short distance to home.

It was now, on the *cnearr*, that Bertr emerged into the new day Pushing her cocoon away, she smiled freely, with dimpled cheeks and clean teeth. Her auburn hair caught Sunni's rays, turning it to glinting copper. She was now a radiant beauty. Kenward loved her and he did nothing to disguise it.

… … … … … … … … …

CHAPTER EIGHTEEN
<u>Þæt Getrýwð rícsians</u>: The Truth prevails

The efficacy of Lífa's potion saw me swim in and out of consciousness for two twilights. I feigned sleep on the third, praying to Nerthus repeatedly for the return of my brother from *Cant*. I stayed in the *Hūs* of my *Mōdor*, guarded against the unwanted and unwarranted intrusion of Gandālfr.

She woke me with a cup of fresh spring water, and yet more potion, saying with some regret that no sign of my brother's return had been seen from the look-outs positioned at the coastline. Gandālfr, she said, was ordering a special hearing to take place at the new hall, presumably to harangue me in front of all the Suevi host. I shuddered at the thought. His power, under the *Cyng,* was indomitable. He bristled with dark energy and I could feel his malevolence weaving towards me on the *wrydstafun. Mōdor* knew the imminent danger I was facing. She did not tell me of "the ordeal", which, in Gandālfr's victory, lay the possible maiming of me. I already knew.

I am not a brave person. Yet when the sword was pulled to strike me down in the world beyond the bright stone, it was anger, not fear that held me. I cannot say if I would hold myself upright with what lay before me. Imaginings sent my belly into torment until I feared I might loosen my bowels. Yet, it is not I, which is important at all. It is the Fate of my people, their life in the love of Nerthus and all we hold dear. If I was maimed, it would alter the whole life of my people. Everything would be changed. That is the power of *Wyrd*. *Wyrd byð swiðost.*

The call came suddenly. It was twilight of the seventh day. I was not prepared and so *Mōdor* bustled the messengers away saying the hearing would not take place until I was healed. She was never a lady to cross, and she became a *spakōna* to harry them away. No doubt this would be relayed to Gandālfr, who would then twist and turn it to present a lie as the truth.

I made ready. I tightened the Suevian knot in my hair, until my forehead was tense. I braided two powerful prayers to Nerthus and Wōden into my falling hair, singing the words softly. I placed my girdle of *drycræft* pouches about my waist. Including within the soft leather, my silvered boar foot. If I was to be accused of black *drycræft,* dark witchery, then I would present myself as the *spakōna* that I am!

So *Mōdor* and I walked the long spear lengths over to *Etdreðecumb* and as we walked on that warm twilight, I saw that Gandālfr had indeed been very busy in hustling the people. As before, the Suevi host were on the move. They nodded to us as they passed, some smiled and sent unspoken prayers over to us. Others just simply passed us by.

I held my head high, and walked on past them. The perfumes coming from the flowers hidden in hedges and filling the meadows released my heart from the pain. *Mōdor* picked jasmine and honeysuckle for me to breathe in their peace. They calmed my nerves and I thanked the *sāwol* in soft words and feelings sent.

The torches of the grand hall crackled in the dimming light. Shadows of my kinsmen wafted past the torches in silence, like wraiths. I nearly doubled up with the fear, a sharp pain that knotted my belly. *Mōdor* held onto me tightly, whispering prayers to our gods and goddesses. *Ealdmōdor* had warned me. This was my test, and I held my Heron wing, gripping it close over my heart.

As we walked towards the *Cyng* seat where Wihtleig was ensconced, upright and stern, to his right stood my *Fæder* and opposite him, the stinking dwarf. Gandālfr was smirking and twitching in anticipation of the show he was about to perform! I could not see Eileifer. I turned my head frantically to find him. *Fæder* slowly shook his head imperceptibly and nodded towards the *Cyng*.

By the gods, I shouted inwardly, he has banned Eileifer! Just within my vision I saw Gandālfr clasp his hands behind his back, grinning with his blackened teeth on show. He was in his supreme moment.

I was made to stand to the left. *Mōdor* left me, reluctantly moving over to be with my *Fæder*. I felt so suddenly, totally bereft, my soul shrank and fear became all-consuming. Without Eileifer, or my brother, it was only my parents who could speak in my defence. It would be viewed as a partisan defence.

Wihtleig stood slowly, panning the audience, his kinsmen within the grand hall. And he spent some moments gauging their feelings. He was a master at commanding an audience and he could feel high drama about to play out.

"Mín ðèodscipe, wè gaderian hèr beneoðan mín diht æt geāscian a hefig oncunnan fram blæc misdæd drycræft began bí Dagrun Wahl stān-warian und kinswif fram þeat Warinni. Þes oncunnan is made bí mín swæs drymānn und gewita!"

"My people, we are here under my command to hear about a serious charge of dark, evil witchcraft performed by Dagrun Wahl, stone-defender and kinswoman of the Warinni. This charge is made by my own magician and is witnessed!"

I heard gasps from my kinsmen coming from several places in the hall. Then total hushed silence, as if the words from their *Cyng* needed to be filtered into their minds. And that he was saying those terrible words at all, for in our world *drycræft* and *wyrd* join and weave within and around all our lives. It was a terrible thing.

"I turn to Gandālfr," Wihtleig summoned in a deep voice, "to put his accusation forward to be heard by us all"

Gandālfr leapt forward, an intense, compelling glaze filled his eyes. He too scanned the Suevi host, whose gaze was fixed upon him. He let forth in a dramatic torrent of words, gesticulating wildly, which left me numb in horror.

"Blæc misdǽd wicci, hǽglesse! Þu āgan ābannan þæt wæterhǽddre bí lèasung und hātan þu Folde Mōdor! Hit onspec þæt sāwol of Elíse! Þu ābannan þæt wuduelfen und þæt wæterœlf hwā býne þæt sāwol of þæt geong spakōna!"

"Black, evil witch, sorceress! You have called up the water-serpent by lying and calling her your Earth Mother. She claimed the soul of Elíse! You have called the wood-elf and water-elf who infested the soul of the young priestess!"

There came loud gasps of horror that rippled alarmingly around the hall. I stared at the floor, and willed the rushes not to come up and meet me again. But as I stared, not able to see those around me, anger began to boil within me. This was an immeasurably huge injustice, on me, my faith, my family and my kin! A lie, and people of the lie cannot be allowed to win!

I looked up and stared right into the glazed, mad eyes of Gandālfr.

I screamed my anger and agony straight back at him.

"Þes is eall ālèogans! Þu are a lèogere Gandālfr, drymānn æt ūre Cyng Wihtleig. Þu are forwyrcan!

"This is all lies! You are a liar Gandālfr, magician to our Cyng Wihtleig. You are forfeit!"

Gandālfr's head seemed to spring forward, his neck stretched and arched. The look that came into his eyes now was pure quintessential evil. And with this energy broiling in his body, he made for me. Then stopped only a few paces away, as if some clever thought entered his sick mind to stop him from attacking me in front of all the Suevian host and his *Cyng*.

"*Hōrcwere fram þæt deofol!* Whore of the devil!" he screamed, spittle building at the side of his twisting mouth, "*Þèos māndǣd willan biscpríce þu maimed!* This deed of evil will see you maimed!

"*Ic gecígan mín gewita.* I call my witness."

Whereupon a man that had been in the shadow, against an oak post, sidled forward into the flickering light. I gasped, as did my *Mōdor,* for we both recognised the squat little figure. It was the priest! Oh, how enemies are made in the seconds' thought and action, I thought, as he began his testimony. He was not of our confederacy. His dialect was strange to our ears, but he spoke nonetheless and he was heard.

"I have had the honour of knowing Gandālfr for many *sumors*", he began and I knew he too, was lying. A passing acquaintance had suddenly built into a hearth companionship.

"And it is testimony that he is magician to your *Cyng*, Wihtleig. Therefore, my testimony bears weight. I was deliberately turned away from the *Drímeolce gerihte.*"

"They made light of their sacrifice of humans to this *serpent,*" he spat the word, "so I doubled back and hid in the forest near to their grove. I witnessed the entire rite in all its gory detail!"

Now the kinsmen in the hall gasped in shock at the irreverence of that fact. This priest was not a pagan. A pagan would never have broken that golden rule. Disrespect for the Goddess was tantamount to devil worship, not the other way around.

"I saw this Dagrun Wahl disappear under a magic spell into the bright stone itself. And that she must have consorted with the devil himself to be accorded such magic! Then I witnessed her coming forward to speak with the serpent who had overtaken the soul of the young priestess. This girl was near death when the serpent left her. This Dagrun Wahl then performed more magic on her, uttering spells and calling in the wood elves. I have been told this Elíse is now a broken spirit."

"And she," he turned to point an accusing finger at me, "is the witch and sorceress who is to be blamed and shamed and maimed!"

My *Mōdor* sprang forward.

"I wish to bear testimony to the fact that all this priest has said is untrue! My *dohtor* is none of those names she has been accused of. She was healing Elíse from *Ælf-shot*, which had invaded her mind after our goddess, Nerthus, left her. Dagrun is a wonderful healer. She has healed many people in our *ceasterwic*. And as to the disappearance into the bright stone. She was given a vision of times to come, where a new religion will conflict with our older and more nature bound one. And this, it would seem, is a rehearsal of those times!"

"What is that which you keep hidden under your tunic?" *Mōdor* pointed sharply to something beneath his tunic.

The priest fidgeted, shuffling his feet as if he would gladly have fled the hall. Gandālfr glared malevolently at *Mōdor*.

"Show us!" the *Cyng* commanded.

The priest gingerly pulled on the leather thong around his neck to reveal a large polished wooden and uneven cross. The symbol of the incoming religion. He then grabbed hold of it and turned about to face the Suevi host, his back to the Cyng.

"Our Christ, our king, died on the cross for our sins to be forgiven! If this *Wicci* would renounce her pagan ways and join us then no harm will come to her! All will be forgiven."

"*FORSTOPPIAN*" roared Wihtleig, jumping up from his throne seat and in two strides grabbed the shoulders of the priest to turn him about, to face him.

"You, priest, are putting your testimony to fault. None of my kinsmen would turn their back to me, their *Cyng* who is in command of this hearing. It is not for you or your Christ to pass a judgement in this matter we are here to discuss."

"Are there others here who would wish to speak in testimony of Dagrun Wahl, or Gandālfr?" The *Cyng* turned to scan the hall.

A voice, slight and barely audible, spoke out,

"Our honourable *Cyng*," said a petite woman in the middle of the crowd, "I have a testimony, spoken on behalf of my people."

"Come to the front *Cwèn*", said Wihtleig, "we cannot see you. Come."

She made her way to stand beside me.

"My lord, I know this woman to be good and kind. She healed my child last *sumor* of a crippling ache in her bones. And if I may speak about this fight now between two religions. My people, the Aviones, though small, are devoted to the Suevi confederacy. We are also believers of this Christ religion. Yet the talk today insults us. We are angry that we may be counted as vicious, hateful people! We are in respect of your ways, Lord, and would honour them. We only ask that you may allow us to practise our way in peace. That is what our Christ talks of.... peace. So, let that lead us!"

"*Giese, Gíese, Giese!*" came the roar of the people, which nearly drowned out the crash made by the massive oak doors being thrust open.

In marched my wonderful giant of a brother, beard swaying and hair flaying at his rolling gait, shouting above the din. His arm stretched upward holding a package "*FORWREGAN, FORWREGAN*! Wrongly accused, wrongly accused! my *sweostor* is innocent."

I breathed in a deep lungful of air. My life had just been returned to me, and the barrel of tears that made their way up to my throat were choked back in my relief and my love for Eystein. He wrapped me in his arms and I released days of anguish. All before the entire Suevi host who cheered and clapped.

Gandālfr had in those few moments shuffled sideways to make his escape. But my *Fæder*, who was more than twice the size of the poisonous little man, tackled him and pinioned him firmly under his massive foot!

I pulled myself upright and turned to see two strangers, a man and small girl standing together, awkwardly, wondering what to do or say.

"My Lord *Cyng*, I do apologise," Eystein exclaimed, "This moment of re-union is very important. We have discovered a deeper plot than anyone could have imagined. These people," he pointed towards the two strangers, "have suffered grievous harm at the hands of this poisonous magician, Gandālfr, your erstwhile companion. Who it now transpires, has used your royal seal and your hearth companionship to conduct acts of deceit, tortuous harm to others, only to further his personal glory and wealth. His coin is evilly accrued. He does not care about allegiance or loyalty. He has conspired with Romans, Rōmānisc, Christians and Pagans to enrich his own pocket."

"Let me give you the witness evidence of my words. Kenward is a royal messenger to your nephew Eileifer, who stands outside, honouring your dismissal of him from this hearing. I would now ask you to invite him back in." Eystein bowed low, knowing his words might anger the old *Cyng*.

Wihtleig stood still, slowly glancing at the prostate figure of his trusted companion. A look of pure sorrow washed across his beaten face, and for a tremor of a heartbeat, I saw him face his own death. Then anger, not unlike my own, seethed within him, but no-one would see the *Cyng* let go. The only sign of the hidden inferno was bunched hands that saw the white of his knuckles.

"Bring him in", he said softly, "I have miss-treated my own blood kin it would seem!"

Eystein signalled to the back of the hall and within two heartbeats, which in my own chest pounded like a drum, Eileifer came in. I could not hold back if my life had depended upon it. I ran to him and was enfolded in his arms, so tightly, all the fear and anger just simply evaporated into the twilight. I was safe. I looked up into his eyes, his soul, and saw tears well up in his.

We turned and walked together back to our *Cyng*.

"When this piece of false drama is played out," Wihtleig said softly to us, "I will have you wed. There will be the biggest and longest hand-fasting celebration this island has ever seen. You have my word on it."

He turned to the couple, standing together, Kenward, whom I later came to know well, had his arm firmly around the diminutive, fragile girl. She held a rare shining beauty as she flashed a smile at me. Then it disappeared, to be replaced by soul-emptiness. I knew then that she had suffered terribly at the hands of Gandālfr. She will require treatment, I thought, as the *Cyng* asked them their names. She was called Bertr and I liked her immediately. They told their story to the *Cyng*, clearly without faltering. Even Wihtleig commended her courage in the face of the suffering she had undergone. I had to restrain Eileifer when he realised his oath-sworn hearth companion had been slain in a terrible way.

"We will call his restless spirit to us," I whispered. "We will be in vigil for his spirit and help him find *Neorxenawang*"

The anger of both the old *Cyng*, who seemed to age visibly these last dramatic moments, and Eileifer, made the air sizzle. *Fæder*, released Gandãlfr from his immense foot, and *Mōdor* came to join us as we waited for the *Cyng's* decree. It did not take long.

He motioned with his arm to our blacksmith. This large man knew exactly what was needed from his foundry some spear lengths away! This would mean a long wait and I looked at Eileifer in dismay. Gandãlfr guessed his fate and lay huddled in the rushes, guarded by two burly Eudose. Yet it was but a short while before the blacksmith returned, although it seemed as if the earth stopped and caught her breath. He lumbered in panting, holding two branding irons, which he then placed in the central fire. He whispered to the *Cyng* that he had raided a fellow blacksmith's store nearby, belonging to an Avione, whom he would reward.

"Stand on your feet, you liar and coward!" Wihtleig hissed at his former companion.

He was bustled forward by his guards and made to stand in the glowing heat of the fire, now white hot in its centre, where the irons lay, already glowing red. Grotesque shadows danced across his face, bringing his grimace into sharp relief. My kinsmen looked on in horror. It was so rare an occurrence in our peaceful world that this awful punishment had to be administered at all.

Wihtleig turned to speak his decree. "*Mín cynnmen, Ic am frèorigferð! Þæt lèasung fãcenfful, wælgíefre gecynd fram Gandãlfr is geresp! Hè willan bí Giefan þæt ceorfingísen on his heafod und his ferhð. Hè willan bí ãdrifan æt þæt wilde weald fram þæt west!*"

"My kinsmen, I am sad at heart! The lying, deceitful murderous nature of Gandãlfr is proven! He will be given the branding irons, on his head and on his heart. He will be banished to the wild forest of the west!"

There was a shocked silence throughout the hall. Again, no-one uttered a single word in defense of the disgraced magician. Then several *cwèns* began to hustle the young out of the hall, Wihtleig signaling that it was permissible. There was a horror about to take place here, and only the hard of heart should be present. I wished I could join the young, but it was impossible. I was to witness the punishment on a man who had tried to destroy so much of my life and those around me.   One Eudose giant held the squat little man's shoulders, pulling his arms behind his back. Gandãlfr yelped. And then he struggled helplessly as the other Eudose pulled the first iron from the fire, white hot. He pulled Gandãlfr's head back, raised the iron and plunged it hard onto his forehead.

The high-pitched scream that rang long and loud around the hall, the sizzling and smell of burning flesh, will stay with me all my life. It ended in a guttural moan as his head slumped forward to hit his chest. They waited until he had regained consciousness. They tore open his tunic to expose his chest. The full *lèasung* branding iron hit his chest and simply fried his skin away, blood oozing from the gaping and smoking wound. Gandãlfr screamed again through gritted blackened teeth until mercifully he completely lost his senses and fell to the rushes. He was branded a liar for the rest of his life, however long that may be. For, in the banishment to the western forest, with no coin or shelter, he would be at the mercy of the Silures, the forest people who guarded *Mōnã*, the sacred Isle of the Druids. And it is said they guarded it mercilessly, seeing all intruders as the enemy. Wihtleig knew this. Consigning his shamed magician to a horrific and slow death was intensely cruel. I saw my beloved slowly shake his head. He looked at me with great sadness in his eyes. We both knew revenge leaves a bitter taste.

Gandālfr was carried away completely unconscious, the Eudose gripping his dead weight by the shoulders, as his feet, still twitching, were dragged along the rush floor. The hall released a communal sigh of relief. Tables were hastily brought forward from their resting place against the walls and the mead soon flowed to drown out those terrible moments. Eyvindr, my lovely younger story-teller brother sprang forward to begin a song about love re-found, in honour of us, Eileifer and me.

Wihtleig banged his heavy mead mug on the table.

"Kinsmen, before we celebrate the commission for change, and our soon-to-be-wed *Cyng* and *Cwèn* all blushing and excited, I must now give notice to the *ðing*, which will take place at *Mōnã's* fullness, three twilights from now. Bring three of your trusted men and women to the stone circle at *Sudmōr,* where we will ask the Gods and Goddesses to bless and confirm the rightness of name and true intention of our people."

And so, the revelries grew to banish the horror. Eyvindr sang us his love song, we snuggled up happily to each other, then quietly disappeared when the mead made thinking obsolete and no one missed us. We made for the trees in the darkness, where only the forest animals, woken by our loving, witnessed the joy.

… … … … … … … … …

CHAPTER NINETEEN
Þæt Sāwol's æthweorfan: The Soul's return

    Eileifer and I had our commitment to release the trapped earthbound soul of his hearth and oath-sworn companion, murdered so brutally and whose body was left somewhere in *Cant*. Kenward asked to be part of the vigil, which of course included the fragile looking Bertr. I had reached the conclusion that this little *Cwèn* was anything but fragile! I had asked Kenward, who knew his oath-sworn best, where on the Isle was his favoured place. His *sāwol* would find it a blessing to be led there. His name had been Wimund, an Anglii. He came from the large farming *tunstede* close to the river on the *Breredingas* lands. His *Godcund* was near the river that flowed to the large sea. An old copse of pussy-goat willow hugged the waterline. And here he made this sanctuary his own.

    It was too close to the Romans for anyone's comfort, so we began our vigil journey at night with little assistance from Mōnā. Our tallow torches were small and smoky, giving off only sufficient light to prevent serious footfalls and we extinguished them completely, in total hushed silence, as we past the Roman holdings, near *Wihtlægsbyrig* where the general was billeted in our once royal home. We could hear laughter and the clashing of metal so close to us, we crouched and crawled our way past. Sentries had been posted and I saw their shadowed forms walk past us not a spear's length away. If caught, we would be made prisoners with a high ransom as royals, to be paid for our freedom.

It was with huge relief that we passed unnoticed, and walked through the pasture land, hugging trees that lined the meadows. Past the Roman building used as a store for grain throughout the valley and which stood nearby the *hūs* of the consul. I noticed as we crept past in the shadows, that he was creating a villa-type building. It had extensions of two-levels, lime-painted and shining white in the night. This was a big Roman footprint sitting on our land.

We reached the sanctuary, laid out our furs, mead, and I untied my pouch of *drýcræft* laying out the stones and herbs before me. Each stone had been taken from our ancestor circle, empowered for use anywhere. Each stone held a part of the *sãwol* of our forebears. I knew each one, and I called to them softly as I laid the circle within the pussy-willow glade. I felt their energy arrive, *Giese! Giese! Ðonc.*

I turned to Kenward whispering to him to silently ask permission of our Ancestors, before stepping into the circle. They would protect the tender bruised *sãwol* of Wimund. He looked askance at me, but closed his eyes and stepped in. I wished to link physical man and spiritual man together by calling to our Goddess Nerthus and her ancient consort and god of the Anglii, Inguz. I hoped together they would guide the lost soul of Wimund home.

I leant forward to Kenward, whispering, "Imagine, please, the place of his burial. Only you know of this. Bind with this torn spirit and help him home, to fly here. It is the very finest gift you give him. Eternal rest and peace in *Neorxenawang"*

Eileifer stood with Bertr, silently in the shadow of the ancient trees, watching me, with an intense gaze. He had never seen me perform as *spakōna* before. I began to hesitate, wondering what he might be thinking or feeling. I turned to smile slightly at him and he returned with a broader one and a nod of approval. I relaxed and drew in power from all around me.

I did not welcome in the forest dwellers but sang straight to Nerthus and Inguz.

I intoned each syllable slowly, gathering in resonance until I reached the perfect pitch and frequency.

"NNNNN.Errrr, thhhh uuusssssssss ssssss,"

The sound rang through the ancient trees, echoed over to the river. And again, I intoned the sounds to reach deep within the watery depths. And after the third calling, I felt her rise.

"Nerthus, Nerthus, Nerthus,

Ūre ælfūenu Foldè Mōdor

Ūre frèond Wimund sūsi sāwol is cirman æt fègan þu in Neorxenawang.

Fultumain Hine!

Nerthus, Nerthus, Nerthus,

Our beautiful Earth Mother,

Our friend's torn soul is crying out to join you in your sacred meadow home.

Help him out!"

I watched the shoulders of Kenward begin to shake uncontrollably, his head bowed to his chest.

"Hold on! Kenward", I said urgently, "You must not let go. Imagine please that Wimund's soul is already rising from his muddy grave in an unknown land. Neither Nerthus nor Inguz can assist if emotion blocks them out"

I hurried on. Taking a large mouthful of mead, I blew onto all the ancestor stones, a gift to them from our physical earth. Then entering the circle, I focused into Kenward's soul and knew it was ready for the journey. I took a deeper mouthful and sprayed

Kenward over his head, his heart and his stomach. It shocked him from his emotions and I knew it worked, as he shut his eyes and took a deep inward breathe.

Inguz would come.

"Iiiiiii nnnnnnu gggggguuuuzzzzzzzz."
I intoned three times. Ending with the rune tone.
"NNNNNnnnnnnnn."

"Inguz, Inguz, Inguz,"

"Gemæcca fram Nerthus wè ãcsian þu æt fēgan ūre Foldè Mōdor æt brengan þæt sāwol of ūre frèond to Neorxenawang."

"Inguz, Inguz, Inguz"

"Consort of Nerthus. We ask you to join our Earth Mother to bring the spirit of our friend to the Meadow of Nerthus."

Silence, the whole woodland held its breath, as did I, for I wondered if anything at all would happen. I had never asked a non-initiate to play such a role. Then, suddenly the whole area erupted in energy. Swirls of wind cascaded around us. And I saw Kenward, deeply in trance, lift his whole body upwards, head taut and his neck straining, muscles bulging out of his skin. His feet were now barely touching the ground. His arms were outstretched to meet the swirling, aquamarine mist that had suddenly arisen from the water. Nerthus was coming! Inguz had entered the body of Kenward. The mist thickened to a fog as it swirled around the stretched body of Kenward. I heard him scream. The mist swirled into a vortex upwards to the night sky and disappeared. Kenward collapsed to hit the earth with a hard thud. He was unconscious, and still in trance.

I put fur hides about him. The pussy-willow copse settled into an eerie silence. For how long we remained, I could not guess? A few heartbeats, or many? We just remained still. Then the fur hides moved, and Kenward shifted his body to sit, watching us all staring at him in grateful amazement.

"He is home", he said simply, "And I have seen *Neorxenawang* and it is indescribably beautiful. My wish is to join him there, but he said I must wait."

He stood slowly, in some pain, and I looked into his soul. This tragedy was more than a companion lost. This was the beautiful and rare man to man love, of a kind that may never come to him again in this lifetime. I hugged him closely and for a long time, while his tears flowed at last and his heart broke. When his heart became empty, he simply walked away into the night. I thought we might never catch sight of him again. Eileifer was desolate also, but refused to show it. I went to him and kissed him, wrapped my arms about his huge chest and waited for the dawn, as Sunni was subtly showing her gentle glow.

Bertr stared after Kenward, and then without hesitation chased after the shadow who had saved her and loved her. She would coax him back, I was sure.

… … … … … … … …

CHAPTER TWENTY
Þæt meolc-hwít augurs: The milk-white auguries

Tacitus (69)

A family debate, a big discussion, had arisen only hours after the most tumultuous time for our Warinni tribe. The dust had hardly settled when tempers rose. I chose to stay silent. Who would represent our tribe at the *ðing?*

My *Fæder*, Folkvarthr was Hèahwita, High Councillor and required to attend. Similarly, Eystein as Chief Thane was expected to bring his presence to the Ancestor circle. But Eyvindr, my younger brother, was a *Wítega* and *scōp*, wise man and story teller. Who would regale our mead hall with those stories for *sumors* to come, if not our Eyvindr?

And then, for the women, it was between *Mōdor* and myself. Only one of us could attend. We chose to simply choose each other and burst out laughing at the whole drama of it! We loved each other too much to quarrel over such a thing. But men have a different blood running through their veins where ego and arrogance ruled. I went to my beloved and pleaded for him to intervene.

"Hah!" he exploded, without hesitation, "my beautiful *Cwèn*, do you seriously believe I would come between two warring

Warinni's? I prefer my two arms intact, and legs to move me forward! Think again, sweeting!"

I did. "Would conferring with a fourth party settle the argument, with all body parts intact, and it would be binding?"

"Explain", Eileifer looked intrigued.

"The white horses of course, horse-talker!" I laughed and immediately saw the answer had been given. Let *Sāwol* give the answer.

And so, it was, that same day, at early twilight, the white horses saw a very rare event indeed. The Warinni host with their *Cyng* traipsing over field and meadow to the paddock where the horses enjoyed their life of leisure and loving care of Eastmund.

The lad had changed greatly, thanks to Eileifer, who kneeled to greet him as ever, and was rewarded by the hugest grin and a warm hug. There was no trace of the embedded fear about him now. New clothes had been made for him by the weaving women and they spoilt him with food baskets and honey. His pale blue eyes glowed, for now we could clearly see them both, as could his friends, the white horses. His wayward hair was kept in check. He lived at the stables. His mother would visit him regularly. She loved him dearly as her only son, but the father never came. Of that we were thankful. I believe Eastmund saw Eileifer as his father now.

"Eastmund," Eileifer said, putting his hand through the lad's tousled hair, "how are my royal chargers? Do they talk with you, and what are they saying, *beorn?*"

"Ahh, we have good times, my Lord," he answered, easily, confidently, "They play games with me. They change their signals, and my mind must skip about, keeping up with them! The old one is worse. But I will get the better of him, sire!"

My Warinni family looked on, and I sensed approval and a warming towards my husband-to-be. he was a Nuithone, of royal Wōden's blood. Yet, our wonderful All Father had many sides, and they saw now, that Eileifer, nephew to the Wihtleig *Cyng* had inherited the gentle aspect of Wōden, the healer and Wiseman.

Most certainly a hearth *Cyng* and not a warrior. "Talk before swords", as my *Mōdor* often quoted in the heat of a man scrap.

Eileifer spoke with Eastmund, who smiled broadly and scampered over to the aging white stallion, who skipped a step when he saw him coming. It was coded language and beautiful to watch. The old horse obviously loved this lad for he bowed his great head down to reach Eastmund, who joined him head to head. Then the dance began, footfalls backwards, stamping foreleg, with muscles rippling and nostrils snorting in an intricate dance of signals and feelings.

Then suddenly they both halted, in a frozen moment, the stallion broke free, muscles juddering in a wave of fear, snorting loudly with a stream of hot breath escaping into the warm meadow air. He galloped to the far edge of the paddock, staying frozen to the wicker fence.

Eastmund ran as fast as his stunted legs would allow, loping from side to side. He reached Eileifer heaving for breath.

"What ails the old giant?" Eileifer asked looking deep into Eastmund's eyes, "The truth *beorn*, and quickly!"

"My Lord, I cannot say for sure. It is all muddled. The fear got in the way for me to know rightly. The Warinni family will face a tragedy. That I know. The old one saw something happening that will injure them forever. Nothing will be the same after this. And it is soon."

Eileifer sighed deeply. "Go tend the old one", he said, "Take some fresh apples from the stable."

He made back towards us, then turned around, "And Eastmund", he shouted, "Well done young sire! You have the full respect of your *Cyng!*"

For a moment, I thought Eastmund would simply burst with pride, as his chest blew out, and the huge smile filled his face. He turned and loped off to the stables and we were faced with the dilemma that could not be answered.

Wyrd flowed in an ever-intricate weave, for Aslaug, who was our *Ealdmōdor* could not attend the *ðing,* her chest was ailing her and I felt anguished that I had not attended her with herbs. Our relations had been poor at best since the *Drímeolce gewita* when Elíse, the young priestess in training, who followed her heart, and recently disappeared from our *ceasterwic* with her beloved, Dægberht from the Reudignians.

So, it fell to me to be *Spakōna* for our ceremonial *ðing*. That set me to focus on all the preparations within the stone circle. *Mōdor* elegantly elected to withdraw from the family fray, to allow my brother Eyvindr to attend, saying she would much prefer to hear the dramatic Telling from him, as the Suevian story-teller, in the new mead hall.

… … … … … … … …

CHAPTER TWENTY-ONE
Ðèodscipe fram þæt Wiht: People of the Spirit

The Wihtwara

Mōnā's full face was shimmering down at me in a cloudless night sky. Her face was clear and I felt my words to her jostle for supremacy: Bring peace, peace for our people. Let the reign of Eileifer be honourable and just. Protect him and my family. All these feelings tumbled around my head until I realised the inner chaos. I was the one that needed peace. Trauma had settled on my soul, sitting there waiting for release and no one but myself could let it go.

I was alone, in the willow copse, whose branches stretched over to hide and protect our ancestor circle. I pushed my palms into the warm earth, feeling the moist soil push up and surround my hands. I needed to bring my soul back to be with the rhythm of the Earth Mother. Her song, I could not hear, yet until that came back to me and travelled with me, I could not be *Spakōna* this night. I needed to prepare for the ancestors. So, I needed to be ready.

I hit the earth with my full face down, taking a deep breath inward. Love washed over me, then the rhythm began, a low pulse that became louder then softer. When it was echoing in waves within me, I slowly got up, eyes closed to keep the inner focus and felt my way to the circle. Each ancestor stone had a sound, unique, and unalterable. As I touched each stone, that sound came and I held it, humming softly to myself. Then another and another, until I was singing the Ancestor's song. I went to the centre where the singing stone stood upright, pointed and close to Mōnã. Placing my hands hard on him, the cool and pitted rough stone patterned on the palms of my hands, I sang with full resonance into his centre. And he answered back with a full echo. My head was clear, my heart at peace. And there I remained until Sãga, our *nigt-gala* joined me there with Lífa. We sang the Ancestor song together. Helping each other to remain completely focused.

The ðing had begun.

Cyng Wihtlæg arrived with Eileifer at his side. It was a mark of respect that he saw him as his equal. Large torches carried by the people, brought a staggering light to the circle, and I fought to keep the focus. Everyone wore the Suevi knot, some braided with prayers to Nerthus, Wōden or Thunōr, and all came in complete solemnity for this was our Ancestor's home. There were representatives from all the tribes.

Wihtlæg walked to the singing stone and raised his hands to the night sky. We hushed our song to a whisper, never stopping. We walked away from the centre to allow our *Cyng* of Wihtland to speak.

"Mōnã, gemæcca æt Sunni, brengan þín ǽht, ǽt bletsian þæt Foldè, ūre eard.
Thunōr, wè standan in ārian fram þín bletsunga fram regn æt ūre bere-wæstm."
"Wōden, Eall-Fæder þu are ūre fǽle foregenga fram duguð, hǽland, scōp und ceāp-man. Þin blōd cernan þurh þín eafora und dohtors hèr on Wihtland. Wè ārian þu þes niht.
Andswaru ūre hātan æt nemnian ūre ðèodscipe in frið und ānnes"

"Mōnã, consort to Sunni, bring your power to bless the earth, our land.

Thunōr, we stand in honour of your blessings of rain on our crops.
Wōden, All Father, you are our beloved Ancestor of tested warriors, healers, poets and negotiators. Your blood runs through our sons and daughters, here on Wihtland.
We honour you this night. Answer our call to name our people in unity and peace"

Giese, Giese, Giese came murmurings through the circle of our Suevi host, standing in reverence within the ancestor stone circle. Each group was holding a torch, the flames flickered in the slight breeze, casting a dance of shadows over the stones. Faces half-illuminated looked expectantly at their *Cyng*.

Suddenly, a harsh wind blew up from nowhere and within that rush, a raven swooped down to sit on the apex of the singing stone, directly above the head of Wihtlæg, who gave the rarest, broadest smile anyone had seen from him in many a moon. His *Fæder* has arrived! People gasped, and one man fell to his knees, praying to Wōden for even rain and sun to bring a good harvest. It was the ever-present prayer of my kinsmen. The winter was nearing and the harvest was close.

"Who amongst you wishes to speak with your All-Father?", Wihtlæg intoned loudly, his face sweeping the circle.

Hesitantly, an aging *cwèn* shuffled from the shadows. Her frail, wispy hair was tied in a tight suevian knot yet still it trailed nearly to her waist and swayed as she hobbled forward. She grasped a staff in her white knuckled bony hand. Her hair held one single braided prayer, intertwined with blue and turquoise thread. She was Nerthus in mortal form. And she surely had something to say!

"My Lord", she intoned in a soft lilting voice, as she bowed to Wihtlæg who in turn bowed in respect to her.

She turned her gaze upwards, a shining glaze lay over her eyes. She considered the night, even above the raven, who stared at her intently, not moving a feather. A moment of complete stillness radiated around the circle.

"All-Father, my deepest love goes to you, child god of beloved Nerthus. She who honours us and makes this island home sacred. We are abounding in all the good Fates. The *Wyrd* swims easily here. Yet it cannot always be so. Ill-fortune awaits us and knowing this, we unite in strength to heal and make good our weakest link."

"That weak link is our Ancestors may be forgotten in the changing of our tribes' common name. My grandchildren will know and honour the new name, but on their lips, I will teach our real name, Avione. And their children's children will know that Avione is where they come from. Our numbers are small here. Most of the seven tribes are still over the Germania Sea. What will they make of this?"

A loud murmuring of *Giese, Giese*! Swept around the circle.

"Accepted", called Wihtlæg, loudly, "Let this be passed also, that we all honour our old tribal names, for the generations to come. Let this not be our weakest link but the strongest, for under these stones lay the Ancestors who are Avione, Reudignians, Anglii, Warinni, Eudose, Suacones, Niuthones! We honour you and will remember you all!"

A great cheer arose. Wihtlæg turned to us, motioning us forward, for it was now the time to sing the Ancestor song. We had been quietly humming the tones. We were practised now.

We each intoned the sacred frequency note, long or interrupted, sweeping high then low. Then we harmonised until the whole circle was thrumming in an earth vibration. This was the Ancestor's song, given from the stones.

WwwwwOooo Wunjō Ōþila
LaLlllll Maaammmm Laguz Mannaz
NnnnnnEeeeeee Inguz Ehwaz
Bbbbbbb Tttttttttt Berkana Teiwaz
Zzzzzzzzz SsssssssssAlgiz Sōwulō
Aaaaaaaþþþþþþþþ Ansuz þurisaz
Hhhhhhhh IiiiiiiiiiiiiHagalaz ísaz

The people began to join in until the whole sacred land was sending us back their echo. We went into trance.

After a while the song began to change of itself. We were singing the notes differently but still all in unison. The power built up, the energy radiant.

WWWWWWWWW IIIIIIIIIII HHHHHHHHH TTTTTTTTT
WWWWWWWWW AAAAAAAAA RRRRRRRRRRRR
AAAAAAAAAAA

WIHTWARA!

The Raven cawed loudly, flew low into the circle, then swooped up and away.

"Wihtwara", the *Cyng* shouted, "our name is now Wihtwara. Let it be so."

So, on this first night of the full moon, the Suevian tribes of Wihtland became the united host of Wihtwara.

Our cousins over the narrow water got to hear about this, almost as fast as a pigeon could fly there in the Meon Valley. They became the Meonwara.

The celebrations at the new lodge began the following night of the second full moon, mead flowed, and dear Eyvindr regaled *Mōdor* with a Telling fit for the Ancestors to be re-told at many twilights. But it was to be his last, his dream of being a *scōp* never came to be. Eyvindr would not be followed by others.

Our memories of him stay frozen, sharp in our minds. I dream of this night of the *Ðing* sometimes. Before the Romans came and shattered our lives forever.

… … … … … … … … …

CHAPTER TWENTY-TWO
Foregísl: Hostage

I remember him choosing to be a *scōp* of the highest quality. He mixed the Ancestor song with the story. He had created a reed pipe from the water meadows that sang notes so close to the ones the Ancestor gave us, tears filled my eyes. It was exquisite. People were hushed, everyone wanted to soak their soul in his music. Then he made high drama of the Raven entering the stone circle, sitting aloft on the singing stone. He almost shaped himself into Raven to re-create our All-father in his shape-shifting. He jumped onto the tables cawing wildly, arms swooping, and it was then that the sound of Romans marching could be heard by all in the mead hall. And stopped my lovely brother in frozen silence. That clanking of metal in impeccable rhythm all its own, challenged the beauty of the Ancestor song. It brought it down like an injured bird to the rushes, there to stay.

A metal monster longer than any dragon stood outside our oaken door.

It was smashed in a thunderous motion. And there stood in his full armour and war helmet, the new legate and governor of the Roman legions on Wihtland. The armoured monster glinted in the firelight. His legs and arms were encased in shining hardened leather, polished relentlessly by slaves to give him the look of a Caesar, a god. His arrogance was bristling around him as he stood, legs akimbo, hands thrust at his hips in a challenging stance.

He began to roar at us in Latin.

"Hic is illicitus congregatio! Vos congregatio enim bellum. Nos volo punio vos!"

Wihtlæg strode forward to face him, speaking in our tongue.

"Þu brecan in ūre meadu heall ealswa git þu āsmiðan beadu! You break into our mead hall as if you are making war!"

And still the Roman continued shouting as if our *Cyng* was not there!

Wihtlæg straightened his back and pronounced every syllable clearly to be heard above the Roman.

"Wè anfeald mǣran þæt ācennednes fram Wihtwara, ūregeðèdes in ānnes!
Wè are ne gearwian for beadu.
Wè ānan frið! Gecwèman fēgan ūs!"

"We are simply celebrating the birth of Wihtwara, our tribes in unity!
We are not making ready for war.
We honour peace. Join us!"

The Roman continued talking and pointing towards Eyvindr.

Suddenly the *Rōmānisc* broke through the crowd gathered around our *Cyng*.

"My Lord," he shouted to Wihtlæg, "it is useless. He does not believe you. He believes you are preparing for war and he will kill all of you. There is a centuria of soldiers waiting outside for his order. He says to avoid bloodshed, he will take a hostage. He will take the storyteller for he is a fool and will perform for the Romans now!"

Mōdor shrieked and charged towards her youngest son, now kneeling on the table, shaking with fear.

Fæder pushed through past Wihtlæg and began to speak in halting Latin, stumbling over many words. The *Rōmānisc* looked at Wihtlæg.

"Folkvarthr is saying to them, that they will be taking the young man whose royal blood of Wōden runs through his veins"

The Legate smiled and pointed again at Eyvindr.

"He is saying he will then be a royal hostage and not a slave. He is taking the storyteller."

I raced towards my brother, just before the soldiers came to grab him. I hugged him tightly, crying loving words, saying rapidly "I will get you back. I am the *Cwèn,* I will get you back!"

"Warian þín heorte" I shouted after him, "Hold safe your heart", as the two soldiers gripped both his arms in a lock behind his back. My gentle, kind *fey* brother held his head high, in dignity, as he walked from us. He smiled at my *Fæder* who had tears streaking his aging face. My *Mōdor* had crumpled to the floor, sobbing, where I joined her, our hearts breaking into so many fractured pieces, they would never quite be mended.

And so, our lives splintered that night. The Warinni family was broken by an exceptionally harsh and evil Legate, who did not even remain on the island for very long. He was after bigger rewards on Britannia, hoping to become, like Vespasian, the next Caesar.

The warrior blood of Wōden fired up within Wihtlæg and he left Wihtland shortly after that night to fight the Romans with the native people in the West. He never did return.

Wihtwara was born and it bled. It was not spoken of for many moons, not in our family. But Time does heal. It was the weaving of *Wyrd*, the river of life that provides the comfort, the understanding and the love of all that is. We came to understand that it was part of a larger plan.

Eyvindr did not become a *scōp* for the Romans, despite being taken by the Legate to Britannia to "perform." It died that night. Eyvindr became a *Rōmãnisc* after many moons away. And we saw him from time to time, when he did return. He became a master craftsman for the growing industries along the river in Breredingas. And he lived his life in relative comfort within that villa complex. Yet he did keep faith with Nerthus and Wōden. He taught his children well.

CHAPTER TWENTY- THREE
Þæt Æcerbot ōlǽcung The Field remedy charm

Our lives, in the Wihtwara tribe were governed by our Gods and Goddesses, Thunōr bringing rain and Sunni heating up the crops to grow to fruition. It was a bountiful harvest this first season. There were no hands that did not grip, shape, and trim those crops. Except for the aged and infirm. They prayed. For in this, we had all offered up our own silent or whispered prayers as we worked. Our lives depended on this good harvest. And we had to prepare for the second crop of horse beans, our hardy winter crop. Eileifer commanded we take all the grain crops up to the new storage on *Etdreðecumb* hill. It was high enough to keep them dry. Barley was our main crop, with wheat, that the Romans brought to us. It was a good grain but not nearly as hardy as barley. Our warm and temperate climate favoured the growing of it though.

We favoured bean crops, as they produced those large green beans that were the staple of our stews and pottage. The children loved to eat them raw, but too many, as was often the case, meant that I was called to treat swollen bellies and intestines that were as raw as scrubbed skins! The horse beans, pinto beans as the Romans called them, grew on long tough thick stalks. We left them to dry in the fields, for all the leftover greenery hardened to tough yellow staves that when gathered, was enough to burn in our kilns for the Wihtwara pottery. Dægberht created our pottery ware in *Chestebeorg*.

When I think of our forefathers, how they lived in the forests, with poor soil that bore little grain crops, I marvelled at how they survived. They became great hunters. Now their children's children had become great farmers. Learning quickly about the soil here in Wihtland. The Anglii seemed to have a greater ability to work that soil to its very best. We looked to them for advice on the best way to sow, when and how to plough the land. They had even created a new kind of plough. It was much bigger and could make fast the work by using two men to pull and one to steer. It made deeper furrows to protect the precious seed. Our larger horses were then used to pull it, needing only one man to steer.

And then, our sacred area, where the precious hemp seed was sown. It held *drycræft*. It held the power of Wōden himself, the All Father. No other crop provided our kin with all manner of things needed to live well and the Romans were not interested in it at all! Above all else, it aided the journeying. Next to our bees, hemp was the most precious life-giver and honoured by Nerthus.

And it was here, nearing twilight, that I came to sit quietly in the field, which was now ready for the second crop to be sown. Mōnã was just reappearing from the shadow time, where all the earth's creatures and the trees simply held their breath. It created a perfect stillness. *Wyrd* became overwhelmingly powerful. It was almost too difficult to breathe, so shallow, low breathes escaped me as I knelt in the centre of the field, waiting. A large Hare appeared, standing up high on his haunches, staring straight at me. We held that moment in sacred time.

Mōnã appeared, the slightest sliver of new light to escape from the shadow to adorn us here on Mother Earth. And the clouds in respect, melted away to show the stars all around the night sky.

And still the Hare remained, linking me to the very soil, staring at me. I barely drew a breath. Then cawing into that silence came a huge raven, the flapping of its wings sending waves into the stillness. And the noise puncturing the night. It settled near the hare, and starred straight at me. I knew the Ancestors had come.

My task, one of many, was to bless the land, the soil with *drycræft* of the oldest kind.

I walked in silence to the East, and dug up a circular handful of earth, warm, and moving with worms. I pulled these out, for there was no role to for them yet. I moved to the South and repeated the task, laying the South turf on top of the East. Walking slowly sun wise, West was added and then finally, North.

These sacred directions, these handfuls of earth became the four corners of the Our Mother, and became the whole field when I had blessed them with fresh and fragrant dew I had collected. Milk from the cows of each herd that had been gifted from all over the Wihtwara steadings. And bark from each soft tree on our land. I looked down on the bundle, from apple and pear to spindle and pine. I remembered with my heart breaking, and tears welling up, that it was my dear, gentle brother Eyvindr, who had collected these, ready for this night. He was gone and for a moment my soul cried out to him, so loudly, and with so much intent and power, I knew he would hear me, wherever they had taken him!

The herbs Lífa had collected lay before me. Together with honey from our bees, I made the salve to bless the earth. I was sitting in the centre of the hemp field, the four turfs before me in a circle. I gave power to each one with the salve, calling out with both hands raised to the sky.

"Erce, Erce Erce, Foldè Mōdor fǽle Nerthus, Mōdor fram ǽll
Āwarian ūre eard
Brengan þæt èacem
Dryhtens Thūnðr und Sunne æt bletsian ūre eard wiþ regn und sunne
Weaxan! Gemænigfealdian! A-Fyllan!

Erce, Erce, Erce, Earth Mother, beloved Nerthus, Mother of all,
Protect our lands
Bring the great gods,
Thūnðr and Sunne to bless our land with rain and sun
Grow, Multiply, Replenish!"

The power of Thūnðr was concentrated in the dew. I sprinkled it on all the four turfs, chanting quietly to Nerthus to bless the fields. It was then that I looked to see a dancing row of torches behind me. My *ðèodscipe* has silently arrived, with Eileifer, our *Cyng* holding his torch high, so I may see him. Beside him stood Eastmund, now his adopted son, smiling broadly at me. And my heart melted and my belly fluttered. By the gods, how I adored that man! He smiled.

I called to him and to everyone,

"*Bletsunga Beorte* Bright Blessings! Whom amongst you has the Wōden rune-marks on the whispering trees?"

"I do, *spakōna,* and my *Cwèn*, priestess and my queen" shouted Eileifer.

He marched forward holding a bundle of even crosses and beautifully worked circles in aspen wood. Four powerful runes had been crafted on and around them.

Inguz, consort of Nerthus, to twin with her energy, to create the balance in nature of male and female.

Sōwelo, the rune of Sunne, calling her rays to the earth.

Jèra, the rune of time and the measure of the seasons, but not those winter months, which no-one calls in.

And finally, Laguz, the rune of water.

"Walk with me", I said softly, leaning into him, "as we place the turf back"

Silently, together, now walking widdershins, beginning in the North, Eileifer placed the aspen *drycrǽft* in the hole, chanting deeply to Nerthus, Ing, Sunne and Thūnðr. I placed the turfs over the symbols in wood, and when all was done, cried out,

"*Wyrda gerynu are for Foldè. Wyrd byð swiðost!*

The runes of *Wyrd* are placed in the earth. *Wyrd* is strongest!"

We heard a drum beat begin, then a chorus of *Giese, Giese*! The beat was loud, then it spontaneously softened, as the following ritual began.

In the silence, the loud cawing of the raven split the air. He swooped down in dramatic fashion, to settle exactly on the circle that lay in the west. He tapped his beak three times, stood erect and proud and then suddenly took off, wings banking to the right. He went high, landing on the top branches of the oak. To sit there and look down upon us. Wōden had left a message. The hare remained, motionless, looking at us: a statue in the night.

A knot built up in my stomach, for I knew what that message meant, as did Eileifer.

It had been foretold to us, twice, once by *Ealdmōdor* and once by the sacred white horse and it meant rain, torrents of rain.

And so, we continued, driving our *drycræft*, our magic, into the land.

I turned to the east and called Nerthus, Wōden, Thunōr and Sunne to us for nine times. I lay on the earth and felt her warmth, kissed the turf, and then stood to call out;

> *"Eastward ic stande, ãrena ic mè bidde*
> *Bidde IC ðone mǽran Wōden, bidde ðone miclan Thunōr"*
> *"Bidde IC ðone hāligan of Neorxenawang,*
> *Eorðan IC bidde and Valhalla,*
> *And ðã sōþan fǽle Nerthus*
> *Þæt IC mote þis Wōden mid gife drihtnes*
> *Tōðum ontýnan: þurh trumne geþanc*
> *Ãweccan þas wæstmas ūs tō woruldnytte*
> *Geffyllan þãs folden mid fæste geleafan*
> *Wlitgigan þãs wancgturf: swã sè wítega cwæð*
> *Þæt sè ǽfre āre on eorpríce, sè þe ælmyssan*
> *Dǽlde dōmlíce, Wōden's þances"*

> "Eastward I stand, for blessings I pray,
> I pray the mighty Wōden, I pray the potent Thunōr,
> I pray the holy Guardian of Nerthus' meadow,
> Earth, I pray, and Valhalla above,
> And the just and beloved Nerthus
> That I by grace of Wōden, this spell
> May my teeth dissolve: with steadfast will
> May raise up harvests for our earthly need,
> Fill these meadows by a constant faith,
> Beautify these farm-turfs: as the Wiseman said,

> That he on earth had favour who his alms
> Apportioned wisely, to Wōden's will."

I heard murmurs of assent through the tribes who had gathered here this night.

Eileifer took the chance to come forward and kiss my hand, giving me the deepest most ardent look, smiling that half smile which never failed to seek out my heart. I took a deep breath.

"And who amongst you has less, who needs grain more than most?" I called out, knowing who it would be, as we had discussed this the morning before, as to her family's needs. They had not yet improved enough and her *beorn* still looked sickly. The diminutive figure of Ingríd walked forward with my little namesake, Dagrun, mewling and hungry. Ingríd came with the offering. It was a pouch of grain from her *hūs* which we had to take from her. That done, Eileifer called forward his oath sworn companions, who carried four huge grain sacks between them.

Ingríd gasped in astonishment, then rushed to Eileifer, curtseyed so briefly and flung her arm about him, little Dagrun in the other arm, becoming quite squashed.

Laughter broke out, the energy, the intense power filtered away, blown by an unseen wind, and in its place, happiness and the joy of union. The Wihtwara were held now in a sacred bond.

"The plough, *Spakōna*, we must bless the plough and first furrow!" came a call from the crowd. Everything was still in darkness. The flames from the many torches casting waving shapes of deep yellow and darkest brown, giving distorted images of the men and women.

But I knew that voice well enough, and he had every right to speak, for it was his crafting that had born the large plough. His oak tree felled for the purpose. The Anglii had given the design to him, but it was our sea-faring giant Ingvar who had built the first giant plough!

Eileifer strode forward to greet his companion of many years.

"You old sea-dog", he laughed, grabbing his shoulders, then dismissing all the reserve expected from *a Cyng*, giving Ingvar an intense bear hug.

"You have returned to us, and that I did not expect. When Eystein released you to seek plunder, or women, both most likely, we all sincerely believed we had seen the last of your hulking big body on this island!"

"Ahh", said Ingvar, ruefully rubbing his beard, "So did I, Eileifer, so did I. But there is a Nerthus line, it wavers and moves, never keeping still, and it grabs hold of you, mostly on a lonely dark night, and she whispers, Wihtland! 'Tis quite enough to drag this old body back home. Yes, it is home. And here I am!"

"Ingvar", Eileifer countered, "We are in a sacred space my friend, and you are lying, or shall I say being economical with the truth. When we are done here, come to the mead hall and furnish me with exactly what happened over there in Gaul if you please. *My* command to you, hearth companion!"

Ingvar's eyes widened and looked as if he might answer, but discretion overcame him and he moved away to help drag the heavy plough forward to the east where furrowing would begin. And we joined them there. Everything had to be completed before sunrise.

Ingvar brought out a thick pointed chisel to bore a hole in the beam. All present were silent. The only sound was his grunts as the metal ground through the now seasoned oak. Eystein stood close with a flaring torch to light his efforts. The shadows cast by the two men and the huge plough danced with the breeze that had suddenly sprung up, and I tightened my shawl about me. This was the darkest part of the night, before the dawn was ushered in by Sunni.

Suddenly I felt a swish over my head, and looked to see a white owl, large and fully grown, glide silently over us all. I gasped, feeling so honoured to have the brush of Owl feather and all our kin were hushed as it flew gracefully to alight on a branch of the huge beech trees that lined the hemp field.

I came over to the plough and bent over the borehole. I placed a small and precious amount of frankincense, from Antioch, or so I was told by the Anglii trader. Over that went our fennel seed and soap made from ash and a pinch of salt of which we had ample. On top went the seed. And I called out;

"Erce, Erce, Erce, earþan Mōdor,
Geunne þè sè Aell Fæder, èce drihten"
"Æcera wexendra and wrídendra,
Æcniendra and elniendra,
Sceafta scíra hersewæstma,
And ealra eorþan wæstma,
Geunne him èce Wōden
And his Dryhtens, Thunōr, Sunne, Mōnā, Ing and Nerthus, þe on Valhalla synt,
Þæt hys yrþ sí gefriþod wið ealra fèona gewæne
And hèo sí geborgen wið ealra bealwa gehwylc."

"Erce, Erce, Erce mother of Earth,
May the All-father, the eternal lord, grant you,
Fields flourishing and bountiful,
Fruitful and sustaining,
Abundance of bright millet harvests,
And of broad barley harvests,
And of white wheat harvests,
And all the harvests of the Earth
Grant him, Wōden,
And his gods, Thunōr, Fríg, Sunni, Mōnā, Ing and Nerthus in Valhalla that be,
That his farm be kept from every foe,
And guarded from each harmful thing."

"Swã, mōtan hit wesan! So, may it be", there echoed a full chorus around the hemp field, with a burgeoning dawn light on the horizon edge, I hurried on.

"And who has the sacred bread?" I called out.

Lífa hurried up to me, curtseying in a way that brought a smile to my face.

"We are not yet hand-fasted dear one", I whispered, "Let us finish this"

Ingvar pushed the heavy plough, now with the bung put back in place, holding forever the *drycrǽft* within, creating that first furrow bellowing out in his own unique cadence:

> "Hãl Wes þu, Folde, fíra Mōdor,
> Bèo þu grōwende on Wōden fæþme
> Fōdre gefylled fírum tō nytte."

> "All Hail, Earth, mother of men!
> Be fruitful in Wōden's embracing arm,
> Filled with food for the needs of men!"

Lífa took the small bread made from all the grains mixed with the milk from cow and goat, honey from our bees to bind it and placed in the furrow Ingvar had made. Aslaug closed it with her hands, calling out in her deep guttural voice, low and lyrical, the complete complement to Ingvar's deep booming voice:

> "Ful æcer fōdres fíra cinne,
> Beorht-blōwende, þu geblètsod weorþ
> Þæs hāligan noman, þe wè on lifiaþ,
> Sè Wōden, sè þās grundas geworhte, geunne ūs grōwende gife,
> Þæt ūs corna gehwylc cume tō nytte."

> "Full field of food for the race of man,
> Brightly blooming, be you blessed,
> In the sacred name of him who shaped
> Heaven, and Earth whereon we dwell,
> May Wōden, who made these grounds, grant growing gifts,
> That all our grain may come to us"

Our kin in the sacred field now erupted in cheer and drum beat, for it was done. The first field of many to have old *drýcræft* placed upon it. My task and that of Lífa, Sãga, Aslaug, was to place this magic on all our fields. Our nights would be filled with chanting and making the salves. Elíse would have been amongst us to ease the burden. She had followed her heart and now lived with Dægberht, as a *Cwèn,* and soon to be mother so I had heard. Aslaug had not recovered well from this blow. Her temper was short and her *spakōna* ways fast deserting her. We all gave her a spear's length distance. She preferred to work alone. But she gave the field *drycræft* her full attention and for that we were thankful.

We processed homeward, Eileifer and I taking the lead, with *Fæder* and *Mōdor* close behind, talking happily, easily, about the coming days, babies about to be born, and the latest news of Eileifer's building plans to enlarge his *Cyng's* lodge to make an apothecary for me and a solar.

As Sunni rose, so the host of Wihtwara melted away into the dawning light, easing back into the *ceasterwic* and *tunstede* village daily life, bleary eyed from lack of sleep. The chores needing to be done without the gift of extra sleep.

"Your task was beautifully executed, as always, Dagrun my love," Eileifer bent down to whisper in my ear, "And now I wish to execute a task of my own, that I believe you will find equally as beautiful, my gift to you, sweeting!" He nibbled the lobe of my ear and sent his arm shooting around my hips to squeeze me tightly.

We made our way, the short walk to his lodge, now expanding, looking new and bright in the sunlight. I loved the light that came into this room, he had created a new structure that had shuttered windows, which could be opened to the full sun. And here as the sun crept into the dark places of the earth to kiss the moist earth, so my Eileifer crept and caressed around me, then entering me, we became one and joy entered my heart for that untold time, an eternity and one second. We slept until Sunni was high in the sky.

… … … … … … … … …

CHAPTER TWENTY-FOUR

WŌDEN

Eileifer went to find Ingvar in the mead hall. It was a meeting he felt entirely uncomfortable about in the first place, requesting as it did, the revealing to Ingvar, of all the gossip of the *ceasterwic*. Ingvar had found a second *cwèn* in the weaving lodge, much to the agony of his first, fully-betrothed Anglii *wif*. A resolution needed to be found. Preferably with Ingvar seeing the error of his ways, but more probably, him leaving for Gaul, taking his weaving woman with him.

And so, it was, we bade goodbye to our loyal friend and hearth companion. But in so doing, Ingríd and her family had the run of his farm. For the first time, they enjoyed all the wealth of the huge steading. His choice, his *wyrd rapas*, changed their lives immeasurably.

But for my life, I had both my head and heart on the fission of tension created by the cruel Gandālfr, and of the gap in the Telling. I had submerged that vacuum of anxiety, whilst in the maelstrom of horror that was my trial. Add to that the prophecy from Nerthus herself, and the agonising loss of my dear sweet Eyvindr. Gandālfr's actions had resulted in a rip tide of *Wryd's* current that cascaded through our lives, changing the direction and our choices, forever. I was so relieved he was out of our lives, but the vacuum urgently needed to be filled.

Ealdmōdor was nudging me that mid-morning, heron wing fluttering, as I walked towards to the Ancestor circle, just down from the hill, deep set on the valley floor, within the crashing sound of the sea and the call of gulls. Shafts of strong sunlight streaked across the circle as I sat at my *Ealdmōdor's* resting place, yet myself seated, just outside the circle. I placed the heron wing leaning up against the multi-faceted stone, which glinted with crystals embedded in the agate and flint. I knelt and prayed to her, words falling out of my head, in a confusion of feeling and deep emotion. Then I took a deep gasp of air and the tears welled up and collapsing on the ground, my face covered by the long grass, I watered the earth with my pain. She took it, as she always does, with soft kindness and warmth. And then I must have fallen asleep, for when I opened my eyes, the twilight had long descended into the blackness of night.

"You will have lost the use of your legs", came a deep throaty voice close beside me. I heaved up, slowly peeling my eyes open, thinking it was Eileifer come to take me home.

"Eileifer, I'm so sorry, I fell asleep", I replied, looking up at him. I gasped as I realised it was not him.

"Who are you?" I asked in some alarm, edging away from this dark figure, who looked uncannily like my *Cyng*, the same dark hair, braided, fell below his shoulders.

"Do not fear, Dagrun, *beorn*, I am a relative, the same blood runs through my veins."

"Here, please take this herb potion, it will assist you. *Ealdmōdor* has made it possible for me to visit you, and give you the Telling."

I took the liquid slowly, and it ran through my veins like fire. It nearly stopped my heart. Then a warm and expansive feeling of heightened vision opened before me. I looked to him, in surprise, and saw him smiling, a beautiful radiance came upon his face, behind which a shimmering light of many beautiful hues grew around him.

"Here," he said gently, "come and sit close to me and I will take you to the Telling, so that you may recount it all to your children and their children's children."

The world spun in a nauseating speed around me. I shut my eyes, feeling a faintness come upon me to a sickening degree. Then it faded. I opened them again, and looked about me. The stranger was still with me. But we were not within our Ancestor circle anymore. We were in a *tunstede* I did not recognise. Nor did I recognise the people within it. The landscape bore steep mountains covered in trees and water lay at its base leading to the sea. It looked immeasurably cold, for Sunni was eclipsed by the mountain casting deep shadows across the water.

"You are now a wraith, Dagrun, you cannot be seen." he said. He thought for a moment and turned to stare intently at me, "Except for those who have the vision, the true ones. They will see you as sure as Sunni rises each morning"

His words, sinking in, stopped my heart. I was fully aware that my physical body was dis-engaged, separate from my consciousness that now had an increased awareness of sight and sound but had a vacuum where touch and movement used to be.

"*Ord æðung*", he hissed at me, "start breathing! Or you will die, right here, right now!"

I heaved an imaginary breath into my invisible lungs and my mind centred and relaxed. I put my hand out to touch a leaf, seeing with deep clarity the skin and bone and sinew of my hand, all sharply enhanced. The leaf, although my hand went through it, had a wonderful the softness of it, and I knew the filigree skeleton that made its unique form. The intensity of this experience, momentarily eclipsed all else, and the joy was breathtakingly beautiful.

My companion and guardian broke into this reverie.

"*Swimman on þæt flōwan fram Wryd. Lifian āna on þæt Nūðā, und gemunan æghwa.*"

"Swim in the flow of *Wyrd*. Live only in the Now and remember everyone. I will leave you now. Do not wander away"

And with that, this tall man, with abundant dark hair, whose plaits swung as he walked, vanished from my side, as suddenly as he first appeared.

He reappeared as a man in physical shape and form walking, or rather striding towards a tall, seated youth with hair and eyes of the same hue. Dark hair, shining with the luminous colours of brown and copper and piercing blue eyes, shaded and mysterious. This gangly youth was seated on a log, working with pieces of wood from different trees and of varying shape that lay before him. He was absorbed in this and only looked up when he felt the presence of my companion before him.

"*Fæder! bletsunga beorte,*" he smiled, a stunning smile that lit up his face, which looked like it would be growing chin hair any time soon. His teeth were astonishingly white, no gaps or brown marks mottled their appearance. He reminded me so much of Eileifer, a sharp pang entered my heart, and the scene faltered. I shunned the feeling of Eileifer, sent it away, realising the words of my companion were not said lightly. I must stay completely in the Now to achieve my task in this Telling.

The boy suddenly looked past his father, and fixed an intense, penetrating stare in my direction.

By the gods, I thought, this boy can see me! Realising he truly could, his powerful stare entered my heart and nearly stopped my heart yet again. Regaining some composure, I smiled shyly back at him, and so very slightly nodded my head.

His mouth curled in a half smile, and he looked down at his wood. So like Eileifer, I thought and yet again I nearly lost the vision before me.

"*Hwā is þeos cwèn sèo becuman wiþ þu, Fæder?* Who is this woman that comes with you Father," the boy asked looking up casually from his piles of sticks.

"Wōden," his father replied, "It is a woman from many, many summers to come, she has travelled on the stream of *Wyrd* to be here, for she is a guardian of the Stones. She is Dagrun Wahl of the Warinni, part of our people……." His voice faded out as I realised who he was, Godwulf, and the boy was truly Wōden!

"And she is pledged to give the whole Telling of the Stones for our distant peoples to remember us."

"Ahh," Wōden murmured half to himself, "she is my Watcher then. She will need protection, *Fæder*, from Loki, who will tell Yngling, who will then plot and scheme and cause all manner of irritation! I suggest you might find both Hjördis and Frídr, to cast a *gescyldnes gealdor* protection spell."

"Well, Watcher," Wōden turned in my direction and pointed towards a high fence, that had an opening, "I had better give you something worth watching! Follow me."

He strode forward, immense long strides, with purpose in his actions, arms swinging in rhythm. I followed in a short-stride run to keep up with him, yet I was met by a wicker-woven gate being swung shut in my face. And that became quite deliberately I am sure, my first test, by the young and enigmatic Wōden.

Passing my hand through a beautiful delicate leaf was one thing, but a sharp, jagged and very thickly constructed gate, quite another. I stood for a moment considering how to achieve the impossible. Everything was new, all unconquered in this new world I found myself "watching." I tentatively pushed my hand against the gate. A sharp pain ran up my arm and I withdrew hastily.

How was it possible I feel pain when my physical body was absent? Then it dawned on me, my mind had not accepted the loss and placed pain there as a given! Recalling the words of *Godwulf*, "Live only in the Now", I cleared my mind, and when I was sure it was at peace, I moved forward with my whole body and passed through that thick gate quite effortlessly.

I opened my eyes to see a chaotic flurry of arms swinging *seaxes* and swords, of legs skipping and dancing around, avoiding a hit, ducking and skimming around each other. It seemed the whole tribe of young boys were in this arena for serious warrior practise. Sunni did not glint off their swords, as she hit the dusty turf with her rays. For all these *seax* and swords were of hardened wood. No blood would be split this day. I had seen the practise grounds of our *Tunstede,* and knew the fury held within those walls, as those young bloods vented steam and anger in their bid for worthy swordsmanship. But true warrior status was never achieved through fury alone, but with detachment and concentration. A cold heart and clear head were words that passed my *Fæder's* mouth more than once.

Wōden glided forward in a thoroughly graceful way, leaning down to pick up a long *seax*, that was almost a sword, and ran his finger down its length, studying it for quite a while. He leant his head to one side, eyes shielded in deep thought, until he suddenly shot a look over to me, those ice-blue eyes piercing into me. Nodding slightly, he moved forward, swinging his wooden practise sword through the air, contemplating his rival, who arrived quite suddenly before him, leaving an erstwhile, confused opponent in mid swing.

"Alfljötr," Wōden exclaimed with a deep voice recently broken, "Ic biscopstōl þu are dōmgeoin! Swā wesan hit" I see you are ready for glory. So be it!"

"*Giese!*" came the reply through the gritted teeth of an older boy, whose eyes were masked with a mass of locks, and who was sturdy and tall. He was attractive and several summers older than Wōden. His movements and gait were slightly slower compared to the dancing, Wōden gave in reply. I sensed clogged energy that was swirling in a deep pit of jealousy. It was an even encounter marred by jealousy and impacted anger on the side of Alfljötr.

The boy suddenly sprang forward with a jab that Wōden sprang well clear of. In pulling back, he danced around the back of the youth, who had to swing sharply to face him, unbalancing him, whereupon Wōden sprang forward to finish the job, and the youth landed hard on the dried turf. Wōden danced on, lightly on the balls of both feet, enjoying the moment. He let the boy retrieve his balance and even allowed him a second shot at his chest with the *seax*. Wōden swung his shoulder sharply away, knowing, it seemed, every move in advance.

Alfljötr let out a high-pitched shriek and ran at him, all manoeuvres forgotten. Wōden was waiting, ready, piercing him straight into his rib cage. But, without warning, the sword cracked and splintered onto the turf. A gasp of shock was released from the crowd of boys, now gathered to watch the feud. Alfljötr grinned, nodding, sensing his victory, when Wōden sped past him to the side of the arena where the clothes were kept in an untidy bundle. With the unmistakable low grating sound of metal on metal, Wōden pulled a forged sword that glinted with Sunni's rays. He held it up to her and gave a prayer. Everyone was hushed to silence now, after the first gasp of horror from a crowd, who realised practise was over and a real battle was about take place.

His blue eyes showed no emotion as he moved towards his now terrified opponent, who looked around for help.

"*Nã fultum for þu Alfljötr*" No help for you!" Wōden hissed, as he caught the hapless young man by the tunic and twisting it, brought him within a hairsbreadth of the sword. Wōden had swung it high, bringing the tip against the quivering neck of his opponent. Alfljötr had sunk to his knees, staring at the cold-steel expression of Wōden.

I turned to see the gate suddenly open. Godwulf entered with two women standing at each side of him, the glare of anger washed across his face at the sight before him.

"Wōden!" he roared. "Stop!"

Wōden ignored both his entrance and his words.

"*Þǽt is nã jãrian in leãs-bregd.*" There is no honour in cheating. You tampered with my sword. You split my sword!" Wōden said clearly for all to hear.

He dug the sword's tip into the lad's fleshy neck, enough to draw blood and scar Alfljötr, blood flowing freely from his trembling neck, missing the life pulse by a fraction.

"It was not I," cried the lad, "but I picked the short straw to fight with you. It was your half-brother who weakened your sword!"

"Þes dolh willan gemonian þu eall þín bold. Fran þín Dryhten þu willan gemunan þes bismer." Wōden growled his reply through gritted teeth. "This scar will remind you all your life. From your god, you will remember this shame!"

He released Alfljötr, who grabbed his bleeding wound and staggered to the ring of boys now gathering around him, leading him out of the gate. Wōden slowly held his sword before him, wiping the tip clear of blood. The look of pride as he stared at the sword was obvious to all, and I realised this was no ordinary sword.

As Godwulf strode towards his son, I felt the presence of the two women beside me. They felt warm and I saw an energy build between them that encompassed me in a light of shimmering white and silver.

"Loki will arrive soon *sweostors*," Wōden shouted over the head of his father, "Be speedy in your work or all be will lost as will the Watcher from *Wyrd*." My vision was dimming and I looked through the blur of mist, frowning at the disappearing shapes.

"Concentrate on your Will to see what is before you, Dagrun, *beorn*", whispered Hjördis in my head, "it is of the utmost importance."

And with effort born of stubbornness at being slow and dim-minded, the clarity came back. And yet even more so, I could witness the energy flow around everyone in the practise ground. Colours ebbed and flowed, changing with expressions and movement. Godwulf was angry at his son and his energy flowed with sweeping red and orange. Wōden's was a deep purple, unchanging and quite beautiful.

Then from behind me, and sweeping right through me with a terrible rush of sticky dense dark energy, came the form of Loki, along with the tall figure of Yngling, the *Elder Fæder* of terrible repute. And as I looked to the women guarding me, standing on either side, a look of satisfaction spread across their faces. This monster in the making, neither felt me nor saw me. I was safe.

My hearing was falling far short of my intensified sight. A mumble was all that reached me. I put all my Will to amplifying the sounds and gradually conversations made sense. Albeit in a stranger, yet vaguely familiar language close to my own. It began to make sense.

"*Giese*," murmured Frídr in my head, "Dagrun, *beorn*, you have succeeded in your important task. From now on, until the Telling is completed, you must live completely in the Now that *Wyrd* has offered you. Give yourself up to the power of *Wryd*. Do you understand?"

"*Giese*", I replied quietly, concentrating on the conversation of a group of young men who were now listening intently to Loki and Yngling.

"Agni, you claim a talent with working in wood", Loki spoke with a cold calculating voice, "Yet the marking of that practise sword was evident to my brother, hence the hiding of his *drýcræft*- forged sword!"

"I swear not," Agni protested, "why was the forged sword hidden in readiness? I say he was forewarned."

"I think not," replied Loki, scuffing his foot into the dried turf, "he has gifted "sight", that we both know!"

Loki was in every way a twin of his half-brother. Except for one aspect. The window to his soul, his eyes were the darkest black, a complete contrast to Wōden's intense blue.

Hjördis spoke quietly, "Loki is Wōden's half-blood brother. He is born of a human mother and Godwulf. Wōden has the eyes of his mother Nerthus and therein lies the difference. They are the two irreconcilable sides of the father's soul, and his eternal conflict."

I watched the Father and son talk quietly at the other end of the combat arena. Godwulf's colours had tempered to a calmer orange-pink. Wōden's was that deep purple, unchanged throughout the fight and the aftermath. I declined to wonder just how he had achieved that. And reconciled the childgod aspect about him and marvelled at it. It was also obvious that Wōden had explained the entire episode to the satisfaction of his father, who looked over to his other son and frowned deeply.

I also noticed a small figure of a youth, who had been standing away from the main group, watching, like myself the whole fight, and now, when Loki spoke of the warning to Wōden, this boy slid back behind the wicker fence and disappeared. Wōden was building his reputation as "the sighted one" but had mundane "help" as well. He was as cunning as he was gifted.

Wōden got up and walked towards us, with his father, chatting quietly.

"It is nearing the time for you, my son, to complete the *Utiseta* all us humans go through to manhood", Godwulf said with some emotion entering his voice.

"*Giese,* yes, *Fæder*, I know and I am preparing," Wōden replied, "Fear not for me. I am nearly ready and very eager to go and find my forest guardians again. My soul yearns to be with them, away from all this *Humanity!*" he hissed the word in exasperation.

Godwulf heaved a deep sigh and looked to the ground. "You mean your brother Loki."

"Yes, *Loki,*" Wōden breathed out, "There will always be enmity between us *Fæder,* you know that. But while I am in the calm, slow heartbeat of my Mother, *Folde Mōdor*, I will harness some forgiveness and compassion as part of my goal."

As he neared us, he spoke silently to me "Follow me, Watcher. Remember all."

And to Hjördis he spoke aloud.

"Hjördis, *Ealdmōdor*, thank you for coming. You can find your comfort hides now, if you wish. Rest." To which she nodded gratefully. For I had never seen a more fragile aging grandmother who was defying her own passing every day. She adored her child-god and simply refused to leave him.

"Frídr," he spoke silently, "stay with this Watcher, if you please. She is a pure novice. I fear for her, truth be told." He looked me straight in the eye to my soul and I found kindness wafting to that part of me that was grieving for Eileifer.

I turned and followed, realising in all of this, that a part of him was a part of Eileifer, his blood running through the ages to bind us.

… … … … … … … … …

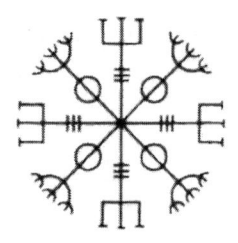

CHAPTER TWENTY-FIVE
<u>Ūtiseta</u>: Vision Quest

I followed as he bade me, with gentle Frídr at my side. She who was *fey* and of the forest folk, her white hair like a spider's web, flowing gently around her elfin face. I warmed to her immediately, and even more so, when suddenly I felt a whoosh of energy and saw her beside me in spirit form, like me, a wraith.

We were nearing the forge, where Wōden had led us.

"I cannot be seen here", she said, looking at me intently. "This place is for menfolk only, and in any case, Weyland the smith does not appreciate the filtering down of male energy at work. It is *drycræft* magic." She sighed.

"I wish it were not so", she continued, "For there are many of us women who would like to learn the magic of casting metal into beautiful things. I cannot stay with you this way for long, though, and will withdraw back. *Ealdmōdor* has need of me. You will be safe here. Weyland has no time for Loki. Yngling would not dare show his face here!"

We both looked on for a while. Wōden had stripped away his vest and tunic, tied his hair back and was busy hammering the hot blade into a straight and perfect form. Back to the fire it went, where the white-hot charcoal glowed and the intense heat brought a sweat to his body, droplets falling into the fire and onto the sword blade, as he bent over. He was muttering prayers as the beads of sweat fell, this being a sacred moment and charged with energy. He was creating *drycræft*. Wayland looked on silently. More hammering, then inspection, whereupon he became satisfied. Wōden held the blade up to the Sky gods and Sunni, exclaiming clearly, "*Sige in beadu, ãrian onþæt æcer, und mōd wæcnan innan þes sweord. Týr, Týr Tyr!*" Victory in battle, honour on the field, and courage born within this sword, Tiw, Tiw, Tiw!

He immediately plunged the sword blade into the waiting vat of water, his whole body becoming enveloped in the billowing steam. I heard him exclaim, then laugh loudly. It dispersed to show him bent over a waiting crucible that was being heated, the fire being pumped with air anew, by a small boy intent on the task of keeping this sacred fire alive. This was the molten bronze that would create the hilt. I was so completely enthralled with the process, so gifted as I was to see it, I did not realise I was on my own. Frídr had left. Nor was I troubled by the intense heat. I felt nothing. Wōden glanced over momentarily towards me, and grinned widely, knowing I must have had a deep and furrowed expression on my girlish face. He said nothing, and I knew I was invisible to the Weyland *drymãnn* also.

The sword of Wōden, charged by prayer to the god of war, Týr, lay cooling, mottled and grey in its birthing. The hilt would be created over many concentrated hours. How it would be emblazoned with guardian animals, no-one knew. If Wōden had any idea, he was playing it close to his chest. Everything would be revealed after the *ūtiseta,* when his manhood would be secured forever and his destiny and purpose revealed. I gasped inwardly at the sheer importance of these days in the child god's life. And in my own, being a part of this creative happening for all time.

Suddenly the stream of Wryd appeared before me in an iridescent glowing white light of filaments interlinking past, present and future. And how we knitted these together, our creativity completely linked to the whole of creation. I could not hold the enormity of it, and it faded as soon as it had appeared. But I held onto the feeling and the memory. For this was the goal. I also realised that Wōden had more grasp of it than I ever would.

He knew I had realised this nucleus of all creation. He had seen it too and nodded perceptively towards me.

What years I could put on this growing man-god, I knew not. He behaved and responded like a grown man in still a young boy's body.

He handled the extremes of temperature and the weight of the craftsmen's tools, like an adult. The molten bronze was lifted expertly by him between iron pincers with flattened ends. He poured the liquid into the waiting mould, glowing white-yellow as it slid effortlessly into the chamber that held the design of the hilt. Now it was patience that would be required of him. He would never be a child, allowed to play with his toys. Nerthus, his mother must have known this the minute she laid him down. And it was why both Hjördis and Godwulf adored him intensely, because of the lost childhood we all take for granted.

All this time Weyland had been leaning up against his workbench, arms folded, looking at his apprentice at work. Eventually, Wōden bent over the vat of water and submerged his whole torso. Rubbing the sweat from his hair and his chest. He surfaced with a gasp of air and shook himself, like a dog who had jumped from a pond. Weyland laughed and came over to join him.

"Clever work! Wōden," he rumbled in his gravelly deep voice, "Now go and prepare for your journey. There is much to organise, and if you overlook ought, you will live to regret it. Be sure to take your smaller sword. It will be seeing more blood than the dribble of this day! And then you can return to claim your true warrior sword here waiting for you."

"You knew!" countered Wōden, looking at Weyland.

"Hah", came the reply, "did you think I would sit here counting nails while my best apprentice took to his new sword for real combat and not some woody practise *seax*?"

"It was purely to teach them a lesson in honour", Wōden said quietly

"*Giese*, I know", Weyland put his grisly arm around the youth and then gave him a suffocating bear hug, just to make sure the child god knew he was loved.

… … … … … … … … …

I waited outside the men's lodge in the *tunstede* part of the village. My energy, even as a wraith would not be welcomed, and I felt Yngling and Loki were present there, as I could clearly hear raised voices. Yngling was the chief elder, older than most. He was highly respected as a warrior, but had been reduced by his own jealousy and resentment, and by the castigation of Nerthus herself, to a barking, quarrelsome man who plotted and schemed with the likes of Loki, mostly against the young child-god.

Frídr was sitting as herself, next to me, quietly humming a *bèo leoð* bee song, to calm us both and to remind her of the days when she was the sole bee-keeper for the whole *ceasterwic*, before she became a *nígt-gala*, night-singer, with Huld, her closest companion. Apart from Vermundr that is, whom I had yet to meet.

She read my thoughts.

"Vermundr is the right hand to my left hand for Wōden", she remarked coyly, "and you will be meeting him very soon, in the forest. We will be staying there for some time to come. There is not a day goes by where I do not miss his smile, his face. He is my beloved, Dagrun."

My heart stopped. I fought with all my will to stay the emotions rising from the deepest part of me, and I silently screamed, *Eileifer!* She must have seen me fading, wobbling, and knew the danger I was in.

I felt the whoosh of her energy spirit fold into me and hold tight. "Do not waver, Dagrun, see Wōden and know, for now, he is part of your beloved. He knows it, you own it. Now!"

Wōden came out of the men's lodge, his copper-brown hair glinting in the rays of Sunni, and I saw Eileifer and knew Frídr was right. The danger receded. He was carrying many articles, hides and weapons about him. It amazed me he did not stagger under the weight of it all but his back was straight, his pace firm. He had very thick wrapped hides about his feet. Thongs woven up his legs to keep the leather in place around his legs that were sprouting man-hair already. I was sure when he returned, he would have grown a full beard.

"Are you sure, Wōden, my friend, you would not like to carry that pretty woman on your back as well", came a voice of a man leaning against the lodge wall, arms crossed, studying the whole scene before him, "She is of little weight."

"Hah," came the reply, "And incur the wrath of my oath-sworn ally and friend, Vermundr, who will certainly cut short my *ūtiseta* not to say my manhood!"

"Not the *fǣge* beautiful Frídr…. *that one!* "replied Týr, pointing straight at me.

"Ahh," cried Frídr, "Wōden cover her!" And with that, both surrounded me creating the protection spell again. I looked over to Týr, amidst the swirling mist and thought I saw him smile.

"*You*", said Wōden quietly, "are becoming a danger to us all, Dagrun. Do not allow this to happen again. For I will not assist you a second time!" And with that he kissed me lightly on the head and walked away, saying over his shoulder, "And that is from Eileifer, take heart, dear one!"

"Týr", Wōden turned to his friend, "exactly when did 'the sight' come to you, and why keep it a deep dark secret from me, old friend?"

"Hmm" Týr rubbed his huge beard, "since that day you were named and to where you are travelling now," Týr remarked, smiling over to Wōden, joining him in the walk towards the forest.

"That long ago!" replied Wōden, nodding slowly, seeming to bring a realisation to him that had sat on the side-lines of his young life. "So, you are behind me then, as Frídr and Vermundr are to the left and right of me?"

"That is so," Týr said, clapping the young god in the making on the back with a hearty thump.

"So, what is it with you and Yngling, then?" he asked his friend.

"Take a leaf out of my knowing, Wōden. Keep your friends close, but your enemies' closer!"

"Hmm, 'tis so, 'tis so indeed," Wōden pondered, then strode off at a pace, anxious to be experiencing his *ūtiseta*.

They crunched onto the shingle along the shore of the lake, deep as it was long. The wind was sending ripples skipping along the surface. Fins of a shoal of fish broke the surface and skimmed away when they knew humans were nearby. The clouds danced into forms of animals and birds. I saw an eagle form above me and wondered the augury of it. Wōden may find his *fetch* animal soon. We knew that Raven held his heart. And I felt he was yearning to see them, to be with them in body and spirit.

I put my arm through Frídr, as much as a wraith can do, and glided along. I walked, but did not feel the touch of the sharp stones at all. Sunni created sparkles on the water, glinting in a merry dance. She was sinking slowly to meet the underworld, and the colours had deepened to orange. A vivid crimson started to streak across the sky. Fine weather was being shown to us for the coming day. I could not anticipate how long this quest would take. I could not think about Time at all, for there lay the danger of melting back into Time and be lost to this world and the Telling gone forever.

Wōden continued ahead of us. We hung back, for the journey was his, solitary in all aspects. Yet the thread that ran to him, from us, remained. We felt it, so did he. At the edge of the forest, he stopped abruptly, leaving us no option but to do likewise. He turned and shouted:

"*Forstoppian, ālǣtan!* Stop leave! You must follow me no more. Frídr, sweet one of mine, go find your love, Vermundr, he is waiting for you. If I have need of you, I will call. You! Watcher, for this part, you must stay!"

He had taken on a truly hard impenetrable look, those ice-blue eyes sending shards of frozen intent my way. Had I known better I would have silently complied. But I had something to say, and say it I would!

"Wōden," I replied equally with steel-barbed intent, "You disrespect me and it does you no credit. My name is Dagrun Wahl of the Warinni. Call me by my name!"

"Dahh! You have "Self" in charge of you, stripling", he roared, advancing back towards me.

That awful word again, once used by the dwarf Gandālfr, was the biggest insult. And he knew it. How? I suddenly asked myself, how could he know? Then, I realised I was being tested. He could see all my life. I was, as a wraith, exposed for "he who has the 'sight' sees all."

He stopped, and relaxed.

"Dagrun Wahl of the Warinni, whilst you are my 'Watcher' that is truly all you can be. And you find this hard to do? If that is so, then go back to your time. *Fèran!*"

"Nã, nã," I looked at him with all anger evaporated, "I cannot do that Wōden. My destiny is here with you, now. The Stones must record your life. They must have it. And I have been given that task, as it was foretold and runs in the blood of my people the Warinni. We are the guardians of the Stones and they in turn are the guardians of us, all *Menniscnes*! I cannot be the one who breaks that eternal bond."

"So be it", Wōden replied, turning and striding off into the forest, as I skimmed over the woody detritus and bushes, keeping up with him as best I could, as a wraith. Exhaustion was never a problem. Mental alertness was. The day was swiftly ending. Birds were passing elegantly, as silver-grey shadows, skimming across the water from lake to nest. Crimson flecks rippled across the lazy water at this twilight, as the orange sphere of Sunni laid her glorious energy to rest. As did our illustrious boy-god, soon to become a man. He began to lay out his bundles and then stalked off noiselessly, to find food, dry detritus for embers, and branches for a shelter. I did not follow.

How does a wraith sleep? I had no body to relax into, to snuggle under warm leaves. And so, I waited, wondering what to do. Then, without any effort, my mind now released from "watching" opened the hidden world to me. I witnessed again the stunning filaments of life-force that flowed and connected with all the forest life. Shimmering in silver waving bands, which vibrated to wind changes, animal entrances and exits. That vibration was so subtle, our physical bodies are quite unable to pick them up. Yet we do in a diminished sense, feel them. It is the vibration of peace we feel when we enter a wood or forest. It is the feeling of union we feel when we enter the energy of a beloved tree. And that is how, as a wraith I learnt to "sleep." By entering this world of peace, and slept.

… … … … … … … … …

CHAPTER TWENTY-SIX
YGGDRASILL

I became conscious again as a shimmering wave of energy, lush and tickling, washed over me. I gasped as I saw a young fox, all eyes and nose, with a green and amber aura, lick my "face." Then to the side of me I caught Wōden, as his spirit self, glowing that beautiful purple colour, changing to bright yellow, as he laughed at my awakening. The spirit of the fox, its colours and energy, sped back into its body and he loped off. Not before giving me one backward glance to offer his acceptance.

I "floated" upwards, or so I thought, as I must have laid out just like my physical body would have done.

"Come, Watcher", Wōden said lightly, "Follow me", as he too loped off into the forest. I spent a few minutes concentrating my vision. The physical world became clearer. It was a crisp-looking morning. Early dawn was sharp, with glistening patterns of early frost on the leaves. And the pattern in spirit was so different from the previous day. Angular, and almost totally still. I understood, in that moment, the feeling we have in the winter world, of time, nature, all creatures reducing movement, standing still. It was *Wryd* that dictated it so. The filigree of *Wryd* was more delicate than the pattern of the frost. I marvelled at the spider-like threads that spun to join all in a static dance of immeasurable beauty.

The light yellow of Sunni gave way to a deepening yellow that became almost amber, as grey clouds grew into a thunderous dark blue. The billowing wind grew to ruffle the smooth surface of the lake, and before Sunni disappeared behind the rainclouds, she sent her colours to dance on the little waves.

Wōden had covered himself in fur. A hood now eclipsing his face. This boy-god looked for all the world like a forest trapper. I urged myself forward to meet his swift pace as he leapt and strode over the forest floor of bushes, ferns and dead, fallen trees. I almost felt the chill set upon the earth, so glad that "almost" was as far I would go. Wōden did not veer left as I had expected him to, for that would surely have taken him to the mountain path where Frídr has led them years ago. His Raven guides and Wolf would be waiting to greet him and it was this adventure I anticipated keenly. Anticipation is a dangerous feeling, for living in the Now forbade it. I squashed it down hard, before it got troublesome. I was learning.

Beyond the shingle of the foreshore, ferns grew and water-loving trees had grown to huge girth and towering branches. Willows dipped their yellowing leaves into the lake water, rustling now in the growing wind. Wōden dipped under them and stopped for a few minutes to soak in the beautiful healing energy of willow. She is Nerthus in another form. And I knew he was silently praying to her. I saw him hold his arms aloft. He had thrown back his hood and I saw clearly the intense expression as he prayed to her. I felt an energy build of deep violet, a deep compassionate love. I saw his colour change to a deep golden yellow. It was the first time the deep purple had left him. The flow of *Wryd* concentrated in a swirl around him. He was receiving her energy and her protection. It was the most beautiful sight I had beheld in a long time. I waited. After some while, and with regret, the energy dissipated and Wōden came out from his willow hiding place. We continued. I kept totally silent for now I was certain that words were not just inadequate, but entirely useless.

He veered left, quite suddenly, away from the lake's foreshore, striding over woody detritus in something of a hurry. There was a definite destination in mind and we wove around the growing number of tall ash trees which peppered this forest landscape. Thunōr had opened the sky. Shards of freezing rain were pounding into the earth and Wōden became a hunched moving bundle of soggy fur as we raced past the trees. The rain came to me in spinning sparks of light. To say it nearly obliterated my vision would be true enough and I had to strain my mind to focus beyond the rain. Ash is the tree of fire, and the rain, ice. Fire and Ice, I thought. The very elements of life, fusion and creation. Was it significant, then, that Wōden's Ancestors were, at this moment, focusing him to that primeval force?

He faltered for a moment, and sat down on a twisting mass of roots from a giant beech tree. She sheltered him from the rain and he paused to take breath. There was a cluster of these queens of the forest. A nurturing feeling of safety lay amongst her branches and curling roots.

Suddenly a filigree of spider-like silver strands came snaking out from each of bulbous roots and twirled around our boy-god. A myriad gathering of *Ælfs* and *Wights* appeared, translucent, shimmering. The women were utterly beautiful and delicate. They came beside him, silently, stroking him with tiny hands or staring with wide trusting eyes. He saw them and smiled.

It was then, I realised, and knew beyond all doubt, that a great trial was nearly upon him. Of a possible sacrifice that would require all his courage. They all knew but he did not: I guessed the primordial forces might pull him asunder. The rune for ice suddenly sat in front of my vision and stayed for a few seconds before fading away. Then the rune for Sunni appeared, glowing in front of me. When I looked to Wōden he was oblivious.

He does not know the runes! I exclaimed, silently. And I knew he was now in the process of re-birth.

He gently lifted himself up bowing to the dryad gathering, thanking them in a strange language. Striding forward again with renewed vigour, we pounded through the ash tree copse. We came very suddenly to an open plain of coarse grass and fern. The air had again cooled, the rain turning to sleet. Moving across the plain, I saw a large hare sitting up looking directly at us, ears erect with whiskers alert. His eyes large and staring with great intent. Wōden tipped his hood in acknowledgement.

Maybe the *Ælfs* has sent knowledge to this patriarchal hare of Wōden's approach.

Beyond the hare was a guardian hawthorn tree, as knarled as any ancient I had ever seen, blood red berries were hanging from its branches in such heavy profusion, the old tree bent and creaked in the breeze. It sent swirls of light snow in a dance of white.

Wōden beat onwards through the growing mist. His staff dug heavily into the ground with each step. The Hare remained dormant. I looked beyond to see his true destination. The real reason for the hare and hawthorn guardian tree.

Then I saw it. Yggdrasill.

Rising like some ancient monster, a huge monument of old wood and knarled branches. It grew in a protected and covered cliff quarry. The largest ash tree I had ever seen. It surpassed the chieftains' oaks in diameter. It was beyond age in mortal time. As we drew nearer, I could see it had survived two lightning strikes. But it had lived on to reach this unbelievable size. Huge sprays of yellowing leaves hung on the topmost branches only barely visible for its unfathomable height. The huge trunk had myriad footholds on its twisted, swerving troughs of ancient bark growth, ascending skyward to a neck-cracking height. Clusters of seed wings, blackening and ready to fly earthward, all the new growth, suspended, waiting, adding energy spirals I could now see and understand their movement. It was the moment of birthing in process.

And I could hear the deep rumbling and rhythmic heartbeat of this ancient ash tree. Knowing too it was the heartbeat of our *Foldè Mōdor*. And it quickened sharply as Wōden began his slow approach, feeling his way forward in reverence to the Ancient One. In return, the tree gave a shooting display of colours from deep within its girth to ascend around its branches in a swirling rhythm of green, pale blue sapphire, turquoise and deep yellow.

This was the tree of creation where mankind was born.

And it was welcoming his son home.

… … … … … … … … …

Wōden had thrown his soaking furs in a pile at the base of the tree and placed an oiled cotton over the top. He was climbing. Each stride taking him into the depth of the old tree, and so high I could now barely see him. Just flashes of his purple aura skipped past my inner vision. It was the only clue I had as to where he was in *Yggdrasill*. And there he remained. I settled myself down to wait. It became the longest test of patience in my life. And there were moments of frustration that I had to fight hard to overcome and not be hurled back into my own time.

I "slept" for several twilights, or so I guessed. It was certainly not my place to intrude. Yggdrasill is male. The Elm is the woman's tree of creation, but I began to feel a tendril of energy wrap around me and a link made, allowing me to enter a little way into this re-birthing. I was certain I heard a rumble of laughter come from *Yggdrasill*!

I was given permission travel down into the depths of his roots deep underground. And so deep for this ancient one that I felt I was near the centre of the Earth! And so, near the lake water, I marvelled at the distance his roots travelled to find that water.

Nerthus! I exclaimed, He is co-joined with our Goddess. His balance is water and his feminine principle is abiding with our mother in the element of water. I remembered so clearly the loving dance that enriched the old oak, when Nerthus came to that old dragon oak by her sacred pool. And how love was born there, in that twilight, so many moons from now in the future time. It is the primordial sacred dance of life.

I was truly beginning to understand and it really came as no surprise when I saw Wōden appear, glowing a deep yellow and transforming into a serpent as he writhed down the enormous root beside me. The only part of him that remained the same were those ice-blue eyes, his whole body now a shimmering cascade of yellow and ochre scales spiralling around his serpent body as he descended into the water to meet with his mother.

"Watcher", came the deep voice, "look, learn and remember, dear one!" I held my breath in wonder.

And so, this was the first re-birthing of Wōden into a god, happening in the depths of that sacred lake, and in the form, that united *Nerthus* and *Wōden*, as mother and son. I saw, all but briefly, a joining of two serpents, one yellow, and one violet, male and female, in the dance of life. And that I imprinted in our *hãlig stãn* for all times to come.

The warmth and love of that encounter radiated outwards, towards all Life, and to me, sitting quietly, as a wraith, I bathed in that energy. The opposing elements of fire and ice colliding in the chaos of creation, was yet to come to Wōden. But here at this moment, all Life was in harmony and balance, water and earth twisting in a carousel of motion that birthed Love upon which all Life depended.

And I also knew in an instant of recognition that this would be waiting for us when we make that last journey to *Neorxenawang*, all of us who walked and lived and prayed to *Folde Mōdor*, our Earth Mother *Nerthus*.

Wōden had achieved the first miracle of becoming a serpent, changing his gifted life-form for another and one that equalled his Mother.

Eventually after what seemed an eternity, they parted. He came back so swiftly, I did not see the going of him, back upwards to the sky. I followed and felt aged and slow even though I had no body to slow me. Perception is everything I decided, in the long moments it took me to breathe imagined air again! He had somehow sharpened his awareness and responses to such an extent he became more than human now. And of course, those ice-blue eyes sparkled with mischief on seeing me eventually arrive at the spot where I had sat for so long.

… … … … … … … … …

Ice shards were forming on the edges of the branches. Everything was still. The earth was holding her breath. The translucence of the frozen water, that icy solid matter, that normally I would think utterly beautiful, was but a dull reflection to what I now saw in spirit. A shining, delicate and complex pattern of light traces wove the building blocks of snowflakes, interlinking, joining up everywhere. The colours of blue, turquoise light yellow danced on the forms, and they were so deep, multiplying in numbers back to *Yggdrasill* who stood large and firm, against their delicate tracing of Life in the deep cold. It was so very cold.

I was worrying after Wōden as he had left his warming furs still in a heap at the base of the tree. He was out of my sight. I concentrated so hard to see him with spirit vision. But there was nothing I could feel or see. I then began to feel frightened. It was this feeling that made my whole vision wobble. It was my emotions again, getting the better of my wraith status of being. So, I quelled it, with huge determination. Fear is the opposite of Love, and it taught me the most valuable lesson. That spirit life is governed by the energy of love in every sense of that word.

He has closed his physical body down, I reasoned to my panicked mind. And it worked. Vision came back. And it was good that it did, for without any warning, the entire world erupted in flashes of lightening that completely lit up *Yggdrasill*. From the very uppermost part of the Ancient One, I glimpsed Wōden, in sharp relief against the white heat. It sizzled down towards him and the tree. I heard the deep crack, and felt the whole tree shudder in shock. It shook as the enormous power of Surt, the giant of fire, coursed down its body and into the ground at my feet.

This is not a re-birthing, I thought. This is the original Birthing of the Beginning!

This is the re-enactment of the Creation. The land of ice, meeting through the nine rivers, the land of Fire, Muspelheim, and the first Jotun was made, called Ymir.

As I thought this, I saw the life-forms of ice and those intricate shapes in spirit begin to melt and dissolve. The shards of ice melted to large drops onto the ground before me, making puddles that erupted with each new drop landing. It became like a shower of rain. The beautiful life-forms, like snowflakes, just dwindled and disappeared as if they had never been.

Then, so suddenly, I heard the crashing of branches. The snapping of leaves, as *Yggdrasill* shuddered visibly. I heard the long sharp scream of our boy-god as he fell from the World Tree downwards, ever falling from that high perch, where he had sat for many heart-aching twilights.

And there was absolutely nothing I could do as he hung, helplessly, unconscious, upside down, blood dripping from a wound, with his leg caught and completely bound by a thin young branch that had twisted around his thigh.

My spiritual heart in my wraith body just stopped. I held breath I did not own. Somewhere deep within my soul a scream began. It echoed upwards and out to the ethereal world I now inhabited.

"Ealdmōdor! Gèoc, Gèoc!
Wōden is be-slægan, hè is forþ-fering!
Gecwèman becuman
Āhreddan him gecwèman"

Grandmother help, help
Wōden is slain, he is dying,
Please come, save him please!"

Within the intake of breath, I felt strong arms wrap around me. I felt her kiss on my cheek, and felt her love simply soak into my wraith body. And I wept spirit tears of relief.

She held me for many moments while I calmed down.

"My child, you must know in your heart, even if your mind forbids it, that Wōden is not destined to die here. Not this day. He is about the business of becoming a god, child. Remember, please, why you were brought here! I will summon help."

"The ravens, *Ealdmōdor*! Call the ravens, please. Ask them to fly to find Frídr. She knows them, remember, you told me that in the Telling!"

"*Giese!* It is already done. Look Dagrun."

Banking sharply around the wide girth of *Yggdrasill* came Huginn and Muninn, their wings beating in rhythm. The rain hurling off their silken wings in a dance of droplets. They were majestic, beautiful, and now as I saw them in spirit form, a full radiance of colours, only hinted at in body. They settled at the base of the tree. *Ealdmōdor* spoke to them, they answered with the tapping of their feet and a loud caw of acceptance.

I saw Wōden twitch, then pull his arms up to cross over his chest. They saw it too and took off to circle gently around him, wings touching him as they banked off at a frightening speed to fetch help.

"Dagrun, *beorn*,", *Ealdmōdor* spoke so softly to me, and I knew she was about to leave, "Be strong, so strong in the coming times. You have much to witness. It will be but a flashing of seconds, and then you can return to your beloved Eileifer. He is waiting patiently caring for your sleeping self to wake up. He knows, so do not fret."

"Now listen, above all *hwæt!* For those sounds you are about to hear must be remembered. The signs you see must be remembered and the symbols. For this part, Dagrun, is the most important for the future generations, it must go the stones, intact. Do you understand?"

"*Giese!*" I replied, as I felt her spirit withdraw. Then she was gone.

… … … … … … … … …

CHAPTER TWENTY-SEVEN
Wuldortanas: The Glory Staves

The Runes

I knelt on the ground after her leaving, feeling emotions far more than was good for me. I was trembling in the aftermath of that shock, and seeing his swaying body dangling helplessly from the World Tree. There was nothing I could do, and in that helplessness, my vision dimmed. And I did not see "Them" come. It was the sound that arrived a mere few seconds after their appearance. I lost seconds in awareness and understanding.

Each symbol, shining and exuding this glow of silver light, had a sound, a low thrum of its own singular identity. Like the beating of a heart, these signs came from deep within the spiritual world, unseen and unknown to even ghosts and wraiths. And with them came complex layers of meanings and feeling, shown in tangible thought forms and colours that radiated feelings. Each one was a moving, audible sculpture of knowledge. And they were making their way towards Wōden.

He remained motionless, save for the slight swaying of his body, as it caught the rhythm of *Yggdrasill*. His arms, still tightly held across his chest, were holding what life-force he had left. Then, the miracle happened, and made me focus so intently, I missed not a second of wisdom growing before my eyes.

The Ancestors were sending the runes to their God. The twenty-four-fold pattern which lies at the very root of the world.

The shapes and sounds of the "Might's" were descending on the prone figure of Wōden.

And as it should be, Ansuz was the first rune to appear in a moving solid rhythm towards Wōden, shining in the violet of his own energy. Ansuz itself, may have spoken first of the dead forebears whose Might was still worked on the living.

And it was so fitting that Ansuz named Wōden as his. The Goths call their ancestor-ghosts Anses.

The living symbol moved closer to Wōden, and so subtly disappeared within him. I saw Wōden move, his body shake, and his head move from side to side. That beautiful violet energy shimmered again around him and I knew he was alive. And that he would live. The gift from the Anses was his breathe.

Yet so much more was gifted to Wōden that day.

Fehu came next, with the soft sound of F, rotating gently and shimmering in gold. There were whirlpools of energy circling around it giving a feeling of powerful energy. This next Rune entered and Wōden trembled with the might of it.

There came a pause. It seemed like an interval, a waiting time for the physical body of the god to adjust. His eyelids flickered for a moment and I thought he would open his eyes. But his vision was totally centred on the inner world. I felt the energy of his brain come alive, working furiously to hold the wisdom. I, on the other hand, was slow and only taking in feelings. I hoped it would be enough.

Ūruz came, slowly, meandering forward, like some slow beast, who could, so it was said, become fast and furious when threatened. Manly vigour was attached to this symbol. The Auroch honoured. And on entering the god figure now, gave him that stature also.

Þurisaz came forward as a skipping dancing giant of a wizard, who sang the sound of þ in a trill alternating with a deep bass. The iridescent colours altered with each turn. This symbol denoted shape-shifting and mischief. As it entered our dormant god, I saw him smile, the creases appear around his mouth and a dimple flash for all to see. A devilish humour came with this rune.

Raiðō swiftly moved in next. A rider taking to the road. The swift traveller and smart communicator. The sound was like a vibrating r, tongue against the roof of the mouth. It reminded me so much of our prayer chant as we travelled to the Nerthus Grove, taking the chariot to her. It entered Wōden to gift him the power of speed.

And with Kènaz came the burning element of Fire. The Rune was a torch flickering in reds and yellows. A symbol for Wōden giving controlled energy. It hovered over his upturned face. Then quite suddenly Wōden moved his arm, took the flaming symbol as a torch, before it entered him to become part of his growing soul.

The cross of the Gebō rune came twirling into view, circles of violet, purple, pink and amber, gyrating around the vortex, as a deep golden hue held the centre. The energy of giving, selflessly, of sacrifice in giving and honouring the brave and good in giving, spun in unison around this beautiful symbol.

They had never been just a symbol, I thought, as we had come to see the runes. Not at all: they were living, sentient beings of spirit. We use them in rite and ceremony, abiding by the lore handed down, but we had lost the vibrancy of *drycræft* magic, they hold. I committed a vow to re-live these moments in my life. And to share it with others.

Gebō spun into the heart-centre of Wōden. With each rune *drycræft*, his body and his soul was strengthening. This rune above all of them, excepting his naming rune, gave him great vitality, as I literally saw him spin with the motion of the "giving" rune, the "Might's" gift to their god.

Wunjō came spiralling in towards Wōden, the colours of sapphire blue and sap green joining together in a dance of balanced colours. Like our *Foldè Mōdor*, Nerthus and the Sky god, earth and air, co-joined. Yet it was the sound of W that opened my heart, for it was the sound of my people in harmony, that precious twilight of the *ðing*, where the gods gave us our name

Wihtwara, the seven tribes joining and uniting in common purpose. Knowing now, the living being that is the rune Wunjō and of the sheer *galdor-drycræft*, I felt a deeper appreciation of the gift bestowed on us that night.

Hœgl and ísaz came together with the low pitch sound rumbling forward as H and I, hurtled towards Wōden. He flinched and took the energy, swift, chaotic and cold, as the first winter rune. And ísaz as the last. Hail suddenly fell from the sky and hit him like tiny arrow barbs. I believe, if he had not been given the strengthening energy of the previous runes, he may not have survived this onslaught. He burrowed his head tighter into his chest, and the cross of his arms over his chest became even stronger. Hœgl and ísaz entered him, the hail passed. I saw him relax.

A few more heartbeats passed before Nauðiz, the bent cross, stopped: hanging in mid-air before Wōden. The energy coming from this winter rune, was perhaps the hardest of all. Negative feeling swamped me, and I was just the "Watcher." There were no colours vibrating around this symbol. Just a muddy mixture of foggy density that carried little or no light. It is the antithesis of Wunjō. It waited. For it was the ultimate test for Wōden. The emotions that accompany the worst deprivation was about to assault his body and his soul. And I felt heart-sorrow wash over me.

It was so sudden, when that rune Nauðiz sped towards him and bury itself within the dormant form. Wōden reacted instantly by buckling his body against the impact. He swayed to and fro, trying to escape it. But there was no escaping it. A long, low howl came from him, building to a crescendo of pain, both physical and mental, taking his battered soul back to his origins. There was no place that rune did not reach. The Mights were testing him to the core. I saw him go limp. I howled for help, silently, cutting across the void, I just hoped the Ravens heard and sped onwards to reach Frídr and Vermundr.

Then the miracle was created, by Wōden, with the will of Wōden and the love of his mother, Nerthus. This would be a

Telling for endless generations to come, I knew for certain he had now achieved the hard-fought status of a god in the eyes of the ancestor Mights.

Before me, as an eye witness, I saw Wōden create a rune of his own making. Wunjō lay at its centre, but he multiplied those to become four-sided and rotating slowly with the rhythm of the heartbeat of Yggdrasill. Colours of green and blue radiated around. Then he added the rune yet to come, and I knew this was from his Mother. Algiz grew on the four corners and was again duplicated. This beautiful structure spun slowly and encompassed the hanging god completely. He was trapped within, and yet safely hanging there. Then I saw him transform into the serpent, his mother's form, those blue-eyes opened momentarily, set against the shimmering amber scales. He opened his mouth wide, shrieking as he did so. Nauðiz, that hardest of all runes, shot from his gaping mouth, disappearing from whence it came.

Wōden had created the first *galdor-drycræft*, the *ægishjālmar*, protection and the great power were now his.

The runes came faster now, almost one upon another. I felt joy for the first time since the hanging. I knew we were seeing the positive energy growing to bring about a completion.

Jèra arrived, both symbols connected in a dance of life. Gyrating around each other the melodious sound of J skipped lightly to our ears. The measure of time and the passing of the mild seasons celebrated in each movement. Wōden smiled with ease as it entered him. I could feel him relax.

Eihwaz came slowly, showing the longevity of its energy. A deep green spun slowly around and called its name: the ancient Yew. The All-encompassing wisdom that old One holds, came into Wōden. This rune symbol altered its shape to the sounds coming from spirit. From the Mights. It changed its form even as it made its way towards him. Straight angular lines now wavered into a liquid pattern. It was mimicking water. Then it became a multi-faceted snowflake giving an energy of purity in its path.

Everything was a story to this rune, Eihwaz. Wōden opened his heart to accept it.

Then the rune Perþ arrived, the Fates owning this one, for it is the symbol of the well of times' past. This upturned well shows the evolutionary forces entering the lives of many. As it entered our man-god, now god in many aspects, I heard his voice clearly, in my mind.

"Watcher, take heed of this Rune, *beorn*. When you clearly see this rune appear on the beech tree, the river of *Wyrd* will cascade into your lives like a whirlpool through a cobweb. That time you fear will be upon you. Tell your children, and their children's children."

I saw him clearly now, conscious, aware and looking straight at me, those clear eyes shooting straight to my soul. I nodded in recognition, and in answer, he swirled on his root binding, a full circle. He had succeeded. Hr had come through the trial for his life. And he was growing stronger with every rune.

Algiz hummed with the sound Z. A pure gold colour danced around the tall shape of Wōden, symbolising the divine protector twins, guardians to the sacred places. It was like the sound of our own sacred bees, protecting the honey which created the mead. Wōden grinned as this one entered him, for he was now the master of the mead cup. There must still be part of him, the young boy, eager to experiment with anything and everything.

An intense light suddenly assaulted all my senses in my wraith world. Too much, too bright, I shouted as the rune sped towards Wōden like a spinning fireball. Sōwulō, I knew well, for I used that energy in my healing so often. Seeing it now before me, alive, pulsating with healing, the disc speeding across the void on the chariot, I loved it even more. Wōden took the full force, its power akin to its opposite Hagalaz. He was swept back, knocking against the large bough behind him. I thought it knocked him out cold. He stayed motionless, swaying, then a warm golden hue grew around his body, and his eyes opened again giving the largest warming smile I had ever seen from him. He tended towards the serious, did our young man-god. But now, he was maturing before my eyes. He was enjoying himself in his sacrifice!

A strong warrior energy entered my world. Pulsating with unexpressed aggression. That thirst for victory and the will to see it through. The war god Teiwaz was represented by this rune. The glowing red-hot rune immediately instilled fear in me. I had to swamp it. The upright spear shape with the shrill sound of T, sped towards Wōden, who, with incredible speed, flicked his arm out to grab the rune, as if to master it, own it and enslave it to his will. Wōden was taking the spearhead of Teiwaz to himself, now and forever.

In contrast, gentle Berkana, representing our lady of the woods, the Birch tree, in all her silver daintiness flurried in with that translucent glow of silver birch gleaming at twilight. The sound B came low and delicate as she spun on her axis before Wōden. Fertility radiated from her. Wōden was captivated, staring, with his head to one side, drinking in this ultimate feminine energy. The counterpoint of Teiwaz, she was his balancer. Working *galdor- drycræft* with these two living energies would bring total balance within, between male and female. It was intended by the Mights that they were together.

I watched Wōden as he assimilated this new energy. I do believe it pleased him very much. For in this moment, the knowledge and acceptance came to him for his seed to be flung far and wide." So, may it be", I heard him whisper. The thought amused him greatly.

Still lingering with that last thought, he was not aware of Ehwaz galloping forward, the colours of ebony and ivory intermingling with russet and brown. All the colours of horse swirled around this rune. The horse is most sacred to us in all its aspects. I tried so hard to concentrate on the moment, but my will failed me, for Eileifer came into view, strong and lucid, and with him the old white stallion from our sacred ones back home. He was head-bent, talking gently, and the old grandfather was answering in kicks and flicks of the tail, rippling muscles and tweaking of his ears. It was so beautiful I was being sucked back.

"Watcher! *Wacian*, Trust, co-operation Dagrun", came a thunderous voice, which pulled me back immediately. Wōden was not happy.

Mannaz, the rune of humankind followed behind our beloved horses. It was as it should be. For this rune linked us to our ancestor Mannus, the first divine human. Yet, fallible and mortal, it entered Wōden as a reminder of his humanness. He took it deep within, his challenge to balance the god and human within him.

Then, suddenly a waterfall of blues, turquoise and deep aquamarine appeared in his world carrying the rune Laguz, accompanied by the sound L, a fast trill ascending, then descending in tone, following the path of Laquz to Wōden. He fixed his stare deeply on the energy coming from it. The river of *Wryd* was at its centre. Everything the Fates knew lay in the rushing waters, and Wōden had to learn swiftly.

His clear voice cried out;

"Becuman āninga þæt brād eorðe þu fæmne Eall-ðearllond ūt þæt èast dimness feolan!
Urdhr! Verhandi! Skuld!
Rūnar rādha rètt rādh!

Come forth the wide world you maidens, All-mighty out the eastern darkness enter!
Urdhr, Verhandi Skuld
Runes rown right rede!"

Some time elapsed. The last runes appeared before Wōden.

Inguz, a shimmering golden diamond, with the sound *ng* thrummed a low beat, rotated slowly towards him. The Divine god Ing and all his primeval energy lay within. A benign and kind god of the green and water. A consort to our Nerthus and friend to the Anglii, who in their homeland are called Ingavonii. I immediately thought of Ingvar and little Ing, on my Wihtland.

The emotion overshadowed the following runes of ðagaz and ōpila arriving to spin and disappear into Wōden.

Everything was becoming misty. I thought my will was fading and losing my time here, yet again. I could not have been more wrong!

Within a flash of awareness, I saw the figures emerge to stand by the well of the Fates. It was the Norns. They had come to Wōden, and as they bent over the water, starring into the depths, all the runes appeared again, simultaneously, blending into different complex forms, each holding immense powerful *drycræft*. These were the *Galdor- runes,* used only in ritual magic, or for powerful healing. Wōden held his arms wide and they came to him. He shook with the power. I tried to memorize them. I heard his voice within my head announce;

"Dagrun, *beorn, þu ãgan tō gōdre ãre cuman. Þes is mæst hefig.*

Cèpan æt þín heorte þæt fãcems fram galdor drýcræft. Giefan hiè æt þín Sãcerde fram seiðr drycræft. Þes is þæt gifu fram þæt Nornir"

"Dagrun, dear one, you have served well. This is most important. Take to your heart these symbols of Galdor-magic. Give then to your priestesses. This is the gift from the Norns."

I sat and asked for help. The symbols appeared before me in my mind, like bright lights. Seared into my memory, one after the other, they were clear and unmistakable, I knew I would be able to recall them at any time in the future.

The Norns looked up from their *drýcræft,* and together they walked with the cauldron of Fate, over to Yggdrasil. They took the sand and filled their bags with it. At the base of the World Tree, they waited, looking up at Wōden.

"*Epandi nam!*" I take the Runes!" Wōden shouted from the depths of his lungs, eyes wide, staring at the Norns.

They flung their arms forward, together in unison, fingers pointing at Wōden. The shot of sizzling light came from their fingers, twisted in the air and hit the tangled branch which sizzled as it broke. The hold over Wōden was gone. He fell to the ground, released, free and very much alive.

The Norns fed Yggdrasill with the water of *Wyrd*, sprinkled the sand upon it branches, for it never to wither or die. They bowed and gave thanks to this Ancient One who had gone through so much pain to gift Wōden his status as a god.

And in the same misty breath as they had come, the sisters of *Wryd* disappeared.

… … … … … … … … …

Wōden lay on the ground, curled up in an infantile hug. Then his hands reached out to grab the soft soil before him. He held the moist pungent earth tightly, then released it to grab more, feeling her softness again after so long. He moved to crouch on all fours, looking around, like a wolf, examining his world. Taking in smell, and touch, aromas, eddies in the wind, all were being processed as if he was born anew.

He moved with agile speed, still on all fours to put his nose to the bushes and plants before him. There lay herbs. I recognised them as chervil and plantain, with some sour apple over to his left. This was deciduous land, where all the forest growth was determined by the flat of the land near to the shoreline. He buried his head into the greenery, flaring his nostrils in a joy of the plant aromas. He crouched. Then he sat back, holding the herbs in his hand, murmuring softly to himself, almost half singing the rune sounds into the herbs. This was his moment of understanding the healing *drýcræft* before him. Of all the legendary things Wōden would become, the healer and *sèconde* using *seiðr* magic, was the most enduring, the gift to his people.

The loud rhythmical swishing and thrumming of black raven wings brought his two spirit guardians before him, each perched on a low branch of *Yggdrasil*. Wōden stood and looked up at them, inclining his head in a respectful bow. They responded with a loud caw, a ruffling of wings before they flew off into the gathering gloom. It was twilight and night was coming.

Then two welcome shadows walked into the glade that made my heart open with joy. Frídr and Vermundr strode forward to greet their young god. Frídr looked hard into Wōden's eyes, head on a slant. He had changed, he had grown taller.

"Well," she said softly, "you are certainly the "One who is stretched"!"

"*Fōdhèrun!*" Vermundr stated with a smile, "And "One who thunders." You certainly have a well of that power now, young sir!"

Wōden flung his head back and exploded with laughter. It was catching, and we all roared with laughter, tears rolling down our cheeks. Well, for me they were not wet, just a tickling sensation that was not unpleasant. That intense crackling energy of spiritual work evaporated as swiftly as it had come. We were in human time again, completely, and all that it held in laughter, joy, tears, and tiredness. And oh! How tired we were. Even me, as a wraith, I suddenly felt overcome with exhaustion, and an empty feeling. I realised it was a kind of hunger.

Vermundr carried a pole holding a young boar, and Frídr had collected herbs and forest food. The fire was kindled with hot embers kept in a pouch and so very soon they were all eating, stuffing dripping meat in ravenous mouths, a silence prevailing as hunger was appeased. Then Frídr remembered me and looked over.

"Imagine you are eating Dagrun, feel the taste and texture, it will appear, I promise!"

And so, it did, in all the lusciousness of imagined food at its best. No burnt edges touched my lips, just fragrant juices and delicious meat. The herbs came with an aura of healing energy and I devoured those.

Tiredness began to overcome us all. I imagined that Wōden was beyond exhaustion. But he held an inner power now. Almost still throbbing with energy, I wondered if he would sleep at all.

Just as I was about to sink into my imagined bed of feathers, he came over to me. I found the intensity of this new energy he had created within him, almost breath-taking. He looked at me for several minutes, remaining silent. Then his voice entered my mind.

"Ðoncian þu, thank you Watcher. You have done important work through these days. But now it is done. You have a choice before you. You can now go home to your Eileifer. He will so surely be overjoyed to have you back. Or.... you may choose to stay. It is for you to decide."

My tiredness suddenly evaporated. I was left feeling stunned, my heart beating fast. I had not expected this. I imagined I would be "watching" Wōden to learn of his whole life. But I suddenly realised that that was not just impossible but undesirable for me. Then what were my feelings, my intuition?

The desire to go home was so intense, I began to panic. Almost immediately the world before me began to fade. It was at this moment I realised I did not want to leave.... not yet. I wanted to learn of the Wōden's *Fylgia*, his Fetch animals, all of them! And how he made the glory sticks and their healing power. *Seiðr drýcræft* was granted to him. How? This was my magic and had been since I was very young.

"Sleep on it, Dagrun Wahl!" His voice loud again within my mind, "Sleep on it."

I did, and dreamt also, for my *Ealdmōdor* came to me. We talked together and when I "awoke" from my wraith sleep, I remembered it all of course, for there are no barriers in this world of spirit. She told me of the times to come. My heart broke. And of my role in keeping the knowledge alive, through the stones recording and keeping. And, the Telling's to come, where I would be given the role left by my lost brother Eyvindr. She spoke of him too. His life as a *Rōmānisc* proved adequate. He learnt skills with the tesserae, creating mosaics. But he loved the *drycræft* of the smithy much more. The joy of his children had filled the aching hole left by that terrible wrench away from his spiritual path. He taught them both the ways of Mithras and the wisdom of Nerthus. He let them choose their way. The magic of the *wights* and the hidden ones, the way of *Wryd*. But also, the mysteries of Abraxas. Above all he made sure they would understand the stones as sentient, ancient beings, who are the guardians of our ways.

"He leaves no stone unturned, Dagrun *beorn*", she whispered as she left. "And your children will bind with his children to form the most powerful Wihtwara yet!"

I sat looking to the brilliant sun that filtered into my world. And through the glare came Wōden, refreshed, grinning widely at me, the one who could not be seen.

"Well, *beorn*," he spoke with a deeper resonance to his voice now. He was every inch a man, the boy had been chased away. "Have you reached a decision? Is it me…. or your "loved" one?"

I laughed. How dare he be so mocking! How dare he make a pass at a wraith, a ghost! If his head were to grow much bigger it would block out that sun!

He laughed, for of course he read my thoughts even before they came to mind.

"Well, it is a straight question," I replied looking at the ground, "the answer to which is as straight…You!"

"*Gōd*", he replied, "But be aware, there will be experiences to test you. Scenes you will wish never to see and which may haunt you in later times. This journey has been very easy. It gets much harder. And please do not judge. That is not your right. Not at all."

With that he rose and joined the others who were busy throwing detritus to cover the fire and leave no trace. Why! I thought.

Then I heard the conversation between Wōden and Vermundr.

"Yngling and Loki have been close on our heels", Vermundr said, kicking at the fire," Yngling is stirring up his hatred of you, Wōden. He wants revenge."

"I know", Wōden replied, "He uses people and he uses *drýcræft*. I know full well that the runes Hagalaz and Nauðiz are his to command. Nauðiz sped out of me, running from Nerthus energy, straight to Yngling who grabbed its *drýcræft* with both hands. We make for the summit. Frídr you remember the way?"

"*Giese!*" she replied, as they pulled their sacks over them, Wōden's furs, now dried, were pinned to his body by the straps of his backpacks. They set off for the aching arduous climb to the summit where Wōden was named in ceremony all those years ago and where Yngling was shamed.

… … … … … … … … …

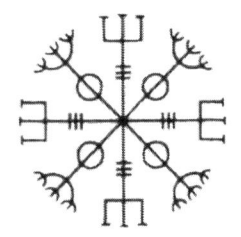

CHAPTER TWENTY-EIGHT
Yngling and Loki

    The trees roots dug deep. Their anchor to the earth was fragile at best. Yet the vertical beauty of the mountain trees, the firs and pinewood giving off thick heady scents of resin, made the climb possible. By their stubborn anchorage to this impossible angle, it made the climbers determined to achieve their goal. The summit beckoned if only to see blazing Sunni again. It was dense and dark, even in the middle of the day. *Ealdmōdor* had made her descriptive of this part of the journey much less arduous. Memory always softens the harsh moments, leaving a glow of adventure that left out the bleeding hands and feet. The grappling with grunts and hissing screams. The next foot and handhold that lurched aching bodies just a half-spear length upward.

    Wōden had, by sheer nature of his acquired power and his youth, spurred ahead and was now completely out of sight. Frídr and Vermundr had stopped, sitting, quietly talking, and repairing their bleeding hands, ripped by the constant grabbing of pine branches to pull them upwards. Frídr applied honey salve to both their hands before wrapping more bandages around them. She tied tough leather to the soles of their feet for better grip. The ascent was cruel.

    Frídr looked over to me, squinting, trying to see me through the sweat glistening on her face. She was weighed down by the exertion. Her spirit eclipsed by the physical need to focus on surviving.

"Dagrun, *sweostor* Wōden is up to something. I feel it. Please make your way up ahead and be *our* "watcher" for a while. Come straight to us if you see Yngling or Loki near."

I floated past them both, feeling sympathy, yet unable to ease their pain. And she was right, for I had a tense feeling starting to wrap round me for the safety of our youthful god. There were two mighty vengeful spirits lurking out there, set against his own newly acquired God status. How much was bravado and how much was skill?

So, I sped around the trees, a mere blurring of images. And I found the speed of movement quite exhilarating. I was enjoying the race so much, I did not see Wōden at all, and sped straight through him in a whoosh of energy that made him look up so very startled, I smiled.

"By the gods, watcher," he hissed, "Never do that again!"

He was crouched in a tight huddle of limbs and arms, his head only slightly protruding over the bush that was his cover. And now I was by his side, and looking over at the two figures that filled me with horror. Yngling and Loki were only a spear length away from us.

"Get behind me *beorn*!" Wōden whispered, "If you are seen, I cannot protect you and do what needs to be done. Am I clear?"

I wanted to ask him exactly what he intended to do but instead I shrunk away from the dark energies before me. I hid behind the thickest fir I could find and I asked the *dryad* to cloak me in forest green. After a while, I peeked beyond the dense bark to bear witness.

Loki had disappeared down a hole in the forest floor.

"Dig deeper", Yngling shouted down to him, "A bear pit is a huge hole in the ground, and it must appear to be just that!"

"I am going as fast as I am able," came the muffled reply. Wooden spikes lay on the ground nearby. Yngling was busy sharpening them to a horrifying point. They were intended to impale through gut and bone. I watched with disgust building, as the scene developed. Yngling was sitting on a large decaying log, his cloak spread wide around him. Sparks nearly flew from the pine he was spiking with the ferocity of his *seax* against the wood. His straggly grey hair moved with the motion of his shoulders bending to the task. He grunted periodically. He was not a young man. He was pot-bellied and varicose-veined. He was bent with anger. He was bent on revenge.

To one side lay a heavy woven latticed bear trap cover. Placed over the hole and covered with forest detritus, the hole would be completely concealed. It lay on the direct path that Frídr had flagged out. Her original coloured ties, though tattered and faded, still hung to the trees. A timeless reminder of that journey so many moons before. And it was about to be violated! It had the stench of cowardice too, for there was no honour here.

Wōden waited, silent, unmoving, watching the scene unfold. I wondered what he had planned. I could not anticipate his actions.

After some while, Loki heaved himself out of the pit using a ragged rush and branch rope hastily entwined and pegged into the ground. His dark hair was now in sweaty strands, his black eyes glowed in an amber light that radiated deep hatred. Why he held such animosity to his brother? Why the resentment that fuelled his energy to hatred, I could not fathom, but it was a reality forever present for the young god.

Loki untied the ragged rope. Now having served its purpose, it was fed to the fire, a burning ember now, the light was fading. *Mōnã* began shedding her faint light upon the pines and fir trees. He had spent some time placing the murderous spikes uppermost in the base of the pit, each one capable of scoring through flesh on impact. Loki's last act before he walked away, was to heave the woven dried and brittle fallen branches over the bear trap and cover it skilfully with detritus to camouflage its presence on the forest path. Then he lay down, wrapped in furs against the chilly night.

I heard Loki muttering outbursts filled with hatred, low and inaudible. But Wōden caught them and I saw him tense and shudder. I nearly spoke out but he calmed his nerves and waited. And waited.

I was doing a wraiths version of "nodding off" when my eyes almost peeled away from their lids. Before me *drýcræft* was happening. Wōden had conjured the *galdercræft* of protection. It hovered around him, while he called in the power before him. It shone and rotated, in golden luminous light before entering the body of the God. Then in total darkness I saw, in spirit, a change come upon him. His aura altered from the deep violet I always recognised as totally his, to a deep green, encased in a smouldering orange. He shook and twisted and I felt rather than saw, his physical form transform into a growling, teeth snarling, saliva dripping alpha wolf. Its head hung low, the large paws flopped silently on the ground as it moved forward. I thought it would head straight for Loki. But I was wrong.

The wolf, now belly down, was scraping noiselessly on the forest floor. He was moving towards the hunched figure of Yngling who was still sitting on his ancient old log, taking first watch, but completely oblivious to the world. He was fast asleep, his heavy breath exploding with each snore, as his head was locked onto his chest. He had tied his long straggling hair in a suevian twist that reached his belly. His neck utterly exposed.

Almost before the realisation came to me, the wolf pounced with lightning speed and ferocity. I saw their two auras merge in deadly battle, but there was no fight from Yngling, old and decrepit as he was, bent with many moons of hatred that hung to his bones. He gave up his life almost without a twitch. The wolf had grabbed his neck, trapped his voice in one crunch and silenced that voice forever. There were no shouts or gurgled screams as the blood spouted out. But he was not dead.

What occurred next defied my mind completely. This lone wolf began to drag the limp body of Yngling over to the bear trap. The old man was heavy and still wearing the long robe that was his signature garment of leadership and ancestry. The wolf silently pulled and heaved, his long canine teeth never losing grip on the tattered fabric. When Yngling was lying at the edge of the trap, the wolf silently moved round and pushed the old priest over the edge. The dry wood cracked and broke. Yngling fell to be scored through in many places on his old body.

The wolf loped off into the darkness, slowly shaking his head and came to sit near my covering tree.

We both saw the incumbent form of Loki shift and slowly move. He had been aware of it all. Now he chose to shift himself. He released himself from the furs, save one, which he wrapped around his body. He knelt at the edge of the pit, craning his neck to look deep within. In the total darkness, he would see nothing, so he pulled some embers from the small carrying sack at his waist and used them to light an oiled taper. It radiated enough smoky glow to bring the twitching and still conscious form of old Yngling into shadowed focus. He turned his head to stare beseechingly at Loki to save him, his student in all things dark. Loki stared back, put his head on a slant and grinned. It was a wide malevolent grin that spoke silently of his disrespect and indifference to his teacher.

"Oh, old man," he purred down at him, "I burnt the rope. What a shame! There is no way down for me. Even if I could, I would decline. Do you see? You have no allies among your recruits of the darker arts. That any compassion was driven out of us when we were so young, by you! How you can expect me to show any towards you now! That is utter conceit on your part. You are a revengeful load of flabby flesh. That flesh will now rot …. slowly. Mark me well old man. Many moons will pass over this pit, the grave you are in, before you see eternal darkness before you. And there will be no Halls of Valhalla to greet you with the mead cup. Your death was never meant to be honourable, old man."

No sound came from within that deadly pit. Loki sat there for some time, until he saw the low glow of dawn edge across the sky.

"Hmmmm, old man, dawn approaches" Loki spoke almost to himself, thinking out loud, "Shall I be kind? Wolves abound here and bears. They would see an easy dinner in you would they not? Shall I show compassion? An easier, yet much more excruciatingly painful death is before you. If I throw this torch into you and fire up the detritus, your blood will sizzle, slowly, your flesh will blister and burst, your eyes will melt and your brain will slowly cook before ever you see the darkness. Shall I? Give me a sign if you cannot speak."

He sat for a while, thinking, watching. Then slowly, with a casual flick of his wrist, sent the flare down into the pit. Loki stood up and walked away into the forest.

My heart stopped, my mind so unprepared for such evil. Nothing in all my life on Wihtland had prepared me for this. Then a surge of anger overcame me.

"Þu ācwellan þæt misdǣd wǣpnedmann!" I screamed into the darkness. Into the void, where I had chosen to live. I looked over to the wolf, but he had silently gone, like his dark brother, disappearing into the forest darkness.

"You have killed the wrong man!"

"*Watcher, be quiet, be still,*" thundered a voice in my mind. The voice of Wōden.

"Do not presume to judge ME, *stripling!* I thought I told you, you do not have that right. Speak to Frídr and Vermundr if you must. GO! Before my dark brother, whom I must never kill, sees you and then it will be you who is slain!"

I fled faster than I had ever moved before, the trees passing me as a mere blur, and the forest floor just faintly tickling me feet. It was not just panic that sped me away. I was shocked, even disillusioned. The anger has been overlaid with confusion. And with it all protection gone. Frídr saw me clearly and caught me fast in her arms.

"Stay still, *beorn,*" she whispered, "Please stay still. Calm down. While I get your protection around you. Daylight is nearly upon us and Loki is close I can feel it."

I resisted screaming, I resisted crying. All these human physical emotions that assist us in release of unwanted energies are denied a wraith, who wished to stay a wraith. I practised some deep breathing and achieved a measure of calm, a level of detachment. The world gradually became clearer.

Frídr and Vermundr had come upon the first piece of level ground. It spoke of the summit being close. Just as the evil Loki and Yngling had found flat ground to create the bear pit.

I sat down and haltingly told Frídr and Vermundr what had happened in the night.

Both sat together on a large log, Frídr poking the ember fire with a stick, rustling up flames which licked the remains of dinner to warm up for their first food of the day. The two hares skewered to the pole which hung between two v shaped pieces of ash, still had good meat on them. I suddenly felt ravenously hungry and willed some of that meat into my world, already warmed and succulent.

We ate in silence for a while, then I continued. Worst of all was the description I had to give of the murder and the evil shown by Loki.

Vermundr sat, elbows on his knees, head down, nodding occasionally and not shocked or perturbed by my Telling.

After a silence that became heavy, he spoke to me with softness and care in his voice.

"Dagrun, *sweostor* our young God is right. You do not have the right to judge him, on any level or at any time. He does what is needful. Always. You, who have the luxury of walking away from this at some time in the future, do not have all the facts before you. That is why you are a Watcher, and only that!"

"It has been a test of his moral strength to have borne the slurs and plotting that old Yngling has directed towards him. From his birth, onwards. Nerthus has watched aghast at his schemes to compromise him and sometimes endanger him. You must have been told by your *Ealdmōdor,* of Yngling's first attempt to endanger the young boy on this very summit!

It was Nerthus herself who asked for retribution as soon as the young man came into his rightful power. Yngling has spent many years pulling young men to his evil schemes. Some were suited, some were coerced. Loki was his favoured one. Look how he has been repaid, Dagrun? Yet Wōden will never kill his half-blood brother. Never. Loki is the dark side of Wōden. Always the reverse side of the coin, *sweostor*, remember that."

I sat cradling my head in my shaking hands, taking it all in.

"It is a coward's way", I said at last, "There is no honour here. Everything that has been plotted, reeks of it. I understand now. It is abhorrent in my world, and it is abhorrent in yours. Wōden was only seeking rightful justice. The honour of fighting on the battlefield runs deep in the blood of our people, and your people. We cannot allow anything less to get rooted in anyone's world."

"It is worse that Yngling has Ingavonii blood, Dagrun. Shameful in his betrayal of his own royalty, his own kind." Frídr said.

"He will be in Hel, now", I said quietly. Then banished the thought away.

"Time to move on, I think", said Vermundr, "we must meet with Wōden soon. Loki is burning for a fight. We will force him to fight honourably at last and not behind the back of someone else."

… … … … … … … … …

CHAPTER TWENTY-NINE
Fylgia: GERI and FREKI

We all felt Wōden had disappeared to be with his beloved *fylgia,* his fetch animals. The wolves lived near the summit, in sunny glades and warm pastures in summer and brilliant snow in winter. It was here that Godwulf, his father had brought the young Wōden, still a baby, to be named with the Goddess, at the summit. And it was here that Wōden met the great white wolf, *Vídarr,* forest warrior, who became his *fylgia* and guardian.

We set off through the dappled sunlit forest, getting warmer as the day grew. Gone were the thick set pines, hugging each other for mutual strength against the impossible incline, and which kept the forest permanently cool in summer and freezing in winter. Shadows played against the bark of elm, ash and even oak had found its way here.

"Shoot on Dagrun!" Frídr pronounced with a smile, "You more than most need some relief. Find it in the glory of the white wolf pack."

"Wōden," she smiled, "will be pleased to see you I'm sure. Tell him we are on our way."

I needed no second guessing and moved my spirit forward at a quick pace. This part of wraith skills I found natural and very enjoyable. If I was not fleeing for my spirit life that is! Speeding through the dappled sunlight created a joy that cascaded into my very sou. Warmth I had sorely missed, yet did not register until this moment. Frídr was right, she knew me. I was a novice, a wraith in training as much as Wōden had been a god in training. An unlikely match, we had been hustled together by the Mights and by *Wryd,* who had sealed our mutual fate in this endeavour.

I burst through into the secret glade, so beautifully described by *Ealdmōdor.* I caused a ruffle of fur, a pricking of ears and a low growl to come from the most exquisite white wolf I had ever seen. He was old, in his later summers. His eyes fixed on mine, an unbelievable piercing blue, a glow shone from them that spoke of deep wisdom.

It was *Vídarr*. And I crouched in respect, looking only at the ground before me. I dared not move. Even as a wraith, I felt vulnerable in his presence, knowing full well he could enter my world with ease and do what he felt he should!

I heard a mixture of human and wolf sounds, dialogue spoken between Wōden and his guardian. *Vídarr's* tail thumped on the grass three times, and then he flopped with ease only years can bring, onto the warm earth. And I looked up. I had heard it said, when I was a child, that certain dogs have a human spirit within. They are in accord with humans so much, it defies their natural form.

Vídarr was one such wolf.

He was grinning at me, with a full display of huge canine teeth, that given different circumstances, would make the blood run cold. But here was a warmth and a simple joy that made me smile back, a huge smile I had not given in many a moon back home.

I started to laugh, and he smiled even wider, flicking his old head from to side to side in sheer mirth of the moment. I came to him, on all fours, sitting beside him, giving him a wraith's version of a good tickle. His tail flopped rhythmically on the grass. It was such a precious moment. And all the fear and uncertainty, sorrow and stretched patience, melted away in the hot sun.

I looked over to Wōden, who was completely entangled, and almost indistinguishable from two skipping, lurching wolves, all legs and tails. It was an unfair match. The young wolves were winning by a large margin. Growls from Wōden did nothing to diminish their playfulness and Wōden was enjoying every moment. After some while, he gave up and lay supine on the crumpled grassland, while his two companions licked the sweat and grime away from him. He patted and stroked them. Then with a suddenness of the instant decision, they both sprang away from him and sped away on a chase for the winner, their white coats shining in the sun, two white-hot thunderbolts.

He leaned up on his elbows, staring over at us.

"*Wacian Wilcume! IC am gecwènlíce þū fegan ūs*! Watcher Welcome! I am pleased you join us! My wolf family welcomes you also, as you can see. *Vídarr* is *fæder* to these two young ones, *Geri* and *Freki*, my *fylgia*. You too can call on them in times to come, Dagrun. Trust me they will come as guardians to you and yours." He paused for a moment, staring intently at me.

"I thought you may feel the need to go home to your beloved. Yet I did warn you and you chose to stay. My respect grows Dagrun Wahl of the Warinni."

"*Giese* Yes, I did choose to stay," I replied firmly, hoping my intent carried in my voice to him, "But I tell you one thing, Wōden, I will not, I truly will not, follow you onto the killing fields. You, who grows into a "berserker" on the fields of many battles! No, I will not do that!"

Wōden bent his head, looking, pondering into the grass land before him. The silence hung heavy in the warm air, the buzzing of flying insects amplified and became loud. Then, quite suddenly, as was his hallmark, he sprung to his feet and pounded over to join me next to *Vídarr*. I braced my fragile wraith spirit for a thunderous onslaught. It did not come.

"Men make of Gods what they will, Watcher," Wōden began, quietly, gently, so I had to concentrate to hear, "Men and Gods, Gods and men, forever entwined in each other's fate. For if man turns his back on a God, then that God dies. If a God turns his back on man, then man will rue the day! It is ever thus, *beorn*."

"So, the minds of men create the legends. They desire a God of war, and all men crave for something larger than themselves. And sometimes they will acquire one by their own imaginations. And I became that war god, overturning the mighty Tiw in their worship of me. Yet you know this, riding as you do on the tide from our future."

"But here before you, lies the larger truth of me…that is why you are here. And yet again I say, watch and learn, remember and commit the memory to the stones."

He sighed deeply, "That *morðor* you witnessed was my first and hopefully my last, Watcher. It was requested of me to fulfil the act, not just for justice but also for me to experience *morðor* so I may take the lessons into my heart and soul. Both are made less, never to return to wholeness. Many thousands of men swim the tide of *Wyrd* as wounded swimmers."

"It is that pity I will take to the fields of blood. I go as a healer first and foremost, and to aid those spirits loosening from their mortal bodies to rise to *Valhalla* or *Neorxenawang*."

"But as a God I have freewill, and must exercise it. My role in battle is to oversee the dead. I can determine who will die and who will live. I have a spear to make, Watcher, here on this sacred mountain. A most magnificent long thrumming spear it will be. Slender, straight and true, so whoever sees and hears that spear overhead will most certainly travel to *Valhalla*."

"No, Dagrun, you do not have to witness the bloody wars, but I will send you something of them in your dreams, which you will know and that they come from me."

"I have other aims in my physical life on this Mother Earth. Huge enjoyment is to be had in plentiful ways… I love a *glèowian* in all its camouflage, I love women…", He said laughing and here he gave me the most penetrating look, "And let me tell you Dagrun Wahl, were you not a wraith and with a *Cyng,* I would be having you right now, this very moment!"

"Ohh." I gasped, "I…well, I am glad I'm a wraith then."

At this, he roared with laughter, and I watched as *Vídarr's* tail thumped enthusiastically on the forest floor.

"And finally, words and the power of them, will overcome the tainted minds and the faulty hearts of men. I will use the power of my mind and wisdom before ever I reach for that spear. You have my word."

Silence fell, but it was comfortable. I became lost in my thoughts, still softly stroking the chief of the white wolves, whom, I swear, I heard purring. A low gravelly sound from deep inside, bringing a look of utter contentment to his scarred and weathered face.

There was truth in Wōden's words. Of the seven tribes who travelled the big sea to settle in Britannia, those remaining in *Cant* had become war-ready, hostile and greedy for land. Having heard of our name-giving during our *ðing*, Eileifer was informed by a messenger, they had named themselves the *Cantwara*.

I longed for Eileifer, I longed for home.

"Stay watcher," came Wōden's voice, clear and calm, already feeling my thoughts, "Stay a little while longer. Your time is nearly here and what you will witness now is but a flicker of your eyelids, on your fur lined bed at Eileifer's newly built lodge. He wishes you to awake in the solar! Think of that my *beorn*!"

NO!!! I did not wish to dwell on that. I would be gone in a second, my feelings eclipsing the delicate balance of spirit. I heard Wōden laughing softly. He was goading me! Dah! I thought, this God has a wicked sense of humour.

But we both ceased in the fun making when *Vídarr* suddenly altered the tenor of his low purring to a deep growl. Within an instant he had changed into a tense and ferocious wolf, teeth bared and snarling.

"Oh, Wōden," I exclaimed," I forgot to tell you, Frídr and Vermundr are near."

"*Nah*, they are not!" Wōden snarled, "Get under *Vídarr*, NOW. It is Loki."

He lunged for his pack and withdrew, with a sharp scraping of metal, the forged sword that had already dripped with young blood in the training yard. Now, Wōden held it two fisted, upright and glinting in the sun, against his own brother. He was swinging it slowly, flexing his muscles in readiness, as Loki burst into view.

Vídarr growled louder and made ready to pounce, his guardian instincts coming into full play.

"*Forstoppian*!" Wōden shouted. The wolf, understanding, flopped down on top of me, protecting me completely from the gaze of Loki.

"Hah," exploded Loki as he too whipped out his sword, "I see you have your lap dog, brother."

The two brothers circled each other, weighing up the time to lunge, gauging the weakness in defensive posture. In Wōden, there was none. I could see clearly, as *Vídarr* had shifted slightly to give me vision, but not enough for the evil Loki to spot me. Even so, my breath was shallow and my nerves taut to breaking point.

"I will finish that straggly old dog, the minute after I have seen you on the forest floor, your lifeblood soaking out of you into the earth!"

"Brother," Wōden snarled, "You are about to learn a hard lesson. Fight with honour or not at all. There is nothing honourable about you. Cowardice reeks from you like a nauseating smell. I will best you brother and clean you up!"

"Honour gets you killed, my twin of all goodness! Tis not I who will bleed" And he chose to lunge, sword held straight at Wōden's heart. The ducking manoeuvre was practised and complete. Swerving round gave Wōden the full width of Loki's back. Loki was fast on his feet and twisted round to block the thrust, metal singing as both swords clashed.

They parried and thrust, both dancing around each other with a lightness of foot that spoke of many years' practise. But Wōden was the taller, and caught Loki with his sword, aimed downwards, in the shoulder. Blood oozed and Loki shrieked in pain, holding his sword arm, which now hung limply by his side. Now the balance had been re-set in Wōden's favour, as he lunged again and again, two hands on his long sword. Loki was forced to defend each thrust with one hand on his own sword, as he continually stepped backwards towards the trees. He did not see Vermundr. He only felt the strangle hold of his arms at his back and a sword held to his throat. It was Frídr who held that sword and had the complete intent to kill him with it, swiftly. Her hatred of Loki showed in her eyes and the twitching of her cheek muscle, as she held herself barely in control.

"You are the coward, brother", Loki hissed, struggling against the vice-like grip of Vermundr, a head taller, and much wider, "What is honourable about this!"

Frídr answered with the drawing of blood on Loki's throat as she fought to keep control. "*Þū forrotian blōma of tord!*" she swore.

"**Loki,**" Wōden roared, reaching his brother in two leaping strides to hold him by his vest, fist clenched, inches away from his face. "You cannot put the word honourable to your lips! You, who plotted and connived with Yngling to give one or all of us a painful death at the bottom of that bear pit you dug!"

Loki now looked white and shriven. His mouth flapped open but no words came. He began to tremble. He realised his brother had succeeded beyond his reckoning in the *Utiseta* and that he was responsible, as the slavering wolf, for the killing of Yngling

"Kill me then!" he screamed.

"*Na brōðor*" Wōden replied, calmly, as he bound the hands and feet of his brother, "that I cannot permit. You are of my blood whether you would wish it otherwise. My oath sworn companions here have no such scruples holding them back. I will have my say with them, but you'd best beware of your dark mind and your runaway tongue. I may return and find you sliced and quartered! Frídr, Vermundr, a word please", Wōden led them both over to the overhanging tree, shaded and cool in the midday sun.

"He needs to learn a harsh lesson, but I must have your oath, sworn to me now, that neither of you will end his life."

Both stared at Wōden with fury sparking in their eyes. They looked to each other in silence and then to the ground, both battling with their emotions.

Then, almost in unison, reaching a grudging acceptance, replied, "*Giese, Wè geswerian!*"

"Good, my faithful ones, Frídr, tend to his shoulder wound, you have the salve. Vermundr, take the rope in my bundle and tie it to the tree yonder, the one leaning over the edge of the cliff top. It is strong... I hope. Then tie the other end to Loki. Throw him over the top. Leave him hanging till I return. I am going in search of my Spear and I will awaken the Glory Staves for the nine herbs."

"Let him experience hanging from the Yggdrasill, and see if it gives him some wisdom. Please make sure he does not end up in the lake. My mother is down there and I really don't believe he will survive an encounter with her!

Watcher! Follow me!"

I sped out from under *Vídarr* following Wōden along the summit path, then veering left back into the forest, we skirted around tall trees growing vertically to reach the light. We travelled back the way we had come to find *Yggdrasil* again. Standing erect and immeasurably tall in shadow against Sunni, now beginning to slowly fade. Descending the steep incline was so much easier both for me and Wōden, who slithered and sped down to reach *Yggdrasil*. As soon as Wōden appeared, the small forest folk came from behind bushes, ferns, rocks and trees, as if his coming had been foretold.

He made himself comfortable at the base of *Yggdrasil*, working his spine into the bark, greeting venerable old friends and companions. Crossing his legs over, he looked well at ease.

"*Hālettan cræftbeornas. Tis a gōd dæg æt gesèon- Gesecgan þín spell!*"

"Greeting craftsmen-Tis a good day to behold. Tell me your story."

"Ah, Lord," said one wizened and curiously bent, twisted old dwarf, "There is indeed a story to tell. But first, refresh yourself with the mead cup. I will call upon our very best craftsmen to furnish you with the story, which I might add, concerns your dark brother Loki!" He waddled away, loping dangerously from one side to the other, his beard swinging on the forest floor and collecting all manner of detritus in its brushing. A swept path lay behind him and all knew where he had travelled that day.

"Oh! By the gods, that Loki", I hissed inwardly.

"Ahh, Watcher," came the amused reply in my head, "Best get truly accustomed to the games and tricks my brother plays on all of us. No-one is left out! Think yourself so very fortunate to be unknown to him!"

The mead came into my world, in a golden goblet sent by Wōden, and I drank thankfully. There was so much to watch. The Dwarfs world was industriously busy. Small rugged bodies were climbing *Yggdrasil* with water and descending with seed and branch. At the base, more were busy with collecting wood for the furnace which, though some way off, still gave a luminous glow, flickering in a dance of beaten metal on anvils and sparking of white heat. The dwarves were master smithies and revelled in working with metals. So everywhere they went, the forge was bound to follow. Small or large, it was an intrinsically creative part of their life. The forge represented their very breath, intake and out. Grizzled and gruff, their humour was spare and dry. Wōden was their favourite demi-god, for his was a rare humour that matched their own.

From the smithy came two dwarves of obvious stature. They walked with thrust and confidence. And behind them came four more dwarves, each holding the long ash pole, taken from the *Yggdrasil*. Alviss, the "All Wise" appeared from behind a bush. He was now very old and very wise. He gave Wōden the nod of greeting, staring at him intently through puffed and wrinkled eyes. The depth of them spoke of a sorrow lasting many summers, all born with grace and fortitude. He reminded me of Hjördis for both were world weary and longing to leave.

"Good day to you, my lord", he spoke with a lump of congested gravel in his throat that made hearing him a matter of deep concentration, "We hear you have triumphed over adversity with your customary panache. What brings you back to the World Tree, this sunny noonday?"

Wōden eased off from the tree bark, and reached forward to clasp the old dwarf in a warrior's clasp of friendship, though Alviss barely reached beyond Wōden's wrist, he clasped his shoulder, grinning widely.

"Ah, dear old friend", Wōden replied, "I come with a task in hand for your very best smithies to create a sacred *wælspere* for me, to last my lifetime on this earth and which will be charged with the magic and wisdom of the Anses and the power of *skaldcræft*. My power on the fields of battle will come from its true throw. Its name is Gungnir"

"Na!" exclaimed Brokkr, now releasing the long ash pole he was carrying, stopping the procession abruptly. They softly cursed him. "But, my lord, your brother Loki has already charged us with creating an even better one, and yet more wonderful gifts for the Gods. We are in competition with the smithies way down yonder, to produce better things than them. Loki passed by here a little while back, before your *Utiseta* at *Yggdrasill*"

Wōden groaned and sighed deeply, "So another challenge greets me from my dark-hearted brother, even while he is hanging by his feet over the summit!" The dwarves burst into hearty laughter at this news, rocking on their heels and holding their bulging stomachs. They had no love for Loki.

Wōden stayed silent for some time, thinking, playing with the grass at his feet.

"This pole you bring", he spoke pointing at the ash now laying on the forest floor, "It is from *Yggdrasil*, yes? Good, this will be my spear...eventually. Alviss, old wise One, charge the spear with these runes, if you please. Going from top downwards, Ansuz, Raiðō, Teiwaz, Mannuz. And on the spear head, Eitri, if you please, incise the three overlapping triangles of the *Fæeldne*.

Now, my friends, fashion an identical spear, but from any other ash you may find. All the runes must be included, but add another one...Nauðiz, a gift to my brother. Alviss, charge the spear with all the power that rune holds."

Alviss smiled, nodding his head, now understanding completely what Wōden was planning.

"And on the spear head, incise the "walk not" symbol but leave out one triangle. I would not wish that death power to be in the hands of my brother on the field of battle. That is entirely my charge and responsibility. I will take that duplicate spear as my own…for now."

Wodan suddenly jumped up, leaving the dwarves to crane their neck upwards to see him. All were smiling as the plan took seed.

"Watcher", he called to me, and all the dwarves suddenly twisted their heads in my direction. I had a sea of sparkling curious eyes on me and I felt quite exposed.

Wodan roared with laughter, "You see Dagrun how you have become accustomed to your invisibility. Tis but a sheer illusion *beorn*, an illusion"!

"Come, we need to charge the *wuldor-staves* and the Nine herbs. Alviss, Wise-One, stay with me, if you please, and oversee what I do. I must get this right!"

I looked over to Alviss, in some amazement to see him shaking silently with laughter, his shoulders bouncing up and down and a hiss escaping from his huge grey beard. I knew then that Alviss loved Wōden with everything his old heart could give. And it was returned.

… … … … … … … … …

CHAPTER THIRTY
The Nine Herbs Charm
And *the Wuldortanas*
Rods of Wonder

The dwarves simply evaporated into the forest greenery. Wōden untied a bundle that had been hanging from his waist. A sacred pouch for sure. I carried one in all my healing rounds. I wondered what was inside, so craning my neck forward I peered over the shaggy head of Alviss, to witness a wonder.

With such tender care, Wōden placed eight fresh herbs in a circle before him, and a small crab apple in the centre. These, I knew were the magical herbs created for him by his mother and kept for this day. I literally held my breath. For what I was about to witness was the creation of healing herbs that was the bedrock of any healing practise and which had saved countless number of lives. I was watching the master healer at work.

He placed at each herb, and touching each of them, the nine *wuldortanas* and on each one inscribed a single rune with a *drýcræft seax*. Both he and Alviss began to intone the sounds that brought the rune into life, although Alviss' tones had the sound of gravel being run down a layer of rock, it nevertheless held great power. The medium is the message, and this "medium" was nearing his own godhead.

Wōden incised M for the rune Mannaz, humming "M" in a song, deep concentration etched on his face. Alviss in a harmonic much lower, joined him. It became hypnotic until a burst of light brought the rune as before, glowing just above the *wuldortanas* and melted into the wood.

He then sang to the spirit of *Mucgwyrt* (Mugwort), and I saw so briefly a lightening flash of energy as the spirit entered the herb.

Next came Ansuz, Wōden's own rune, so he sang the A with a deep and booming voice, the sound vibrating across the forest. When Ansuz appeared, Wōden smiled, welcoming that rune with open arms, while it too disappeared into the wood.

The *Attorlaðe* (Betony) spirit came in a deep purple, the herb flowering in an instant.

Galdor- drycræft was happening here in all its glory. I felt truly humbled witnessing it, promising to *Ealdmōdor* that I would never depart from this, in the Telling.

Stune (Lamb's cress) followed on with the rune Sōwulō, which literally brought that brilliant white light again to flood the forest for just a moment. Then the rune Wunjō was incised for *Wegbrade* (Plantain), that profuse, soil hugging and much trodden on herb that had so much power in its humility, above most healing herbs. A master healer all its own, I thought, as Wōden intoned W in a sweeping song covering two octaves, with Alviss holding the bass notes. The incantation continued. I watched spellbound as Sōwulō was incised again for *Stiðe* (Nettle) and the hissing sound of S rose high into the branches of *Yggdrasil*. *Fille* (Thyme) and *Finule* (Fennel) both were accorded the beautiful rune Fehu, for Nerthus and the Earth. Both Wōden and Alviss gave it their all, singing this incantation. Last came the mighty *Wergula* (Crab apple) which Wōden inscribed Wunjō for joy, into the *wuldortanas*, the rune appearing in white and golden yellow, melting into the wood.

The *Wergula*, with its star centre held powerful healing. A beautiful spirit came and danced its way into the fruit in a wild circular motion. And that, I suddenly realised is how the origin of our women's Seith magic was created, the trance-state that keeps us wildly spinning in a circle is a truth now and is ever thus!

Wōden realised as soon as it had entered my mind, and he looked over to me, curiously, with an intrigued expression on his face. I blanked it, for I knew. But it was for him to find out. At last, I thought, I have a rare jewel of information about his future. But I cannot, must not, release that to him. It would spoil his fun!

We rested for a moment, Wōden deep in thought. Alviss watched him through those grizzled old eyes. If eyes truly were a window to the soul, then Alviss was ancient, older than the soul of this God sitting before me, who was twiddling with the ties to that pouch he had kept so close. Like some lovesick young one, on the search for his heart's desire. Oh! If only I could tell him. But that would change the whole future of our world. He would expend much energy and his seed, searching. This had been passed down in our own telling. Who was I to change that?

"*No! My dear beorn, you must not*", came that familiar loving voice of my *Ealdmōdor*, who wrapped her arms around me. I turned to see a beautiful face before me. Not with parchment skin anymore, but radiant and young.

"I think you are in some danger here. You have become very fond of our God, have you not? This is most unwise, Dagrun. Your duty as a watcher is to remember. Not become entangled with emotions that can only do you and Wōden harm. It was rash and challenging of him to suggest he would like to have you. And he could, wraith or not! He will sire half the royal houses of the confederacy, before he finds his true love!"

"Oh, *Ealdmōdor*! I am missing Eileifer so very much. This is becoming too harsh for me!" I spluttered out the words that had been trapped within me for what seemed almost a whole summer.

"*Giese*", she replied, holding me tighter, "I am very aware how much this has cost you. You are a true *Spakōna* in our eyes, Dagrun Wahl, but you do not acknowledge it at all. Your innocence is what attracts Wōden. I am taking you from here to visit *Neorxenawang*. You need rest above all and you have earned it. But first I wish to take you back to the *Tunstede* and *Ceasterwic* of Wōden. I want to you meet someone."

She whisked me back through a dazzling tunnel of light and colour, until we slowed and came to rest outside the women's lodge, the evening light fading to twilight. I saw everything in a blur, realising how right she was, that in my exhaustion, I did not have the will to focus.

Eventually my world began to clear. I saw an old woman bent nearly double, with white hair hanging to the dusty ground beneath her bare feet. Knarled and bent, she was forced to shuffle in short steps, one foot on its side holding a wafer-thin body only just upright. I had never seen a walking ancient before. *Ealdmōdor* had lain flat for many summers before her passing. This one had the most powerful stubbornness I had ever witnessed in some one still breathing our sacred air!

I realised, gasping, that it was the powerful, most wonderful *Spakōna* of all, Hjördis!

"My dear *beorn*," *Ealdmōdor* whispered to me, "she sees you better than you see her. And we all end our days this way. I was just lazy!"

"Oh, never a truer word spoken!" came the croaky reply from Hjördis, "Let me look more closely at this wraith, this Watcher in our midst. Is she up to it *sweostor*, do you think?"

"Ahh, she would think not, that is her problem. She is exhausted so I am taking her to *Neorxenawang* for a short while. I wished her to meet you, dear one, for you must be remembered in all hearts to come, as a true guardian of our God. And this, Hjördis, is Dagrun Wahl of the Warinni, whose family are guardians of the stones."

"Oh, I am honoured to meet you, *sweostor*," came the reply that nearly made me meet the ground.

"Ðoncian þu", was all I could reply.

Ealdmōdor touched my arm, "Look Dagrun, look over there. You see that child, that lovely *beorn*" *Ealdmōdor* wore an enchanted expression I had never seen, a warm smile as she shook her head in astonishment.

Hjördis cackled.

The little girl came skipping up to Hjördis, holding some flowers picked in the heat of the sun, now visibly wilting in need of water.

"*Ealdmōdor*, I picked these for you in the meadow past the trees. Look, aren't they beautiful!" she cooed in delight and Hjördis smiled, "*ðocian þu,* Arnbjorg. Thank you kindly," she said as she took the flowers carefully from the little girl.

She turned to Dagrun.

"Watcher, behold the ancient soul of a mighty *Spakōna*, and be sure you remember her too in all your prayers and Telling's to the people!"

It was then that I realised. I turned to see my *Ealdmōdor* whose face was marked with tears falling to the soft earth. The little girl was her! Arnbjorg. I had never spoken her name. She had always been ancient in my life. Always *Ealdmōdor*. Her years counted beyond measure, as did Hjördis'. Now it was my turn to wrap my arms about her, as we sped through space and time on the river of *Wyrd*, to rest in the most indescribable place of peace. The meadow of Nerthus, *Neorxenawang*.

… … … … … … … … …

CHAPTER THIRTY-ONE
Gungnir And
The Trickster Loki

I was kept in a soothing halo of light yellows, turquoise and pink. I rested and dreamed. I was back home on Wihtland. Was I truly there? I shall never know, but it was real enough to sooth my heart and I had such a loving space given to me with Eileifer, who most probably dreamt this and awoke from it when *Ealdmōdor* drifted gently in to talk with me.

"Dagrun, beorn, I am so pleased you are rested", she intoned with a voice much softer than she ever had on earth. I liked it very much. She was renowned for her sharp tongue and blistering truth-giving. It was all for our benefit, but then it never seemed so.

"We shall be travelling back again soon. To a time that sees Wōden fully engaged on the battlefield."

"Na! *Ealdmōdor*," I answered too quickly, and she frowned, "I will not follow him onto the killing fields!"

"Ohh," she sighed, "Did I say that, *forðgeorn lytling* Perhaps if I refrain from calling you a child, you may start to behave like the brave *spakōna* you are!"

I remained silent. She had not lost her sharp tongue.

"He has promised to give you dreams, has he not?" she continued, "A much kinder way of giving you a memory you can send into the sacred stones. Nã, your visit now is your last. But we will be covering very many miles. He is travelling to fight other peoples' wars in Gaul. He is becoming an accomplished Talker, a smoother of the way. People are calling him Mecurius, and he will be remembered far and wide for his smooth tongue and quick mind. But first he finds his true love, and it is there that we will join him, in the mead lodge for a grand Telling. Many people will be there Dagrun. It will be crowded. Frídr will protect you, as no doubt Loki will be present.

And regarding that more unpleasant man, I need to give you a Telling of the trickster and his cunning ways, which Wōden most certainly bests him on this occasion. He is learning fast to be as cunning as his dark brother. Loki is a good teacher."

… … … … … … …

"Wōden waited while the copy spear was being created by the two dwarfs, Brokkr and Eltri", Eald Mōdor intoned in a soft level voice, *"The spear had been incised with the faulty "walk not" symbol and the major rune for negative and harsh tests to the bearer had been inserted. It would take a very practised eye to notice the omission and inclusions of this beautifully made spear.*

He took it and bade a grateful farewell to the dwarves, who immediately set to work finishing the genuine Gungnir spear. Loki had spent an excruciating night hanging from the precipice. He had begged, pleaded with Frídr and Vermundr to be released, yet they knew it would be at an appointed time, just after daybreak, the following day, before they eased him up, laying him flat on the earth. He lay there, breathing in air to exhausted lungs. He tried to sit up but almost lost consciousness in the blood-battled raging to revive limbs, nerves and his mind. They quickly rubbed his legs and arms vigorously and pounded his chest to get the blood flowing. After a while he moved to sit up and looked about him.

"Where is he?" Loki growled, his lower lip shaking in a fury not spent, but building. He had learnt little in his own Utiseta. Nothing had been gained except a deeper hatred.

He strode away, shakily, into the forest, after the silence metered out to him from Wōden's own oath sworn. That silence was loud and clear in their unswerving loyalty their God. He made it to Yggdrasill as noon day approached and missed Wōden by a hairsbreadth. The dwarves gave nothing away. They gave him the Gungnir spear, and waited for payment. None was forthcoming. Loki just laughed with his back to the dwarfs, as he disappeared into the forest. They swore a vengeance I cannot repeat here in the Nerthus meadow.

Back in the Tunstede, he strode in, the following morning, with the spear, holding it aloft, calling for a contest to take place. His being the skaldcræft spear, it would be lengths ahead of all others.

He was soon joined by his sparring companions, all with spears of varying lengths and thickness. But none were like this one. They felt outdone and envious before the contest had even begun. One of them saw an aging man, standing alone at the edge of the Tunstede. He was a stranger. A large dark cowl hood covered his face. He was nearly bent double with age, and a long staff seemed to be the only thing holding him upright. He shuffled forward, with old, worn leather boots that flapped as they let mud, water and air in. His threadbare cloak let the wind in. He was a sorry looking apparition of a man gone to seed.

"Does anyone want to throw this old spear here, for a wager? I need the coin to fill my belly with warm food this day!" he said clearly, holding the spear up and waving it at the young men. They bunched together, laughing, challenging.

Then one of them shouted back, "Old man, do you take us for fools? That old spear will never best THAT spear," and he pointed to Gungnir, Loki holding it high in bravado and conceit.

"But I will take it just to please an old man." The young man strode over to the cloaked figure.

"Your name, old man if you please, so I may give it to the serving women. You will feast today whatever the outcome."

"Ōfnir," came the grizzled reply, "And what is your name young man so I may remember you?"

"Bjartr", He said with a wry smile.

"Here take it," said Ōfnir, "and throw your best shot for me. I favour Kornmjölsgot for my supper this twilight."

With that the old man wandered away, taking the quickest possible path to where the spears would land, and stayed out of sight.

Soon, the spears came thrumming through the air, some sizzling with speed from the strong young throwers, some twanging with a miss shot that ended with a dull thud in the soil, spear lengths before the rest. And of those few, only two were still in the air, competing with a superior energy holding them aloft. Gungnir was still in the air when the false spear hit the earth, two spear lengths short.

The old man was no longer old, but a vibrant excited young God, who sped between the two, exchanging the false for the real, which he took up and sped from the field to disappear into the forest gloom.

Wōden made his way to the Yggdrasil, calling up the Dwarves in a loud voice.

Alviss. Brokkr, Eitri, I bid you make yourselves seen. Come good friends, I bring excellent news!"

A loud rustling of leaves and branches being parted brought the three dwarves before him. Wōden was grinning widely, holding Gungnir with outstretched arms, offering the prize to the magnificent craftsmen who had fashioned it with such care and love.

"I wish to hand this into your care for now, until I have need of it on the battlefield. Hide it well my friends. And I thank you for creating this Gungnir. Never let this fall into the wrong hands. It can only be given back to me. Test me too for if I can disguise myself, so can Loki."

"My lord, it is your will we obey." growled Alviss, beaming widely with immense pleasure at seeing the success of the young God's plan.

"Oh, and bring all your wights and sprites to bear onto that sycophantic crew my brother sidles around with, save one whose name is Bjartr. He holds honour and respect."

"And where might you be going lord?" Alviss asked,

"Oh, I'm a going a-hunting, old dwarf, to find me a cwèn", replied Wōden with a huge smile that spoke oceans of the fun he was about to have.

Wōden the child-God was gone. The God as man had arrived.

… … … … … … … …

CHAPTER THIRTY- TWO
Freyja of the Vanir
And the *Seiðr*

So, in this world of spirit, we sped after Wōden. In the place of the Telling, the most exquisite mead hall I had ever witnessed, in the place where *seiðr magic* flowed with the Fates and Destiny was changed, I saw Freyja, as a woman priestess appear within the crowd. It was so sudden, I nearly missed her, as she melded with all those gathered to hear the story. But she was tall, a giantess, like myself, regularly unable to hide amongst a throng. Her golden hair, wrapped in many plaits intertwined with small delicate flowers, simply glowed like a gently swaying flame as she gracefully swung and moved through the crowd, heading for the Mead pots in the corner of the hall.

It was difficult not to feel captivated. I, who knew of her, her legend imbedded in our Tellings in the woman's lodge felt drawn into her *seiðr* magic. If there was any woman who could curtail Wōden's wanderings of the *Ceasterwics*, it would be her.

I looked over to Wōden and saw his intense gaze follow her every move. I turned to comment to my *Ealdmōdor* but her space was vacant. She had gone. I felt suddenly alone and horribly conspicuous. Before the thought had firmly settled in my mind that everyone could now see me, Frídr glided in around me weaving her own *seiðr* magic of concealment.

"You are safe now, *sweostor*," she whispered, "look and observe the Fates come into play. Wōden's whole life is about to change, and will empower all who follow him and Freyja in *Seiðr*."

Wōden was in the throes of his Telling, yet his gaze kept wandering to the mysterious priestess amid the crowds in his hall. People began to shift uneasily where they stood, some even turned to see the cause of his distraction. This immediately pulled him back to the story, his gestures and voice took on the drama of an accomplished *scōp*. He was, in truth, giving a lesson in Runic law, masked as a drama, with acting that made the memory thrill and the pictures embed into the deeper mind. *Yggdrasil* became the centre of the Nine Worlds, and the Norns, those powerful *Völva* women who re-wove destiny. The atmosphere was charged and silent as his descriptive wove magic into their lives. Then, with the flick of an eyebrow and a broad grin, Wōden released the electric silence with comedy. Laughter rippled through the hall as he described his eventual landing back onto the earth and how he thought he was a dog, sniffing the soil, the roots and the herbs. And here he was on all fours mimicking his actions that day. Yet through all this he kept his one eye on the flaxen haired woman.

The Telling came to an end.

The oak beams shook with the banging of tables by many, and the hollering of thanks by the rest. Wōden jumped from his impromptu stage and gracefully wove through the crowd to the mead barrels, where the mysterious woman was standing quietly in half shadow, her eyes shaded with long lashes. She wore an inscrutable look. Flashes of her white blonde hair caught the firelight and set Wōden's own heart ablaze. He had not seen a beauty such as this lady from another country, another world…

Frídr moved forward and I followed, not wishing to expose my fragile spirit to the glare of Loki and his kind. Although I had not seen him in the lodge at all. Wōden saw me and most imperceptibly bowed towards me. And so, did she, with a flash of energy from her eyes, I knew she was a *Völva* as practised as any and more than a match for Wōden.

And it was she who spoke first and made the connection that *Wyrd* had destined for them both.

"*Dryhten,* my lord", Freyja intoned with a deep voice that was barely intelligible for the foreign land she came from was far from here, Wōden's homeland, "*skāldkapar mjaðar* attends you here. Who will you favour with a welcome draft?"

"None but myself this twilight, fair *Cwèn*. From where do you come?" he asked, moving closer to study her.

"From the lands of the Vanir, lord," she replied, "It is part of our pact of peace to travel and unite with those of the Æsir."

"By the gods, but you are fair of face for such a dangerous mission!", he retorted, reaching out to gently stroke a strand of that delicate but abundant hair, which, he guessed when unravelled, would reach near her ankles. He made a wager with himself on that question.

"Why dangerous? why so!" she replied, staring intently into his eyes, reaching into his soul, which I felt sure was open and receiving, "The war is finished and we cannot lope about in a pretend peace. We will not incur the wrath of the higher gods. We must do what is destined. So, tell me more of your mead of poetry and your victory over it!"

It was a diversion away from an argument and it worked. She is as agile of mind as he is, I thought, and I turned to Frídr and saw her smiling. I stayed silent and forced my mind to remain blank, for I knew how this would progress quickly into a marriage of great wealth and fortune. Although Wōden, to my knowledge, only ever took her on one famous travel through Gaul, they stayed devoted to each other. But I was from the future and a Watcher. I could not influence any part of the events. I was watching.

"Well, a victory of sorts," Wōden grinned, altogether pleased to recount a clever exploit as one of his many guises he loved to create to fool humans, giants' trolls and dwarfs, "*Ōðr* came to claim me, we met and devised the plan. The spirit of Kvasir needed to be at peace also. There was never any doubt that justice played a part in this. Suttung became obsessed with the guarding of his stolen juice. He wanted to be *Ōðrœrir* and he trusted no-one except his daughter Gunnlöd to guard it. She became a prisoner under that mountain. It was a dense and challenging task to get through."

Wōden reached to the mead barrel and scooped a large wooden *drynefæt* into the amber fluid. Resting on his haunches, while Freyja sat gracefully on a pile of furs, he offered the cup. She bent her head to one side, questioning him, then smiled. A beautiful radiance, an inner light shone from her face as she stared silently at Wōden, who was by now, entirely smitten. She took the cup and sipped carefully. It was her first taste. She smiled, then took a full draft. It pleased her and she moved closer to her *Dryhten*.

"I made it my business to know those slaves of Baugi", Wōden continued, staring into the mead cup for some moments, "Freyja, there is always a need for justice to be served. I created a whetstone for them to quarrel over, kill each other for. They met their own deaths but I devised it with the knowledge that justice lay at the core."

"And then there is no denying my motives were entirely selfish. I wanted, no, I desired the mead to assist in the learning, acquiring wisdom at any cost it would seem. So, I went in search of Baugi, Suttung's brother and disguised myself as Bölverk. They were his slaves and he complained bitterly at his loss. I offered to do their work for the whole summer in exchange for a draught of mead.

That Suttung was a *yfel hornungsunu*! He refused to offer even a sip. So, we tricked him. I tricked then both. Rati, my drill, dug a hole into Hnitbjörg Mountain.

But then I shifted into my serpent form and entered the mountain.

Gunnlöd was a mournful, beautiful captive in that dark mountain. And I laid with her, she was happy and gave me the three drafts of mead. But I swallowed it all and became eagle to fly back to my homeland. It was hard fought Freyja, and I can only gift the mead to truly gifted ones…. such as your good self."

Freyja sat silently, looking deep into her soul, before she confronted Wōden with a steely look, a powerful energy. I clearly witnessed the golden beams and violet rays speeding over to him, rendering him quite speechless. She was so much older than her beautiful youthful looks. Her *galdor-cræft* was working on him.

"I have no need of your mead of poetry, *Dryhten*", she intoned in a low soft voice meant to beguile and admonish equally, "I find it delightful that is all. As for your exhausting adventures. Well, young sir, all *they* are is a great expense of energy. It is time you put aside these youthful escapades. Why did you think the Mights and the Norns gifted you with such powerful ancient wisdom, if all you do with it is play the fool?

They can easily take it all back into their domain and render you useless!"

"Dahh Nah", Wōden exclaimed, anger flashing across his face. Yet he did nothing. He remained silent for in his heart he knew she spoke the truth. All his instincts had guided him towards the gift of knowledge. Knowledge is true power. He had been misusing the gifts. No-one had dared to confront him about it except this utterly beguiling young woman who may even be, by so many twilights, older than him.

"I am here to teach you *Seiðr*," she continued staring into his eyes, "it is women's magic gifted to us by the Mights and the Norns whom you know guard and administer destiny with the will of *Wyrd*. All this is known to you. But it is needed for you learn *Seiðr* so you may enter that realm guarded so fiercely and known to but a few, where the Fates themselves can be brought into guide and alter any situation or person they deem necessary. Do you understand Wōden?" she asked finally, moving ever closer to the man God who had won her heart also. "And it will not necessitate you expending all this energy. We do this in trance, we do this with our souls, our mind and heart linked to the power of *Wyrd* directly!

"*Giese*," he replied quietly, truthfully, opening his heart to her.

"Then we must join, and join totally with each other," she whispered.

And so, it was that God and Goddess met, and loved with a power gifted to them both.

"We must leave", Frídr announced, "I need to ask you some questions."

I followed behind Frídr as she wove walked towards the door, now barricaded with heavy oak, as all those gathered in the hall were seated and getting steadily drunk with the same mead that was meant for the poets and the *scōps* to enliven their prose and visions.

She veered a sharp left where a thick hide was placed over an opening, hidden by a wide supporting oak post. I was aware of some tension in her and I guessed the reason for our escape. Loki was near.

The night air was very cold. Vapour releasing from her mouth into the dark as she told me Loki may have seen me. "I cannot be sure Dagrun," she whispered, as we moved further away from the hall. Mōnā was casting a bright light of silvered grey and gentle shadows. We hid amongst the deepest of these, by the tall slated roof of the smithy.

"He looked over and seemed to look past me with a serious scowl. But that could be purely his hatred of me, you know. He is swallowed up by it. I believe he revels in it, finds what joy he can in hurting others in ever more evil ways. When it is directed to him, which Wōden can do, he is consumed with thoughts of revenge!"

"I think I felt it too," I answered, glancing over the surroundings swiftly assessing any presence.

"I must keep you safe," Frídr whispered, "Come follow me, and I will call for your *Ealdmōdor*."

We slipped away from the smithy and I followed as she hunched to the ground and with long deep strides of the practised hunter moved away from the *Tunstede* and into the forest. She found an ancient yew, which had long since separated and provided a safe woody haven to hide within. Frídr hunched up wrapping her arms about her knees. It was bitterly cold, but as the human heat warmth circled around the inner trunk, I felt her relax a little.

"I will collect detritus for warmth", she announced, "Stay very still till I return."

And off she disappeared into the night. As a wraith, I had no problems with the cold, just an awareness of a change in the forms of night and frost that were ever caught up in this exquisite play between spirit and physical form. I did not register the rustling of leaves, nor the shadow that crossed the opening. And it was with total shock I realised it was neither Frídr, nor any friend.

Loki bent his head in to stare in menacing coldness at me. Huddled as I was in the bend of the yew cave. He grinned with shocking amusement and shook his head slowly. I did not have *galdor –drýcræft* to work with. I was helpless.

"*Ic cunnan ãfyllan þu Wōden-weardian*! I can kill you Wodan-watcher", he growled, "You will become just vapour, your soul to wander aimlessly through eternity never to reach Nerthus Meadow or your lover Eileifer."

I gasped so deeply, and froze so completely, the fear enveloped me and I lost the control I had over my mind. I prayed I would be hurtled back to my time before he could complete the action he had started.

"*Þu forrotian blōma of tord*", came a loud shout from behind Loki, who turned to have his face smashed by the blunt end of a large sword, held by Vermundr. Loki sank to the forest floor, leaves and much soil mixing with the blood oozing from his face.

Frídr appeared and summarily kicked the prostate figure of Loki in the gut several times before her husband pulled her away. An anger so deep held Frídr, and for several more heartbeats she fought to gain control. She calmed down to breathe heavily, swearing in ancient Norse, most probably a dreadful curse.

I felt a warm presence beside me and looked to see my dear Ealdmōdor smiling gently.

"'Tis time to move on, *beorn* my dear one", she said quietly leading me away from the scene before I witnessed something more, "You were never meant to witness such things. Wōden would be most disturbed to know you carried this to the *Cenningstān*.

We must go to a further time in which Freyja and Wōden both practise *Seiðr* magic and visit Yggdrasil together. It is with his horse Sleipnr. You will find comfort in this Dagrun as your troth to the sacred horse led you to Eileifer and runs true in your blood."

"But Frídr wanted so much to ask me things about the future time," I countered back, staring intently at Ealdmōdor. I had formed an infinity with Frídr. I loved her as a *sweostor* and would miss her.

"Dah!" Ealdmōdor exclaimed, looking at me with that harsh expression which now went straight to my soul, undiluted, lacking a physical mind there to block it.

"She does not have the right to ask those things of the future for herself, however mundane and inquisitive. It might alter her Fate. And you would be her accomplice. Had you thought of that?"

"Nah", I muttered looking to the forest floor, "It would have been wrong. She would need to learn *Seiðr* for herself to bend the Will of Fate to her choosing. I practise *Seiðr galdor-cræft Ealdmōdor*. But I have only ever done this for healing others and curing their pain."

"There you have it, Dagrun," the old wise-woman intoned, "there you have it. No need to say more. Now hold on, we will travel fast!"

We sped fast along the river of *Wyrd*, just flashes of colour and indistinct forms to show the passage of time.

"Face forward, Dagrun!" *Ealdmōdor* commanded, for she knew I would never see Frídr again.

CHAPTER THIRTY- THREE

SLEIPNR: Slipper.

I opened my mind's eye to the bright haze of Sunni, her rays melting the grass land into a wilting dryness. Waves of heat shimmered above the meadow. Cornflower and vetch drooped towards the cool of the earth, as if seeking just a drop of precious water.

The land was in drought.

Shifting colours of red, orange and yellow wafted across my vision. They were in charge, they dominated the air. And I knew if I were in physical form, my lungs would feel the searing heat of those rays.

Freyja and Wōden were standing together, his arm around her waist and they were looking at what was before them. Both were now older. They were comfortable with each other and gave that feeling of love in companionship.

"We must work *seiðr* to break the grip of Sunni on our land." She turned to speak to Wōden, who looked grim and unsmiling, a furrow across his brow, "Are you willing?"

"*Giese*", he replies quietly.

"You see that grey mare over yonder by the trees, trying to grab hold of the shade. She has a foal who will not leave her side. Together they speed faster than any I have witnessed.

You need to make them yours, Wōden. Become a horse-talker. I will tell you more when you have succeeded."

As I watched the tall man-God lope over the meadow, crunching on the dried grasses, a bolt of sorrow charged lightening hit my heart and I nearly crumpled yet again as Wōden became Eileifer heading off to the sacred whites on Wihtland.

"Hold fast Dagrun", came the voice of *Ealdmōdor*, "you have so nearly completed your mission. So very close *beorn!*"

She gave me strength as I watched Wōden near the grey mare. With her foal near, his appearance made her skittish. She pounded away from him and settled at the far end of the meadow. This was not going Wōden's way. He would need a gentler tack, *seiðr* was needed. He too settled on the dried earth, two spear lengths away from the horse who was, with head bowed to a patch of green hidden by a bush, munching with her foal, the much-needed food.

Wōden remained still for some time, until he melded with the stillness of the earth. I could feel he had become one with his mother, Nerthus. She was guiding him. I heard the chant, gentle and slow coming from his lips, like a soft caress.

He held the rune Ehwaz aloft, which had been inscribed on Ash, and sang in a faint voice, becoming louder.

Eh byþ for eorlum æþelinga wyn
Hors hōfum wlanc ðǣr him hæleþas ymb
Wellie on wicgum wrixlaþ sprǣce
And biþ unstyllum ǣfre frōfur

Steed is noblemen's joy before heroes
A hoof proud horse, where about it warriors
Rich in stallions
Exchange words
And is always a comfort to the restless.

And so, this continued into the evening. It was becoming twilight, long shadows cast upon the meadow meant a cooling of the day. A welcome break from the heat made the horses relax. They were now used to his presence sitting before them.

Wōden stood slowly, his tall body casting a long shadow. He began to trance, swaying rhythmically in a slow circle making his shadow move with him creating a slow dance on the earth. From his pouch, he had brought out a herb mixture and with the mead pouch he swigged a mouthful, spraying it out in to the twilight air where it hung unable to move in the stillness. He moved forward slowly repeating the action with the sound of Ehwaz taken to the horses in high notes. This made the mare's ears twitch, and when she smelt the perfume coming towards her, she and her fowl slowly moved forward, towards the waiting man-God, whose trance had become so rhythmical it had set up its own breeze in the still air.

They moved closer to each other, the foal just a finger's breadth away from its' mother. Soon their shadows met, Wōden's still gently swaying, and the grey mare offering a still point in this dance of souls. Without so much as an intake of breath, their heads joined and the union was made. Tails swished, hooves pounded the earth, as the two horses learnt was what needed of them. Wōden stroked the young foal whose understanding was less, and needed comfort. The grey mare understood everything. As twilight became night and *Mōnã* graced the meadow with soft light, Wōden mounted the horses, astride both, his giant's leg length sufficient to the task. They cantered about the meadow feeling each other's needs and abilities. They were perfectly matched. She was, as they moved ever faster, the horse with eight legs. Freyja was smiling broadly. She was delighted.

He came up to her, laughing, saying as they twirled about her, hooves pounding up clods of dry earth and dust.

"They are perfect my *Cwèn*. Her name is *Sleipnr*. Come join us, if you will!"

Two horses, two giant riders. They set up a speed so fast I lost them from my sight. It was then I realised with a shock that they had literally disappeared from the apparent world. Within a flash, they were here in my spirit world.

That had been the instruction, the pact between horse and man.

"You must join us, Watcher," shouted Wōden, turning his head towards me, briefly, as they sped forward, the energy rays so brilliant I had to nearly shut my mind's eye from them.

"*Hraðe, Hraðe*!! Quickly Watcher," he shouted, "There is room for one more. You must witness this."

I jumped and landed with apparent ease on the widest girth of horse I had ever felt. I am a giant also, but it was a shock nevertheless.

"We are heading for Yggdrasil," he shouted at me without turning his head, "To travel between the worlds and speak with the Norns. We must end this drought."

Freyja turned to me and smiled, her inner radiance undimmed by the years. She was also going home to Vanir and I could feel her happiness.

It was not long before Yggdrasil loomed before us towering into infinity. Its breadth so immense it felt like the earth's horizon gone sideways. We did not stop to greet the dwarf guardians, there was little need. The Norns held the key and Nerthus held the means. We sped upwards through clouds and rain, sweet sunshine and twilight.

"Where are we going?" I whispered to Freyja, who was now gifting a smile that gave me the answer.

"To my homeland lucky Watcher. We are going to Vanaheim."

So, before I could collect my thoughts, awash with wonderment at the thought of visiting Vanaheim, our speed slowed and a world I had only imagined, opened up before me. We had left a scorched earth to view a landscape of sap green leaves dripping from tall trees and grassland weaving a swaying pattern to a gentle breeze. Beyond lay the shimmering dance of a sea bathed in strong sunlight. Its turquoise blue was exactly the hue of our sea at home, of Wihtland. My home was Vanaheim!

"This is my home" I exclaimed, "Are you sure we have not landed on Wihtland by mistake?"

"Hah HA!" roared Wōden, "Now I understand, Watcher. Your homesickness is not just for your *Cyng* but for your land also!"

"She may stay here with me while you visit the Norns," said Freyja, spoken clearly, as more of a statement than a request to her *Dryhten*.

Wōden stayed silent for a while.

"Hmm…. perhaps she will not wish to return. Perhaps she will lose herself in this paradise of yours, my *Cwèn*." He pondered for a moment.

"Nah, she has to come with me. I need her to witness our *seiðr* with the Norns so she can give the knowledge to the *Cenningstãn*."

My shoulders slumped with disappointment, yet I knew he was saying the truth. And I would be hastening back all too soon if *Ealdmōdor* had anything to do with it.

We left Freyja skipping at a run over the lush meadow presumably to see her kin and bathe in a sea that just simply tore my heart apart in want of my own home.

… … … … … … … … …

We sped in a circular route, with *Sleipnr's* silky coat rippling with the rush of air. Wōden's long copper-brown hair was sent backward and I wished he had put it in a suevian knot.

He circumvented Yggdrasil to visit his sacred guardian animals, forever in his trust. With the Norns, they safeguarded the tree of life, their roles permanent and eternal. I had heard of the four harts, learnt of their role in many childhood Tellings in the women's lodge. Now I was to meet them. Dãinn and Dvalinn, always together, came into view. They were eating the leaves from the tree. It was said they kept Yggdrasil alive with the feeding. Never too much and always within the cycle of renewal. They stopped and loped over to us. *Sleipnr* whinnied and nuzzled Dãinn. Wōden leant over and whispered in the ear of Dvalinn, who threw his large antlered head back, bared his teeth and roared.

I wonder what was said, I thought.

Wōden turned around to face me with a large grin.

"I simply instructed him to get Dāinn with Fawn as soon as possible and I expected to hear the rut chorus from Midgard! No-one can best him, not even Duraþrōr"

With that, we sped off again to meet with Ratatoskr, the ever-vibrant busy squirrel who was messenger between the Eagle who lived at the top of Yggdrasil and the Wyrm Niðhöggr who lived in the roots and was close to the Norns at the Well.

"My friend", shouted Wōden, "Speed your way to Eagle and tell him to fly down to greet with me and then scamper as only you can, down to Niðhöggr to tell the Norns I have important things to discuss with them."

The ever-mobile squirrel shot off, soon out of sight amidst the green foliage of the giant tree. We waited while *Sleipnr* fed on the lush greenery. Then hearing the rush of heavy wings, he looked to see the largest Eagle I had ever seen hove into view. Majestic and slow, the beating of his wings, to keep him aloft, seemed effortless. And he settled with graceful elegance on the bough before us, so he was at level eyesight with Wōden.

"Eagle, we welcome you," Wōden intoned deeply, holding his gaze level to see into Eagle's heart, "This is my Watcher, who has come to witness, then record, within the *Cenningstān*, all she feels and sees. There is an imbalance in the world of men. Drought is gripping the land in a death throe that threatens animals and men alike. They cannot endure much more. I have come to gather *seiðr* amongst the gods and Norns to bend Fate in their favour. I ask you to fly to Thör and ask for his compliance in bringing rain back to earth. Our beloved mother, Nerthus, is crying for the need of it and her sorrow is only shedding but small dry tears. We need his help."

"*Giese*, it will be done", replied Eagle, who then lifted slowly to bank sharply over our heads and headed off upwards to the higher heavens.

We headed downwards at a sharp angle to arrive at the well of Urd quickly. I think Wōden was racing the squirrel out of sheer devilment. It would not have surprised me at all.

The well was located at the first of three roots that met and nurtured the other parts of the World Tree.

I felt apprehensive. The three sisters of Fate carried enormous power. They held destinies in their hands which could alter and change at will. What would they make of me? I thought. Yet when I first saw them, their rays of colour about them, so beautiful and ever changing, there was no feeling of power about them at all. They were busy tending the tree. That task was pure in action and showed ultimate devotion. They were in effect servants to Yggdrasil.

"*Heālsung! Valkyrie sige-wif. Ic āgan becuman æt ābiddan þin fultum in Seiðr.* Greetings Wise women, I have come to ask for your assistance in Seiðr.", Wōden greeted the Norns.

They looked up and stared at him. Urðr spoke plainly,

"We know why you here, Wōden. Of course, we do! Now introduce us to your Watcher, *gecwèman.*"

Wōden was put on the back-foot, he fidgeted and looked ill-at-ease for the first time since I had become his watcher.

"This is Dagrun, Urðr, a Völva and *cwèn* from a future time. She has chosen this because she is one of the Warinni and guardian of the Stones. She is to place her wisdom in the stones for all generations to come."

"This we also know, Wōden", Verðandi spoke, whilst ladling the precious water to the tree, "Have you learnt nothing from our gifts to you? We know all the Fates, including yours *Dryhten*. And it is fluid at that. The river of *Wryd* is ever changing to the whim of human and God alike. You are no different from each other. This brave woman, however, is!"

"We wish to talk with her," Skuld announced, "so we suggest you visit your mother, Nerthus who would welcome you greatly."

"And we need to speak with Freyja," Urðr said, "Send your *Sleipnr* to fetch her. I fear if you go, she will be returning kicking and screaming at leaving her homeland. The horse will beguile her. You have lost that ability long since!"

"And go before we change our minds about *Seiðr* for your humankind." Skuld added.

I was left utterly speechless. This was our God they had admonished in a way unheard of in any realm I had visited.

"*Dah, fīras!*" Skuld muttered as Wōden left at speed, "These men make our job endlessly hard!"

"Now, *Cwèn*", Urðr moved forward holding out her hand to have me sit by the well of Urd, "We would like you to share your experience with us. Leave nothing out."

My mind froze for a moment. There was a uniqueness about this moment that left me floundering for thoughts that needed stringing together. Here I was, sitting before the Fates, and for them to give *me* their time and space to recount my experience to *them*!

"Ahhh *sweostor*", Urðr smiled gently, "You really do not know who you are, do you?"

"You are of our blood", Verðandi said, "a giantess whose ancestors like us, hail from Jötunheim. You, and you children's children carry the Fates, the power of *Wyrd* in your very souls. It is you who carry the wisdom to the stones, who know them so closely. You who is alive and recording all human endeavour for all time."

"And you do not know your power!" said Skuld quietly, "and that is a good thing…for now."

"But instil it in your children *gecwèman*", Skuld continued, "For in their time, it will be greatly needed for them to draw on, for courage and strength."

"I know," I countered, "I have seen what the future holds for my children. It is harsh and terrible!"

"*Giese*, indeed it is so. The flame of the soul of all your peoples will be all but blown out, a waft of warmth and a trail of smoke. That is why you have been chosen to lay our lives and the memory of them, in the stones, the Guardians of our Souls. Without you, the memory dies and we will not exist anymore!"

"So," Urðr said, "We are eager to hear all, and as we said, leave nothing out!"

From their intense stare, I knew I was being tested. And so, the story of my time as a Watcher of Wōden was spoken for the first time. When I came to recounting Loki and Yngling, there was a gasp of exasperation from Skuld and a smile from Urðr.

"Ahh but that Loki is a good teacher," she interrupted with a smile. "We know all his tricks that keeps Wōden on his toes. Forever checking against his brother, his own motives, in case they match in any way that evil. Loki is entirely necessary in the larger tapestry of Life, our duality eternal and seemingly permanent."

"And we give you the name, Cædwalla", Skuld insisted, looking at me intently, "Remember this name. Give it to your children to know he is their Loki!"

I suddenly thought of the nasty Gandālfr who called me "the stripling" and tormented me with lies and half-truths. On telling this to the Sisters I suddenly realised why he had come into my life in such a way. I lost consciousness for days after knocking my head on the hard ground. It prompted a dangerous travel for my brother to *Cantium*.

"But you now realise, do you not, *sweostor*, "Verðandi said, smiling, "Your "sleep" at that time actually prepared your Eileifer to accept what is happening to you now. And know this also Dagrun. It will be just a twilight or two at the most in his time. When you open your eyes again to your world, little time has passed. Here, you believe it is almost forever!"

"Now, your story is nearly complete. We will describe to you now, notable events in Wōden's life that does not necessitate you witness. But there is but one final very important event you must witness before you leave us as a wraith and re-join your sleeping body."

… … … … … … … … …

CHAPTER THIRTY-FOUR

MECURIUS: Þæt èacen specul

The Great Talker

"Wōden found the urge to travel away from his homeland too overpowering to ignore," Urðr began, "And he took his Cwèn with him on just one occasion. He left Freyja behind mostly, as Seiðr did not blend well with the fields of war. He did little killing. He was the "Talker" the scōp who made diplomacy his guide between the warring tribes. He earnt the title of Mecurius, as the early Romans dubbed him. He saved much blood being split needlessly with a few wise words spoken at the right time.

He became known as Mecurius the Giant. The inventor of letters. Well, that is open to debate. They have belonged to the Mights since the beginning of time. However, it is certain that Wōden brought them and his silken tongue to the notice of many a leader, warrior and downright troublemaker in his extensive travels. He rarely stayed in one place for very long, the Great Shifter was more appropriate. It would have sent your spirit reeling Dagrun, beorn, had you tried to follow him. As it was, Freyja soon palled of the journeys and only came with him on rare occasions. Besides she had their son Baldur to care for, and if you can imagine another Wōden in the making, it took her full might of mind and heart to control the lad. Yet he was as fair as Wōden was dark. Fair of face and of mind, they say. He took after his mother in many ways and she adored him fully.

Pass this next Telling to the Cenningstãn, Dagrun, as it will foster a greater understanding of Freyja, who was more than a match for Wōden. This story proves it. You will like it…

In the eastern part of our lands, far from Gaul and in a very temperate climate, there lived a race of "small people", peaceful and Sunni-loving. They were ruled by a woman named Gambara. They were named the Winnili. Gambara had two sons, Abor and Agio. They were fiercely loyal to the tribe and adored their mother, who ruled wisely and with care. Respect flowed amongst the people and they thought this was how it would always be. This attitude has always vexed us. As the Fates, we know, as do you Dagrun, that change is the creative force we must all honour. It is the only constant.

The Winnili turned their back on that Truth. So, it came to pass that a warring tribe of vandals happened upon this idyllic little country and saw plunder and wealth mixed with woman and sunshine before them. Abor and Agio were horrified, seeing their mother and all the women threatened and they, being so much smaller than the Vandal warriors, were hopelessly inadequate to defend their people, their queen and their country. Nevertheless, they did not broker a deal for the huge tributes that were demanded to avoid war.

Ambri and Assi, who ruled the Vandals, were also shocked at the apparent bravery of the "small people." The Winnili went to Wōden and asked that he use his seiðr galdercræft to bend Fate in their favour. Suffice it say, this soothed the God's ego. And in return he played the game of chance with them.

"Swã hwã swã Ic biscopríce ǽrest hwonne æt dæg-rèd æt híe Ic willan gifan þæt sige" Whom I shall first see at sunrise, to them I will give the victory!

"And so, it was left to pure chance, that lord of change, to decide the Fate of many in a peaceful way that prevented so much shedding of young blood, "Urðr sighed deeply "I wish it were ever so in the dealings with mankind.

But Freyja immediately saw that possible outcome to be wholly terrible. The vandals would immediately ransack the dwellings, rape *and kill the women, drive the children into slavery and simply dispose of the old. Abor and Agio called upon Freyja, who constructed a plan that would edge the Winnili in favour of victory. If Wōden could play the game of chance with whole peoples, then so could she!*

She counselled in a wise and clever way. The Winnili should come to an appointed place in the East and that their women should come also. The women should let their hair down and place it over their face like a beard.

At sunrise, with Wōden still blissfully asleep and snoring, Freyja turned the bed to face the east. She woke him, reminding him of yesterday's deal of chance. So, when he focused on the window and saw all the people of the Winnili gathered in their vast numbers, he asked, "and who are those Long-beards?" Freyja replied with a wide knowing smile, "As you have given them a name, give them also the victory!"

Wōden roared with laughter and looked askance at his clever wife who had easily bested him. So, he gave the Long-beards their victory, "that they should defend themselves according to his council and obtain victory. From that moment forward the Winnili were known as the Langobards (Long-beards)

… … … … … … … … …

CHAPTER THIRTY-FIVE

Wōden: Þaet èacen hǽlend
The great healer

Skuld rested back on her haunches, hair straggling to the ground, as she created an elaborate design in the earth with a stick. She suddenly looked upon me, intently searching my soul.

"Dagrun, *sweostor*, you must pay great attention to what I say now," she spoke with mounting feeling in her voice, "For men's minds are just like this", she pointed, then stabbed at the intricate design before us, "plotting and swerving this way and that. Never, ever straight and true. Well most men's minds are as such!"

"There are always exceptions dear *sweostor*," Urðr replied, digging Skuld lightly in the back, "Baldur, son of Wōden and Freyja is one such, as well you know."

"*Giese!*" she replied, "And look what happened to him. Too good, too pure for this realm of man!"

"Agreed."

"Dagrun, you must know that in times to come, which you have briefly glimpsed, there will be lies laid down in the written word, against our god Wōden and our goddess Nerthus. Many men will feel withered by the power of these words, written by men with dark intent and greed as their companions. Layer upon layer of lies will grow to become the warped truth. Many spear lengths of time will see many moons pass before enquiring and honest people will dig and dig to find the hidden truth. And it is your messages in the *stānwurþunga* that they will find."

"But the Runes are a gift from the Mights", I countered, "They can never be used to grow lies!"

"The written word is not from them at all", Skuld countered, "Look to your Romans when you return. Learn their language of written words and you will be prepared. Teach your children too. For their knowledge of it will save lives."

"And now we left Wōden enjoying his travels, but with all the healing knowledge kept within. And it is as a great healer that he achieves his height in Valhalla. Not in killing. He will not be remembered for that great healing, in the realm of me. So pay great attention Dagrun, for this is one important truth of our God Wōden."

Skuld stopped creating the tangled design in the dirt of the human Will and smiled at me slowly.

"Listen well Watcher", she whispered.

"Wōden travelled widely, many cultures heard his persuasive dialogue and his acute humour that could scourge one man and leave another bent with raucous tears. His mind expanded as did his wisdom on treating difficult encounters with warring countries and arrogant chiefs and thanes. He became known as Mecurius throughout Gaul and beyond. He became the wandering god, which he will be remembered for. He was also victorious in battle, he never took a blow that injured him or so it seemed. He bestowed that same magical hand on his army!

But in all this, a void was growing within, his spirit was not growing at all. His true gifts lay unused within him. He was, as granted by the Mights themselves, a true healer.

One of the more peaceful days within the arena of war saw Wōden and one of his oath-sworn companions take off into the forest. Sleipnr taking Wōden far ahead of his companion, Phol, who lagged, no matter how hard he drove his steed in a furious gallop. Wōden and Sleipnr ducked and swerved around and beneath overhanging branches in a blurred speeding fury.

So, it was the greatest shock for both Phol and his steed, as he rounded a bend in the path to come upon Sleipnr grazing with rested foreleg near a fallen tree. He skidded to a halt and fell from his horse. Over yonder was a fallen horse, and Baldur, Wōden's beloved son, leaning over his steed, muttering and moaning low. Kneeling, holding out their hands in supplication and chanting galdercræft of the highest level, was Sindhund, Sunna and Volla, invoking the healing powers.

But they had not the drycræft of the galderstaves granted to Wōden as he hung from Yggdrasil.

So, the God came forward and reached for his pouch that contained the glory rods. He went into trance, the Seiðr magic taught to him by Freyja, and brought the healing of the Mights to the injured horse.

"Thu biguol en undam, so he uuola conga:
Some benrenki, sues bluotrenki, souse lidirenki:
Ben zi bena, bluoda,
Lid zi geliden, sees gelimids sin!"

"Then charmed it, Wōden did, as he the best could,
As the bone-wrench, so for the blood wrench, and so the limb wrench,
Bone to bone, limb to limb, so be glued."

"Dagrun, *sweostor*," Skuld, in halting her narrative, looked directly at me with an intensity which made my heart falter for a second, "This is of the utmost importance. Do you remember what happened when we released the young god from Yggdrasil?"

I thought for a moment as I summoned pictures into my mind.

"Why, he immediately went to the herbs, to the bushes, as if his life depended on it" I answered, "He muttered to them, touching and feeling their energy."

"*Swiðe gōd*," Skuld enthused, "The Mights in all their wisdom granted Wōden, through the power of the runes and the glory rods, the means to talk to and understand directly, the voice of the plant spirits. Their union with him, their compliance and help brought the highest *drycræft* to all he did in the healing of his people and animals alike.

So, mark this well, for this special magic needs to be recorded in the *Cenningstān*."

"And so, it was that Wōden healed the horse of Baldur, "Skuld continued, "And his spirit rejoiced and came back to him from the void. He knew his healing powers must always be honoured on the battle field and in time of peace.

He talked to the plants directly.

"Remember, Mugwort, what you revealed to me, what you set out in mighty visions, "una" you are called, oldest of plants, you have the might against three and against thirty, you have might against poison and infection, you have might against evil that travels around the land."

"And you, waybread, mother of plants, open from the East, mighty within, carts may have run over you, ladies may have ridden over you, brides may have cried over you, bulls may have snorted over you, you withstood all then, and you were crushed so you may withstand poison and infection, and the evil that travels round the land."

"This plant is called cress, it grew on a stone, it stands against poison, it drives off harmful things, and it attacks against pain."

"It is called nettle, it attacks against poison, it drives off harmful things, casts out poison, this is the plant that fought against the serpent, this one has might against poison, it has might against infection, and it has might against the evil that travels around the land."

"Now, attorlothe-the lesser shall drive out the greater, and the greater the lesser until the cure for both be with him."

"Be mindful now, Maythe, of what you made known, of what you finished at Alorford, so that he should never give up his life for disease, one maythe was prepared for his food."

"This is the plant that is called crab apple, a seal sent this forth across the sea's back, as a cure for the bite of another poison."

I was listening intently to the words spoken, the wisdom that lay deep within them. I knew above all else that my memory must not fail me.

Urðr shifted to come and sit close to me. She put her arm around my shoulders and smiled warmly.

"Dagrun, you been chosen to be the Watcher over Wōden. In so doing you have been given wisdom beyond your earthly years. What you now carry within your mind and your soul must be used, else the circle be broken and the river of *Wyrd* forks away elsewhere."

"*Ealdmōdor* taught you all she knew, which was a great amount and you have used that knowledge in your healing work. Now you must listen carefully, for your healing must absorb Wōden's *drycræft*. You must re-make the nine glory rods and fashion them in the way of Wōden. Ash for the *kinsmen* and Elm for all the *cwèns*. Empower them with the highest *galdercræft runes* so that you too can call upon the Mights for assistance only when it is sorely needed. Do you understand *sweostor*?" Urðr bent her head to one side looking deep into my eyes. She wanted to find my soul's recognition. My heart was fluttering wildly. I was excited and fearful together at once.

She smiled and nodded. "So now your lesson is nearing its end. Listen well and when it is done, your *Ealdmōdor* will whisk you within a heartbeat to your last and most important meeting with our young God. We bid you farewell now, Dagrun. You are indeed of Jötunheim and our *sweostor*. We will watch over you, be certain of that."

Skuld leant forward and finished the last Telling.

"*These nine spikes against nine poisons, a worm came crawling, he tore a man apart.*"

"*Then Wōden took up the nine glory-rods, struck the adder then so it flew into nine. There apple ended it and its poison, so that it would never bend into a house.*"

"*Chervil and fennel, two of great might, that Wōden shaped these plants while he was hanging from Yggdrasil, he set them and sent them into the seven worlds, for the poor and the wealthy, as a cure for all.*"

"*It stands against pain, it attacks against poison, and it has the might against three and thirty.*"

"*Against foeman's hands and against lordly sleight, against bewitching of harmful beings.*"

"Now these nine plants have might against nine powerful diseases, against nine poisons and against nine infections."

"Against the red poison, against the running poison, against the white poison, against the pale blue poison, against the yellow poison against the green poison, against the pale poison, against the dark blue poison, against the bright poison, against the purple poison."

"Against worm-blister, against water-blister, against thorn-blister, against thistle-blister, against ice-blister, against poison-blister."

"If any poison come flying from the east, or any from the north should come, or any from the west over the tribe of men."

Wōden stood over the ancient trace and said

"I alone know the running rivers and they enclose nine adders, all weeds may now spring up as herbs, seas slide apart, all salt water, while I blow this poison from you."

"Mugwort, way bread which opened from the east, lambs cress attorlothe, maythe, nettle, wood sour apple, chervil and fennel, old soap, work the herbs to a powder, mix them with the soap, and with the apple's juice: make a paste from water and from ashes: take fennel, boil it in the paste and warm it with the mixture when I put on the salve, both before and after: I sing the charm on each of the herbs, thrice before they will be used, and on the apple likewise: and I sing the same charm into the man's mouth and into both ears and onto the wound before I put on the salve"

I was listening so intently I barely noticed an arm wrap around my shoulders and then hold me tightly. *Eald Mōdor* pushed me forward and I spun, with her, into the void of *Wryd*.

… … … … … … … … …

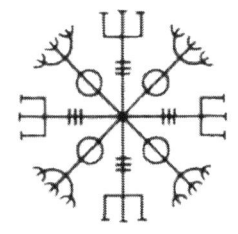

CHAPTER THIRTY-SIX
Þæt dèað fram Baldur
The death of Baldur

"For this part of the Watching you must be strong, Dagrun, stronger than you have been so far. Remember, if you falter and let your feeling and emotions get in the way, you will lose your presence and be gone."

My mind was still dizzy and with eyes still shut, I nodded. When I opened them, she was gone and I felt the piercing of sudden loneliness hit my heart.

And where I had been sent, this sent a shudder through me.

I was looking upon a scene of impending misery. The sky was thunderous as if Thunor himself was furious. Sunni was blotted out with dark rolling clouds, sending the earth below into the early darkness of twilight.

But there was one shining light amongst this strange darkness. It belonged to the angular, aquiline face and the noble stance of the brightest lord, Baldur. He stood amongst a gathering crowd of men and boys. He simply shone and from my invisible space in the spirit world, I had to half close my eyes against the brilliance of his golden and deep yellow aura. He was like his mother, Freyja, fair of face, and from the good-natured way he stood to the taunts of lesser men, he was a God.

I felt a presence and turned to see *Ealdmōdor* with me again, and I sighed audibly with gratitude.

She smiled and I felt the slightest pressure of a kiss on my cheek.

"Before you, Dagrun, is the *Wyrd* acting out a terrible twist in Fate which will have a profound effect on our god Wōden. His beloved son is about to die and he is not there with him. He cannot save him. It will break his heart and Freyja's heart too."

"It will begin the Ending."

"Watch, Dagrun, but do not join in at all. Loki is behind all this and he is watchful. It is why I am here to cast *drycræft* around you for the last time."

And so, she spun her magic while I watched with an aching heart.

"Why are they throwing stones at him?" I asked, "and arrows, spears. They are bouncing from him and he is laughing at them all!"

"Both Baldur and his mother Freyja had the same dream on the same night. This then, becomes a prophecy dream and it is taken very seriously. Freyja is a *Völva* in her own right and very powerful. She spun *drycræft* on all the weaves of all living things so that none will harm her son. This you see here is sport! It is the new pass time."

"Ahh, *Ealdmōdor*, look over there!" I pointed to a dark figure making his way towards the circle of men. A raven cawed in alarm, but Wōden was not there and it took off, banking away from the gathered men and into the deep forest, lost, gone. It was as if he could not stay to witness what happened next.

It was Loki, looking black and intensely hateful towards his beautiful nephew. He was guiding another, smaller man beside him. It was then I realised, this man was sightless. A silver film covered both his eyes entirely and there was no movement in them.

"*Giese!*" whispered *Ealdmōdor* "It is Höðr, Wōden's blind son, Baldur's twin brother."

"Look, Loki is handing Höðr a sharpened mistletoe branch. It's like a spear. Why so?"

"Because that is the only living thing that missed the *galdercræft* set by Freyja. Loki found out and he is using Wōden's injured son, Höðr, to kill, without knowing, his own twin brother."

"*Nāāāāh!*" I screeched, as *Ealdmōdor* gripped me tightly to silence me and stop Loki from seeing me. He was too intent on his murderous task to notice me.

"I will kill him myself! Let me go!" I screamed and struggled but her grip tightened until I was left breathless in my spirit body. Her will was ever intent on overcoming my own.

"*Þū cunnanne forstoppian þes misdæd! Dagrun*", *Ealdmōdor* hissed in my ear, "you cannot stop this evil."

I bent my head into my chest and heaved deep breaths into my lungs, to calm me, and slow my rushing heart. I knew I was on the verge of losing my spirit-self entirely.

"Calm yourself," *Ealdmōdor* said soothingly, stroking my hair. I felt the slightest sweep of her spirit hand on my head. Everything came back into focus.

"You must be a Watcher, Dagrun, look now, *gecwèman*," she coaxed.

I watched, as my heart began to bleed. I had become so attached to Wōden, his adventures, his spirit melded into mine sometimes and I knew him almost better than my beloved Eileifer. He would, in some ways, always be a demi God to me, more man than God.

Loki hustled the poor Höðr forward, who was totally unaware of his impending crime. Baldur meanwhile was laughing, throwing off the stones hurled at him with good natured curses and half promises of the fight that would ensue that twilight, with some of his erstwhile friends. Much mead drinking was being promised in the grand mead hall, Breidablik. Baldur had designed and built it to be like heaven on earth. It was as glowing gold as he was himself. A beautiful place constructed for him and his people.

Loki bent forward to whisper in the ear of Höðr, then stepped forward to hold and guide the arm of his nephew.

As the spear was thrown and thrummed through the air towards Baldur, Loki stepped back into the shadows. I believe I saw a wolf slink back towards the forest that curtained the open ground on the edge of the Tunstede.

That unsuspecting mistletoe spear rammed into Baldur's chest, into his heart. Loki's aim was accurate. What happened brought a hushed silence to the crowd, a heaving sigh of unexpressed horror wafted in and then out, as the stricken Baldur crumpled to the ground, a look of disbelieve and pain locked on his beautiful face forever.

He was carried away, amidst the cries and mourning of all his oath-sworn companions and the people of the *Tunstede*. They wrapped him in clothe of gold. Swathed in white linen, his ghostly form now waited for Freyja and Wōden to arrive. Wōden would take several twilights to come home. But Freyja came and crumpled to his side and stayed weeping inconsolably for days. There is no repair but only the slow, agonising march of time for a grieving mother. He was her shining light. Now snuffed out by the evil Loki.

We stayed and followed. *Ealdmōdor* did not leave my side. She dared not. For in one more instance of seeing Loki again I would have killed him, and she was sure of it.

We walked around the *Tunstede* as twilight grew to darkness. *Mōnā* did not appear, the clouds of Thunor gathered deeply and seemed to descend to the earth. *Ealdmōdor* nodded, feeling my thoughts, and we both wondered what might happen next.

Those following days seemed endless, all waiting for the return of Wōden. We could do little but pray for the spirit of Baldur to find peace.

When Wōden finally came home, what greeted him was the mourning silence of the whole *Tunstede*. He knew before he even entered the great mead hall that it had been sucked dry of all joy.

He had shrunk before my eyes, shoulders hunched in immeasurable pain. He turned to me in a sideways glance that brought cold horror to my heart.

"Well Watcher", he whispered in a choked growl I could barely hear, "Have you had your fill of Watching, then?"

"Wōden", I began, "I am so very sorr…"

He shot out his arm, he held his hand, palm towards me for silence.

Then he turned and shuffled slowly into the Hall to see his dead son and comfort, if he could, his distraught *Cwèn*.

We retreated then, into the forest. I was ever watchful for that wolf, hand on my *seax*. I could not relax. How I was expected to see off a real wolf, in spirit, I did not contemplate that. *Ealdmōdor* smiled indulgently at my youth.

Thunōr was ever present. No sun came to greet us for the following days. The clouds broke to give tempestuous rain.

"This, my child," *Ealdmōdor* said the following noon time, "This is the beginning of Ragnarök, the end times."

I hunched inwards and realised she was right. All that had been shown to me as a Watcher needed to be kept, recorded within the *Cenningstān* for it may well become a fading memory in the minds of men all too soon.

"If Freyja can compose herself sufficiently and ask Hermod to plead with Hel to release Baldur, if all men and gods and all things alive or dead, weep for him, then we have hope."

It was hard to keep hope alive, hiding as we were, in the damp forest. Our time there became muted into hushed whispers, while we prayed to glimpse the shining golden form of Baldur in spirit, like us. I longed to see him, even talk with him to feel his wisdom upon us. His humour and his smile eluded us. He was locked in the underworld.

And Thunōr remained rumbling in supressed fury.

… … … … … … … … …

CHAPTER THIRTY- SEVEN
Hringhorni

    The day came for the funeral rites of Baldur, beloved son of Wōden and Freyja. Nanna, Baldur's wife, had died of grief only a day after her husband had been murdered. Of Höðr, the blind brother, there was no sign of him. And of the evil Loki, nothing.

    Thunōr loomed ever large in the descending skies. Deep shades of grey filtered through ominous blue/black clouds that shrouded the *tunstede,* and over the Breidablik, a sweeping tunnel of cloud began to build. The wind increased to gusts. There came a whirlwind of rain that pulled hair and cloaks around men and women, who braced themselves from being swept upwards in the tunnel. The roar on the wind grew and from the swirl entered the solidifying form of Thunōr, the God. And roar he did, in anger at the stupidity of the humans and demi-Gods alike. He strode, Mjolnir grasped in his huge hand to the entrance of Breidablik and put his hammer to the door. It trembled and shook at the force of it. The whirlwind had dissipated to a breeze, as his long cloak in deep blue, settled about him. The people, who had all turned, ashen faced, to peer at him, pulled hair and cloth back into place.

    He swept into the hall and disappeared.

    We had already walked from our forest hiding to be close to the magnificent Hringhorni. *Ealdmōdor* had re-enforced my cloaking *drycræft,* knowing that at some point Loki would appear to gloat at his handiwork. We could see the hall and the pathway, already lined with the mourners. They were a full two-spear length deep, waiting for Baldur and Nanna to make their last journey together. Many were grieving and the sound of wailing echoed across the valley floor, ever louder as the moment of the procession grew nearer.

Hringhorni lay on wooden rollers, desolate and silent, waiting for its last voyage. It was holding under its massive sails, the largest pyre I had ever witnessed. The boat was elegantly built, the largest boat I had ever seen. Ingvar would have been silenced in awe of it. Upon the bow and carved in intricate detail on the oak centre beam, was a teeth-baring dragon and underneath was attached a shield of power symbols, eagle, wolf and bear amongst them.

The hull stretched backwards forever to an incredible length and I guessed would hold nearly an entire *tunstede* of rowers. This boat was designed and built by Baldur. His achievement was, as with all his endeavours, close to perfection.

And all too soon it would be put to the flame.

A cry went up in the gathering and soon we saw the huge oaken doors grind open to reveal a cart pulled by oxen, carrying the two shrouded bodies of Baldur and Nanna. Gathered around them were many shining articles of gold and silver, *seax* and sword, shield and loom, all to go with them to their resting grounds. Beneath the white shrouds, I could glimpse the jewellery that adorned them both.

Suddenly Sunni burst out through a cloud and flooded the pair in bright sunshine. The people gasped and muttered words of shared surprise amongst themselves. The rays hit the shrouds and brought them alight with reflections on the gold and silver until they were both wreathed in a golden light. And it remained so, until the oxen were pulled away and the shrouds placed on Hringhorni. The boat shuddered on its rollers, like a living being.

Both Wōden and Freyja stood desolate and hunched beside the boat. Both shielding their eyes against Sunni, whom they had not seen for days and which blasted their sleep deprived minds. A low moan came from Freyja, as a new wave of grief hit her and Wōden grasped her closer to him.

Thunor stood close by, towering over both, breathing heavily and causing the trees to bend in his outbreath. Mjolnir was ready to consecrate the fire, but all this was waiting for the boat to be rolled onto the water. It was too big to move. It stayed heavy and laden on the rollers. On the boat, too, was Baldur's steed, fitted for the journey in all its saddle and finery. Wōden had bent over the body of Baldur and whispered to him, prising his own golden ring, Draupnir from a frozen finger and gifting it to his son.

A call had been sent out for help. And it came so swiftly, I was in no doubt they had been waiting in the forest for just this moment.

Into the arena of grief came a spectre I would wish to forget. On the back of a growling, grinning wolf, saliva dripping from its mouth, came the giantess from Jötunheim, one of my Ancestors, Hyrrokin. She flung at the ship so violently that sparks flew from the rollers, as Hringhorni careered, shaking and rolling down to the sea where it hit the water with a huge splash that drenched those on board. Baldur's horse whinnied in fear. Thunōr exploded in anger and everyone shrieked before him. He expressed his grief through mounting anger.

My anger was growing sharp again: *Ealdmōdor* looked swiftly at me.

"Be still! Dagrun", she hissed. But it was too late. I knew beyond a shadow of a doubt that the wolf was Loki. It was so obvious that he had planned this move, presented himself to this terrible scene. Loki had to be the final instigator of chaos and sorrow. It was his hallmark.

My hatred pulsed into intense anger. He suddenly shifted around, turned his wicked wolf face to stare straight at me, and growled a long hideous threat that stopped my heart in fear.

"Nāāāāh!" shouted *Ealdmōdor* in a shriek I had never heard from her, "quick, we must go, go NOW!" as she took my arm and we sped away into the spirit world, away from the danger of the evil Loki.

CHAPTER THIRTY- EIGHT
The well of Mimir

We stayed in a quiet type of hinterland, a place between lands, that I came to realise was the veil itself, where even the thrum of *Wyrd* came to a pause.

My *Ealdmōdor* gave a deep outward breath, and I felt her spirit body sag.

I bent my head and whispered an apology, for I knew her extreme fatigue was my fault alone.

"Perhaps it is for the best, Dagrun", she said, after a long pause, which had her wrestling with her own thoughts, "For you missed witnessing the conclusion to this terrible event. A dwarf came skipping into the sombre gathering, dancing and skipping. I believe he was spurred on by Loki, who had created this whole epic of tragedy and shame. Thunor kicked him screaming into the flames which he had just consecrated with Mjolnir and of course Baldur's poor horse died in the flames.

But the evil Loki had not finished with them all. Everything living and dead cried for and mourned for Baldur, except the giantess þökk, Loki in disguise, who refused. Baldur would remain in Hel, in the underworld until Ragnarök, when the new world will begin."

There remained a long silence. I could not find the words. I was shamed by my own emotions.

"This is your lesson, Dagrun Wahl of the Warinni, the *spakōna*, our Völva in the making. At least one of your children will carry the gift. Would you want her to become a victim of her own hatred? Would you want her fail because she expressed her growing wisdom in emotions created to destroy rather than build harmony and peace?"

I jerked up and stared at my *Ealdmōdor* with understanding growing.

"*Nā*," I whispered, "I will do anything to stop that coming into being."

"Then," she said firmly, "You must learn to detach. You must learn, *now*, that evil is the mirror we must consider, that it will always be present in the world of humans. You must learn and know the essence of the prayers of your enemy."

"But never live in hatred. For that is their food which keeps them alive and with which we die. They are victorious if we live in their hatred. And would you want Loki to laugh and be happy knowing you had unwittingly come to join him?"

I nodded, for I was really beginning to learn.

"That is why our kinship is so important to us. We hold that above war."

"Yes, we do. But not always do we honour it. Wōden became besieged with grief. He left the *Tunstede* and went to the battlefields again, but this time with Fury at his side. He sent his spear over the heads of hapless victims in the killing fields, and they died as surely as Sunni rose the following morning. He came back to Yggdrasil through whispered words of the Norns, bent and exhausted, his spirit weak. They bade him come to the Well of Mimir. The only place where Wōden could talk directly to the God. His severed head had been lovingly healed by Wōden with his nine herbs and his glory rods. In return, Mimir counselled him as no other could."

"We are about to greet him there. Are you ready for your final Telling, Watcher?"

Ealdmōdor pierced straight through to my soul with her ice-blue eyes.

"*Giese!*" I said firmly.

… … … … … … … … …

We entered the spirit world of Yggdrasil at its root. Where sat the Well of Mimir. It was dark, with encroaching overgrown ferns of enormous height. The darkest green fronds towering over the well's entrance, hid the well from view. The ground was damp, even muddy, and there were pockets of still water laying in deep puddles.

The water from the Mimir well was sought after. Wisdom was carried in its spirit.

A deep sense of foreboding entered my thoughts. I tried to dispel it.

Then I glimpsed Wōden, lying semi-conscious, with one arm draped over the well's edge. He was muttering in a low whisper. Words I could not fathom. *Ealdmōdor* hugged me tightly, whispering in my ear, "Gain strength Dagrun, you will need all of it!"

The ferns moved and shook, a rustling that brought Wōden's head up to twist around. He looked ravaged and unkempt. Dark circles locked his eyes in tiredness and they seemed almost lifeless.

His dwarfish guardian and oath-sworn friend Alviss appeared. His long beard swinging in rhythm to his loping gait. He squelched over the puddles and cursed softly. This was not his favourite environment. He peered over the well, his feet dangling in mid-air and his beard moving to inaudible utterances he sent down to the pit of hidden water. It was many spear lengths down. He dropped a stone into the well, and counted, until he heard a splash, then a curse. Slowly but surely Mimir entered the world of Yggdrasil. He was a dis-embodied head wreathed in herbs and salve. His eyes were dark and deep. So very deep inside his parchment covered skull, they looked like dark sockets. If ever there was an image of Hel, it was Mimir.

Alviss bounced back onto the firm earth, thinking not without reason that Mimir might fancy Alviss to join him in the depths.

"Hmmm," "Alviss coughed," Wōden has need of you and your wisdom, Mimir. As you can see he is laid very low."

The head swivelled round to stare at the bent form of the god, in all his suffering, now frail and human "He was given a great and awesome gift from the Mights", Mimir growled.

"That needs to be gifted back with sacrifice if he is to achieve the full wisdom of a God"

"But has he not sacrificed and suffered enough already with the death of Baldur, his son?" Alviss asked, rubbing his beard as he did when unsure of his ground. "Pah!" retorted Mimir, "That was nothing to do with us. That is purely the workings of Loki!"

"A sacrifice is needed" he repeated, as he slowly descended into the gloom.

… … … … … … … … …

CHAPTER THIRTY-NINE
LOKI

Alviss reached out to the hunched figure of Wōden, his beautiful curling hair now dipping into the mud puddles that his knees had sunk into. It seemed as if all physical sensation had left him.

"*Wōden, mín Dryhten,*" Alviss whispered, bending to reach his ear, now caked with mud, stroking his hair like a father would,
"*A word in þín eare, fram þín hold ãðswornian ambyhtscealc,*

Besèon dèop be-innan æt gewitan þín geweald **Nūðã!**

Forðǣm ðe þes lāc willan oððe ãsmiðian þu deād-lic oððe cèpan þu æt þín rihtwís stede wiþ þæt Dryhtens!"

"Wōden, my lord Dryhten, a word in your ear, from your loyal oath-sworn servant,

Look deep within to find your power, NOW,

For this sacrifice, will either make you mortal or take you to your rightful place with the Gods!"

Wōden shifted up, swung his head towards his friend and ally, and, looking deep into the dwarves' old grizzled eyes, clapped him on the back, nearly sending him slewing forward into the stagnant water. Then a hug from Wōden saved him and they stood for a moment, waiting.

They did not have to wait long.

With a great swishing of ferns and heavy footfalls, the dwarf, Alfrigg, who had assisted in creating the spear, Gungnir, and its counterfeit, burst through the dark greenery to warn Wōden.

"Wōden, Loki is near", he shouted with some alarm, "And he had evil intent upon you my Lord."

Before anyone present could react, as if all were suspended in the river of Wryd, unable to move of their will and intentions, Loki, with a great cloud of darkness swirling around him, entered the glade that held the well of Mimir.

He was holding Gungnir aloft, level, with his straight focus on Wōden.

"*An èage forðǽn an èage, Brōðor!* An eye for an eye, Brother," Loki growled, advancing forward, slowly, carefully measuring his footfalls like that of a wolf.

"This is your spear, Brother, except only you and these dwarves know it is counterfeit, it will mark you brother for all time."

And without a fraction delay upon those words, the false Gungnir thrummed through the air between them. Blood of half-blood, resentment piled upon hatred, fuelled its path straight and true.

Wōden had but a moment to respond. As if knowing the target, he put both hands to his eye. When the spear impacted on him, he stopped it from going through him like a honed shard of flint. He held it momentarily within his eye. Everything was still. No sound came from him at all.

But Loki howled, lifting his head up to his dark gods in fury at the outcome of his plan to murder his brother. Not maim or injure. His was a plan of annihilation.

He turned and left. It was my last siting of the vilest presence I had ever encountered. But I knew the essence of the prayers of my enemy in that moment. It stayed with me, and went to the *Cenningstān*.

Wōden now heaved a huge intake of breath, held it, and then pulled the false Gungnir from him and with it, his eye hung on its tip. He flung it into the well with a cry of pain and let the blood flow from his empty eye socket into the pool of brackish water now fast becoming red.

Mimir appeared with a look of compassion and care on his wizened face. He had brought sacred water for Wōden, who drank veraciously and then poured the remains into the socket. Alviss had collected all the herbs needed from Mimir and he packed the cavity with the poultice.

"Keep our God here, Alviss, till all is healed. I wish to talk with him now. We will have a wonderful Telling."

Wōden, who had been crouching down, his head to the earth, lifted his face, and looked straight at me. I gasped momentarily for what I saw was magnificent and not at all the gruesome sight I had expected.

"Well my faithful Watcher," he said with a growing smile, "What do you see now?"

"Oh Wōden," I exclaimed "I can see your eye! It is shining and wonderful to see! It is blue and silver, changing colours, but all bright, and it has all wisdom with love shining from it! You have one eye in Spirit and one eye on earth in the world of men."

"Ah Dagrun", he replied, "I can see much more than that! I can see my son, my beautiful son. All the anger is gone. No bitterness now. Your watch here is done, Dagrun Wahl of the Warinni, may you and yours flourish in peace. And thank you, from my heart."

I felt a touch on my shoulder, and knew without needing to see, my *Ealdmōdor* had come to take me back home. The rush of love and excitement that flooded my whole body goes beyond any words here. My Watch was truly done.

… … … … … … … … …

CHAPTER FORTY
WIHTLAND

I had dreams, many of them, before I finally came back to my body. They were very real. It was as though I had to gain soul retrieval. Wōden was as good as his word. I saw him on the killing fields, older, wiser, and with his spine bent wearing a huge hat that shaded his face. I thought that quite deliberate to hide his spirit eye. I always knew he was a vain sort. Or perhaps it was to protect it from the glare of man. He was a guide now for the dead souls whom crowded round him on the battlefield. He sent them on to Valhalla or to Neorxenawang, for there were women too, who died in battle. No-one was left to flounder under his watchful eye.

Then came the day of my awakening back into the world of man. It was twilight, a fortuitous time as the light was dimmed and subtle. At first, I saw a flickering misty kind of light, then my sense of smell came to me, and I grimaced at the acrid smell of wick smoke. It stung in my nostrils and I tried to rub my nose. That was when I realised my body was a heavy, leaden, slow, aching pile of flesh and bones! I was not prepared for that. I drew in all my will to just move my arm. I must have achieved some movement, as I heard that voice I had been longing to hear for so very long.

"Dagrun, my *Cwèn*, you are back!" Eileifer exclaimed, as I felt his hand on my arm, then his cheek on my face, and finally, his kiss. It sent a jolt of energy through me that brought with it all the love and excitement I felt when my spirit knew we were coming home.

Then I felt my body again. And with it came a great feeling of empathy and gratitude. Of being in physical form again. It was as if my spirit yearned for this and was so very happy. Our lives in physical form is, I realised in that moment, a great gift from the Mights, our Ancestors.

I opened my eyes to his face. It was so very beautiful, handsome and full of love shining towards me. And I achieved my first smile in human form again. It ached. And he just hugged me, tears flowing from him in silent shudders of his shoulders, tears catching my cheeks and my mouth, I tasted their saltiness and warmth. I joined him, our sorrow and our joy, bled out onto the furs, hugging tighter until I could feel the pulse in my arms and his.

And when we were done, we laughed. It had always been our way out of pain.

At last, I asked the burning question, "How long have I been gone, Eileifer?"

He looked down, gathering the pain within him and said slowly, "Over four full moons Dagrun!"

"*Nā!*" I exclaimed, "*Ealdmōdor* told me it would be like the blinking of an eye!"

"Well look for yourself, *mín freogan*" Eileifer said softly.

I turned my gaze to my body, and gasped. I had become like a glory rod. Flesh now thin and wrapped around bone with fast reducing muscle.

"Lífa kept your body alive, Dagrun. We owe her much. She sat with you and after failing to give you even the slightest amount of food, achieved a remarkable way of giving you water and broth. You must talk with her when you are stronger. Now speaking of food, I will get you some of that bone broth. Do you feel like taking some?"

"*Giese!*" I replied, "I need to walk and very soon. I will tell you all there is, Eileifer, for *Wyrd* is most wonderful. It stretches time beyond our understanding. I have been in spirit for countless moons, many seasons!"

Now at least my eyes were working for me, and I looked around. And gasped quietly, for this room was new to me, and for a moment I wondered if my memory was failing me. Smiling, I realised this was my "solar", the place Eileifer had promised me. It had an opening to my precious land outside, that brought Mōnā shining gently into what was the largest room I have ever seen. The opening, showing the outside, was a long wide space, with what seemed like wooden planks that could move. Huge pegs rammed into hemp loops made them moveable. I was in awe. Then turning my aching neck around, I saw another similar opening, with those planks shuttered. I knew this was to the East, where Sunni would be rising. What if both were open, I wondered? Then it would feel as if I were outside, the breezes flowing though.

The furs were piled beneath me, but I also felt I was laying on something so soft I could not feel solid wood. I craned my neck to look down and saw hemp cloth filled with feathers, so soft I laughed at the luxury of it all.

"Oh, Eileifer, you are indeed spoiling me", I muttered quietly.

"That he is, but don't be angry with him, Dagrun, for he is learning the *Rōmānisc* ways!" came a voice I knew so well.

"Lífa", I exclaimed, as she came forward to me with the widest smile. We wrapped our arms around each other and her tears too graced my cheek.

"Lífa was it terrible for you all?" I asked peering into her eyes for comfort.

"Nã,", she smiled, "It was torture, *sweostor!*"

"You may not want to know this," she continued "but after we all failed trying to give you water, I became desperate. We all did. Even Eileifer became withdrawn and morose. We did not recognise our *Cyng* at all. So, one evening I went to the water meadows, to the rushes, and found a good strong length of stalk. I softened it to make it pliable. And I coaxed it down your throat long enough to reach your stomach and fed you through the stalk. It worked *sweostor*! For here you are. And we can use this in our healing. You *Fæder* and *Mōdor*, Eystein, Eyvindr, Eileifer and myself, we all went back to the water meadow to gift Nerthus our precious talismans and brooches and our prayers of gratitude."

"Eyvindr!" I shouted, "He is here on Wihtland? Have they freed him?"

"*Giese, ond Nã*", Lífa said smiling, "He is still a *Foregísl,* not a libertus, and was here to help with the new villa. He has returned to *Cantium* where he is apprenticed to the builder of the largest villa in Britannia. He is learning to build the Roman way, Dagrun."

"Please tell him to come and see me!" I implored Lífa, grasping her hands tightly.

"*Giese* when he returns to us,", she replied, "very soon, but now take your food, Dagrun. All in valuable time *sweostor*, in enjoyable time. I am so very happy you are back with us."

The bone broth was the most beautiful tasting food, almost better than in my spirit world. And it was this world that came flooding back to me, now, memories, recollections that I must keep close to my heart. I fell into a deep sleep, the smiling face of Wōden coming to greet me.

… … … … … … … … …

Sunni came bursting into my consciousness, as my first meeting with a new day. I had to shield my eyes against the glare. Both openings were now open, light cascading in and meeting me at my resting place. A breeze, light and gentle, caressed my face. It was a glorious welcome to Nerthus. But, however much I yearned to be out there in the sun, I could not move from my furs. I spent a while admiring the lodge Eileifer had built, and I knew it was on high ground because I was looking straight upon where sea met the sky. We spoke of the prophesy from the white horses, of famine and he always believed it would be flood and to have the grain stores on high ground meant we, as a tribe, would not starve.

This solar was a world away from where I had made my dark, damp home. I now realised the wisdom of it all. My herb *Hūs* was truly meant for herbs to thrive within that dampness and sometimes the freezing cold. But not for me. Eileifer saw what I could not. It would have made me very ill. And what good is a healer and *spakōna* who is lying on a sick bed! He saved me in every way that is possible. The truest love I would ever know.

And now I saw our special place. He had adorned the walls with fine woven hemp, and must have asked the weaving women to create beautiful designs in deep-coloured threads. There was one on every wall, to hide the rough-hewn timbers. And on the floor, fragrant rushes had been laid out, strewn with sweet smelling herbs of rosemary and meadowsweet.

And someone had collected wild flowers from the pasture land and placed them in my favourite jug.

All I had to do was get well and get up. I heaved a huge intake of breath and fisting my hands on the furs, I tried to raise myself to twist round and get my feet at least to the rushes. A cry escaped me. But I achieved it. I heard the creaking of new wood, and realised quickly that I was in effect on a higher level and someone had heard me.

The thick oaken door heaved open, grating on the dried mud packed floor. And I heard a soft swearing of exasperation.

Then I saw a face I had not seen in many moons.

Aslaug appeared, looking as stern as ever, as ill-tempered as she always was, and she stared at me, erect, as if a broom had been rammed up her back. Hands clasped in front of her, head to one side, she stared at me in silence.

I did not feel the old fear at all, just a mounting irritation and a wisp of anger, which I swallowed instantly. I had leant well enough the outcome of that emotion!

Then, quite surprisingly, a rare and wonderful smile lit up her lined and haggard face. It reached her eyes, and they shone in affection towards me.

"Dagrun, *beorn*," she cried, striding forward to reach closer to me, "We thought we had lost you! I found you slumped by the *stān* of you *Ealdmōdor*, soaked through and seemingly dead to the earth. I was given a vision to seek you out, Dagrun. I believe this came from your *Ealdmōdor*."

"You saved me", I replied, reaching out my hand to squeeze her hand, "*ðocian þu,* thank you."

"You must share what happened to you, Dagrun", she declared.

"*Giese,*" I struggled to my feet, holding onto the wooden post holding the furs, "If you will kindly help me to the solar opening, so I may fill my lungs with the warm sea air!"

But my legs simply crumpled beneath me. So, holding all my weight, Aslaug took me to the stool just by the opening. And there I looked out to see exactly where Eileifer had chosen our *Hūs*, our grand lodge to be.

I leaned my head out and immediately my hair caught the breeze. After some grateful huge intakes of fresh air, which made my underused lungs full to bursting, I scanned the scene before me. I felt light headed with the purity of the air.

It was the birdsong that assailed my ears, before my eyes took in the blazing yellow of gorse that stretched around the rim of the *dūn*. And which tapered down almost to the *botms,* where a lake of spring water lay, rippling in the wind and catching Sunni's rays in an ever-intricate, twinkling movement. I was as captivated by that sight as I was of the piercing exquisite lark song, as they danced to the rhythm of the wind, catching thermals and swooping down to then ascend in their majesty. I breathed in peace and expelled yet more of the friction and sadness embedded in my soul.

But as I drank in this perfect scene, a sharp jolt of words came thundering into my mind…

"Watcher, remember all that you have seen and go the *Cenningstān*" that ancient voice intoned.

I knew then, that the Watcher was being watched. I would not have expected anything less.

"Aslaug", I turned to watch her for a moment before saying, as kindly as I was able, "I cannot tell you what happened to me in the *Wyrd*, not yet at least. As a Warinni, and guardian of the stones, I must give all knowledge and happening to the stones, so they may be kept for all seasons and all moons. It is important. The Norns made me pledge this, and as an oath-sworn *sweostor* I cannot gainsay them in any way!"

"The Norns," Aslaug exploded, taking a shocked breath inward, "*Sweostor* what do you mean?"

"I leant that I am, I mean we, my family, indeed the Warinni, being giants, are of the Jötunheim, as are the Norns" I blurted out, feeling that old smallness before my priestess, which had haunted me before. I shook myself. This was absurd.

Aslaug bent her head in silence, before whispering an apology. She turned to leave as the oaken door opened and I cried in delight as Eileifer appeared, all smiles, behind a young maiden who was carrying food and ale.

"Aslaug," he beckoned, "Do not leave on my account! Come join us in sharing this super"

"My *Cyng*," she turned to face him, "I don't wish to outstay my welcome."

"*Nã nã*, please stay", I begged, smiling and offering a seat to her, "Aslaug, you saved my life, I am indebted to you. Eileifer, I have just explained to our priestess why I cannot share my Telling yet. I have sworn to take it first to the stones. But I know you cannot join me for much of this time. Your *Cyngship* does not allow it. I need strong arms and a strong spirit to help me in this."

"Aslaug, please will you join me and Lífa in the journey across Wihtland?"

"*Giese!*", she replied, happily without a second's hesitation.

"And after we have completed the pledge, then we will call the biggest gathering, all the Wihtwara, to hear the Telling together, with much mead and song."

We sat and eat a full supper together and for the first time in my life, I felt a union with Aslaug, a levelling and a strong bond building to entwine itself around us. She became, as she was always meant to be, my *Ealdmōdor*, until I departed to meet my blood grandmother in Nerthus' meadow.

As Eileifer and I settled together to allow sleep to waft over me, and being too frail of body to join with my *Cyng,* he stroked my hair, his beautiful smiling face resting on his arm, hearing my words before sleep overtook me,

"*Líðe ferhð*", I whispered, "This beautiful place, our home, this seat of *Cyng's* needs a name. I wish it to be called, *Eileifer dūn* and over where the larks fly, *Lœwercedūn.*" "*Giese*", came the whispered reply.

… … … … … … … … …

CHAPTER FORTY-ONE

Ðã þæt Hãlig Stãns grèotan

When the Sacred Stones Weep

When the day arrived for my first journey to the *Hãlig Stãns*, Thunōr was bubbling up clouds to block out Sunni. Deep greys and thunderous blue shapes were building to remind us that *sumor* was nearly over. I had spent the best part of a *mōnaþ* and a further *wice* beyond that, struggling to get my legs to behave in a rhythmical manner. I braved the wind and the rain that our mighty Thunor sent to test my resolve and strength. Eileifer did his level best to dissuade me from that first journey on my own, believing it was too soon. But I did gainsay him. Something that would be unthinkable when I had adopted the full royal role of *Cwèn* in Wihtland. Yet he was right. He kept shaking his head as he wrapped yet another kirtle round me to warm my weak legs, and muttered something in Old Norse, before twisting me around, with a gentle slap, bade me go.

I needed to touch the earth again, pull my fingers through the dirt. Just as Wōden had done when he had collapsed back to the earth from Yggdrasil. It was instinctual. It was heaven! The smells of a wet hedge, twigs embedded with green lichen that I brought to my nose and breathed in the perfume. It was intoxicating to my senses that had been dormant, unloved in the world of spirit. And fallow fields with flowers still swaying, limp with rain, almost whipped their heads up to greet me! Or so I wanted to believe.

Everything seemed to hold an intensity of physical power I had allowed to diminish in *Wyrd*. I had assumed the ethereal energy in the spirit world to be perfection. Yet it would cease to exist without the beauty of the physical to accompany it. I now knew what Wōden had learnt at Yggdrasil.

On this first day, I planned to reach the *botms* of *Eileifer dūn* where the rainfall was deepening the pond by the day. Enough had gathered to allow the wind to dance ripples upon the surface. It had beckoned me daily. Nerthus was calling me. To reach there I needed to descend, but it was steep. So, I decided to follow the pattern and the spiral dance of the gorse as it gently swept in a downwards curve towards the water. Huge droplets were dancing on the surface, sending sprites into the air, to take a breath before descending to the watery depths. The rain tickled my face. Droplets landing on my neck to find their way to dampen my clothes. My hair was in dripping ringlets. I had long since loosened the knot. And I was deeply at peace, so much so, I stopped several times within the cluster of gorse, to touch, squash and breathe in the heady perfume of the deep yellow flowers. The colour of them made me feel that I was in the centre of Sunni.

Eventually I neared the water and without any prompting, felt my heart open wide to receive the love of Nerthus. I collapsed and knelt before her, sweeping her waters up into my face, drinking fully of her. And it was then I knew how precious our physical world is to us, to our Ancestors, to our Gods. We are in union with the love of it. We are in union as caretakers of it. We are co-creators of it.

I looked to see a silhouetted figure on horseback, waiting at the top of the ridge. I knew instantly it was Eileifer. I waved him down to greet me, knowing he would otherwise leave me to my solitude. I was glad and relieved, as my weakened legs had betrayed me.

He too swung a gentle descent down, his beautiful piebald stallion kicking up wet clods of sodden earth in his wake. Eileifer's suevian knot bounced and swung energetically as he came nearer. I could see him smiling, dimples fixed in his cheeks. He pulled his horse in and bounced from him with a high swing that saw him land close by me. I laughed and tried to stand, but crumpled again by the water's edge.

The smile I loved so much instantly left him and he pulled me up in a swift sweep of his arms and held me close, breathing hard but saying not a word.

"You are displeased, my *Cyng*," I spoke at last softly, waiting for some rebuke.

"*Giese!*" he replied, holding my face in his two strong hands and making me look straight at him "That I am, Dagrun. We truly believed we had lost you towards the end. Now we see you risking illness again. You are trying too soon to be well. I can see your spirit is full, Nerthus has come to you, but your body needs rest, Dagrun! You will obey me on this!"

"Look," he continued, reaching into his pouch he kept tied to him at all times, "I bring a gift, an offering to our *Foldemōdor*. Allow us to make our offering together for your health to speedily return and for our hand fasting to be blessed with child!"

He showed me the beautiful silver filigree brecciate, copper inlaid with a shining silver leaves entwined around the whole circle. And I gasped at the workmanship. We both knelt by the water and said a prayer softly, quietly, before allowing it to drop gently, disappearing from us to the depths below.

"How come you by this?" I asked
Eileifer took a long inward breath before saying simply and quietly,

"Eyvindr, my love, your *brōðor*."

"*Ahh*," I shrieked," Is he here on Wihtland?"

"Na! but he will be soon. Your brother, Eystein has gone to talk with him. He is still in *Cantium*, still a hostage by name. But more relaxed Dagrun. He has done well. But he will be returning as a

Rōmānisc, to the new Villa. He will not be joining us, the Wihtwara. He is not *libertus.* But that may change."

"I must see him as soon as my pledge is completed," I replied, grasping his arm, as my excitement grew, "You see we must, that is, our people, the Wihtwara, learn and become proficient in the Roman words, and their tongue. I was given that by the *Norn Sweostors"*

"I am seeing that you have indeed told me very little of your time in the *Wyrd",* Eileifer replied, "We are all waiting to know."

"I am pledged to hold everything I witnessed in abeyance until I can meld my spirit with the *Hālig Stān*s. They above all others must know everything for the future times. If I recall it to you now, it will diminish. Please be patient" I turned from him in regret, but he took hold of me and held me tightly, then jumped up onto his stallion, he reached down to hoist me up before him. We galloped up the *dūn* in silence to reach the higher ridge where our lodge sat resplendent on its own summit. Nothing more was said, but I knew he understood. It took several more twilights, much sleeping and hearty eating before I was allowed the journey to the *Halig Stāns.*

I had already sent messages to my Kin asking for their forbearance in giving me time to complete my pledge to the Norns, to Wōden, before welcoming me back into the *Ceasterwic.* I had to do this alone, except for Aslaug and Lífa, who were my right and left hand.

"Dagrun, *dohtor,"* Aslaug leant down from her horse, studying me carefully, "Have you got good provisions? You will tire easily in this sharp wind."

"*Giese*, that I have," I replied, noticing with an inward smile that she had provisioned for an army and her poor horse was sagging under the weight of it all. I saw furs which I was entirely glad of. I found that I could not keep the biting wind from reaching my bones. I had so little flesh and muscle.

We were in fact travelling but a short distance to *Sudmōr.* Beginning with the *Cenningstān* where I might also sit with my

Ealdmōdor, giving thanks for my return to the very place where it all started.

"You know we will be enduring at least two cold nights, Dagrun", Lífa confided, "Aslaug is well prepared, bless her!"

I heaved a breath inward and started to feel apprehensive for the first time. It was the wrong season, the cold was setting in. Although I had never hesitated at the thought of nights spent with the earth mother, this time it felt vaguely wrong.

"We have each other for warmth, *sweostor*," I replied.

We set off, like three *Spakōna* on a mission, taking our horses to *Plæsc Bearu* for deep drinking, before the long trot over *Ceofodūn Scyte*, *Rægecumb*, and *Etdreðecumb*. Roe deer nibbled lazily at the last of the meadow grass, their tawny coat glimmering with raindrops now Sunni had appeared at last. The clouds diminishing under her growing heat. I was ever thankful that the time of beetle gathering on *Ceofodūn*[JH1] was past. Our horses would have surely thrown us in the plague of flying, clicking insects. I kept quiet council as we gathered speed towards *Sudmōr*.

My home, my place of my birth on this Isle of Wihtland. My *Ieldran* were close, yet I could not run to greet them. A knot formed in my throat and I had to fight the tears away. So hard it is, I thought, so very hard to be a *Spakōna*. A seed was planted in my soul at that instant, when watered with love and conviction might grow into a change of direction for me.

… … … … … … … …

We reached our Ancestor stones nearing twilight. Hidden away by a circle of low-lying goat willow, we tied our horses to the trees and gave them each a leather pouch filled with oats to eat. Sunni was sinking low in a cloudless sky. The colours deepened and reached into the circle, laying a delicate tone on the stones, whose shadows lengthened with the sinking golden globe.

After gaining permission, I walked straight to *Ealdmōdor*. Where it all began. Aslaug and Lífa left me alone there, walking the circle quietly, giving whispered invocations to our Ancestors. I placed the heron wing before me, watching to see even the slightest flutter. The stillness clamped my heart for a moment. Then suddenly I felt a shadow pass over me, and looking up I gasped, for there flying so low and peacefully caught on a gentle thermal of wind, was Heron. She banked her head round as she passed and the connection was made. My heart burst open and tears came. I knew beyond a doubt, it was *Ealdmōdor*.

A truth came hurtling in also, the kind that is unexpected and deep in its meaning. She was showing me I no longer needed to connect with spirit, with *Wyrd*. I was being given permission to be wholly in body, mother to my children and wife to my *Cyng*.

My job was done, I no longer needed to be a *spakōna* to the tribe.

I looked straight in the glow of Sunni as she sunk below the sea, and a great weight was lifted from me.

As Lífa and Aslaug came over to join me, I said to Lífa, looking directly at her, almost imploring for her assent, "*Sweostor*, I know we have been together in our journey. You are like a twin-soul to me. I have just been given permission from the Ancestors to become a wife and mother. I have taught you all I know and if it is your wish, you may take over my role as *Spakōna*."

"Ahh, Dagrun!" she replied smiling warmly, "If only you knew how much I wanted you to say those words! It is my dearest wish to tread this path in your footsteps. The *Ealdmōdor* knew, and now so do you."

"It has, *beorn*, been staring at you in the face", Aslaug said smiling ironically, "And it has taken this supreme sacrifice which very nearly saw the end of you, for you to wake up to it!"

"Dah!" I exclaimed, feeling both embarrassed and chagrined that as ever, I had been slow in understanding, that I was the last to know.

"Come, my dear Dagrun," Lífa took my arm to hoist me up, "May you finish your pledge now with a clean and a light heart."

As we neared the *Cenningstān*, we entered its long dark shadow. Soon it would be in darkness and we waited for *Mōnā* to join us, making a four. We joined our hands together, after we had made our offerings. They hugged the stone's base, half hidden by deep green, bending grass. All our Ancestors from the Warinni and Eudose, Nuithone, Anglii and Aviones, sheltered under the power of the *Cenningstān*. There are so few us, I thought. We are the first. But the power remained constant and soon I felt waves of energy build around me. I began to sway, knowing there was contact being made. Then and only then did the ancient one, the Might, show himself briefly, and for an instant I knew, believed, it was Wōden himself, old and hunched with the wide brimmed hat covering his face. Then he retreated. I visioned everything I had seen as a Watcher, swept those images and feelings into the stone itself. I felt the power grow until we were all grasping each other's hands so tightly, it hurt.

Then, very suddenly I felt the flow alter. It shook or shuddered, and then it was gone. I opened my eyes. Before me, in the gentle light of Mōnā, I saw unmistakably, glistening water flow from a crevice into the grass below.

"Þæt Hālig Stān grèotan" I said softly to my sisters, who nodded in silence and bowed their heads.

… … … … … … … …

Twilight was fully upon us so and it did not take much hesitation in bedding down for the night in our most sacred of places. We left the circle, and made our way to the horses who were now with bowed head and foreleg rested, fast asleep. My dear gelding raised his head and snorted softly as I approached. So, I gave him a caressing rub down to take away any moisture, and covered him with a woollen overclothe. He was a spoilt gelding, no doubt, but he rewarded me with deep loyalty.

And Aslaug came into her own, as she swept the furs from her horses back and we gratefully hurled them round our bodies, which by now were feeling the chill. A fire was made and soon we were huddled in our warmth, eating cold meat and hunks of dry bread.

The calls of the night kept me awake. The owl swooped low to catch his prey, very close to us. Then calling to his mate, they both silently winged their catch home to their young. The aroma of damp earth and lichen never failed to calm me. And I fell asleep to the low rhythmical snores of Aslaug.

I awoke to the scuffing of my horse's hoof by my head, tangling my hair into a muddy knot. He certainly knew how to get my attention. The others were already packed, Lífa scraping the fire embers and digging them into the dirt with her heel, muttering under her breath, words I could not catch.

"What ails you, *sweostor*?" I asked leaning up on my elbow to see her frown and slightly shake her head.

"Ahh, my bloods have arrived in the night along with a pounding ache in my head," she replied, "With your permission, Dagrun, may I go back to the *Ceasterwic*, to lie in the women's lodge till it passes?"

"*Giese*, of course, I have Aslaug, and I will be fine, really," I answered.

"And I need not worry about such things happening now to me," Aslaug replied drily, "I am in my crone status and very happy, thank you very much!"

I suddenly came to wonder about my flow. It had dried up completely since my body was sent into slumber. I resolved, now I was a free woman again, to eat much more and get my health back quickly. I felt an urgency to be with child. It was such a new feeling, I revelled in it for quite a few minutes.

We left Lífa trotting homeward, looking miserable, her head bent.

We left *Sudmōr* heading up the trail of *Brocbeorg* to meet with the track that would take us to the *Mōtstān* where I needed to complete the next part of the pledge. It was placed on the ridge by the ancient peoples, much older than our ancestor circle, where we held our *ðings*.

We knew it held many secrets, much knowledge and could hold the wisdom of Wōden.

On our upward journey, slow and comfortable, rocking easily on my gelding's back as he gained steady hold on the rocky climb, I looked around and chose this time to soak in every part of my Wihtland. We saw the sea glistening, for there was full sun this day. And as we were heading for the high noon day, shadows were short and the light intense. It picked up the detail of our farm workers, bringing in the barley, sheathing it and making high piles of it. Wagons were being loaded to take it to the dry barns. The gulls were everywhere, dancing to a tune of their own rhythm, swooping to collect the grain, with crow butting in to gain supremacy of the feast below.

I noticed some Roman ships making their way to *Breredingas hýð* where they would offload merchandise bound for the new *Berandinzium* villa, as the Romans likened to call it. And I thought of Eyvindr who would be there soon.

We reached the top track, turning left to spur our horses into a canter, which we all enjoyed. Almost before we could take breath, the long barrow of the ancients came into view and the leaning stone just beyond. The wind picked up, tugging at my knot, flurrying the horse's tails. It was always windy up here on *Mōtstāndūn*. The gorse bushes bent forever from the harsh sea wind. They were hardened and tough. I leant against the leaning stone, away from the wind to collect my thoughts.

"Are you ready for this?" Aslaug said quietly, putting her arm around my shoulders, "We can forgo this you know. I made a serious pledge to your *Cyng* to bring you back in the same state in which you left. He gave me authority to stop this if I felt your health diminish in any way. You are, my *sweostor*, getting close to me making that decision."

"I will be up to the task," I replied, squaring my shoulders, "But may we have some food before we continue. It is after all noon day. We can sit here against the stone, away from this wind for a while"

So, we sat to eat the remainder of the food. I was determined to see this whole pledge completed by twilight. Even if we had to plod home in utter darkness, with no-one but *Mōnã* to guide us.

I breathed in deeply. Aslaug had recounted the days I was asleep. The days of Wōden watching. And it filled me with a growing sense of peace and stability. Our home was secure, people led their lives in peace, our culture and our tribes were united under Wihtwara. We had, as a migrant people, settled well.

Sunni burst out from behind a cloud that skittered across the sky. The *dūn* swept gently downwards to the copse of trees below, still in full leaf and swaying to the dance of the wind. Oxen were chewing on the grass below, and colours of russet and deep yellow peppered the upward hillside leading to *Chestebeorg* where our small *tunstede* of Reudignians had settled, with some recent arrivals of Niuthones. They were making a name for themselves for their fine pottery and metalwork. The Romans were pleased to have them here on Wihtland. Or Vectis as they likened to call it, which in our tongue sounded Wectis, after our warrior *Cyng* Wecta, grandson of Wōden. They used their skills, and they were paid for it, and so I saw that the peoples there were building solid hūs'. And they looked full of health. I drowned my thoughts about the Romans. The pain of that evening was still acute. My brother was hauled away by that Roman governor, who did not last long here, but long enough to ruin part of my life and that of Eyvindr and my family. Then my thoughts passed to them, whom I had not seen since I awakened.

I sighed and pushed myself back to the present.

"Come, Aslaug," I said, "Let us do our work here."

We pulled ourselves up, dusted down our clothes and gave our offerings to the ancient ones, the Mights. This leaning stone, pitted and dark, stained with mould, uneven curves silhouetted against a glaring Sunni, was so old, it nearly stopped my breath. So, I passed through the heavy curtain of the *Mōtstãn* to meld and find his heart. The stone felt cold, hard against my face as I pinned my ear to him, and heard the faint thrum of the earth heartbeat. As it grew louder, and the resonance deepened, I gave myself up to the energy. Images, feelings, all the recent Watching, became a Telling and fled into the heart of *Mōtstān*. I was not aware that my tears had wetted the stone, was not feeling the iron grip I had on the deep crevices of his surface.

Then so suddenly without any warning, a stricken image, the most fleeting of pictures flashed before me, of a metal helm, leaving only black eyes crazed with killing staring at me, and then it was gone.

"Ahh", I shrieked, pulling away from the stone, and collapsing on the ground. Aslaug was with me in an instant.

"*Beorn*! What ails you?"

"Aslaug, I saw that killing image again. The one that came in a dream. Only now it is real. It is intense. The killing will happen here. I am now certain!"

"Maybe, but that is not for you to worry about, Dagrun," there was a sharp tone in her voice, as she felt enough was quite enough.

We left the *Mōtstān* with all its Tellings deep within. We briskly cantered to the *Beorht stān* over *Mōtstāndūn*, and *Beorhtstāndūn* to gallop down *Scorawella Scyte*. We tethered our mounts, and walked to the secluded place where the great and tall *Beorht stān* rested, within a copse of beech, shadowed by their great branches that swept to earth in a celebration of love for the earth and for humans too. The beech was the *Cwèn* of the forest.

We both walked towards this giant of a stone with some nervousness. Unspoken were the fears from our last encounter which saw me disappear from body into a terrifying day in the future. And they came forward to claim my mind, again fearing the same might happen. Aslaug circled the stone, looking upward and around, feeling the energy all round. She lay her hand upon it and then produced the offerings to gift to the Ancestors. Finally, she stopped, looked up and smiled,

"I think it is clear for you, Dagrun."

I came forward and offered my hand, "I will feel safer if you hold me here in this present, Aslaug. You will be my foothold and my guard."

And so that last pledge began. It was indeed easier and there were no hidden shocks waiting. Twilight was descending as the shadow from the *Beorht stān* grew beyond the beech copse, settling on the dried ferns beyond. We hastily packed our belongings onto the horses, who, sensing that we were homeward bound became skittish and edgy. It suddenly occurred to me, now my freedom from spiritual commitments had been gained, I would visit my *Ieldran* so I gave Aslaug leave to head back, with a message to Eileifer to make his way to *Sudmōr*, if engagements allowed, and I kicked my gelding into a fast pace before the sun went down completely.

… … … … … … … … …

CHAPTER FORTY- TWO
Þæt Cynelíc Ǽwnung
The Royal Wedding

I gave my gelding to the stable boy, who led him away, fairly skipping with delight, as he loved my horse and it was mutual. I knew he would be receiving the most thorough rubbing down, the best hay and many strokes and murmurs. He would repay with those big dark eyes pouring out love and affection to the boy.

I was hoping for a similar welcome. And it came in gasps and smiles and hugging from my *Mōdor* who fought back the tears unsuccessfully and an even tighter hug from *Fæder* who fought back his tears with his Adam's apple moving erratically. And that fixed smile on his face that refused to give in.

And I simply cried, in relief and exhaustion combined. I hoped Eileifer would understand this need to unite with my blood, to feel the unconditional love waft over me so I could at last let go. And if he joined us this twilight, I would at last give the Telling. It would begin the process of detachment and letting go of Wōden's mystery to become Wōden's story. I would become the *scōp* of the tribe for a while. But I accepted the role readily.

"*Mōdor*," I announced, "I have been given leave to end my time as a *spakōna*, by our *Ealdmōdor* and I want you both to know I am happy."

"Why *Dohtor*, that is some relief!" my *Fæder* announced, who never minced his words, "So when can we announce your hand fasting to the *ceasterwic* and the *tunstede*?"

"Folkvarthr*!*" *Mōdor* exclaimed, knocking him far from gently on his shoulder, "Give our Dagrun some breathe, she has only just returned from the dead!"

"*Fæder*, even Eileifer does not know of my release from those obligations," I replied, rubbing his shoulder in sympathy. My *Mōdor* was nothing less of a giant and stood head to head with him.

"I have come straight to you this twilight. For in truth you are my blood kin and should be the first to know. I have sent a message to him to come here. I'm sorry if I have surprised you. Do you have enough food for supper this twilight?"

"*Giese*", *Mōdor* answered, smiling quietly to herself, a look of sheer happiness radiated from her. It was then I realised how much worry I had placed upon my kin. Healing the sick had been a goal for me since childhood, but the entry into *drycræft* had slipped in alongside. Finding I was good at it, my Warinni blood became excited and took me over into a passionate search for more wisdom. It culminated in my "death" that must have terrified them all. And here I was facing them in their relief and my guilt. Why is it then, I asked *Ealdmōdor* in silence, that in working for the higher good, we always sacrifice, first and most acutely, our kin and loved ones?

"I'll fetch Eystein," *Fæder* announced, breaking into my thoughts, "This is time for feasting and celebration. Our Dagrun has returned for good!" As he whipped the hide away to stoop down into the night and the inevitable rush of chilly air hurled smoke and ash into our faces, he turned to gift me the biggest heart-warming smile I had ever seen from him. His Adam's apple began its work again, and I knew his tears would fall privately, in the walk to my *brōðor,* who remained in his small *hūs*. Even though he was now *Ealdorðegn*, our chief thane, he preferred to keep close to his family. And he always had to duck under the low eaves.

We heard the pounding of their feet before the hide was raised. They both came straight to the fire, blocking the warmth, by heating their backs and grinning like a pair of over-stuffed bears.

"*Þurh þæt Dryhten!*" Eystein growled through his thicker beard than I remembered, "But you are a sight my *sweostor*! Did they not feed you where you have been?"

The roar of laughter that produced brought him forward, to wrap me in the biggest brother hug that left me gasping for breath. It also relaxed the energies enough for me to realise my kin were shocked at the sight of me.

"This girl needs feeding up," *Fæder* cut in pulling me gently to the hearth where the cauldron hung, softly bubbling with *Kornmjölsgot* and roots. And I sat thankfully on the fur covered stool, gratefully taking the bowl filed to the brim. We all sat in relative silence eating and murmuring appreciative words at *Mōdor's* clever cooking. She never failed to bring aromas of herbs and lately spices coaxed from the *Rōmãnisc* to enrich our plain fare. I was mopping up my second bowl when we heard the horse's neigh, and the heavy footfalls of Eileifer. He entered smiling, chill vapour escaping from the frosty night, and we all felt at our ease. He came forward and kissed me gently on my head then moved over to give the Warinni bear hug to everyone else. He came and sat close to me, pouring the hot porridge into his mouth. I knew he had not eaten at all this day.

"I am more than glad your pledge is completed Dagrun" he turned to stare into my eyes. "I for one, and indeed many others, have been waiting anxiously on the side-lines of your life, knowing this may have been one step too far."

"But you don't know my *sweostor*, Eileifer," my Eystein joked, "her stubbornness outmatches all else. Everything takes second place when she has a mind. Are you sure you want to be hand-fasted to this maiden!"

"Well, since you put it that way Eystein, May I decline?"

I flashed a look at him, then seeing his dimples completely give him away, I rammed my fist into his ribs, very nearly causing his recent porridge to make its re-appearance on the hearth.

"I look to you, the Wahl's and your kin, to arrange for our Hand-fasting on the twilight of the new moon" Eileifer stated "We are fast moving into *Winterfylleth* and *Hālig-mōnaþ* is still a time of gathering in of the bounty. Sunni is still smiling down on us too."

I looked aghast at *Mōdor*, whose primary role in this, our big celebration, was the greatest. Her expression equalled my own, and Eileifer looking from one to the other, as if we were secretly communicating with each other in an unknown language, coughed and shifted about.

"My lord," she said calmly, "Of course this is all possible but I need the total support of not just our *ceasterwic* but the *tunstede* within our Wihtwara bounds. If this is given, then we can celebrate our happiness in the full manner on the eve you request!"

"Ahh, *Gíese*… timing" he looked to his feet, pondering, "I will get a messenger, nah, two messengers to alert all the people. With coin if it is needed. That will bring help to us. Nothing like the rattle of a few coin. These days it seems my people are getting more like the Romans they constantly moan about!"

We left my kin scratching beards and pulling pot and pans from safe places, as the enormous task before them settled firmly at their feet.

We cantered back at a fast pace, needing to take the much longer, but well beaten path of the meadow lands and shoreline that afforded us enough light from Mōnā for our horses to guide us home. We pounded up *Eileifer dūn*, scraping clods of earth in our wake. Never had I wished to be under those fur covers more than at this moment. We both felt such great desire from pounding our thighs against the horse's flesh.

We leapt of our steaming mounts, who were gratefully led away to the stables by the waiting boys, while hand in hand we rushed for our solar. I could feel the surging energy course through my body, now awakened from its deep slumber, to know every nerve was alive and waiting.

Eileifer turned and held my head in his hands, uplifting, to seek my eyes deep in his, and our souls to meet. Our breath came in short bursts as he explored me, ripping away my garments as if they were gossamer from a chrysalis. I was, amidst burning passion, being reborn back into this world. My world, our world. As I felt him harden against me, and I replied with juice anointing my thighs, we came into each other, living in the tumult and rhythm until totally exhausted, we came to rest completely entwined. As I brought my breathing back, a truth hit me with a pleasure that brought a smile.

"My love", he whispered "That smile has a meaning. What is it?"

"*Mín frèogan*, my time in *Wyrd*, in the spirit realm, I was, at first, speechless with the beauty and magnificence of everything. Every tiny thing. Everything was in perfection. Or so I thought, until I realised that my body was gone and everything about it became nothing more than a memory. I was in mourning. And there you have it. This, now, is beyond anything I experienced there. This is perfection!"

"Dagrun, *Cwèn*! You are my perfection. You are my wife, now and until we draw our last breath. And in *Neorxenawang* we will continue our blissful joining. I pledge to you now I will never see you in mourning over that, my love."

And with that I finally began the Telling. Of Wōden, the child-god and his battles with his peers. Loki and his treacherous, murderous intent towards Wōden. The *Utiseta,* part of which at Yggdrasil gave him the *drycræft* of the Runes and *Galdrastafur*. His *fylgia,* those magnificent wolves. And the murder of Yngling. This brought angry tears at the memory. Eileifer calmed me, reminding me, quite rightly, that Yngling had it coming. So, as he stroked my leg, lovingly, beginning to explore me, my stomach exploded in an unquenchable fire, as he brought his hand to my *cwið*, and played me beautifully until I begged for him to enter me and ride me like the thumping of the horsed back between my thighs.

And that is how Eileifer learnt of the Telling, in a scattered, loving, drowsy way, until dawn broke and we eased ourselves into a new day. Our beautiful, wonderful daughter Lãfa, was created that night and was brought into our Wihtwara world on the day of Nerthus within the *nigon mōnaþ*.

… … … … … … … … …

I smoothed down the layers of gossamer fabric, the weaving women had created for my hand-fasting. Eileifer had equally beautiful garments sewn for him. The day became a stunning affair, after storm clouds came, and then just as suddenly disappeared. Eileifer said it was Thunor coming to bless us, and I knew, after remaining so close to Wōden, to be completely true.

I marvelled at their skill, those lovely, quiet, dedicated women, who gave their service to others in the dark weaving lodge. They prayed as they wove the threads into garments and kept alive the *Wyrd Rapas* for us all. And so, they had done this for me also, for I felt the energy bristling as I moved. They had spun the most delicate hemp thread I had ever seen. These were soaked in urine, vinegar to whiten them and make them more pliable. Added to that were the lemons, they must have coaxed from the *Rōmãnisc*. Then, they dipped the threads in a woad bath for various times, creating a waving sea of blue. Weaving it together, they created these small waves after wave. As I moved, they floated into each other, and came alive. They knew how much I loved the sea, from the first moment of arriving here as a small child, I ran into the rolling waters and stayed there until my skin had wrinkled like *Ealdmōdor's* parchment hands.

Sewn into the cloth, edging the bottom, neck and sleeves were hundreds of tiny garnets and sea pearls radiating outwards and upwards to form a glistening sunset on the sea of gossamer cloth. I had chosen to keep the suevian knot in my hair, tied tight and hanging to my left, which had nearly reached my breasts, how much my hair had grown during my Watching.

I reached over to grab my waist belt I always carried, with pouch and *drycræft* tools. I suddenly felt a hand grab me gently to pull the belt away. I turned to see Eileifer in full *Cyngly* robes and the most beautiful royal garments I had never seen. And he completely took my breath away, leaving me staring wordlessly at him. He had grown in stature. There was Wōden's blood coursing through every vein, and that power manifested the God himself, before my eyes. This was the rightful *Cyng* of our people. Not the shy deprecating horse-talker whose dimpled smile melted my heart. This was altogether a different man before me.

"Dagrun," he whispered, "Please do not wear this belt on this day of all days. It is a mark of your life now past. And it spoils the skill and *drycræft* of all the women's work."

"And you are the most magnificent woman in Wihtland" he added, pulling me close him, and kissing my hair, my face and neck. I pulled away, laughing, "Hold off now! You will disassemble a whole morning's work!"

The women waiting to fuss over me some more, burst into a chorus of giggling, whereupon Eileifer retreated smiling, slowly shaking his head the way he does when bested by a gentler force he cannot compete with.

The midmorning light cascaded into our solar, both openings were gifting mote laden shafts of Sunni rays that hit the rush floor, which still had mote dust flying up from Eileifer's retreat. I was thankful my robe was light, for the day was becoming hot. We had a long slow journey gathering the tribe from all *ceasterwic* and *tunstedes* to march behind the hand-fasting wagon carrying us both. Eileifer was weighed down in his robes.

We both left arm in arm to the cheers and ribald comments of our lodge kin. His oath sworn hearth warriors were the worst. And I sucked my cheeks in to stop laughing so much, I might halt the procession.

We climbed up onto the ox-drawn cart that had been draped in colours and streaming ribbons of cloth. The last of the flowers still honouring us with their blooms in *Hālig-mōnaþ* lay strewn about us. A hoop of twining cloth held by a strong wreath of grasses and flowers bobbed over our heads as we headed down *Eileifer dūn* to meet the straighter track that intersected the *tunstedes* and *ceasterwic* of our kinsfolk. As we made our way, people joined the procession, with rattles and drum. The singing of hand-fasting songs grew ever louder, as the numbers grew.

Our people had settled over a wide area of southern Wihtland, even to the far south at *Selins* and *Sernclinz*. I saw the *Hūfeinga* kinsmen, our royal *Nuithone* tribe which was Eileifer's own, appear in the throng, chanting loud and strong. They had come on horse and ox-carts. Our *Anglii* kin from *Meolodūn* and *Ceofodūn* were the near neighbours and were travelling close behind us. I could hear their words above the heightening din, and murmured in tune with them, smiling over to Eileifer who was grinning over to me and singing louder. I joined in with him. It was perfect.

The honeysuckle and some late jasmine lined the hedgerows. The oxen and the swaying hoop above us brushed the flowers which sent the headiest perfume over us. Eileifer looked so very happy as he, on the right of me placed his arm over my shoulder and twisted my suevian knot in his hands. At that moment, with the perfume swirling about us, our spirits joined. Nerthus had blessed us both. The rhythmical swaying of the hoop and the two oxen's rump sent me into a carefree peaceful place.

Sunni had graced this day. Thunōr had brought but the gentlest of winds. Even some lazy bees hopped around the late flowers. By the time we had neared the seaward track, our Wihtwara kinsmen had swollen in number until I was sure everyone of the *Suevii* on this Ilse had turned out for our hand-fasting. It was a great confirmation to the popularity of the *Cyng*. The *Eudose and Nuithone* now numbered more than all other kinsmen of the *Suevii*. They are a priestly caste for the most part. Though some are warriors as oath sworn to the high priests. They first arrived in *Cantiaca,* with the first migration, most of whom made their allegiance to the Romans, and those remaining became oath-sworn companions to the priests. News of our sacred Isle reached them and our peaceful ways in honouring the Earth Mother, and they migrated here.

As I watched them walk in solemnity, their heads bowed down, I noticed their hair was loose and flowing. They had chosen not to honour the suevian knot and a cold chill ran down my spine. I felt the *wyrd rapas* touch me, its flow edging my spirit into the future where the clash of our beautiful spirit world of Nerthus would clash with the new man dominated religion.

Eileifer looked over to me, realising I had stopped singing and the smile I had joyfully worn, now lost.

"What ails you *wíf?*" he asked, looking around me to find the source, his deep grey eyes puncturing the happy scene around us. I said nothing but pointed to the high priests.

Then after some thought I said, "There you see the future for our children's children. Their might against the might of the new religion, *mín Āðum.*"

"*Giese,* my love, but do not dwell on this. Not this day of all our days to come!" he put his strong arm about me and held me close. I willed the feeling to be gone. As we rounded the bend in the trackway, the open sea burst into sight, celebrating the twilight with deep crimson and orange colours. A shimmering dark blue and glittering surf was punctuated by white waves toppling languidly onto the golden sand. I released the sore vision and sent it forward to its home in the future.

We were nearing *Sudmōr,* my home, the place of my Ancestors. Soon we would be guided into the stone circle. Our Wihtwara kinsmen crammed shoulder to shoulder within the circle, holding high the tapers and torches to deepen the twilight shadows as we waited for *Mōnā* to grace our hand-fasting.

At the time of the Sunni and Mōnā union in the sky, we will, in our ancestor sanctuary be tying our knot of love and honour and fidelity.

Aslaug walked before me as high priestess accompanied by the Nuithone high priest Ælhstãn, who stood a full head above her and equalled Eileifer in height. As we neared the stone circle the songs and chants dwindled, as our kinsmen turned to issue a hush that was sent backwards to the trailing Wihtwara. We came to a standstill, the silence broken by the low swish of a large bird's wings. I knew, with a pounding heart, even before I looked up, that Heron had graced our ceremony. *Ealdmōdor* had come.

A few gasps issued from the crowd now gathering tighter as those behind joined us. Heron flew gracefully over our heads. She swooped down to gently rest on the head of the *Cenningstān*, the centre stone, which stood erect and much taller above the circle of ancestor stones.

With one of her long legs relaxed and gently bent, she turned to look us straight in the eyes, into our hearts and into our souls. Eileifer and I stood motionless. The connection came in a searing moment of aged wisdom and intelligence. There is no other bird like her. She is our guardian, our mentor and caretaker of the ancient knowledge. She is Nerthus, the earth mother in another form.

If she had not seen pure love in our souls, she would have immediately taken flight. But there she stood for many moments longer, as I bent down with Aslaug to offer gifts and prayer at her stone. Eileifer and Ælhstān offered their gifts to his ancestor.

Sunni was descending, sending intense waves of colour onto the darkening sea. A glow of deep orange crept into the circle and the shadows lengthened. The tall thin form of Heron became a silhouette. Her shadow crept down the Cenningstān until she became totally united with the rough flint and quartz crystal. She became a stone statue. My love for her was overflowing as the priest and priestess began the chant to our Gods and Goddesses.

Ælhstān, as the *Weofodthegn,* and Aslaug moved forward to stand together before the *Cenningstān* for the invocation to the Gods. And to Freyja, our goddess of marriage and fertility. As they stood quietly chanting, and then gathering strength in voice and cadence, my mind was immediately taken back to my Watching time. On hearing her name, I saw again that first meeting with Wōden in the mead hall and how their love sparked, ignited between them from the first instance of meeting.

The priest and priestess began the invocation:

"Gyden, Freyja wè ācsian þu æt cuman ond bletsian þes cynelíc æt halig ǽwnung betwèonum Eileifer Cyng ond Wōden ācenned ond Dagrun Wahl fram þæt Warinni.
Hit willan gestrangian ūre geðèode Wihtwara und betýnan æt gǽd betweonum æt Eudose und Warinni.
Wōden ūre Eall-Fæder, wè ācsian þu æt cuman ond bletsian þes ǽwnung wiþ þín wif, Freyja æt brengan ānfealdnes und cræft æt gaderscype."

"Goddess Freyja, we ask you to come and bless this royal and sacred marriage between Eileifer, Cyng and Wōden-born, and Dagrun Wahl of the Warinni. It will strengthen our tribe Wihtwara and close the ties between the Nuithone and Warinni.

Wōden, our All-Father, we ask you to come and bless this marriage with your wife, Freyja to bring unity and strength to the union."

As Ælhstān and Aslaug intoned the words, I experienced a powerful change in the energy. It became thicker, it almost crackled. And a surge of feelings swamped me as they travelled to my heart and soul. They exploded. And in that instant, I became spirit again. On either side of the Cenningstān, still with the Heron motionless on its summit, stood Wōden and Freyja glowing in an iridescent light. They were smiling at us. I hoped Eileifer could see them also. I dared not look round, for in breaking with that power, I would lose them. I heard exclamations, isolated and low from some lucky kinsmen in the gathering.

Then, as suddenly as they had come, Wōden and Freyja faded from us. In the brief time it took, I saw, and will remember all my days, our All Father nod towards me in thanks. I knew then that all the work had been accomplished and completed. I was being formally released. And it was in this moment that Heron, my *Ealdmōdor*, gracefully rose and banked away from the circle, flying into the twilight sky. She was briefly silhouetted against Sunni, as *Mōnã* appeared, the crescent moon from behind a wispy cloud.

Our ceremony began in earnest with *Weofodthegn* asking for the exchange of *handgeld* and *brýdgifu* with Ælhstãn reciting to Eileifer,

"`Dōn þu ãgan æt handgeld þu ãð æt ãgan?
Do you have the *handgeld* you are in oath to gift?"

Eileifer turned to his oath-sworn, who had been carrying the ornately decorated box, clasped in copper with a filigree design around the top and bottom edges. The Wihtwara symbol has been embossed into the leather and tinted with blues and blood red. It was exquisite. He turned to smile shyly at me as he lifted the lid to present to my *Fæder*, who had silently woven his way through the tightly packed crowd. *Mōdor* was somehow at his side also, smiling with a radiance I had not seen since Eyvindr had been snatched from us.

"*Giese*", he replied, "IC Giefan þu þes handgeld swã Ic ãð æt dōn" I give you this handgeld as I am in oath to do."

My *Fæder* held out both hands to take the box. He lifted the lid and a surprised hiss escaped his lips. He smiled his broadest and winked at me before closing the lid. I was on my tiptoes in curiosity to know what incredible gift Eileifer had gifted me in safekeeping within my family for ever.

I looked at him as he held the most suppressed, enigmatic smile I had ever seen on him. And he winked too and held me ever closer.

Now it was the turn of my *Fæder* to come forward.

The *Weofodthegn* boomed over to my *Fæder* in a way not possible with the *Cyng*, for he was relishing his role and plumping himself up.

"Dōn þu ãgan æt brýdgifu þu ãð æt ãgan?" Do you have the bride gift as you are in oath to have?"

"**Giese!**", my dear fæder roared in response, making Mōdor take a step back and cover her ears.

"Ic Giefan þu þes brýdgifu. Hit is þins æt ãgan und gehendan eall þin dægen" I give you this bride gift. It is yours to have and hold all your days"

He came forward in great solemnity to hand me a large leather pouch. When I went to take it, my hand dropped at the weight of it. I gasped in surprise, for it could only be holding coin. And many coins at that. I looked up at him, for my *Fæder*, like Eileifer still towered above me, and searched his eyes to find his heart. And it was bursting with pride. My family, indeed the Warinni, had never in all my years here, held coin. We were happy to exchange whenever the need arose. It was a very effective way of sharing our kind of wealth that could not be measured in metal discs.

Now our world was turning. The Romans had made their mark on us. We had to deliver our wealth to them in coin. So, it was, that our foundries stopped making swords and began creating coins. And breacleats, buckles and ornaments the Romans craved. We were becoming craftsmen and we were getting very clever at it.

My *Fæder* has seen the way our world was turning and gave me, as my bride gift, the most precious bundle he could. And I guessed it had cost him dear.

No sooner had I recovered from this, the exchange of swords came upon us. My big burly brother Eystein came forward, quite brusquely, with a unique new sword resting in its scabbard that had been elaborately designed with copper inlay and garnets. It was a *Cyng's* sword. He held it proudly to him and went to stand next to Eileifer, who had just removed his own sword and was now holding this new sword. He passed it to me as a gift, both hands gently resting under the blade.

"*Ic Giefan þu þes sweord æt āhreddan for ūre eafora æt āgan und æt brucan.*" I give you this sword to save for our sons, to have and to use."

I took it from him, resting it in both my arms, as I would a baby. He smiled at me, and I realised had I been a warrior *Cwèn*, I would have held it aloft and screamed a warrior cry. But I was not one of those and never would be. He was marrying a healer, a *spakōna* and soon to be mother. Although I had not even thought much about it, intuition told me I had his seed growing in me.

Now it was my turn to gift him. Eystein stepped forward holding out this magnificent newly beaten and crafted sword. In the growing twilight, shadows had lengthened and the torches flared, held aloft to give us light. This sword now taken from its scabbard came alive with cascading colours across the blade as Eystein held it forward. All our kinsmen were silenced by the beauty of it. It was huge. It's long blade wide and engraved. The way my brother looked, holding in such deep emotion, I knew somehow it had been created within our family. Yet none of us were ever a *smiððe*. I turned to face my *Cyng*, looking deep into his shaded eyes, now dark from the intense waving shadows dancing around us from the torches' flames. I felt the love pouring from him. You could have sliced the air between us with his new sword. I made my pledge:

"*Æt gehabban ūs gebeorglíc þu sculan acennan an íran. Wiþ þes sweord gehabban gebeorglíc ūre hãm.*" To keep us safe you bear a blade. With this sword keep safe our home"

As Eystein handed the sword to him, he unexpectedly burst out with all he was holding within.

"My *Cyng*, this sword has been created and crafted by your brother now gone, but never, ever forgotten. Eyvindr has brought this beautiful sword to life, for you Eileifer!"

We both gasped, I felt my knees give way. Eileifer leant forward to support me, smiling deeply and kissing me on the cheek. "Hold fast, my love" he whispered. "All is good, very good this night."

He produced the rings which we gave to each other.

The *Weofodthegn* quietly stepped forward, holding the two-coloured bands that would tie us to each other. As he bound them round our wrists we uttered the vows in turn, privately and quietly.

Ælhstãn bent his head low, muttering his own prayers. Then after a heartbeat of silence, when all were hushed and the only sound came from the hissing tapers, he threw his head up and shouted:

"*Hit is ǽrgedon! Bí æt gifu fram Freyja und Wodan und ūre Ieldran, Eileifer, ðèodcyning und Dagrun Wahl, dohtor fram Folkvarthr are ǽw-fæst!*" It is done! By the grace of Freyja and Wōden and the Ancestors, Eileifer King over a nation and Dagrun Wahl, daughter of Folkvarthr are now married!"

Our kinsmen, the Wihtwara, erupted into a cacophony of cheers that near deafened us both. The flames from the torches and tapers swinging and spitting in the joyous expression of our people. Hand clapping, drumming and singing soon followed as we made our way from the circle. There would be a night-long celebration followed by a lazy day and another feasting to follow on. It gave everyone the chance to forget the daily struggle, the worry about the impending harvest, too much rain or too little rain, and too much wind and cold. All this was forgotten on these, our special celebration days.

… … … … … … … … …

CHAPTER FORTY- THREE
Sceatt Æht
Coin Wealth

I lay relaxed and coiled around the warm body of my husband. It was the full morning and I could faintly hear the movements in the hall below, dogs shuffling around for morsels left after a full night of revelry, songs, stories and then after the mead had taken control, bawdy talk and coupling in the shadows of oaken pillars and eaves that lent a little privacy.

This was the third morning of celebrations, and the last. I still felt the echo of our delightful coupling and knew it would not take much to be set afire again. I delicately drew my fingers down to his already erect tool and looked up to see one eye open and a large smile in that dimpled face that made me hopeless in his arms. His smell was intoxicating, better than any perfume I could name. My *Cyng* swung over and enveloped me in an embrace which brought me to a pitch as he deftly stroked and licked me until I arched for his union and we became one in a rhythm slow and relaxed, both languid with so much love. When our climax came, it was together and long.

As we lay relaxed, our body sweat mingling with each other, there came a timid knock on our door, built heavily and designed to make me feel safe and to keep others out.

"Nah!" came his low grumble, "who dares knocks on the *Cyng's* door when he is busily getting his *Wif* with a royal son and heir!"

"Ohh!" I retorted, "So I am just the brood mare now am I!" as I went to thump his chest, he deftly caught my arm and wrestled me into another embrace that kept the messenger standing on the other side of the door for several minutes. It did not occur to either of us that it may be urgent.

Eileifer heaved himself out of my embrace and quickly wrapped a fur about him as he padded over to the door. Sunni was sending a strong shaft of light across our solar, dust motes flying everywhere as he moved across the room. The mid-morning heat was growing. All the languid laziness of a late *sumor's* day drifted past my consciousness. I snuggled back into our furs and linen cloth, soft in the bird-down mattress made especially for the marriage bed. I suddenly felt ravenous and was about to call for food, when I saw the tight and worried expression grow on my *Cyng's* face and knew instantly that royal matters had overtaken and indeed squashed our laying-in.

The messenger was speaking to him, in a low intense manner, gesticulating at phrases he needed to emphasize. He looked well-travelled, muddy, dishevelled and anxious. I caught a whiff of stagnant water and bog land about him. I quickly realised he must have travelled through the near impenetrable land of the north. In all my years, I had never travelled there. I had grown up to feel it was forbidden. Stories of wild boar lent horror to the prospect.

It was dense forest, interspersed with inland waterways and bogs, navigable only by narrow boat of the kind my ancestors used in the Cimbric peninsular for navigating through the fjords and inland lakes. Since the Wihtwara had become arable farmers and left the hunter status behind them, the only person I knew knowledgeable enough to take on the north, was our dear friend Ingvar of the water people, the *Ingavonii*, a notorious womaniser and master boat-builder. Eileifer forgave him much.

Eileifer turned around to stare at me with a questioning look on his face, head tilted to one side, as if he was deciding upon something. He then dropped the fur wrap which crumpled to the floor at his feet and I watched the sinews and muscles move on his naked body, marvelling at the beauty of him. He was of Wōden's blood. He was a giant of Nuithone blood. And he was my beloved. I just stared in silence as he leaned over a pile of washed and clean clothes picking out under garments and woollen leggings and jerkins. I suddenly realised that these were not the clothes of a royal, but those of a *thrall*, or *villan*.

"Eileifer, please tell me what has happened" I insisted, leaving our marriage celebrations behind me.

He looked at me, intently for a few seconds.

"If I tell you, "he said softly, "you will want to come with me. And I know you enough Dagrun, my love, to say it will be passionately insisted upon!"

"And?" I asked.

"I will have to deny you" he answered shortly, pulling his scabbard and sword about him.

"Eileifer, I am not a simple woman," I insisted.
"I would not have married you if you were!" he retorted back before I could continue.

"Then furnish me with the truth if you please and let me decide how I may proceed!"

"If I do, I fear it will proceed to our first marital argument," he lashed his seax in place, for all to see he was in a warring status. It was an overtly dangerous thing to do as the Romans had forbidden the wearing of swords since the rebellion by Britons up in the Eastern part of Britannia.

"Tell me, *gecwèman*", I implored. "And if the Romans see you like that, they will take you, like my Eyvindr! I will then be lost forever!"

My *Cyng* stopped and sat down, beckoning me forward. He put his fingers through my long and loosened hair, knowing it was, to him, a very special part of me.

"Dagrun, you have barely recovered from your most dangerous undertaking for the good of all our kinsmen. What I must do now is dangerous and physically intense. I do not wish you to be exposed to yet more danger and to try your body more. You may be carrying our child."

I did not intend to tell him just yet that I was almost definitely carrying our child, conceived I believed, on our very first lovemaking after my return from *Wyrd*.

"Eileifer, you must tell me", I insisted, "Our marriage must never be based on half-truths or things hidden. I may lose trust in you. Do you understand that?"

There was a silence, heavy and impregnable. I sat at his feet, my arms curled around his waist. As I looked up at him I wondered what on this earth had made him so defensive.

"Eyvindr" he said simply. I shot back.

"What do mean *Eyvindr*!" I half shouted my brother's name. I was now standing looking down at the bent head of my husband.

"What has happened?" I asked slowly, trying to keep control of my hurtling emotions.

My beautiful, gentle little brother was in trouble.

"He has escaped from *Cantium*. I do not know the exact details yet, only that Ingvar assisted in the escape. And that he managed to elude detection, and reached to our northern coast on Wihtland."

"*Oh, Bí eall þæt Drytens und Grydens āhreddan Hine. Nerthus āwerinan Hine!*"

"By all the gods and goddesses save him! Nerthus protect him!"

I fought to gain back my breath.

"I must come with you, Eileifer. I will come. He is my brother" I panted the reply to him. We both knew I would not, could not, be dissuaded.

Eileifer's shoulders sagged in recognition of my determination. I did not want him to think he had been defeated. I hugged him hard and with all the feeling of a grateful *sweostor* about to be reunited with a *brōðor* who had never left her heart.

I dressed quickly, putting on several layers, even though the day was warm, I knew we would be heading for a darker, colder territory. I followed Eileifer down the oaken steps to the hall where the odorous smell of festive detritus hit me and my stomach heaved. I choked my mess back, pride forbidding me to add to the stench already there. And I certainly did not want attention drawn to my "delicate" state.

The mead had flowed well last twilight, and the revellers, both men and women were paying the price. They were slowly becoming haggardly upright, shuffling around mumbling and chuckling to each other as the night's Tellings got re-told, probably ever wilder than before.

Our bee hives were very productive now with copious quantities of mead produced, aided by the warm season that was so much longer than usual. It promised a large harvest soon. Of that we were all thankful.

I saw the serving maidens begin to clear up the mess. All of them freed on my very first command as *Cwèn*, they appeared more lively and ready to work. They now knew their work would be paid for in kind or in coin. And that was a matter of some discussion within our tribe. That matter of coin. Little did I know then how much importance it would have on my brother's life? I was soon to find out.

At the far end of the hall I saw a welcome sight indeed. Ingvar strode forward to greet us. He had just arrived after the messenger had relayed the news. He looked almost the same as when we had parted at the field harvest rite. Except he now had an elaborately braided long beard, braided hair twisted back to reached half way down his back, and symbols inscribed on his forehead and each side of his neck. He looked like a Norseman. I had to turn my head when we gave our bear hug.

"Ahh, dear Dagrun", he growled with a wide smile, "I know… I look like a wild Norseman and I smell like a wild hog's backside!"

"*Giese*", I replied tugging at his new beard, "But why the new countenance old friend?"

He placed his hand over his heart and pulled his woollen over-shirt outward.

"Ahh" I smiled nodding, "the old story of Ingvar and a woman."

"Oh, not this one, Dagrun", his smile became broader, "This one is very special. She matches me in all ways. She comes from the North and I travelled there for a while. Her people are now my people and I have adopted their ways."

"And the love of the sea, Ingvar of the *Ingavonii,* what of that?"

"Oh, I shall never leave the open waves hitting the sides of my boat", he answered, "and her name is *þrudr*, should you ever ask"

"I hope we may meet her in happier times than now"

I looked over to Eileifer, "We are completely happy, except for this latest news of my brother. Come, sit and eat with us, then tell us all you know."

We all moved over to the trestle, where a serving of cold foods was being laid. Ale in an earthenware jug with wooden cups appeared and we all began to help ourselves to mutton, hard cheese, and yesterday's bread. Hild, my favoured servant maiden came with a small jug of honey, knowing my craving. I took her to one side and quietly asked her to hurry and pack food provisions, enough for us and my brother, ointments for skin and oiled clothes with the tinderbox filled with hot tinder.

With his face still full of food, I asked Ingvar the question that had brought sharp bile to my throat.

"Why did Eyvindr run from *Cantium* when he had been given leave to come here to *Berandinzium* Villa?"

"Dagrun!" Eileifer shot a warning look over to me, "Give the man time to finish his food!"

"*Ic sarig,*" I replied head down.

Ingvar swallowed hard and swift. He leant forward to look me deep in the eye.

"From what Eyvindr has shared with me, hurriedly I might add, the poor man. Gentle to the tips of his fingers. He was pushed beyond his control. He is a very clever and creative young man, and they recognised his talents early in the construction of this lavish, opulent villa in the *Cantium* countryside. The chief architect, after seeing his work on tiling, placed him with the mosaic craftsmen, as one had fallen fatally ill. Being a royal hostage and not a slave, he was treated with some deference and he had free time. So Eyvindr was drawn to the foundry. He saw *drycræft* in the working of liquid metal to create refined artistic work."

"He saw himself as a waylander!" I joined in seeing the pleasure it would have brought him.

"Indeed!" said Ingvar, "The sword gifted to you was created there. Right under the noses of the Romans who had banned the making of swords. I sent that sword to you under cover while it was still warm! He took a huge risk in the creating of it, but he made it his personal statement of love to you both."

I held my hand to my heart and gritted my teeth to stop the sob that nearly escaped from me. My poor dear brother who would not harm any creature, let alone a human.

"I could tell you stories of the uprising that are truly brutal, but I must move on in the Telling.

This large villa was built for the relaxation and recuperation of the military elite. Generals come there and governors of Britannia. Top level meetings take place there. I have visited this villa to see Eyvindr, before the clash happened. It is eye-popping my friends. It is like being in Rome itself. I think the word is luxurious."

"Whatever does that mean?" I asked, feeling the false nature of it already and wondering how Eyvindr coped with extreme wealth.

"How is Eyvindr?" I asked simply, leaning into the trestle to watch Ingvar.

He starred into his ale for several heartbeats.

"Sweet *sweostor*", he said, looking me deep in the eye, "You will find him much changed. The Romans got to work on him as soon as he set foot in their territory. He is theirs now. They like to believe they own him body and soul. And it is his soul that has had to dig deep for courage in the face of it. That gentle, sweet, story-telling nature is gone. No more."

I gasped and reached out for Eileifer, who grabbed my hand and it tightly.

"They really do not understand our ways", he continued "and make little or no attempt to understand. We are the barbarians in their eyes, so we are the ones that must change! Eyvindr, from what I can gather, bent his Will to match theirs. It worked, for they rewarded him with clever work and responsibility. So much so, that when he asked for a transfer to *Berardinzium* villa, which is still a bare shell and not progressing at all, they agreed. All was set. "

"What, by all the gods, happened?" interjected Eileifer, sounding amazed and frustrated that something so promising had gone fatally wrong.

"A Roman general from the East named Aquila Augustus arrived wounded from the uprising. Not fatally, but enough to warrant an extended stay in this "Roman resort."

As soon as this man was fit to walk, the trouble brewed up into a crisis. He was brutal by nature, his mind twisted by too much blood and gore in the killing fields. It was not his body that was fatally injured, it was his mind. He must have been *Ylfa gescot,* elf-shot, badly I would say, by some *wuduelfen,* while camping overlong in the woodland in the East. But he was very clever. All evil men are, in great need to cover their nasty doings. Of which there became plenty. It seemed he preferred both the pretty girls and pretty boys."

I gasped again, knowing what was to follow. And instantly the face of Loki came into my mind. And Eyvindr was very *ælscienu,* just the kind of face to attract a Loki in his midst.

"Of course, he had to protect and defend himself," Ingvar continued, "I believe had his Will been smashed completely by the rigours of slavery, he may have succumbed. Many do, in the punishing life of a Roman camp. But your *brōðor* fought back, Dagrun. With the gods' good fortune, he did not take the life of Aquila Augusta, but left him less of a man and more wounded than when he first arrived. Had he killed him, and been caught it would have meant crucifixion for sure."

I choked and gagged at this thought, a tragedy which may still happen if we did not secure his release somehow.

"He is in a very hard place, a vulnerable situation, so how can we secure his life which may still be forfeit?" I cried in desperation, looking rapidly from one anxious face to another. I had never seen Eileifer so distraught.

A long silence followed, the only sound was the rasping of the hunting dog's tongue on a stray bone left overnight.

Suddenly Eileifer thrust out his fist and banged the table so hard it shook the oaken trestle and sent tremors over the surface of our ale. The dog jumped up and flashed across the rush floor, threshing it as he went, sending stalk and husk up into mid-air, to be caught by Sunni's ray's, fogging the hall before it all fluttered back to earth.

"We must seek out the weakness in the Roman heart," he said firmly, "Find out what makes that heart beat the faster,"

"They have no heart," I hissed through clenched teeth.

"Well, my *Cwèn*, they have a heart that speaks to their Gods. What is it that they offer to their God?"

"Gold", I replied, "Of course! We must pay them in coin."

Ingvar nodded enthusiastically, "*Giese*! welcome to the second hundred, my dear friends, for it is through coin-wealth exchange and bartering that laws change, kinsmen grow and peace is brought…at a price."

"And you can help us?" Eileifer looked over at his once oath-sworn companion.

A broad grin covered the big man's face until everyone could see his remaining teeth, blackened and in need of pulling.

"I can," he replied, "Dear friend, since we parted I have been a trader in metal of all kinds from Gaul to my Friesian homeland and beyond. People admire my boats, and I have built one or two, always insisting on payment in coin. Then I began collecting all discarded ornaments, bracteates and torque. I have in my boat at this very moment many sacksful of metal, copper silver and some gold. There is a handsome trade here, Eileifer. And I will offer it all up to you."

"Can we secure a hiding place for Eyvindr?" I jumped in, whisking up a solution in my mind and testing the feel of it.

"*Giese!*" Ingvar replied looking suitably pleased with himself, and realising I had jumped into his mind and seen the solution for myself.

"I left Eyvindr safe in woodland near the *Stithes fleots heafod* not far from *raeccbroc*. That is where we are heading. And from there we will hug the coast to meet with the Durotrige on *frescewætr ealond*. I have met with them on several occasions. It is where I get discarded metals. They are productive in metal coins and jewellery. They are prolific traders and welcome us. They go to the Romans to trade and in return the Romans leave them alone. It is an amicable arrangement. It is not so on the mainland where their kinsmen are allied to the Britons fighting the Romans"

"They came to *Ealdmōdor's deað gerihte.*" I said softly, "I know they will help us."

"Eyvindr can remain with them, have the use of their forge to build coin wealth. He can create his own freedom. His "libertus"!"

"Ahh, we have it", Eileifer declared, "Now we must hurry and prepare."

At that very moment Hild appeared carrying my bundles and scurried off to the gather the food for us and Eyvindr. Eileifer looked over to me and smiled, nodding in that subtle way of his. I moved over to wrap my arms about him. He whispered, "I know you are more than capable my love. I see you have planned already. Well done!"

"We will take the horses as far as the water", Ingvar stated, "then give leave for your servants to bring them home. We will be gone for two twilights. Let them know to bring horses and wait for us by the noon of the third day.

It was after Sunni had reached her highest point, when the shadows slowly began to lengthen, that we departed, aiming to keep away from any Roman clusters or travel ways. We took our horses over the downs sweep, cutting diagonally across from *Eileifer dūn* to meet the estuary where Ingvar's boat was kept near *Nīwbrycg*. Eileifer had earlier raced over to our *tunstede* at *Sudmōr* to bring his loyal horse talker and guardian of the herd, Eastmund, to care for our horses and bring them back ready for our return. He must have visited Eardwūlf, the boys *Rōmānisc* father, to harness his support and bring expertise and knowledge to our cause.

As we set off Eileifer looked over to me and smiled, nodding, saying quietly, "*Giese*, we have his loyal support. I am feeling strongly now that we will succeed!"

I wished I felt the same. But having witnessed the harsh, unremitting cruelty those Roman generals were capable of. In snatching an innocent man from his home and enslaving him, whatever their excuse to the contrary. I knew this whole bid for Eyvindr's freedom could go badly wrong for us all.

I dug my heels into the gelding, who responded in a flash, as we sped down the *dūn* to *Plæsc bearu* where the horses had a deep drink from the fresh pool there. It would be their last before their return, as we wanted full speed to get to the estuary. We had packed all we needed in leather bags, corded with strong hemp rope to go around our necks. We would be wading through the muddy water. A land of bogs that marked the beginning of the estuary. I did not feel confident and was becoming anxious. I prayed to Nerthus to protect us in her territory. Yet, squashing those feelings, thinking of Eyvindr, who must be feeling a hundred times worse. He was trapped in hiding and uncertain of his future. His very life might well be lying in our hands.

We cantered past *Froggalōnd*, our horses' high-stepping through the marsh land, sending up spray and clods of sodden earth and cress. By the time we had reached the drier incline of *Etdreðecumb*, our feet were soaking. We would become much wetter very soon. Sunni dipped behind the gathering clouds. I looked up and realised we would be denied even Mōnã's rays this night. I gave silent thanks that I had brought the hot tinder box.

We passed into forest along *Rūhbeorg,* swinging below overhanging branches, still in leaf, as our mounts swung along a little used trackway, used only by the forest hunter of deer or boar. I bent down and hugged my gelding's neck through this wooded maze. I trusted him completely. He knew his way. So, at last we emerged to gallop down, in the fading light that scudded along the downs valley, reaching *Wykendeshylle.* We had halted briefly at *Gemōt Hearg* to take breath and rest our horses. Eileifer and I bent down to touch our Mother Earth near the ancestor's mound, to offer up deep prayers to our Ancestors', the Mights, Nerthus and Wōden to bring our brother safely home and free from the fear of death by crucifixion.

What a very tall order, I thought, as I raised myself up on my horse to pull him round and head off towards the end of our gallop and the beginning of our water-journey. The silted end of the *Stithes fleots heafod.*

When we reached the end of the estuary, I realised exactly why Ingvar insisted on wading through to his *sǣnaca* which lay moored and hidden from view. On either side of the narrow waterway clogged with reeds, lay, as far as I could see, impenetrable bog land. Even before we had reached this part of our journey, the odour of stagnant and fetid marshland, unmoving and silted water, assaulted my nose. It nearly made me puke yet again, but I fought it back, keeping my head low so no one could see the internal battle with my stomach. Tiny crane fly hovered everywhere, their paradise was our hell.

"This is a country of *Wæterœlfadl,*" I stated, reaching for my sack, "A danger of *Ylfa gescot* is strong. We must cover all of ourselves and put this salve in our ears and nose and inside our mouth!" Memories of dear Elíse suddenly came to my mind, on that day of all our days. And how dangerously ill she became from elf-shot.

Murmurs of gratitude came from Eileifer. Ingvar, who denied the danger, being a son on Ing, politely, if hesitantly applied the salve, which stank stronger than the bog.

I saw Edmund grin in great relief that he was spared, as he tied our horses on a rope to his own mount and waved us farewell, shouting back that he would cosset them and return them on time.

"Bind your feet well, Dagrun", Ingvar knelt and wrapped more waxed leather around both my legs up to my knees, tying it very tightly with leather thongs.

"Now we can begin" he stated quite solemnly.

Immediately I sank very nearly up my knees and pulled hard to make just one step. The mud was warm and sucked around my legs.

"Nah!" shouted Ingvar, "follow me. Don't be so hasty!"

Eileifer dragged me towards Ingvar who had found the shallow pathway and I followed closely behind him. Eileifer took the rear more to keep an eye on me. We waded slowly forward, the light dimming very rapidly now as clouds blocked the last of Sunni and hid *Mōnã* from view. I had put the warm tinderbox round my neck, and the ointments and tallow in a larger leather sack that hung like a large teardrop.

"*Forstoppian!*" I shouted, "If we light the tapers, it will help keep the flies away from us."

"We cannot possibly light anything in this water-bog Dagrun, my *Cwèn*," Eileifer hissed in my ear.

"I asked Hild to fill my hot tinder box." I said evenly, "Here, we have enough to light us throughout this night!"

"Well Nerthus be praised, "he exclaimed in delight, "You are more than wonderful Dagrun!"

He helped me pull the sack over my head and as he held the torches out. I reached in with small metal prongs and placed the glowing tinder in the woven reed and flax waxed head. Each one spluttered, smoking, then bursting into a good flame. They would last until we reached Eyvindr. Unless they needed to be extinguished quickly. Upon that thought, I did not tarry long and sped it from my mind. We continued in better spirits now, looking more attentively at our immediate surroundings. The torches caste long shadows that danced upon the brackish water. I noticed eddies made from sunken creatures and from this I now felt their skin brush against my legs. Were they small water serpents, or toads or frogs? I did not need to investigate. But felt that vision acquired made the mind work faster. I saw many spirits lurk in the shadowed reeds. Long shadows danced to the rhythm of the swaying reeds as we disturbed their water home.

It was only when we emerged from our water journey that I noticed the leather had come away. I started in shock as leeches as black as night were feeding on my blood.

"Eileifer, "I cried sharply, "I need help. Leeches have stuck to my shins. Look!"

He knelt in the darkness and peered at my legs. There were several of them dotted around my left leg. "My," he replied," they are having a feast. Let us put a stop to it right away."

He reached for the tinder inside the nearest torch, still intact and burning. I looked away as each sizzle on the leech made it drop away until my leg was free of them and the only mark left was a small puncture mark. I put some protective salve on each one and bound the leather back in place.

We were now on a sound pathway by the edge of the water, which made a rippling sound, not just of deeper water but of a tidal reach. We had entered the estuary. We kept low and decided to extinguish all but one of the torches. We hung together as we made our way forward in the deep night that had now descended on us. My thoughts went to Eyvindr. What must he be suffering right now? I longed to put my arms about him and hug him tightly. We travelled silently for some time.

"Down!" hissed Ingvar, "Hit the earth NOW, Romans!" We crashed to the sodden earth. It was marshy and soft with river water trapped within the clumps of cress and reed. The torch was crushed, and I, falling on my hot tinderbox, issued a silent scream as it dug into my tunic and was heating up my skin. We saw the rippling of waves made by oars, several of them, in perfect unison. The Roman legionnaires were disciplined to an edge of their young lives. The brow of a long narrow *sænaca* glided into our view. If any of those soldiers cared to look to their left, they would see us prone on the muddy earth. I stopped breathing.

They were too busy talking. It seemed to be a narrowboat taking troops to their next station or that they were returning. It was not a patrol boat. Their helms glinted and their metal vests clanked as they moved. It was now at this moment I remembered the *Norn* sweostors telling me I needed to learn their ways, their language. I understood completely now and pledged to learn. I could have discovered much from their conversation right now. Even so, I was too scared to remember much, and it was only when we all saw their backs receding into the gloom, that I relaxed enough for my mind to start working again.

"Hurry", hissed Ingvar again, with a worried look, "We must reach my boat quickly. It is too exposed. I never, ever, expected to see Romans on this godforsaken stretch of water. It worries me much. Why are they here?"

Without lighting any torches, we hurried after him, trusting him in the darkness to know his way. We sped. We made for the looming silhouette of the *sænaca* before the Roman narrow boat appeared. We dragged it back further into the bushes and low trees until Ingvar whispered for us to stop and we relaxed. Hiding behind the hull, we saw again the Roman boat. This time I counted and reached twenty-five young Romans soldiers. My guess was these were raw recruits joining a much bigger force at the head of the estuary. Perhaps boarding a boat to take them to Britannia. But why in the dead of night? And where had they camped? This was hostile land even our kin refused to dwell.

Ingvar leaned back on his haunches, studying the sodden cress for a few tense moments.

"A precious few moments to take a breath my kin, but that is all we have. We must get Eyvindr out of this region and to the Durotrige with all speed!"

"Why are those Romans here in this swamp-invested backwater?" I pleaded for a sensible answer.

"I do not have the answer to that", he replied solemnly, "Unless they have been conscripted to find your brother. In which case, our bid for his freedom is impossible and his crucifixion a certainty! Remember, if you will, that my departure and his escape coincided, and that their discovery is as old as our travel here. Time enough for them to get a messenger here."

"But they have no idea he is here!" Eileifer interjected, swamping me with his warmth and love by wrapping his strong arms about me.

"Indeed", Ingvar replied, nodding, "That is our best hope. How could they possibly know? I have taken not one soul into my confidence. So onward my friends."

We hurriedly pushed the *sænaca* over the wet and crushed greenery, the slide to the water made easy. As its name suggested, it had a keel and sail stored aboard for sea going ventures. The keel was narrow and Ingvar dropped it down and made it fast before we hit the water. The boat thrummed through the estuary, the oars slipping rhythmically down and up. It was a fast boat and I thought I saw the Roman boat ahead of us and whispered for the men to slow to a crawl. Indeed, I was right and we stopped altogether, resting awhile.

"I must make a note to bring your off-spring onto my boat journeys, Dagrun" Ingvar muttered softly, "If their eyes are as good as their mother's they will make excellent look-outs!"

He cursed softly at the slowing of our pace but there was little we could do. We hoped the Romans were not anywhere near *Ræccbroc,* where Eyvindr was hiding in woodland. According to Ingvar, the Romans had not frequented this creek before. Their huge deep-hulled long boats would get stuck in the tidal waters. The soft slap of the oars against these gentle waters nearly lulled me into a tired sleep. My head kept hitting my chest as I thrust my mind to stay awake.

Ingvar's boat was weighted down with sacks of discarded metal and ornaments. So, our efforts to row were made even slower. So, when eventually the boat began to shudder and sway with each swing of the oars, we knew we had reached the real tidal waters. The bank quickly disappeared and the estuary widened.

Ingvar commanded to softly steer towards the bank opposite. As we veered right, Eileifer hissed, "Lights ahead, a large Roman boat!" Sure enough, in the distance, moored on the left bank at the very mouth of *Stithes fleots heafod* lay two Roman boats, sailed hoisted and ready to go. Torches flared and it was clear that centurions were embarking. The boat that had overtaken us must have moored alongside.

We all let out a huge sigh of relief. My dear Eyvindr was safe. But for the Britons across the water, it was far from true. These Romans from our Wihtland were amassing an attack on what must be against the Durotrige.

"We must wait no longer," said Ingvar, "Our neighbours must be told of this so they may warn their kin on the other coast!" Now that our immediate threat was gone, we all bent our backs into rowing on this moonless night. Before long we felt the grind of gravel on the hull and we came to a stop.

"Eileifer, my lord," Ingvar whispered, "please will you assist me in pulling up the keel. We can then drag the boat into those tall bushes yonder"

We heaved the *sænaca* up the narrow beach and into good dense cover. It would not be remaining there for very long, as we needed to be turning westward before dawn, with Eyvindr aboard.

Ingvar let out a series of high pitched whistles. Silence. I stood there, feet sinking in the mud, hardly daring to breath and clutching Eileifer's hand. Suddenly, to my right, the bushes began to rustle and I saw a familiar hand push the briar away. The shadowy figure of my brother bent down to emerge freely in front of us, straightening and standing seemingly much taller than I remembered him. I had to halt a cry building in my throat at the sight of him. A stranger to my eyes looked back at me, serious and hesitant. His beautiful raven hair cut so close to his skull, square and straight and tamed. His Roman clothes were muddied and torn. He looked like the fugitive he was.

But all that swept over me and past me as I rushed forward to hug him tightly, tears escaping now in shaking rasps of breath. I could find no words. I hoped my feelings would transfer to him. But while he held me, I could feel a resistance. He was taut like a strung bow, eager to be released. There was so much emotion in him he could not release, not even to me, his *sweostor*.

I pulled back, and looking into my *brðōor's,* eyes, I could see only a faint love returned to me. I saw pain, deep unremitting pain, and I could do nothing but hug him again, this time gently, with compassion pouring from me.

"Eyvindr", I whispered to him, "We will win your freedom. I promise. All this will be put behind you. Wihtland will become your home again."

"All your kin are gathered round you, Eyvindr", Eileifer added, "We are united as Wihtwara now and there is nothing we will not do for you. Your *libertus* is waiting but we must hurry to the Durotrige at *Frescewætr Ealond.*"

We took long bent strides back to our boat, creeping low in case another riverboat full of Romans might glide past us. I looked to the horizon and saw the night was still with us. With the *sǽnaca* safely bobbing on the tidal water, she came into sail to become her name, a boat worthy of the open sea. I don't believe Ingvar would ever create one that could not hurl him and his adventurous nature into sea spray and high waves. And that is exactly what we encountered, as we sped out onto the open water. Poor Eyvindr had his head over the side shortly after we hit the first large wave. Eileifer looked over to me, smiling, as I had a strong stomach for the sea. I loved it in truth. So, it would seem, did my *Cyng*. Another match, I thought to myself, as we sped towards the western edge of Wihtland. The *Sǽnaca* lifted and dived over each wave with beautiful elegance. With the sail angled into the wind, that was becoming fresher by the minute, I caught my first glimpse of the white cliffs rising in splendour and the needle shapes spiking out of the turbulent water at their base.

"We have to be right canny here my friends" Ingvar shouted above the clap of water against the rising hull, "Rip tides live here. *Wæterælf* rule these waters, stirring up hidden death for those not wary enough!"

"The Druid preside here", he said simply.

"We will down the sail very soon. Then it is pure strength that will take us to the beach yonder," he pointed to large cliffs streaked with colours that deepened and shone as the light grew. I had not seen anything so magnificent in my life, and I just watched in silence as Sunni, gently rising, began the paint the most stunning wonder.

"To the oars!" Ingvar shouted, as we scrambled to sit and begin the big push to land.

Eyvindr overcame his sickness as we neared the beach. The cliff grew until it towered over us in coloured majesty and eclipsed the skyline completely. Sunni disappeared behind its' colossal height and I suddenly wondered how we would scale that height.

I looked over to Ingvar for direction and without saying anything he pointed to his left as we beached the *Sænaca* and started walking along the narrow-pebbled beach. As we reached the point of the headland, I saw the opening to a large cave. And even more surprisingly, a figure standing motionless before it, in hemp-woven robes, the hood of which, hid his face completely.

"We have to gain permission from the Druid to stay here on *Frescewætr*. This is their sacred Isle." Ingvar said to us quietly, as he moved forward to stop and wait some two spear lengths from the white figure who stared at us silently, from within his hood.

Then he began to speak loudly, with deep resonance, in the Briton tongue of which I knew not a single word.

"*Cyfarchiad tua chwi Gwedd Rhywun.*
Ni dyfod yn derbyn wyneb ac anrhydeddu.
Ni chwilio eich cymorth ac amddiffyniad tros ein brawd."
 "*Greetings* to you Wise One.
 We come in respect of persons and honour.
 We seek your help and protection for our brother."

The Druid extended his arm, pointing at us, showing knarled and bent fingers.

"Paham cael chwi dyfod yma tua ein cysegredig ynys, yn cyfrinach ac dan o dan tywllwch?" The Druid answered, his voice full of gravel as if he was from the very cave itself.

"He asks why we are here on his sacred Isle, furtively and in the darkness," Ingvar said without turning his head. He could not see my gaping mouth, which became even wider, when he proceeded to answer this priest in the halting but understandable native language.

"Ein brawd Eyvindr has dihangta oddic wrthy Rhufeinwr yn Cantium. Ef has dioddef treisiad ac anghywir cyhuddo."

"Ef chwilio cysegr."

"Ef dwyn gallu arbennig yn smithy ac ef dwyn aur māl. Grda cymorth oddi wrth Durotrige. Ef ewyllys ennill ei "libertus.""

"Our brother Eyvindr has escaped from the Romans in *Cantium*. He has been violated and wrongly accused. He seeks sanctuary. He brings a talent in Smithy and he brings gold coin. With help from the Durotrige, he will earn his "libertus"."

The conversation continued. At one point, this priest gesticulated with his arm, flinging it outwards so I could see the wrinkled and aged skin of an elder of many seasons.

"Eich brawd ewyllysio dwyn yr digofaint gan yr Rhufeinwr mynydd-dir ni! Ni bwa yr prenfroed ceidwad gan ein pobl. Eton i amgyffred ei dioddefaint."

"Your brother will bring the wrath of the Romans down upon us. We are the last guardians of our people. Yet we understand his suffering", his gravelled voice left its echo on the air.

There was a prolonged silence. Sunni was growing in the sky and still we stood, waiting. The outcome unknown.

Ingvar spoke some more to the aged priest, who looked to the sky, before nodding briefly, turning on his heels and disappearing into the black mouth of the cave.

"Well?" Eyvindr asked, with tension in his voice.

"I have given him everything I can give" Ingvar stated, looking uncharacteristically worried, "Half of the intended coin must go to the Durotrige now that they are under attack. They are hesitant because we are bringing a Roman threat to this Isle. But they understand Eyvindr had been dealt a bad outcome from a heinous crime. He is going to call a meeting of the high council. We can do nothing but wait. It is in the hands of the gods my friends!"

We all slumped to the pebbled foreshore, feeling exhausted and deeply anxious. No-one spoke, each one of us going within, to reach for yet more courage, hiding within the pocket of our souls. Then tiredness overcame us and we reached for the furs and some sandy ground. We prayed to our gods, silently, searching to reach a truth the Gods would hear. Then, eventually as the wind died away and the sea tide lapped gently against the tiny pebbled beach, sleep came, gratefully releasing us from the torment for my beloved brother.

We were all awoken, abruptly, by rough feet kicking us into the early dawn day. It was two Durotrige Britons, both in cloaks of a different hue to the high priest. They were stick-thin and neither smiled or gave us any sign of hospitality. Ingvar knew their tongue and asked them what news there may be for our brother Eyvindr to have a haven here on *Frescewætr Ealond.*

Neither spoke to us, or gave us any indication of the meeting's outcome. Their silence worried me, and as I looked over to Eyvindr, I saw his shoulders droop, he became hunched with fear.

"Fear not *Brōðor*", I whispered, "Maybe they are learning to be priests and they are committed to silence."

We followed them into the dank and dark cave, feeling the wet slime on all the walls, trickles of water found their way to a wet and mushy floor. My feet soon became soaked, then numb with cold. It worked its way up my leather wraps until I could feel nothing below my thighs. The young apprentice priests lit torches to guide us, as light from the cave entrance left us, and deep, black, darkness met and joined with the cold to test us.

As we rounded a corner we had to hunch up, the ceiling suddenly descending to meet us. Glittering crystals abounded in this cave. It was sacred and I understood why the Druid's met here. The energy became thick and vibrant. The more we moved inward, the more powerful it became. Suddenly it opened into a grand cave with a high roof that had crystals hanging down in profusion. I gasped and held Eileifer excitedly, forgetting the damp and the cold. A feeling of peace crept from my soul and joined with all my senses, to wonder at this magnificent sight.

"Eileifer, this is the most sacred place I have ever witnessed in my life! It reminds me so much of the Telling from *Ealdmōdor's* journey with Hild through the cave of Nerthus!"

"I am honoured to see this", he whispered, "We are being treated well, despite the rude awakening."

Indeed, I had heard stories that filtered back to us from traders, of what the Druids might do a person they did not respect. It did not make easy listening.

We squinted through the darkness, with wild shadows snaking from the dancing flames, into the gloom, giving brief catches of figures, standing in a half circle, hands held loosely and hoods enveloping their faces completely. They seemed dignified, in repose and not at all menacing. We were gently pushed forward until we stood within hearing distance.

There was silence. We waited, not even daring to shuffle our feet against the biting cold. The crystals emitted an energy that simply overwhelmed me. And it that state I barely heard the High priest call out to us.

"*Pwy ymhlith chwi mae offeiriad?*" intoned the priest figure in the centre of the group, in his own tongue.

Ingvar stepped forward and haltingly, carefully, explained and pointed towards me.

I was pushed forward. He had a deep voice, this high priest. I gathered an ancient energy from him. He was gentle and kind. He had past his younger days however they were spent, and had reached a high maturity of spirit.

"So, you are a guardian of the Stones, Dagrun Wahl of the Warinni" he said in our tongue, faultlessly. I gasped quietly and smiled to him, nodding and giving a bow to his status.

"We have heard of you" he continued, the voice without a face, "and we acknowledge you." He came forward to gently place his hands on my heart and on my forehead. I caught a glimpse of ancient eyes half closed, contemplating.

"So, you must now give up your *Völva* days and nights. You can no longer be a *spakōna* for your people. And why have you undertaken such a dangerous journey now, as you are with child?"

I heard a loud gasp behind me, and a shuffling of feet, knowing it was Eileifer in shock.

I had wanted to tell him after all this, in private, on a night when Mōnā was full, by the fire in our solar! Not now, not this way.

"Ahhh, I see the father knows naught of this!" the High Priest replied, softly chuckling to himself.

I answered the priest in a faltering tongue, "I have come now because the man we ask to keep safe on your *ealond*, is my brother, Eyvindr. I will do anything to keep him safe!"

"We have reached an agreement. We will safeguard your brother, but he must earn his keep. He is a talented smithy, so I hear. You must now secure his life in your land. The Wihtland you love so much. It was decided anyway, before this meeting. We knew all along. We just wanted to meet in person, the *Cyng* of the Wihtwara, and your oath sworn companions. As for you fair maiden, dedicate your life to your children. Teach them all you know. Learn the ways of these Romans, and teach that to your children too. But all this you know, given to you by your own Goddesses, I believe. I am here to remind you!"

I was lost for any words. I smiled and sent my heart to him. The faceless one who radiated so much love I knew I would never repay enough. He saw my thoughts

"Come to me here, child, if ever you need reminding again!" I returned to a beaming Eileifer who was simply ecstatic and wanted to hug and kiss me but refrained, with difficulty. We were led away, yet I turned back to see once again the priest who had seen my heart, and quite deliberately, he pulled his enormous hood away and I caught sight of his face, a beautiful smile lit up his face, and his old eyes sparkled with joy!

We took a very different path to the one we came on. It was much shorter, drier and before we knew it, we glimpsed daylight streaming in through the mouth of this entrance. It led upwards to the cliff top. A winding path through dense elderberry, gorse and ancient hawthorn made our journey difficult, but pleasurable, after the swamp land and the dank cave.

Eileifer kept shaking his head and smiling in that soft way that made me love him so much. He guided me upwards, his hand in the small of my back, ready to catch me if I stumbled. Eyvindr became more talkative, even eloquent. His old story telling gift reaching to the surface at last. I believe he had finally seen a better future awaiting him here on our sacred Isle. But there was still so much to achieve, to make the victory happen. We had bargained with friends, as these illusive Druids proved to be. Now we needed to bargain with our foe, for the intractable Roman was a much harder nut to crack.

At last Sunni graced us. From a seabird's eye, we looked like a weaving serpent, as we snaked up the cliff. The two young druids leading us upward, were still silent. They radiated a powerful energy that surrounded us and we too became silent. It was a procession in prayer. My leather leg bindings were now tacky and I longed to take them off. I became observant of detail, and watched intrigued, as I passed a spider completing her web, dewdrops still hanging in the early *hālig mōnaþ* sun. The harvest was nearly completed and the rituals would soon begin. In my mind, I sped back to *Eileifer dūn* and wandered down to the lake where my *Cyng* first captured me from the big sleep, and won me. Relishing that moment, I looked over to him and saw he too was savouring that meeting. We were so close in spirit, our souls forever touching. There was no parting us. He turned and stared into my eyes, reaching my soul. No words were needed.

Ingvar was smiling to himself also, but his images were of a place far from here, in the cold and immense mountains of Götland where his love now sat and waited for his return.

As for Eyvindr, the expression on his face brought me sharply back to this present time and the trials that lay ahead. Our bodies may have been warmed by Sunni but our spirits contracted at the thought of facing off the Romans and winning a victory so rare, it would be forever told in the mead halls of our children!

Soon the arduous climb gave way to flatter land, meadowsweet reached our senses. Tall grasses swaying in the noon day sun glittered in a mosaic of deep yellow and bronze. I gratefully ran my hand through the delicate soft strands making the awful bog land and swampy water retreat into the mists of the past. We quickened our pace, following the priests, past these lush meadows, into furrowed land, barley stacks already tied and waiting to be threshed and stored for the winter. I could see a *ceasterwic* in the distance, then two. People were on their daily work routines. But their *hūs* were of a different shape to ours. They were all circular and much taller and larger. I was intrigued and as I looked over to Eileifer. I could see he was staring intently at them.

Smoke was escaping from the tip of the steep-thatched roofs, which descended to the ground so great, I wondered how they were built. The opening was only just tall enough to let a small man through. We were giants, and bending down would be difficult and awkward. The Durotrige looked at us as we passed by. Our height marked us as odd.

Not for the first time, I had felt we were a totally different race of people.

We were only the second generation of Wihtwara, and there were very few of us. We kept to ourselves as the Durotrige kept to theirs. But we were not enemies.

The two priests beckoned us to enter the biggest lodge. We bent nearly double to enter, but as we straightened and looked about us, a mutual chorus of surprise and awe escaped our mouths.

"By all the gods" Ingvar exclaimed, waving an appreciative arm as he circled the lodge, taking in every detail, "How in the name of Wōden did this roof rise so high?"

The timbers holding up this great structure had a girth so wide, whole trees were used, spaced evenly in a wheel-type construction. They were held by strong upright beams that were held in place by interlocking joints which circled the whole roof.

"Look at the designs carved into the beams, Eileifer" I exclaimed, "They are so intricate and balanced. The colours so deep!"

Eileifer nodded, looking up, clicking his tongue and nodding. I knew he was taken with this lodge to the extent we might be seeing one or two in our *tunstede*! The central fire was circular and very large, the smoke trailing lazily up to the smoke hole. And there was no eye-stinging smoke to be felt at our level. There were furs and sheep pelts scattered all around the edge, with laid rushes placed on a circular pathway around the fire pit. Flames danced as the breeze blew in, and I stood watching them awhile, as we waited to be directed to the elders of this tribe. A huddle of men broke away at the far end, and in facing us, I marvelled at their appearance. All had their hair braided, like the Northman, but with beads and bones woven in. Woad and a deep brown dye was painted over much of their skin and it seemed the older ones had the more intricate patterns everywhere. Their wrinkled skin became part of the design, as if their *drycræft* moulded them into a moving *galdercræft*. In our world, I saw them as a moving higher runic magic. In their world, I knew not what they meant, only that I felt their power as they moved towards us.

One stepped forward and spoke clearly in our own tongue, asking for Eyvindr to come forward to be accepted into their tribe. As he moved forward, straightening his back, I saw Eyvindr's jaw tighten, the muscles clenching. He looked so Roman. He knew he was now Roman, and in their eyes, an enemy. Those Romans had sucked all the pagan spirit from him.

But I sensed he kept his soul intact from them.

If I had seen this, then so must the Druid high priest and the Elders now beckoning Eyvindr forward?

Taking deep breath, my brother spoke elegantly in his native tongue,

"Ðèodscipe fram þæt Durotrige, Ealdors und þin kin. Ic ðoncian þu fram þæt dèopnes fram mín ferhð in ālūfan mè und mín kin þín giestlíðe frèondlíc. Ic wordbèotung an āð æt æthweorfan þin fremsumnes bā wiþ gold und mín helde. Ic āgan micel to gefrignan þu ond ic āgan micel to gedǽlan."

"People of the Durotrige, Elders and your kin, I thank you from the depths of my heart in granting me and my kin your hospitable friendship. I pledge an oath to return your kindness both in gold and with my allegiance. I have much to learn from you and much to share."

Eyvindr, my gracious and beautiful brother, knelt with head bowed, waiting for whatever reply was to come. The elder, certainly one of advanced seasons, slowly moved forward. In his hand there nestled a skull. The surface was shiny and stained a brown colour from many hands that had rubbed the crown, praying, giving allegiance. And so, it was with my brother. He knew intuitively what he must do. He laid his hand gently on the skull, was then prodded to place both hands and the elder intoned a prayer. Eyvindr answered, quietly almost under his breath, with a prayer of his own.

As if on cue, the Durotrige elders emitted a high-pitched chant with the banging and clashing of circular drums and the jangling of skulls. We looked over to the entrance, and on cue came a line of men and women carrying all manner of dishes, a spit and a half-roasted pig. Platters of bread, dishes of stew and steamed fish. Not least came the mead and the barley ale.

We were invited to feast. And I have rarely enjoyed food so much as on that day when the Wihtwara joined with the Durotrige.

We were placed near the Durotrige elder who knew our tongue. We were at the head of the table, Eileifer being *Cyng*. I complimented them on the delicious food and the craftsmanship of their pottery in which it was served. I told them of our clay at *Chestebeorg*, the four-colour clay found at *Broc*, which produced fine clay sediment that fired well, and was strong and pliable.

"Did you see the cliffs upon which beach you first landed on *Frescewætr Ealond?"*, Our translator laughed, "That is our source. It is magnificent, no?"

"We have settled over yonder, because it is a sacred isle, a beautifully rich place to farm and raise our families", Eileifer explained, "Our homeland became impossible both from flooding of the lowlands and from invaders from the east. We took the brave decision to escape and begin anew. We are a very small community but it is of the seven tribes in a confederacy with priests and priestesses to oversee us in all things."

"It is indeed rare to have such close-knit tribes living in peace", declared the elder whose seasons on this earth, defied my reckoning.

"We are bound by our Goddess Nerthus", I said looking directly at him, "She is our *Fodör Mōdor,* our Earth Mother. He smiled at this and nodded.

"We are indeed close then, Sister of the Wihtwara!" he replied.

"Why are you friendly with the Romans?" I ventured to ask him.

"Why are you!" he shot back within a hairsbreadth. "We trade with them of course. We are doing this to safeguard these islands. And the Druid who shelter upon them. You have met with but one Grove. There is another far to the east on *Everlant Ealond.* The Roman generals come and they go. It is upon the whim of one or two generals that all life can change here, as it has in Britannia. They see us as peaceful and cooperative, making coin for them, trading our crafts with them, as we do with the Gauls. And whatever wealth we gain, and we do, trust me, it goes to our kin on the far shore, to assist them."

Eyvindr sat bolt upright, smiling, raising his beaker to the Elders,

"I pledge my whole spirit and body to assist you in building coin aplenty! By the spirit of Waylander, I will fill many a bag for you!" Beakers crashed to the wooden table in a beating of approval, sending splash after splash of mead and barley ale to soak the platters of food.

Soon we were all satiated with too much food and ale. The scraps were withdrawn, some fed to the wolf hounds, and the tables collapsed and stored. We withdrew to the sit on the furs and rest while Sunni descended to the depths. It was not long before sleep overtook me. A peaceful and full sleep, with no tension and worry to harry my mind. Eileifer curled around me to keep me warm. Eyvindr relaxed beside us, and just before I closed my eyes, he gave me a smile, a broad relaxed smile. He felt safe at last. Ingvar was snoring abundantly loudly, as only he could do!

The morning gave us rain. Clouds amassed in the sky, Thunor was gathering strength. We left the warm lodge, and gave Eyvindr great hugs to support him on his way. The drooping leather bags laden with metal and gold were slung over a horse gifted to him by the tribe. He cantered away with an assistant, to the smithy, which would become his home, his life and his reparation.

Ingvar's boat had been taken, as we slept, to a much easier inlet. Eileifer hugged those responsible as it meant an easier journey for me. Ingvar informed us that another estuary was nearer, with no surrounding bog land, and we would be safely to *Eileiferdūn* by sundown.

We said our farewells to the ever peaceful Durotrige, and their Druid priests. We pledged a return and an open offer of hospitality from the Wihtwara. We left feeling a deeper unity on Wihtland.

"Visit the Druid on *Everlant ealond* ", the priest called out, "It is important to seal the energy for your children and your children's children."

"We will!" I shouted back, as we took to the path, heads down and hoods up as the rain increased and I prayed our harvest had been kept safe.

… … … … … … … … …

CHAPTER FORTY- FOUR
Berandinzium Villa

We arrived back at our lodge, wearily treading the stairs up to our solar, and warmth. A comfortable bed had been made for us. The night was well advanced. We shed our much-stained clothes. We washed in tepid water, and sunk into a dreamless sleep, Eileifer cradling me in his arms. My last image was of my beloved *brōðor*, straight backed on his high-stepping gelding, as he cantered towards his new life.

The morning brought more rain from Thunor, not a deluge, just a warning. And if I was not involved with saving Eyvindr, I would have been out at first light to work the harvest. As it was, Ingvar remained for now, to bark orders to the lazy ones and bend his back in bringing in the barley. This season some wheat had been grown, the seed we got from the Romans. They preferred it and we complied readily as it made superior bread.

Eileifer turned to me, "We need to see the *Rōmānisc* before we go to *Berandinzium Villa*", he said as he pulled on a clean tunic, "I need to feel my way through this problem, gently. Our success depends on the right approach."

I had just finished pulling the many tangles from my thick hair, which was so naturally curly, I resented it for the challenging work it involved. Eileifer loved it for pulling his fingers through "his ebony copper jewel" as he called my locks. My bone comb was broken in several places and I committed quietly to carving a new, sharper and finer one.

"I believe we should see Eastmund", I turned to see Eileifer, watching him as he pulled on a woollen over tunic and clasped his leather belt with *seax* and pouch hanging from it. "We can visit the white horses and be horse-talkers for a little while."

"*Giese*, I know this to be the right approach. I may be *Cyng* but Ærdwulf is more *Rōmãnisc* than Reudignion. He will know how to approach the lord of this villa. He would rather kneel to them than to me."

"That is disloyal", I exclaimed pulling my hair into the tight knot that would tame it for the day ahead. I tied it just above my left ear, still feeling that *spakōna* affinity.

"Nah, we are broad of mind enough to include other ways of living."

I sat quietly for a moment, watching Sunni as she poured into our solar. Suddenly an image appeared. It was of a tiled floor being created at the villa, in which my Eyvindr would be assisting. It flashed brightly, then was gone, but etched on my mind was a figure with the head of a cockerel, the body of a man and legs of a serpent. Its symbolism was potent, I knew this had been sent.

"I believe our visit will be breath-taking", I replied softly, "And I have been given a good feeling around it. We will be successful, Eileifer, I know it!"

As we trotted gently down *Eileiferdūn,* suddenly and without warning, my morning food came back to greet me, I did a *spíwãn* down my dear gelding's leg onto the rough grass. "Ahhh," I groaned and wiped my mouth. I leant down to the water bag and lifting it to my sticky throat, swallowing long and deep.

Eileifer turned about, nudging his stallion to obey. He came up and put his hand gently under my chin, pulling my head up to face him.

"I do not suppose it would do any good to order you home?"

"Nah", I replied, smiling, "Wōden himself would not succeed in turning me back. Besides, I have been given a Sighting, *Wyrd* is at work here, change it and the whole outcome will alter. You know this!"

He nodded slowly and with one backward glance turned his horse around, but proceeded at a slower pace. We ambled our way to my *ceasterwic* at Sudmōr. We were so slow I could lean over and pick hawthorn leaves to sooth my empty stomach and when I saw mint clustered by the hedgerow I stopped and picked a large handful to chew slowly. It calmed my sickness so by the time we reached that familiar turn in the track, and my old *hūs* came into view, I was feeling fine again.

Old smells assailed my nostrils, suddenly, the weaving stink from the women's lodge where the yarns were dyed. The metallic smell of burning metal and charcoal heated to that intense white that gave power to the *drycræft*. We dismounted and gave our horses to the stable boy. I moved swiftly to my *Fæder's hūs*, my heart singing. I found *Mōdor* where she always was, cooking by the fire. I hugged her for a long time, then shared my news. I was with royal child. She shrieked and then laughed, rushed over to Eileifer before he had even properly entered and hugged him without protocol. My *Fæder* entered, swinging back the hide flap and bellowed at his *wif*, hands on his hips, legs apart in a real stew.

We laughed, and I told him why *Mōdor* was so excited. He bellowed even louder, and came to give Eileifer another grand bear hug, slapping him most unroyally on the back. When he turned to me, his dear face softened and I saw his eyes glisten as he swallowed hard and came to gently kiss me on the forehead, cupping my head in his huge calloused hands.

He then suddenly disappeared out of the *hūs,* calling behind him, that Eystein needed to be present. A family celebration was under way. My big brother entered smiling, shaking Eileifer's hand, pumping it madly. We sat together sharing the food *Mōdor* had prepared, skilful in the mixing of herbs, and now spices she had got from the *Rōmãnisc*. I whispered to her, I was getting *spíwãn,* so she took my bowl and put another mixture of herbs in with the rest and told me to take a plentiful supply back with me.

I enjoyed every mouthful. I hoped my children would grow to love cooking as much as I did with *Mōdor*.

In between mouthful's, we shared the telling of Eyvindr, how the Druid priests had prayed for him and how wonderful and hospitable the Durotrige had been in accepting him into their tribe. The work of creating coin for the Romans was crucial to buying his *libertus*. He simply had to be freed to create the life he deserved here on Wihtland.

Fæder remained silent, thoughtful. Then he looked up straight at us.

"If it is Roman coin you are needing I can lay my hands on more. Your bride gift was just a portion of what I have amassed over these years. And I refuse you to use any part of your bride gift. No, I have more. I knew many seasons ago that coin wealth will become important to us. Trading in grain is good, but bulky. And it cannot be depended upon during the famine seasons that hit us when the Gods see fit to try us."

He raised his great frame up, for at his tallest, he nearly reached the eaves of our *hūs*. Lumbering over to the far side, he bent down to scrape away the rushes to reveal a door in the floor made of metal. He produced a metal spike I had never seen before, with notches at the end. In the door, a metal plate had been bolted in. There was an opening which this metal spike fitted and when he turned it, the door lifted. He bent down to his full arm's length and pulled up, not one but two leather sacks. I could plainly hear the jangle of coins as he heaved and grunted them to the surface. We all sat in stunned silence as my *Fæder* produced a coin fortune before us.

I looked from him to the coin wealth, thinking I did not know my *fæder* at all, and as I peered across to *Mōdor,* her expression matched mine. She had been kept from this deep secret. Only Eystein looked accepting of the fact and I realised quickly, he knew.

I raised my eyebrows at him for him to explain.

"We have been trading with Romans since I think, oh, ten *sumor's*?" he looked over his father for support.

"The *Rōmānisc* aids us a great deal", *Fæder* continued, heaving the wealth over to hoist the sacks onto the table which groaned under their combined weight.

"Anything we could create, handsome bracteates they admire greatly, our pottery from *chestehyll* has gained a reputation for sturdiness, has also been traded. Above all our fertile land has given a surplus of grain for many seasons now, even after we have given tribute to the Romans. So, you see, our coin wealth is well-earned. And it will help my son gain his rightful freedom, achieve his *libertus*!"

"But Ingvar has given his wealth for Eyvindr needs. He needs to know of this!" Eileifer burst in, looking not a little angry.

"*Giese*, of course," *Fæder* replied, grabbing his arm, "All that wealth will be returned to him in kind, if needs be. Honour within our kinship is more important than any wealth gained."

I sat still, quietly tossing all this new revelation over in my mind, and I was very disquieted indeed, by the feelings that came with this sudden coin wealth. The feelings of greed made separate those of sharing, of the hungry and needy people who did not have the talents to make this coin wealth throughout their hard lives.

I thought of our field ritual, of giving sacks of grain to the poorest, not judging them for their lack. And I turned my head away from that coin wealth in disgust and fear. If those Romans were not in our land, would we be so greedy for it?

I turned to face *Fæder* and Eystein, "Why is it then that you felt the need for a metal cage, with a lock to keep this coin safe? Do you fear having that much? Do you fear it getting stolen from you? Fear is the absence of love *fæder* and you betray Nerthus!"

I got up to leave, to suck some clean air into my lungs. But my *brōðor* hit back before my *fæder* could react.

"I did not notice your reluctance in accepting your bride gift Dagrun!" he shouted at me as I swept out of our *hūs*, my feelings overwhelming me.

I stomped around outside, folding my arms into my chest, hunched with head down, battling with this torrent of emotions that had so suddenly swept over me. After a little time, I began to feel the cold seeping in and no-one had come for me. I turned and went to go back inside. *Mōdor* was waiting, standing quietly by the side of our *hūs*, looking over at her *dohtor,* who had become a pain. She came forward and gently put her arms around me rubbing into my back to chase the cold and the hurt away.

"*Dohtor*", she said softly, taking my face in her hands "Listen well. You have faced many trials in your young life. The river of *Wyrd* flows so strongly in you that you have swam in its current without complaint. Ever. We all admire and respect your courage. But you are yet still young to have wisdom.

The *wyrd rapas* flows through us all, connecting us to each other. The spirit that lives is much too strong to be denied. And at the heart of that spirit is change. It is why we flow, better in the stream than at the edge clinging to a never changing muddy bank!

This coin wealth is coming to us all. Better we learn to embrace it, use it wisely and know that it too has a spirit. It lives. If we deny that, it will corrupt us. The highest good this spirit is serving us now, is the freedom for your *brōðor*. This spirit of coin wealth does not judge us, we do that! Let the spirit live in your heart for the good it will do."

She pointed to our *hūs*, "Inside there are three men, who also live in your heart. Eileifer is angry at both your *fæder* and Eystein. Eystein is angry at you. But the one who is just hurting, whose heart is breaking, is your *fæder*. Please go and give him your love and ask for his forgiveness."

I released and let go a huge gasp of pent up feeling. The air escaped from my lungs and I was reluctant to fill them. I then gasped in huge belt of air and strode back inside, blocking the tears for as long as it took to reach *Fæder*, who opened his arms in ready forgiveness and swamped me with his enormous size and strong arms. I spluttered several apologies before the tears dried and I sat quietly down next to Eileifer, who turned to smile and look sheepishly over to his father-in-law. He bent his head in a silent apology.

"The *Rōmānisc* is our most likely ally, a good go-between with the Roman at *Berandinzium Villa*", Eileifer put forward, "With that in mind we were about to visit Eastmund, to secure a private meeting with his *fæder*, Eardwūlf."

"Eastmund will not like that too much," ventured my *Fæder*, "No love lost there. Nah, let me do the asking. Eyvindr is my son. I will do everything to bring him home to us!"

"The new moon will an appropriate time to visit the villa. Three twilights from now. We will go together." My *fæder* banged his mug on the table and we all echoed in agreement.

Eileifer and I gave our farewells and walked to our horses, who had been well cared for with hay and a good rub-down. I gave the boy a coin, and he looked at me in sheer amazement, tossed it in his hands for a while before placing it in his pouch. Sharing coin is better than hoarding it.

We gave the rest of day to our white guardians. Eastmund nearly tumbled over himself in his rush to greet his adopted *fæder*. They both ambled away together, Eastmund bending Eileifer's ear with much telling of the horses' wellbeing and his own progress with them.

The old white mare snorted a loud greeting to me. I was so glad to see her still with us. I had not visited since my time in spirit and even before then, horse-talking was a rare thing, left to our talented son, Eastmund. Nevertheless, our horses do not forget us, even as we pass them by.

I stroked and talked quietly to her, as she snorted and gently tossed her head this way and that, flicking her tail and scraping the ground with her hoof. I knew she wanted me to connect with her, so I leant forward and buried my head in her neck feeling the way forward. I felt love swamp me, and in opening to her spirit, images flooded in. I felt a rippling of her muscles. I suddenly saw symbols appear before me. Too many to know what each one meant, save one, which I had seen before. It was the cockerel headed figure again, only this time, as the panorama enlarged upon itself, I saw people gathered in a huge room, wearing long capes and carrying long shaped tapers I had never witnessed before. They were chanting in a language unknown to me. They were circling all these floor mosaics in prayer and honour. It was a ceremony. It faded as quickly as it came. I continued to hold our white guardian in my embrace. I loved the smell and feel of her. Eventually I walked her over to the stable and dug my hands in to find an apple, then two, for her to munch. She told me she was bored. Needing no more encouragement, I jumped on her wide old back and we cantered away, through adjoining meadows, me holding onto her mane in a freedom run just for us. She did not go fast. She knew. There would always be an affinity between us. We doubled back as we reached the end of our flat land, which bordered onto the *chestedūn*, its high escarpment too much for either old mare or *cwèn* with child. We trotted back enjoying Sunni's rays on our back, as she descended, bringing us into deep shadow that undulated along the tall grasses we had flattened in our wake. Eileifer stood waiting for us, holding our mounts, who were nibbling at the lush grass.

"Needs must we head homeward", he shouted as we drew near. I dismounted with a happy spring in my step and hugged him, nuzzling my head into his neck, catching his smell and breathing it in.

"Homeward we go husband" I whispered, "Thank you for giving me this chance to help my *brōðor,* and for this little freedom run. Both mares appreciated it!"

He laughed and patted our favoured white spirit horse. Eastmund took over, and I thanked him for caring for them so well. We promised to visit again soon.

As I was helped onto my gelding, I turned to Eileifer, "She gave me another telling, Eileifer. Another vision. There is something very important will be happening at the villa. It had no timing given to it but I feel it will change our lives and that of Eyvindr. I do not know anymore, but I do believe it is about their religion, their higher calling. It will affect us."

As we made for home I suddenly felt the fluttering of butterflies in my stomach. It was not my child making its first movements. It was far too early. No, this was the deep inexplicable fluttering of anticipation, of excitement. The flow of *Wyrd* within, was moving me ever forward in the centre of the river to something totally new.

… … … … … … … … …

CHAPTER FORTY- FIVE

ABRAXAS

Fæder was as good as his word. Ærdwulf, the *Rōmānisc* was called upon and he went to visit the lord of the villa. His name sounded very strange to my ear. His name was Vrittakos Eluskonios. These sounds I had to roll over my tongue many times as we made our way to *Berandinzium Villa* exactly on the new moon, as pledged. I felt open and excited about this meeting. I trusted in *Wyrd*.

Eileifer kept beside me, looking over to see if I would lose my morning food. We were dressed in our ceremonial clothes and I had taken a large draft of herbs to quell any sickness. *Mōdor* had squeezed my shoulders, saying with a huge smile, "It will be a *dohtor* for sure Dagrun. You fought inside me for many moons, we struggled together to find our unity. That balance came, you came easy and that is how I know, dear one!"

We were heading east, towards the mystical *Ælond* of *Everlant* where the *Diviciacos* from Gaul still lived among the wilderness with the wild boar as guardians. I had pledged to go, as the Druid from *Frescewætr Ælond* had asked of me. But this time, with great determination, my *Cyng* forbade it. And in truth I was relieved. The thought of creeping though forest claimed by wild boar did not excite me.

And keeping that wild vision in mind, the air was sucked from my lungs as we rounded the *hyll* and caught sight of *Berandinzium villa*, only partially constructed, sitting in a vast valley floor, its walls built to accommodate a small family. The remainder stretched away as stone markers, to give a tantalizing glimpse of what would be a great palatial villa. It nestled beautifully by the estuary that saw boats come and go, merchandise piled high on the banks, ready to be taken elsewhere.

As we trotted forward, the land easy and level, I saw such an intense activity by many workers, seaman, builders and craftspeople, all working to build *Breredingas* into a thriving port. The Romans had claimed her. She was no longer part of the *Wihtwara*. I doubt she ever had been and for the first time in my life I felt I was entering another country altogether, another culture greeted me on my small homeland.

I needed to embrace it and not feel alienated but I knew not why.

Eileifer suddenly reigned in his stallion, we stopped. Behind was *Fæder* and the *Rōmãnisc*, who had not shared many words with us, but kept quiet council with *Fæder*. This discomfort may be due to Eileifer adopting his only son from him. But he was a rotten father. Of that, there was no doubt. I did not trust him. But I trusted *Fæder* with my own life so he was invited to come and would ease our introductions. He was well known to these people who did not even own Roman names. I was intrigued and it was my curiosity that pulled me forward after Eileifer had had his fill of the villa and all the surroundings.

Eileifer had reached over to pull my gelding to him, leaning over to plant the most tender and long kiss. "I think it best you stand behind me *wif*. They are renowned for looking down on women. They will not recognise you as a *Cwèn*. When in Rome, Dagrun, when in Rome…"

I clamped my tongue to my teeth and sucked my cheeks in. I was not known for remaining silent for very long. But it had it merits even so. I could observe much more. And my eyes were never still.

The day had been overcast, so when Sunni graced us with her shining heat, that small part of the villa lit up and became like the shining white cliffs of *frescewætr ealond*. It would become a temple to the Gods. `It was being built, with many hands labouring on the walls of a new construction to the north side of the land which rolled lazily upward, with grazing sheep on its slopes. Their white coats were dotted amongst the grass upland giving their ownership to the white villa and made a scene of near perfection for me. The cloudless azure sky completed this picture.

We cantered down the last incline and brought our horses to a trot. A boy immediately came forward to take our horses to hay and rest, as we made our way towards the front entrance. I was marvelling at the depth of the limestone frontage, the neatness of beams dovetailed together in precision craftsmanship. But what stopped me in my tracks were the openings, long and rectangular that had a kind of green crystal in small squares fitted into a frame, like our sea crystals on the beaches but shinier and more translucent. For the first time, I was looking at Roman glassware, remembering the telling from Eystein in his journey to *Cantium*.

I dragged my gaze away to see a man come out to greet us. The large door held open by a slave boy. I caught a brief glimpse of the interior, a mixture of shade and light, like our solar on a good day. I could also see a woman waiting in the shadows. I instinctively stepped back behind Eileifer and saw *Fæder* and the *Rōmãnisc* step forward.

"*Ego invitovos omnis salvere iubeo ut meus domicilium.* I bid you all welcome to my home" the swarthy olive-skinned man intoned in a deep voice. He spoke in Latin but I could see clearly, he was no Roman. His thick raven hair curled around his tanned face, and those near black eyes surveyed us with an intense stare. Then he suddenly smiled to show a row of perfect white teeth.

"*Meus nomino is Vrittakos Eluskonios et ego et meus familia Venio propta Gaul. Nos are dies the verus fundmentum construction of Berandinzium Villa.* My name is Vrittakos Eluskonios. And I and my family come from Gaul. We are, as you see, in the very basic stages of our construction of *Berandinzium villa*."

"And you are the king and queen of the tribe Wihtwara, I hear from my friend here," he pointed to the *Rōmãnisc*, who was quietly translating to Eileifer.

"We are both emigres from a distant land, so I feel an affinity with you already. I am not Roman, as you can plainly see. And where is your queen?"

I stepped out from the shadow of my husband and considered this man's eyes. I am forever direct and the *spakōna* spirit was still strong in me. Suddenly his expression took on a much deeper imprint. We stared at each other in silence, both our souls meeting and acknowledging the other. I knew we were both swimming in the mid-river of *Wyrd*, and my heart began to beat faster.

He broke away first and beckoned us into a large entrance hall. This was only partially completed. It was my first sight of the intricate mosaic floor patterns and painted walls. Two men were kneeling on the floor adding the small coloured squares to a twining rope design that edged a square not yet begun.

"I do apologise for the industry," he commented, as he led us to the left and into a room that had been put aside for the meeting.

He turned to beckon his wife forward. "This is my wife Venitouta Quadrunia. If it pleases you, queen of the Wihtwara, my wife will show you the plans for our villa, as I feel it will mean a great deal to you. While we men discuss the business in hand."

She stood before me looking up and bowed gently. I was humbled by her grace. She too was dark and olive skinned. Her eyes were pure jet, framed by twisting curly raven hair. I instinctively felt drawn to her.

As we left, I shot a look to Eileifer, conferring silently with him to succeed in all things for my Eyvindr. He nodded at me imperceptibly.

She turned and spoke, delighting and shocking me in one breath, "*IC ãgan lang wana gemèlan þu....er... wè nèahgebūr*. I have long wanting meet you. We.... neighbour."

"Forgive my faltering and poor grasp of your tongue. I will call for my daughter who was born here and knows your language far better than I."

"By the love of Nerthus, nah!" I exclaimed, "It is I who is wanting. I am ignorant of Latin. I do wish to learn very much."

She smiled and shrugged. I was going too fast for her. But I felt so happy that this barrier had been swept away, promising a good dialogue between us.

"Venitouta, I am in respect of your leaning and wisdom" I bowed to her.

"Call me Vinita, please," she said in my tongue, turning to issue a command to a waiting servant girl in flowing Latin. I was being drawn to the sound of this language already.

We waited as the girl flapped off in hard leather sandals on the smooth marble floor. These new sounds and the huge room unfinished, overwhelmed me into silence. The villa echoed with many sounds carried from afar, with no hangings or furnishings to muffle the sounds, it was an empty space under construction.

I was forever drawn to the tiny coloured squares set in hard clay that depicted scenes of a God and Goddess in nature. This then, I realised, were their living spirits here in the floor. But we would never consider trampling over our Gods, never! Then as I looked around there were slim pathways bordering the figures, also beautifully decorated but with no images set in them.

I looked up to Vinita and pointed to both the figures and the borders. She nodded, understanding my unspoken question.

"Queen of the Wihtwara," she said falteringly, "This will be our temple."

I was staggered at the implication of those three words.

"Oh, my name, please, call me Dagrun! I am Dagrun Wahl of the Warinni." A young girl appeared, holding her arms out to her mother, whilst the servant took up her place by the painted wall.

"Ahh, this is my daughter, Aia," Vinita said, embracing her warmly. She was of slight build, but I guessed her age to be the same as Eastmund. Around twelve summers, no more. She turned to me and held out her arm, to give me our traditional welcome of a forearm clasp and a bear hug. I laughed and hugged her well.

"She has learnt much," I said to Vinita.

"Ic am welðungen æt gemèlan þu", she said in near perfect Saxon. "I am honoured to meet you."

I had a hundred questions lined up, waiting in a queue.

"Why have you come to build a temple on Wihtland?"

She translated to her mother, who thought for a moment before replying.

"This will not be the only temple on your island. We know, as do the Romans, that this island is very sacred. The Druids from Gaul have occupied sacred land here for aeons. There will be five other temples that are planned."

"Our temple holds secrets known only to us. This one will be the last journey for those in their final initiation. We have given over part of the temple to the Roman god Mithras, whose initiates worship below, "in secret", she pointed to a narrow, darkened walkway that led downwards into the depths of the land below.

"We will also open it up to the followers of Bacchus. But our God, the very ancient one, who precedes all others, and who oversees all others, is Abraxas. We are Greek and we are Gnostic Basilides. They were Ancient peoples. We intend to keep their wisdom alive here."

She stopped and let her daughter catch up in the translation. My mind was working so fast, nearly tripping over these revelations. Yet deep in my soul, a thread was being woven that spun out to join with these new acquaintances. And again, my butterfly stomach was working letting me know deep truths were being shared.

"Why are you sharing these secrets with me?" I asked, the next burning question slipped out of my mouth.

"My husband gave permission for me to share with you and answer all your questions without pause," Venita said, smiling, her eyes glistening with warmth and some excitement, "he told me you live your life in the other worlds, as well as here."

I nodded, "This is true. I have been shown this place in vision and I know it is very important to us all."

"Come, let me show you the plans. And I will explain."

We walked past the room set aside for the negotiation over my brother. I could hear muffled talking taking place, a laugh most certainly from my *fæder* filtered through and animated talk continued. It felt very promising.

Venita led me into an undeveloped area, that had partial floor mosaics in place. At the far end was a completed figure in colours of red, black, white, brown and yellow. I screwed up my eyes in concentration, for I had never seen anything like it in my life.

This figure had the head of a cockerel, yet the body of a human warrior in armour, like the Romans wear. But what made my breath stop were the serpent legs, curled and stretching ending in two serpent heads. It was like seeing Wōden and Nerthus together. These people worshiped serpent energy of the Mother Earth as we do! I did not understand the meaning of the cockerel, nor the symbols being held in both hands, but I realised suddenly without any hesitation that our spirit ways had a link to each other: we held common ground!

"You are looking upon Abraxas", Venita said reverently, through Aia, "He is our god, the power above all others and the first archetype. He holds all 365 heavens within him and connects to us humans as we also have 365 parts to us. Through him we can connect to the stars. He has seven letters connecting us to the seven major planets. Each letter holds the power A=1, B=2, P=100, X=200, A=1 S=60. The angels of the last visible heaven are the makers of this world here, now."

"Take a moment," Aia said quietly to me, "I know something of your Nerthus goddess and your affinity to *Wyrd*. We are kin, you and I."

I let out a breath of astonishment. So much to take in! The numbers fuddled my thinking. But intrigued me nonetheless. And of the stars, their knowledge of the heavens surpassed our understanding.

"How do you know so much about the workings of the heavens?" I asked, as I was beginning to feel overwhelmed.

"Ah, that is the accumulated wisdom of Alexandria!" she said, "The astrologers and theologians worked together, and then wrote everything down for future generations, for us! They studied the stars in detail, made maps and diagrams. Our physicians became interested and found the magical affinity all humans have, with the cosmos."

"The number seven is a sacred number to us."

"And to us also!" I burst in with some excitement, "In our homeland we lived together in a confederacy of seven tribes. We worship Nerthus, the Earth Mother, who can become a serpent, as does our god Wōden"

"Now I see," Venita replied, gently taking my arm at the elbow and leading me towards another room half-completed. "You see here, we have the room of initiation and introduction. But it is way behind completion. I believe your brother has shown a notable talent for mosaic design, yes?"

"I believe so", I replied, hoping all was proceeding well with the men.

"Do not worry Dagrun. I have overheard the talk and there will be peace of sorts made with the *Cantium* Romans. Expensive, mark you, but your brother will claim his *libertus!* Although it may take years," she added.

I turned and hugged this wonderful lady. She laughed and took me by the shoulders, her silken drapes falling onto her wrists.

"I am feeling a friendship forming, Dagrun. I would be very honoured to have you come and visit us whenever you feel the need. Our house is open to you."

"And you also should visit us at *Eileiferdūn*. I would love to show you and Aia our sacred white horses. They have their ears to the spirit world." I had a mind to bring Eastmund forward for Aia, who seemed to enjoy learning our ways.

"Look at the figure here," Aia said, "He has the cockerel head but if you look closely you can see he is wearing a pendant. It is magic, like your *Wyrd drycræft,* it has great power."

"Ah yes", Venita pointing to the pure white triangle, "Firstly the cockerel is the messenger of the sun. He is for us the most sacred of animals. And the pendent, well that is truly magical. What is written is:

Ablanathanalba."

"We think it is from the original Alexandrian text, it is the same spelt both ways."

"When it is chanted, it is reduced to the sound Ba, bringing the magic of Abraxas, into this world."

Immediately, I could feel *Eald Mōdor* by my side, nudging me to remember. In the Telling of young Wōden, the magic that was woven into the sacred braids for the young demi-god was a reducing chant.

I suddenly felt faint.

"Do you have a seat?" I asked.

The servant girl was called and flapped over with a stool.

"Tighten your thongs, girl!" Venita snapped, "And fetch some water for our guest."

I rubbed my belly, feeling a sickness appear suddenly.

"My dear lady," Venita exclaimed, "You are with child, like me!"

"By the goddess! *Giese*" I exclaimed, "When are you due?"

"Oh! it is early, seven months at least. I am praying this villa will be completed by then. We have conscripted more labour. Boatloads full of supplies are on their way from Gaul. Meanwhile we are using local stone and clays."

"I am for a long wait also. Maybe our babies will come close together?"

"Wonderful! I am hoping for a boy child."

"I really do not mind" I replied, hoping quietly for a daughter to pass on our wisdom of stone guardianship.

Suddenly noises from the far side of the villa, of men slapping shoulders and laughter. Eileifer and my *fæder* came out beaming wide enough to get one of Ingvar boats inside their mouths. I knew we had a victory.

"It is done my love!" Eileifer called out to me, striding over the mosaics without a thought. I rushed forward to stop him creating an embarrassment, leading him carefully around the narrow walkways. Hissing at him, "I'll tell you later" as he looked nonplussed at me, as if I had lost my mind.

I turned to Aia, holding both her hands in mine and said "I thank you from my heart, for your assistance. Your skill with our tongue is so strong, you must come and meet our people. Feel free whenever you wish."

I looked over to Vrittakos, and I felt my heart open. He knew it instantly, and smiled. I nodded to him in respect. The *wyrd rapas* had been truly honoured.

… … … … … … … … …

CHAPTER FORTY- SIX
Ealdmōdor

This is a rare moment, to be left alone with my thoughts. Mōnā sent slivers of light through my window, which I had insisted upon remaining open, this twilight of the beginning of *Þrimilce mōnaþ* which I knew I would not be witness to its end.

Þrimilce mōnaþ, I sounded those words slowly, each syllable hushed on the outtake of my laboured breathing. This was the *mōnaþ* of my spiritual birthing. In greeting Nerthus in the grove, she gifted me the sight to view the future of my kin. How terrible it seemed. Elíse was her host and I learnt so quickly the remedies for *Ylfa gescot* that had invaded her so quickly after Nerthus left her.

It was the birthing of my love for Eileifer. How he suddenly appeared and sent his love arrow to me. Such moments are to be honoured and savoured forever. It was the most magical of times when we honoured our Goddess and gifted her the May queen.

It is that indestructible loyal deep-spirited love that has endured. We named our *dūn* after our beloved daughter, Lãfa…Love. It will forever be known as *Lãfadūn*.

Now this moment has given me the chance to re-live all those memories clattering to be seen, remembered and lived again. Lãfa, Eastmund and Aia had quietly left. I was so rarely left alone, as just as *Ealdmōdor* kept me by her side, so my Lãfa had taken my place in the vigil for my spirit's leaving.

Mōdor was quite right, I birthed a daughter. She came as easily as could be expected for a first-born. Lífa and my *Mōdor* were constant in their care of me and my daughter, but *gealdor drycræft* was never used. Lãfa gave no complications and she was supremely loved by her *fæder* and as for me, I revelled in her joy to be alive. She was a skipping, singing child, instinctive and open to nature.

Her smile, and her sparkling eyes has come to me now, like a bud opening fully to the full glare of Sunni, when first she heard the stone's heartbeat. Her little head rammed against the giant stone, her hand slowly caressing the rough surface.

"They are alive as we are, Mōdor", she exclaimed after a long time in peaceful contemplation, "They have decided to remain in the earth, closer to Nerthus and to guard us!"

"We are their guardians too, Lãfa", I said, "It is a mutual two-way alliance. I think of it as a marriage. We cannot live without each other, so we help each other.

When you can, sweetheart, you must come to the guardian stones and listen. Practise it. One day they will amaze you!"

And so, they did! Several seasons went by, as she grew into a tall giantess in her own right, she came bursting in to tell me the *Cenningstãn* had shown her husband to be.

"Describe this wonder to me Lãfa", I replied.

"He is tall like a giant so he must come from our ancestral lands. He has the darkest hair, like Fæder, and he has piercing blue eyes. He smiled at me and held out his hand to me."

"Was there anyone else in this vision from the stone? "I replied, trying to contain a smile that was itching to cross my face.

"Two ravens and a wolf", Lãfa chimed in the lilting song-burst way she had about her.

"Lãfa, that may have been a husband you were given, but sweet daughter, it is more likely our Eall Fæder Wōden has come to greet and welcome you to his realm. It is more likely you are being given notice to begin your training. He would want you to be a spakōna like me."

I remember so clearly Lãfa gasp, her eyes, balls of pure astonishment as she soaked this news into her spirit to see how she felt.
"*Giese*", she replied at last.
My smile never arrived as I hugged her tightly, tears unbidden watered my eyes.
Lãfa, so profoundly meant to love, directed her purity to Nerthus, the trees and stones, her animals. I know Wōden guided her, as did I and her *fæder*. But it was he, the All Father, who fed her imagination, soaked her spirit with energy and fed her, his love.
 At last I realised my sacrifice as a Watcher, for nearly a season, planted a seed for my people to gain wisdom directly. To become the Wihtwara "people of the spirit."

… … … … … … … … …

EPILOGUE
Lãfa

The day is as grey as the heron wing resting on my *Mōdor*. I prayed to Thunor to swallow those clouds so we may glimpse Sunni. But he did not hear me.

I breathe in deep and again prayed to the *Eall Fæder* to gift us benevolence and bring us warmth, to give some heat in our sorrowful procession.

I know full well my Mōdor is nearly at peace, for she will be reunited with my fæder, who had journeyed to Nerthus' meadow a full two sumor's ago. I had felt pulled apart when I realised part of her died with him. She mourned in that silent unspoken way, and gave up the will to live.

All the Wihtwara kin has gathered. Everyone. My brothers are present, leading the oxen up to the leaning stone. Lífa, now our *Ealdmōdor*, is waiting for us there to begin the *deaō-gerihte*. *Wítega* women massed in a protective circle, so loved was she, my *Mōdor*. And my adored man, whom she said was "my Wōden" whom I chose, like her, over my *spakōna* dedication, walks by my side. She did not know I was carrying his child, which I know is the daughter she would have longed for. But I know she is present. I look around to see kin as far as the eye could see. And several who are not, but they come in respect.

The Durotrige come from *frescewætr ealond* surrounding one remaining Druid, an ancient and wonderful old man defying mortality. My guess he was the welcoming priest who met my *Mōdor*, *Fæder* and *Ingvar* at the entrance of the cave. A Telling that had worn around the edges, with so much glorious repetition.

The saving of my uncle Eyvindr warmed many a heart around the mead hall fires. And he is present also, with his family of four *beorns* and a beautiful *wif*. He has prospered and learnt skills at the Villa. He still looks more Roman than Wihtwara, but we forgive him. *Mōdor* was proud she learnt their language. She passed it on to me and I am grateful. Dear friends have been made at *Berandinzium Villa,* which lay unbuilt for many seasons. In fact, until Eyvindr earned his *Libertus* with coin wealth he made himself.

Together we learnt some of the creation mysteries. Of the planets and the stars in the midnight sky. Far beyond our knowledge, it is ancient teachings of Abraxas. They have come together, the whole family and their kin, lifting hands in salute to us. And I find myself smiling back. With them is Eastmund, now betrothed to Aia.

Arkyn squeezes my arm and drags me back to the ever present. My heart takes a leap. We are entering ritual ground and Lífa is beginning the death rite for my mother. The leaning stone claims presence above all. My dear friend and ally. We have spoken often and now I see moisture dribbling from the rough surface. My mother claimed it to be so. "When the stone weeps", she said, "The Gods are in mourning." It is still grey. And now I know Wōden weeps.

The pyre is before her. My brothers lift her so lovingly to lay her to her final resting place.

And I am being asked to come forward, as did she, before her *Ealdmōdor's* pyre, to claim the heron wing. It rests gently on her chest, lifeless as she. I am loath to remove it, for all my life I loved and feared that heron wing. The power it holds is beyond words. I gently lift it and hold it to my heart. I can hear sobbing behind me. I pray to hold my tears for never would I wish to lose dignity at this moment.

My brothers move forward to place the torches around the piled wood. As the flames take hold, the chanting begins and grows ever louder until I feel the stones and the trees tremble. All kin on our sacred Wihtland joins in one voice for our queen, our *Cwèn*.

Without any warning, I see her appear faintly before me, she is smiling and young, with her my *fæder* by her side. I know her spirit is free. I feel a rustling of the heron feathers and the power returns to become the bridge between us forever. Until we meet again. I grasp it tightly, my heart opening to bursting point, as the vision fades and they are gone.

For the briefest moment, the clouds part and brilliant Sunni shafts down to us and I know she is gone. The peace of *Neorxenawang*, Nerthus' meadow, enfolds them forever.

… … … … … … … … …

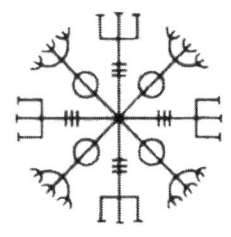

AUTHORS NOTE

This book is a work of fiction, yet, in delving deeply into the history of these ancient peoples and discovering in the process, a new aspect, highlighting a different and earlier time frame to the accepted 5th century, for their migration to these lands and the island, I discovered they were indeed what their name implied: Wihtwara, "People of the Spirit." And Wihtland: Isle of Spirits, became their home.

They were a deeply spiritual people whose connection to the land, the spirits who dwelt therein, and their Gods and Goddesses formed a union we can only aspire to, so far have we removed ourselves from the heart and soul of our land and our birth right. These beautiful people were the true guardians and caretakers of the land. Their lives revolved around the seasons, the successful harvest and the honouring of their Gods, whom they knew to be active and bound to them as they were in return, bound to them.

I have tried to remain authentic, using old Saxon English, especially in the invocation and prayers spoken. I have come to love this language, as a link to our Ancestors.

This book is the first in a trilogy charting the lives of an ancient peoples from the 1st century to 686 A.D. and the relentless march of Christianity over the Pagan world. The deep union, understanding and rituals these ancient peoples held towards our Earth were stamped upon, ridiculed, and the peoples violated for their beliefs. It was for the most part an ingenious cover-up. Clever minds assigned and re-invented Christian holy places on pagan sites of worship. Pagan names for these special sites were demonized. An important Pagan burial mound on the Isle of Wight was renamed "the devil's punchbowl"!

One aspect stands out above all others. That is the subjugation of the feminine within this Pagan world by Christian missionaries and with it, the subjugation of the Earth. Mother Earth was paramount in the minds and soul of all Pagan peoples. For without her acquiescence and that of the Gods aligned to the sky and weather, they felt alone.

Those missionaries sought and succeeded in burying underfoot every link and aspect of feminine honouring. The replacement was for the one male god to be deified and worshiped. I have not found one reference in the book of words they carried, of any respect and veneration of the natural world, neither plant nor animal, sacred soil or mystical sky or to the equality afforded to women. In this book of words, Man is above nature.

Yet if we go to the discovered Nag Hammedi gospel, quite another story is written.

I am indebted to the work of Tylluan Penry whose book: The Magical World of the Anglo-Saxons painstakingly pares away Christian dogma to reveal a Saxon world honouring the feminine principle and the power therein.

… … … … … … … … …

I was born in Kent, a Kentish lass, big of bone and quite tall. I relocated to the Isle of Wight in 1976, the year of the big heat. I thought I had moved to the Costa del Sol. I had a pocketful of plastic that flipped to the ground on a Saturday and not one spiritual genome in my body.

But the ancestors of the island had other plans for me!

After a very traumatic event whilst living in Bembridge, the key to my spiritual world opened a door, and I went through, never to go back. I soon made wonderful friendships with like-minded people and I joined the ever-growing network that live here on the Isle.

Over twenty years ago, I found myself, with two friends making the third attempt to find the Longstone, our ancient Bronze Age standing stone sitting askance on Mottistone down. It was revealed to us that magic abounds there and being sent off on a wild goose chase was quite normal!

It is steep. I stopped to take breathe putting my hand on an ancient stump, where a very old oak tree used to be. What I was then shown has changed my perception and my life, though it has taken many years of digging, researching and questioning to reach this point of writing.

I was no longer in 1995, but in a time long past. I was someone else completely, and I was terrified. I was seeing into the eyes of a frenzied warrior, whose eyes had long since become wild with killing. They were black and piercing and they were staring at me with gut wrenching coldness. They glared at me through an elaborately designed helmet that covered his whole face.

I was about to be murdered on the field of battle. Yet I was not taking part in it. Just standing, waiting. It is remarkable how much detail is remembered in the last moment of life. The silver filigree designing on this helmet is as clear today as when it was first shown to me. And his eyes will never be forgotten.

I came out of that shaking and upset. It was so real. And I walked away from it.......

But that was the beginning of the journey.

Several years later I was again at the Longstone with the same friend. We had become regular visitors, so it was with a great shock that putting my hand to the Longstone, I became that woman again. I was looking over to the Chessell down ridge, it was sunny but very cold and the wind was blowing. Over the ridge came an army of warriors, dressed in leather, thongs wrapped on their legs and carrying shields. They were intent on killing us.

I knew it was the last day of my life and the life of my people. We were going to be wiped from the land of our island home, forever.

Then I was shown where she was buried, in a forest, the season was winter, and the beech leaves lay all around. Again, I came out of the vision very upset and disturbed and again I walked away.

It was only after an extraordinary visit to the Longstone cottage with Druid friends, one winter's weekend, that I finally realised I had been shown a real record of events. That my Ancestor was real and lived on the Isle so many centuries ago.

The cottage was cold with no electricity and as I have Rheumatoid Arthritis, I stayed in keeping warm. On the second morning, early, I looked out onto the Longstone and saw the form of a woman, tall, like a giant set against the stone, looking out onto those Chessell downs. I took a photograph. She was there: I have it still.

My Druid friend then offered, at the end of the weekend, as a kind gesture, to take me to see an unexcavated disc burial mound in the middle of the forest. As we neared the spot I became quite speechless with the discovery that all those years ago, my Ancestor showed me where she was buried and now, in 2006, I was being guided to the sacred place. It was in the right season too, for all the trees were bare and the beech leaves lay strewn on the ground. I recognised it from that vision. And there it was hidden in the forest, a wide beautiful disc barrow, implicitly female and subtle. It was Bronze Age. We marvelled at it and stayed for a while meditating and sending prayers to her.

But because of its age, it threw me off the scent as to who she was and more importantly, when it was.

So, after many months' research I came to realise, with the help of a truly wonderful archaeological friend, who cleverly combines a great understanding of spirit with grass-roots archaeology, that Saxon burials of very prominent people were interred in bronze age burial mounds. A very prominent female priestess has been discovered close by. And it sent me into an intense search for more clues.

... ...

Was it the Dark Age? Clearly Not!

There is so little known about this time in our nation's history, (I feel her-story is far more appropriate) we call centuries of life here, the dark ages. History lessons going back for generations instil this in the minds of our young. We write it off as unfathomable and get onto the Romans who were sophisticated, exciting and very definitely over here!

Yet there is mounting archaeological/genetic/ linguistic evidence that is highlighting a totally different and exciting story. The migrations of peoples from the Cimbric peninsular to our shores in pre-history, through flood and war in their homeland to make Albion their new home, is gaining ground.

The work of Stephen Oppenheimer in his book The Origins of the British creates a doorway through which we can look upon a world long since denied our examination. And it is wonderful and plausible.

The Germanic people had a sophisticated culture, a society built on laws that today, in this country, are still enforced through our own democracy. Their craftsmanship was extraordinary and they delighted in trading. Their spiritual base was so strong it was intrinsically the deepest pagan culture, with a respect for women that was not suppressed until Christianity appeared.

Within the broad sweep of Germania, there was a confederation of tribes, seven in all, called the Suevii, or Suevi. They were a strongly spiritual federation, who worshipped

Wōden, or Mecurius as he was called by the Romans, for his mastery of healing and diplomacy. But equally, they worshipped the Earth Mother goddess Nerthus, of which Tacitus mentions because of the peaceable nature of the tribes that endured when she is present.

But she has been obliterated from our present knowledge. In the trail of finding her again I came upon startling references of her in the May queen celebrations we still do today. For Nerthus loved humankind, and agreed to appear at certain times driven by oxen on a chariot, through the villages to present herself to her people. And as Tacitus mentions, she had her sacred grove on an island in the big sea. Could this be Britannia?

There is mounting evidence gaining ground amongst both historians and archaeologists that the clean break between Rome leaving our shores and the "murderous Saxon hordes" arriving was not "clean" or even breaking. It is more likely that migrations from Germania were steady and over a much longer time frame. And they co-habited with Romans, who enjoyed trade above most things. In fact, Europe, then, which included the British Isles, was much more cosmopolitan than we ever imagined.

So, the "Dark Ages" it certainly was not. A bit like London today, in fact, without the Wi-Fi! And the traffic jams.

... ...

Whale...aka Wahl
Guardian of the Stones

Throughout my childhood, I have been acutely aware of my birth name Whale. Alternating between bemused and embarrassed, (especially embarrassed in my early years!). My aunt who loved genealogy claimed it as ancient Saxon. What good that was to me in the playground was anyone's guess. I was several inches taller than anyone else and very big boned. My father was a giant at 6 feet 5inches. That, I was told, came from the Whale family. We were a race of giants.

So, I placed it all under lock and key.... until now.

In the years of research that followed that extraordinary weekend up at the Longstone cottage, and my deep belief that not only was the Ancestor of this Isle, real, but that she was quietly present in my life, and I was edging closer to a personal discovery that confirmed my name and answered many questions that had been closeted away.

I began walking the island, seeking out ancient trees and creating a unique collection of tree essences I called Wihtyar essences, after the ancient name of both isles of Wiht and Yar. I became known as the "tree lady." I loved that journey and knew the Ancestor was guiding me to many a sacred tree as I learnt a great deal about the spiritual energy of our beautiful island. She loved this island home so much her energy is ever present. One sharp winter morning when I was up at the Mother mound creating the Imbolc snowdrop essence, in old Blackgang (Knowles farm), a stunning National Trust area, she spoke for the first and only time. "For every drop of this mother's milk is a drop of my wisdom." That snowdrop essence became used so frequently for women in search of their own creativity.

The ancients knew this island was special. It has a rare and powerful mineral seam running its entire length from East to West and many of our ancient sites and monuments, including the Longstone are built upon it. We call it the dragon, our Earth Dragon.

In researching the ancient peoples of the Cimbric peninsular I made discoveries that spurred me on further. The confederation consisted of seven tribes who were each different but maintained a powerful unity that spoke of elaborate and sophisticated social laws and customs. Each had their own individuality but came together as the Suevi host. Within their number came the Anglii and the southern Jutes, under their true tribal name of the Eudose. Together with the Reudignians, Aviones, Warinni,

Suacones and Niuthones, they were a formidable Germanic group.

Yet their purpose, for the main part, was peaceable. And their society spiritual. It was within this framework that I found the biggest clue to my name. The Warinni tribe were a very tall people, giants in fact. It was a genetic trait quite a few Germanic peoples shared, but these people were very tall. And in their customs and beliefs was a strong adherence to stone worship. They built stone circles and venerated this space in funerary rites and law-making. Their close relatives were the Geats, also given to producing tall and wide, strong people.

Recent archaeological digs on the island, discovered giant-type skeletal remains at Brading, a thriving port in the days of the 2nd and 3rd centuries.

The slow steady migration of these peoples to our British shores brought the Eudose, Nuithone and Warinni to settle specifically in Kent and the Isle of Wight. Others followed as the sea lanes became known and navigable. There is a section of the North Sea called the Whale Road. Frisians also made the journey here.

It was a gradual process of integration and co-habitation within a very fertile land mass.

So, these migratory people who made the south their home, became known as the Cantwara in Kent, the Meonwara in the Meon valley and the Wihtwara of the Isle of Wight known then as Wihtland, (Isle of Spirit).

And of the Wahls, there is still a family who live near the Meon Valley, there is a family of Whales who live in Avebury Trusloe near to the Stone circle and there is me…. on Wihtland, who was born a Kentish lass. I spent a whole two years of my life travelling abroad creating stone circles in troubled lands, bringing people together in ceremonies for peace. I had no idea then, I was doing something that was "in my blood" to do anyway!

The Meonwara are mentioned in the Doomsday book, and the Cantwara are evidenced. But of the Wihtwara there is very little. I believe they were the highest priest and priestesses who lived here, then. I believe there was also pagan royalty, for it is known, that in the march of Christianity, Wihtland was last place in Britain to be Christianized. They refused to recant. The venerable Bede makes an unusual and very specific mention of the bloodline of Wōden in relation to the royal line. And it is traced very clearly to Wihtland, with Wihtlæg and Wihtgils related to Witta and Wecta who were sons and grandsons of Wōden.

"We still honour Wōden's name in the word-stem *Wednes*-in English place-names and one of the days of our week. So, we read in Book 1 of the *Anglo-Saxon Chronicle*: "From this Wōden arose all our royal kindred." This text from one of our oldest surviving English histories, was no routine description of descent but a deliberate statement. The gap between each of the main English founders and Wōden was but a few generations. For instance, The Jutish (Eudose) leader Wihtgils, whose name is attached to the Isle of Wight, was claimed to be Wōden's great grandson through Wecta and then Witta. Wihtgils was also claimed as the father of the fifth-century and earliest semi-legendary invaders Hengist and Horsa, which would make him already resident in the British Isles when they invaded!" (*pg. 387: Old English perceptions of ethnicity. The Origins of the British by Stephen Oppenheimer.*)

If we take this genealogy to its logical conclusion, (and why would Bede veer away from his stolid Christian ethic to pay respect to a Pagan God) this makes Wōden a true living God closer to recorded history than we have been led to believe. This puts him in the realm of other living Gods around the time of the new millennium, Christ, Mohammed and Buddha. Christ was removed from our lives as a living God when the Synod at Constantinople created the edict of Christ as God, making Gnosticism heretical. It was at this point, that it became fundamental in outlook and began the purge of Paganism. This is the subject of the second book in the series, *Berandinzium Villa.*

The final book in this series, *The Healer Queen* takes us to the climax of that terrible invasion in 686A.D.

… … … … … … … … …

I have a personal theory that both Witta and Wecta lived and fought in Britannia. That their great grandsons Hengist and Horsa came to Kent because their grandfathers had lived on these shores. Moreover, Hengistbury head is an encoded place name and it overlooks Wihtland. There is evidence that Witta fought here, or up on the Scottish boundaries against the Picts. The Romans could not pronounce or even recognise W. So Wihtland somehow became Vectis. If we replace the V with a W we get the tantalisingly close name of Wectis…. After a legendary king Wecta.

The Wihtwara were massacred in 686 in a bloody battle that is forever imprinted in the stone on that high hill. King Arwald was the last pagan king of Wihtland.

Just east of the Longstone is a place that has become known as the Black Barrow. It is said the dead lay bundled and buried there. I have visited there. It is a heavy dense area where nothing grows well. It has never been excavated as it is on private land.

I performed ceremony near the barrow mound, to try and give the spirits there, some peace.

My Ancestor was amongst those who were killed that day. These books are being written for her and all her peoples.

Lest we forget.

Bletsunga Beorte

Bright blessings

GLOSSARY

Saxon…English

Adlian síclian…become sick

Áðum…sister's husband

Æðele…high born noble

Æðeling…prince

Æðelu…noble family

Ægishjālmar…helm of awe

Ælf gescot…elf shot

Ælf…elves

Ælfscyne…elf-fair

Ælfsiden…apparition, nightmare

Ælscienu…beautiful

Æmta…quiet

Ālfablōt…elf-blessing

Ārtèas…dishonourable

Attorlaðe…betony

Bæc bord…larboard

Bèahgifa…ring-giver

Bèam…wooden ship

Bebod…decree

Belene…henbane

Beorht stān…bright stone

Brim…sea

Brimfugol…sea bird

Brōðor…brother

Burgstede…city (m)

Buriel…bury

Byrg…to bury

Byrgels…Burial place

Cealcstān…limestone

Ceaster…city (f)

Ceasterwic…women's village

Cenningstān…touching stone

Ceorl…husband

Cnearr…small ship

Cnèomagas…kinsmen

Cōlian…become cold

Cwèn…Queen

cwèn…wife

Cýððu…native land

Cynecynn…royal family

Cynedōm…kingdom

Cyng…king

Cynn…family

Dæg weorþung…celebration

Dæg…day

Deaō…death

Deaō-gerihte…death rite

Ðèodcyning…king over a nation

Dèore brōðor…dear brother

Dohtor…daughter

mín drihten…my lord

Đoncian þu...thank you
Drímeolce Cwèn...may queen
Drímeolce intrepettan...may dance
Đrūh...coffin
Drýcræftig...magically skilled
Drymānn...magician
Dūnælfen...mountain elves
Ealdorðegn...chief thane
Ealdorman...earl
Èalond...island
Èam...uncle Maternal
Eard...homeland
Eatenas...giant kin
Èðel...family's land
Fæðe...father's sister
Fæder...father
Fædera...father's brother
Fædera...uncle Paternal
Fæderansuni...cousin
Feferfuge...feverfew
Fille...thyme
Finule...fennel
Flot...Sea
Fōdhèrun...the stretched one
Forðgeorn lytling...Impetuous child
Foregísl...hostage
Forlidennes...Ship wreck
Forstoppian...stop
Forwrègan...wrongly accused
Friþ-spott...vigil
Fylgia..." Fetch" animals
Galdrastafur...binding runes
Gebroðor...brothers
Gebroðor...oath-sworn brothers

Gebūr...farmer
Gecwèman...please
Geðèode...nation
Gefreoge...tradition
Gehwilian...become poisonous
Gerihte...rite
Gesib...Kinsman
Godcund...sacred
Hālig mōnaþ...September
Hālig stān...sacred stones
Hālig wielle...Sacred well
Hèaburg...capitol
Hèahfæder...patriarch
Hèahwita...high councillor
Heorð Cyng...hearth king
Hlýda...march
Hū...hut
Hūs...house
Hwata...soothsayer
Hymlic...hemlock
Ieldran...parents
Kornmjölsgot...barley porridge
Lācnung...medicine house
Lǽringmæden...female pupil
Lèasung...liar
Lenctenmōnaþ...spring month
Leof frèond...dear friend
Lèogere...liar
Ljōð leoð...spell song
Londlèod...native people
Lytel spere...little spear
Mæden...girl
Mæden...maiden
Mædmōnaþ...meadow month

Mægðe...mayweed
Medowyrt...meadowsweet
Menniscnes...humanity
Mín frèogan...my love
Morðor...murder
Mucgwyrt...Mugwort
Næhfædras...close Ancestors
Nefene...niece
Neja...nephew
Neorxenawang...Nerthus meadow
Neorxenawang...Spiritual home
Nigon mōnaþ...9 month's pregnancy
Nigt-gala...night singer
Niht...night
Onflyge...flying venom
Ordœðung...Start breathing!
Popina...local wine bar
Pypelian...become pimply
Rihthand...right-hand
Rōmānisc...Roman
Sācerde...priestess
Sǽ genga...sea-going vessel
Sǽ naca...sea vessel
Sǽ...Sea, Ocean
Sǽl lida...sea farer
Særima...coast
Sāwol...spirit/soul
Scip...Ship
Sciprap...ship's rope
Scōp...story-teller
Seax...domestic dagger
Seiðr...feminine magic
Slæn wyrhta drymānn...blacksmith
Smiððe...smithy

Soctunga...succubus
Spakōna...high priestess
Spíwān...vomit
Stefn...ship's stern
Stiðe...nettle
Stune...lamb's cress
Sumor...summer
Sweostor...sister
Swustersuna...sister's son
Þearu...copse
Tunstede...men's village
Utiseta...shamanic vision quest
Völva..high priestess
Vördhlokkur...Warlock
Wacian...prayer vigil
Wælspere skaldcræft...sacred spear
Wæterfæsten...camp by water
Wæterœlfadl...water-elf disease
Warlocan...wizard
Wealte...ring
Wegbrade...Plantain
Wergulu...crab-apple
Wice...week
Widwe...widow
Wíscwèn...wise-woman
Wita -wítega...wise-man
Woruld scamu...public disgrace
Wranga...ship's hold
Wryd rapas...magical weaving
Wuduelfen...woodland elves
Wudufæsten...camp by woods
Wuduwosan...wild spirits of the wood
Wuldortanas...rods of wonder
Wynstra...left

Wyrt-hūs...herb-house
Ŷðfaru...sea journey

English...Saxon
"Fetch" animals...*Fylgia*
9 month's pregnancy...*Nigon mōnaþ*
apparition, nightmare...*Ælfsiden*
barley porridge...*Kornmjölsgot*
beautiful...*Ælscienu*
become cold...*Cōlian*
become pimply...*Pypelian*
become poisonous...*Gehwilian*
become sick...*Adlian síclian*
betony ...*Attorlaðe*
binding runes...*Galdrastafur*
blacksmith...*Slæn wyrhta drymãnn*
bright stone...*Beorht stān*
brother...*Brōðor*
brothers...*Gebroðor*
Burial place...*Byrgels*
bury...*Buriel*
camp by water...*Wæterfæsten*
camp by woods...*Wudufæsten*
capitol...*Hèaburg*
celebration...*Dæg weorþung*
chief thane...*Ealdorðegn*
city (f)...*Ceaster*
city (m)...*Burgstede*
close Ancestors...*Næhfædras*
coast...*Særima*
coffin...*Ðrūh*
copse...*Þearu*

cousin...*Fæderansuni*
crab-apple...*Wergulu*
daughter...*Dohtor*
day...*Dæg*
dear brother...*Dèore brōðor*
dear friend...*Leof frèond*
death rite...*Deaō-gerihte*
death...*Deaō*
decree...*Bebod*
dishonourable...*Ãrtèas*
domestic dagger...*Seax*
earl...*Ealdorman*
elf shot...*Ælf gescot*
elf-blessing...*Ãlfablōt*
elf-fair...*Ælfscyne*
elves...*Ælf*
family's land...*Èðel*
family...*Cynn*
farmer...*Gebūr*
father's brother...*Fædera*
father's sister...*Fæðe*
father...*Fæder*
female pupil...*Lǽringmǽden*
feminine magic...*Seiðr*
fennel...*Finule*
feverfew...*Feferfuge*
flying venom...*Onflyge*
giant kin...*Eatenas*
girl...*Mǽden*
Druids...*Diviciacos*
hearth king...*Heorð Cyng*

helm of awe...*Ægishjālmar*
hemlock...*Hymlic*
henbane...*Belene*
herb-house...*Wyrt-hūs*
high born noble...*Æðele*
high councillor...*Hèahwita*
high priestess...*Spakōna*
high priestess...*Völva*
homeland...*Eard*
hostage...*Foregísl*
house...*Hūs*
humanity...*Menniscnes*
husband...*Ceorl*
hut...*Hū*
Impetuous child...*Forðgeorn lytling*
island...*Èalond*
king over a nation...*Ðèodcyning*
king...*Cyng*
kingdom...*Cynedōm*
Kinsman...*Gesib*
kinsmen...*Cnèomagas*
lamb's cress...*Stune*
larboard...*Bæc bord*
left...*Wynstra*
liar...*Lèasung*
liar...*Lèogere*
limestone...*Cealcstān*
little spear...*Lytel spere*
local wine bar...*Popina*
magical weaving...*Wryd rapas*
magically skilled...*Drýcræftig*
magician...*Drymānn*
maiden...*Mǽden*
march...*Hlýda*

may dance...*Drímeolce intrepettan*
may queen...*Drímeolce Cwèn*
mayweed...*Mægðe*
meadow month...*Mædmōnaþ*
meadowsweet...*Medowyrt*
medicine house...*Lācnung*
men's village...*Tunstede*
mountain elves...*Dūnælfen*
Mugwort...*Mucgwyrt*
murder...*Morðor*
my love...*Mín frèogan*
nation...*Geðèode*
native land...*Cýððu*
native people...*Londlèod*
nephew...*Neja*
Nerthus meadow...*Neorxenawang*
nettle...*Stiðe*
niece...*Nefene*
night singer...*Nigt-gala*
night...*Niht*
noble family...*Æðelu*
oath-sworn brothers...*Gebroðor*
parents...*Ieldran*
patriarch...*Hèahfæder*
Plantain...*Wegbrade*
please...*Gecwèman*
prayer vigil...*Wacian*
priestess...*Sācerde*
prince...*Æðeling*
public disgrace...*Woruld scamu*
Queen...*Cwèn*
quiet...*Æmta*
right-hand...*Rihthand*
ring...*Wealte*

ring-giver...*Bèahgifa*
rite...*Gerihte*
rods of wonder...*Wuldortanas*
Roman...*Rōmãnisc*
royal family...*Cynecynn*
sacred spear...*Wælspere skaldcræft*
sacred stones...*Hālig stān*
Sacred well...*Hālig wielle*
sacred...*Godcund*
sea bird...*Brimfugol*
sea farer...*Sǽl lida*
sea journey...*Ýðfaru*
sea vessel...*Sǽ naca*
Sea, Ocean...*Sǽ*
sea...*Brim*
Sea...*Flot*
sea-going vessel...*Sǽ genga*
September...*Hālig mōnaþ*
shamanic vision quest...*Utiseta*
Ship wreck...*Forlidennes*
ship's hold...*Wranga*
ship's rope...*Sciprap*
ship's stern...*Stefn*
Ship...*Scip*
sister's husband...*Ãðum*
sister's son...*Swustersuna*
sister...*Sweostor*
small ship...*Cnearr*
smithy...*Smiððe*
soothsayer...*Hwata*
spell song...*Ljōð leoð*
spirit/soul...*Sãwol*

Spiritual home...*Neorxenawang*
spring month...*Lenctenmōnaþ*
Start breathing! *Ordæðung!*
stop...*Forstoppian*
story-teller...*Scōp*
succubus...*Soctunga*
summer...*Sumor*
my lord...*mín drihten*
thank you...*Ðoncian þu*
the stretched one...*Fōdhèrun*
thyme...*Fille*
to bury...*Byrg*
touching stone...*Cenningstān*
tradition...*Gefreoge*
uncle Maternal...*Èam*
uncle Paternal...*Fædera*
vigil...*Friþ-spott*
vomit...*Spíwãn*
Warlock...*Vördhlokkur*
water-elf disease...*Wæterælfadl*
week...*Wice*
widow...*Widwe*
wife...*cwèn*
wild spirits of the wood...*Wuduwosan*
wise-man...*Wita -wítega*
wise-woman...*Wíscwèn*
wizard...*Warlocan*
women's village...*Ceasterwic*
wooden ship...*Bèam*
woodland elves...*Wuduelfen*
wrongly accused...*Forwrègan*

BIBLIOGRAPHY

The Origins of the British by Stephen Oppenheimer
Pub: Robinson: ISBN 978-184529-482-3

The Elder Gods: The Other World of Early England
By Stephen Pollington
Pub: Anglo-Saxon books: ISBN 9781898281641

Leechraft: Early English Charms, Plantlore and Healing
By Stephen Pollington
Pub: Anglo-Saxon books: ISBN 9781898281474

The Magical World of the Anglo-Saxons
By Tylluan Penry
The Wolfenhowle Press ISBN 978-0-9570442-2-7

Rudiments of Runelore
By Stephen Pollington
Pub: Anglo-Saxon Books: ISBN 9781898281498

Peace-Weavers and Shield-Maidens: Women in Early English Society
By Kathleen Herbet

Pub: Anglo-Saxon books: ISBN 9781898281115

The Spine of Albion:
By Gary Biltcliffe & Caroline Hoare

Proceedings of the Isle of Wight and Archaeological Society Vol.18 2002

Wihtgarasbyrig Explored
By David Tomalin

Proceedings of the Isle of Wight Natural History and Archaeological Society vol.21/22 2006-2007

Anglo-Saxon Charter Boundaries
By David Marcham

Wordcraft: New English to Old English Dictionary and Thesaurus
By Stephen Pollington
Pub: Anglo-Saxon Books: ISBN 9781898281535

Useful Websites:

Bosworth-Toller Anglo-Saxon Dictionary
Abraxas: Wikipedia

VETTA F. VICTA Witta son of Wetta
www.home.comcast.net/~cwitzjr/vetta.html

TheHistoryFiles.co.ok/featuresBritain/England
Sussexmeonwara07.htm

www.Wilcuma.org.uk

Printed in Great Britain
by Amazon